W9-CGM-150

THE HOUSE OF ELIOTT

The HOUSE of ELIOTT

JEAN MARSH

Thorndike Press • Chivers Press
Thorndike, Maine USA   Bath, Avon, England

This Large Print edition is published by Thorndike Press, USA and by Chivers Press, England.

Published in 1994 in the U.S. by arrangement with St. Martin's Press, Inc.

Published in 1994 in the U.K. by arrangement with Macmillan London, a division of Pan Macmillan Publishers Limited.

U.S. Hardcover 0-7862-0230-0 (Basic Series Edition)
U.K. Hardcover 0-7451-7741-7 (Windsor Large Print)
U.K. Softcover 0-7451-3610-9 (Paragon Large Print)

The text of this Large Print edition is unabridged.
Other aspects of the book may vary from the original edition.

Set in 16 pt. News Plantin.

Printed in the United States on acid-free paper.

British Library Cataloguing in Publication Data available

Library of Congress Cataloging in Publication Data

Marsh, Jean.
      The house of Eliott / Jean Marsh.
         p.   cm.
      ISBN 0-7862-0230-0 (alk. paper : lg. print)
      1. Costume design — England — London — History —
20th century — Fiction. 2. Clothing trade — England —
London — History — 20th century — Fiction. 3. Sisters
— England — London — Fiction. 4. Women — England
— London — Fiction. 5. London (England) — Fiction.
6. Large type books. I. Title.
[PR6063.A6599H6   1994b]
823'.914—dc20
                                                            94-14264

THE HOUSE OF ELIOTT

CHAPTER ONE

'Take it off.' The voice was loud and sharp but clearly attempting to subdue underlying emotion.

The slender figure silhouetted in the window wearing top hat and tails turned. 'I wasn't being disrespectful,' the girl said hesitantly, slowly taking off the hat.

Beatrice looked indulgently at her younger sister. 'Of course you weren't. I'm sorry.' Evangeline's grave beauty lit up with a lopsided grin and swooping on Beatrice she hugged her. Beatrice smoothed the long dark hair which fell like wings over Evangeline's forehead and gently pushed her aside as she turned to the bed which was strewn with men's clothing. 'Who would have thought that Father would have so many clothes?' Beatrice had picked up a canary yellow slub silk cravat. 'I don't remember him wearing this.'

'I can't *imagine* him wearing it.' Evangeline looked around the large, gloomy, high-ceilinged bedroom, its heavy dark Victorian furniture placed against equally dark patterned wallpaper, and thought how well it matched their father's sombre presence. Her memory of him did not include the wearing of a canary yellow cravat.

'Look at this.' Beatrice had opened a drawer in the massive mahogany tallboy and was holding up a handful of scarves. 'Silk,' she said incredulously, letting them slip through her fingers. 'All of them.' She pressed her lips together firmly, a sure sign to Evangeline of trouble to come. 'These aren't going to be given to the poor of London,' she said. 'It seems *we* are the poor of London.' Evangeline examined herself in the long mirror again. Could something be done with this coat if the shoulder pads were removed and the tails cut off?

Beatrice irritably picked up a dark grey overcoat and started to fold it. 'No, I can't believe it,' she exclaimed. 'Now, I'm really angry.'

'Why, what is it?' asked Evangeline.

'What is it? It's cashmere. This would have cost more than Molly's wages for a year.' Throwing the coat on the bed Beatrice stormed angrily to the window. Her slightly sharp, neat features framed by reddish hair and now inflamed by anger had assumed the look of a spirited cat. 'I don't understand. He left nothing, but he had all this. Well, these aren't going to the poor either.'

Evangeline tried a little laugh. 'The East End Mission won't get much at this rate.'

Her sister was not going to be teased out of her ill-humour. 'We could use some of these clothes — we can turn the dress-shirts into blouses, and all this silk,' she said, picking up the scarves and almost caressing them, 'we can do something with these.'

Evangeline, joining in her sister's excitement, had taken out of a wardrobe an armful of brocade and velvet waistcoats. 'Oh, Bea, these are beautiful.'

Beatrice looked at them in amazement. 'We could wear them almost as they are.'

'Would you dare?'

'I am going to dare doing a lot of things now that we have no one to answer to.' Bea looked at Evangeline challengingly. 'Father's death has considerably increased our wardrobe.' She returned to sorting out clothes on the bed. 'Any shirts we're not keeping I'm going to cut the buttons off.'

'Oh, we can't, Bea. What will they think at the Mission?'

'They can think what they like,' Bea said with some asperity moving to the chest of drawers on which lay an ornate silver tray containing cuff-links, a pair of ivory-backed hairbrushes engraved with the initials H.L.E., a spectacle case and nail scissors. She put out her hand for the scissors, paused a moment and picked up the embroidered spectacle case and looked at it, her eyes suddenly full of tears.

Evangeline dropped some shoes into a large cardboard box; they had been hand-made, she noted. This was all rather macabre, she thought, picking through his clothes, like worms stripping his bones. She shivered. 'We're not keeping any shoes or trousers, are we, Bea? They are all to be collected, aren't they?' There was no answer. 'Bea?' She turned to look at her sister. 'Oh, darling Bea, what is it?'

'It's so odd,' said Beatrice stifling a sob. 'I'm so sad about him and yet so angry with him, too.' She remembered how any little confidence in herself could be stifled by his disapproval or lack of interest. 'He allowed us hardly anything, no real education, no social life, no clothes, no money of our own and left us nothing but the house and now we find all these expensive grand clothes, it's a mystery.'

Evangeline hoped she wouldn't talk about being a spinster again. There was so little encouragement to offer: thirty was too old to expect to marry. She passed her handkerchief and Beatrice dabbed her eyes with it. 'You made him that case, didn't you, Bea?'

10

'Yes.' She sighed, distractedly scraping a fingernail across the knots of the embroidery. 'He's left us penniless and unprepared. I don't know what we are going to do and yet I suppose I loved him.' She dabbed her eyes again.

'Is this yours?' Beatrice looked with surprise at the tiny lawn handkerchief liberally trimmed with baby blue lace that Evangeline had handed her. 'I found it in this pocket.' She indicated the tailcoat which she was still wearing. 'It couldn't be Mama's after all this time, could it?'

'No, it couldn't,' said Beatrice thoughtfully.

Lydia, Lady Eliott sat with her son Arthur in her large ornately decorated drawing room in Kensington. She was perched uncomfortably on an overstuffed shiny sofa. Uncomfortable it might have been, but at least it was fashionable, it was right, and that mattered more than comfort to Lydia. The right accent, the right clothes, the right house, the right friends, it gave one a sense of security and that was what Lydia needed.

'You know they won't have enough to live on. We will have to help them.'

Arthur turned from the sleek, modern cocktail cabinet. 'You mean, give them some money?' He was surprised.

'Good Lord, no.' She laughed. 'Of course,

they won't need much — they aren't used to much. For a doctor with such a successful practice his daughters led remarkably quiet lives.'

'Uncle Henry believed a woman's place was in the home,' Arthur said, rather pompously for his twenty-five years.

'So do I, but he did hold the poor things on a very tight rein.' Lydia spoke with a vestige of sympathy: no such rein had ever been imposed on her either before her marriage by her financially strained but indulgent parents or afterwards by her rich and indulgent husband. She smiled at Arthur and took the cocktail he'd been mixing for her. 'Oh, deevy, a White Lady.'

'It isn't a White Lady, it's a Maiden's Blush, we're out of Cointreau.'

'Well, deevy, anyway. What are you having?'

'Whisky, of course.'

'Of course.' Lydia's smile was now tempered with disapproval. 'Is it your first?'

'It isn't my first and it won't be my last and you're a goose to worry about my drinking. I drink far less than any of the chaps at the office.' Arthur took her hand between his, pressed it and gave her his special direct, honest gaze. He was aware that his mother thought he was a very superior being and wasn't inclined to disagree with her. He also knew exactly how to get round her.

She smiled at him affectionately and sipped her cocktail. 'It's delicious, this Maiden's Lady.'

'No, Mother, Maiden's Blush.'

'Well, talking of maidens, were they surprised how little your uncle left them?'

'Little Evangeline didn't quite take it in, but Beatrice was surprised and angry and rather rude.' He remembered with discomfort his cousin's reaction to the news. Beatrice had demanded proof and brushed aside his offer of sympathy. 'Were you?'

'Was I what?' Lydia looked up.

'Were you surprised?'

'Not that much. I have a shrewd idea where some of the money went.'

Arthur had long wondered how much his mother knew but there was no point in asking her; she was as good at telling other people's secrets as keeping her own. 'So do I. The good doctor wasn't always so good, was he?' Lydia looked at her son quizzically and turned away to the mirror, smoothing the silk over her ample but firm hips. Arthur was disconcerted, his mother looked like the cat that got the cream. Uncle Henry couldn't have . . . No, no, of course he couldn't have. Another whisky, that was what one needed. Never-

13

theless, he looked hard at his mother again.

'Now, about the girls,' she said. 'I've done some thinking.'

'We're tired, we've done enough for today, Evie.' Descending the stairs, which were as gloomy and intimidating as their father's bedroom, the sisters carried down the last of several large cardboard boxes. On each landing the brown and green stained-glass windows, typical of the Victorian Gothic architecture in Highgate, shed a light that increased rather than diminished the gloom.

'I'm hungry,' said Evangeline. 'Let's eat now.'

'But Molly isn't back.'

'We can eat what we like and when we like now, and we can cook for ourselves,' Evangeline said gleefully.

Beatrice looked fondly at her sister. Evie was hardly out of her childhood with an innocent impulsiveness. 'All right,' she said and marched into the kitchen. On a dark brown painted dresser their supper sat covered by a wire mesh frame. 'Cold boiled chicken, doesn't need much cooking,' she lifted a jug, 'and barley water.' Evangeline looked crestfallen for a moment. 'I know.' She beamed, and darted into the larder. 'This will cheer it up.' She was carrying two bottles of stout and a jar of Indian chutney. 'Molly won't mind, there's plenty more.'

'Chutney or stout?'

'Stout,' Evie said laughing. 'We're really breaking all the rules.' Oh, those rules, she thought, our food was as bland as our lives. No fried food, no friends, no pastries, no parties, no spice . . . 'No, no, no,' Evangeline exclaimed, 'I don't believe all those rules are good for you, not all of them. Papa,' she said daringly, 'was wrong.'

'Well, possibly he wasn't right all the time but, nevertheless, he was a good doctor.' Beatrice carved the cold chicken and put it with an undressed salad on the well-scrubbed kitchen table while Evangeline poured out the stout.

'I'm going to have chutney with chicken, not chicken with chutney — and if he was such a good doctor why didn't he move his practice to Harley Street?' Beatrice, amused by Evangeline's vehemence, watched her put half the jar of chutney on her chicken.

'Oh, you know Papa. He liked making people come to him, and living here in Highgate made it difficult for Mama to visit friends.'

'But did she, Bea? Were you ever allowed out? Where did she take you? What did she wear?' Evangeline already knew the answers to all these questions and had heard every detail of each visit to London, but hearing them again she would note new details and hoard them in her memory.

Her mother, whom she had never known, was as real to her as her father. Bea's descriptions of her appearance and clothes, her delicate elegant hands, her talent in water-colours and her originality and wit had coalesced to form an image as clear to her as that of any living person.

Beatrice, too, was thinking of her mother. Yes, they'd been allowed to escape for an afternoon occasionally to visit the dreaded Aunt Lydia and Uncle Richard, although sitting dutifully with Aunt Lydia with all her desperate pretensions to gentility was hardly an escape. After tea they were sometimes able to go to the National Gallery, the Portrait Gallery or, best of all, one of the smaller modern galleries with their explosion of colour and freedom of form which her mother wanted her to look at with open spontaneous eyes.

On days when they could leave Aunt Lydia early her mother would take Beatrice to different parts of London and show her where she had lived and where she had been to school. Chelsea, where she had studied painting, was Beatrice's favourite, and sometimes, for a glorious treat, they would have a second informal tea with one of Mama's Bohemian friends where Beatrice was treated like an adult and spoken to as a person of interest and intelligence whose opinions were worth having. A far cry from home where even her mother was treated like a slightly wayward child. My little pony, he had called her. Beatrice remembered the note of anxiety bordering on hysteria she sometimes heard in her mother's voice. When that happened her father's hand would fall heavily on his wife's shoulder, he would rub her back and it would quieten her. But Beatrice had always felt it was threatening rather than kind. 'Things between husband and wives,' Kathleen, Molly's mother, used to say, 'are not always what they seem to be.'

Evangeline sighed. Suddenly she felt quite deflated. 'Oh, Bea. I wish it hadn't been me.'

'Evie, Mama knew she was taking a risk having another baby after all her miscarriages and she did see you. That made her very happy.' They reached across the kitchen table and touched hands.

Evangeline sipped her stout. 'I like this.'

'So do I,' said a voice with a strong Irish brogue, and Molly, their young maid, came into the kitchen. With her bright elfin face and lively manner she brought a gust of fresh air into the gloomy house. 'I hope as how you haven't had me bloaters and you've left me at least one bottle of stout for me tea.' She bustled around the kitchen putting the fish into a pan and cutting bread. Her free and easy manner with the sisters wasn't impudence but familiarity. Although she was their maid now, she had been brought up in the family almost as a sister to Evangeline. Kathleen had been allowed to stay in the house even after the birth of her illegitimate daughter. This wasn't so much kindness from Dr Eliott but a case of expediency after the death of his wife when Evangeline was born.

'Didn't touch your bloaters, Molly. How was your cousin?'

'Very low, Miss Evie. The young boy who was shot died too. They're burying her father on Saturday — the whole family will be going over on the night ferry. It'll be a grand turn-out.'

'I expect you'd like to go too,' said Beatrice.

'Yes, Miss Bea, I'd really love to.' Molly spoke eagerly.

The sisters looked at each other awkwardly and Beatrice, assuming responsibility, said, 'You know we'd send you if we could, but since Father . . .'

'Yes, yes, Miss Bea, I know you would.' Molly was aware of the precarious state of their finances and much more besides. She was too good-natured and too fond of the sisters to sulk and, lifting her bloaters out of the pan and onto a plate, she carried them to the table and joined the girls.

'This smells a bit better than cold chicken,' she said and, lifting her glass, 'This tastes a lot better than barley water.' At this the front door bell jangled in the large row of brass bells high on the kitchen wall. 'Wouldn't you know, as soon as I sit down . . .'

'It's all right, Molly,' said Beatrice. 'It will be the woman from the East End Mission. We'll deal with it, you finish your tea.' Molly sat down but curiosity took preference over the bloaters and she went to the basement window. There was the young woman from the Mission and there also was a motor car.

Fancy, she thought. Only a young woman but a motorist, or would it be a motoress? The young woman seemed older than Miss Evie and younger than Miss Bea but dressed quite differently. Was that what you wore for driving? Quite like a riding habit somehow with that divided skirt, but what was the point? You didn't have the machine between your legs like a horse. Molly laughed to herself. But whatever she was wearing, the young woman was a lady just like the Eliotts. Funny how you could tell. It was born in them, she supposed, and she also supposed it was time she finished her tea and cleared away. Friendly

19

as they were to her, it would never do to 'take advantage or take for granted', something her mother had drummed into her before she returned to Ireland. She turned away from the window.

'How d'ye do? Penelope Maddox, East End Mission. Stuff ready? Motor outside, tried to get a lorry. Army wouldn't budge, got used to that lot during the war.' Evangeline and Beatrice were left breathless by the onslaught from the angular but attractive young woman.

'Well, there's quite a lot but I don't think a lorry will be necessary,' Evie said awkwardly.

'Not just collecting here. People give up, y'know.'

'I'm afraid we've cut off some of the buttons. Give up?' Evie felt embarrassed.

'Don't worry about that, volunteers will deal with it. Most of it's sold. Our people need dinner, not dinner jackets.' Penelope paused and looked directly at the sisters, assessing them. She took one of the boxes of clothes and carried it to the car. 'Yes, people give up hoping he'll come back, then they don't want to be reminded, so the Mission benefits.'

'Oh, I see.' Beatrice followed her to the car with another box. 'You can drive, how wonderful,' she said.

'Had to, ambulance driver. And you, did

you do anything? Doctor's daughters, aren't you — nurse?'

'No, I mean, no, I didn't do anything in the war or nothing that counts and, yes, my father was a doctor.' The three women continued to pile up the clothes in the car's dickey.

Evangeline felt they were old-fashioned and inadequate beside this example of the 'new woman'. 'She could have,' she blurted out, tilting her chin towards Beatrice. 'But she had to look after me and the house — and she was Father's receptionist.' Well into her stride, she added, 'She would have been a huge asset to the war effort,' quoting from the *Lady* — or was it the *Sketch*?

'But, anyway, Father wouldn't let me,' Beatrice said with an affectionate smile at Evangeline.

'Wouldn't let you, eh?'

'Father wouldn't let us do anything,' said Evangeline glumly.

'Going to do anything now? We always need volunteers.'

'I'm afraid, since our father's death,' Beatrice said, 'we have to earn a living.'

Penelope beamed at them, 'Good for you. Anything in mind?' She looked at their blank faces. 'No? Well, I'll keep a look out. Thanks for all this — even without the buttons.' They watched her jump behind the wheel and drive off.

'Isn't she extraordinary?'

'Yes, and the motor started straight away.'

It was a sunny day, but it wasn't the sun that put the two pink spots on Beatrice's cheeks, nor was it the speed at which she was striding down St Martin's Lane, a speed with which Evangeline was finding it hard to keep up. She was also ignoring the theatres full for their matinées and the buskers now seemingly playing for each other, and the sandwich-board men advertising doom, clairvoyants and tea-rooms with equal impartiality.

Evangeline's attention was caught by a young girl, perhaps her own age, singing quite sweetly, 'I Dreamt I Dwelt In Marble Halls', an incongruous dream, she thought, for a girl making her living singing in the streets. Even more incongruous was her size, her stomach was enormous, she was obviously pregnant, too obviously, perhaps.

Evangeline had never seen anyone quite as pregnant as that. The young girl caught her eye and, with a conspiratorial wink, shifted her 'baby' to a more comfortable position. Laughing, Evangeline ran to catch up Beatrice who had now reached Trafalgar Square.

'No,' she said suddenly, 'no, we are not taking in lodgers and that is final.'

'I agree with you, Bea, but please calm down, and slow down, too.'

'I will, I will.' But Beatrice continued at her rapid pace. 'Lodgers. We'd be trapped, we'd be servants. Arthur is trying to run our lives, just like Father did. I'm thirty. I want my life back.' She thought of the gloom of Arthur's office, so like the gloom of her father's house, and she remembered her rage when he had explained, slowly and pompously, that he was to be Evangeline's guardian, officially. The look he had cast at Evangeline had been proprietorial. No, more than that. It made her feel uneasy.

'You will probably marry. I mean Evangeline, of course.'

'Of course.'

'And you, Beatrice, could be a governess.'

'Well, that's settled, then. Let us know when you've found us a husband and a position.' Beatrice gathered together her gloves and handbag and stood up.

'Don't be facetious. You must now understand that your situation is far more financially precarious than we had previously envisaged.'

Beatrice glared at him. 'It seems to me that our precarious financial situation was created by the men in the Eliott family, Father lost all his money and you didn't envisage it.'

23

'We are looking for work,' Evie said, trying to placate them.

'You are ladies. Eliotts. It is out of the question — and what could you do? You were not educated for any profession.' Arthur sat behind his desk again, he felt safer there from Beatrice's rather accurate barbs.

'We were not educated,' Beatrice said.

'I wanted to go to art school,' Evangeline joined in softly.

Arthur laughed and looked at her fondly. 'Silly gel, we don't want a Bohemian in the family.'

Ugh, Beatrice thought, what a stupid condescending smile. 'We must go, Evie. We mustn't waste any more of Cousin Arthur's time.' She turned to the door and informed him, 'Actually, we've decided to sell the house.'

'Oh no, my dear, one never sells one's only asset. I forbid it.'

'You forbid it, Cousin Arthur?'

'I forbid it, which, as Evangeline's guardian, I have the right to do. But Mother and I do have another proposition . . .'

Having negotiated Trafalgar Square and crossed the Haymarket, still walking briskly, Beatrice suddenly stopped at the corner of Jermyn Street and faced Evangeline. 'We'll work something out.'

'Yes, we'll think of something else.' They had stopped by a newspaper seller whose placard read 'COAL MINERS ALL OUT ON STRIKE'. 'Well, that won't bother us. We won't be able to afford coal.'

'Oh, Bea, that's a hard thing to say.'

'Hard times make hard hearts,' she said, mocking herself. Evie laughed, relieved that Bea's good humour had returned. They strolled on down Jermyn Street. Men, Beatrice thought, even here they rule. Trumpers for their hair, Lobbs for their shoes, Hawes and Curtis for their suits.

'Mmm. I like that.' Evangeline paused by a window.

'For you?' Bea was amused.

'Yes.' Evie was looking at a man's cricket sweater in the window. 'I'm going to try it on. We can't buy it — don't worry, I know that,' she said and went bravely into the shop.

The shop was hushed and smelt slightly of sweet tobacco. All the fitments were in rich, highly polished walnut and glass. At the back an elderly assistant was helping a customer choose a tie, a difficult task, Bea thought, seeing that all the ties looked alike. A younger assistant approached. 'Can I help you?'

'Yes, indeed,' said Evangeline rather grandly. 'We would like to see the sweater in the window.'

25

The young man opened a drawer in one of the large chests.

'Would it be this one, madam?'

'Yes, it would be.'

'Jolly good. That has been in the window for the Eton–Harrow match. For a brother?'

'No.'

'Your father?'

'No,' said Evie with her most enchanting smile. 'For me. I would like to try it on. Where is the fitting room?' The young man stared at her, overwhelmed by both her smile and her request.

'I say — er — how topping . . . but I don't think — that is to say, I don't know —'

'You don't know where the fitting room is?'

'No, or not so much know, but know if . . .'

The older assistant approached. 'Is there any problem, Mr Jenkins?'

'Not at all,' said Evangeline brightly. 'I am interested in buying this sweater and I would like to try it on.'

The older assistant pursed his lips, which perfected his likeness to an old prune, Beatrice thought, and said icily, 'There are no facilities for young ladies in this establishment,' and inclining his head towards Beatrice, 'no changing facilities for ladies of any age.'

Evangeline drew herself up to her full

height, which wasn't considerable, and said haughtily, 'Then you will never receive our patronage again.' They swept towards the door which Mr Jenkins opened and, Beatrice bowing graciously, the sisters left.

Evangeline looked at the two street-walkers standing on the corner of Curzon Street near Gunter's. In a way they were really very attractive, both with unnaturally pale skin accentuated by dark red lipstick and certainly more smartly dressed than the average Englishwoman. Maybe they were French. That sort of thing was done more by the French than the English, even in marriage, or so she'd learnt from books. Not the sort of books she had read in Papa's medical library. From these she had learnt what they did. Funny that they were called street-walkers, they didn't seem to walk very much.

'Now remember, Evie, this treat extends to one ice-cream each and no more.' Had they gone to another tea-room the treat could have been extended, but Gunter's was the most fashionable and therefore the most expensive. Sitting on hard, uncomfortable gilt chairs they surveyed the room. Women who thought they were smartly dressed, *à la mode,* but who all looked basically the same, dictated to by today's fashion experts just as they had once been dictated to by Nanny, and some up from the country for the day who wouldn't have known if they were fashionable or not.

'You were very Duchess of Kent as we left, Bea.'

'Anyone would think we were asking to remove our clothes and do the Dance of the Seven Sweaters.'

'Look, I was right, wasn't I? It would look wonderful with a long narrow chiffon skirt.' Evangeline had been sketching on the back of the menu.

'Oh, two strawberry ice-creams, please.' Beatrice ordered from the waitress who, being the only other woman in the room dressed in black, looked almost as chic as the sisters in their mourning clothes. 'Evie, I love it. You do have good ideas.'

'Oh dear.'

'What?'

'A woman has just come in — no, don't look now — looking like a cottage loaf. Plump women shouldn't wear fitted clothes.' Evangeline returned to the menu and started drawing rapidly giving quick glances at the woman.

'Can I look now?'

'Yes, she's talking to a woman wearing a hat like a chamber pot, extremely plump.'

'She can't help her shape, Evie.' Beatrice

turned discreetly to look at the two women but quickly turned back stifling a laugh. Her sister's description had been accurate.

'She could help her shape, if she wore something like that.' Evangeline held up the menu for Beatrice to see her sketch.

'Yes, you're right.'

'Yes, indeed, miss,' said the waitress, crooking her neck to see Evangeline's drawing as she delivered their ice-creams. She, too, was trying not to laugh. 'Perhaps I'd better leave the menus with you.'

'I'm going to try and make this ice-cream last.'

'If you do, it won't be ice-cream, it will melt. Do you think these sort of women come here every day, Bea?'

'They have nothing to do but spend their husbands' money. They'll eat cream cakes here and then go to the Dorchester Hotel and get rid of the fat in the Turkish bath.'

'They might not all be rich, but you won't find any miners' wives here. Could we have iced sponge fingers?' Evangeline was enjoying this rare glimpse of luxury.

'Not unless you want to walk home.'

The street-walkers were still there as they left. Evangeline wondered if they had had time to earn some money while she had been eating ice-cream, and if the street singer was still dreaming she dwelt in marble halls.

How stubborn, how stupid, how inconvenient of her nieces to refuse to take in paying guests, and why did they insist on calling them lodgers? They needed that three pounds a week and it was not going to come from her. 'Arthur darling, why do they insist on calling them lodgers?'

'Does it matter what they call them? They still don't want them.' Arthur topped up what was already a rather large whisky.

'You're drinking too much,' said Lydia automatically. Blast those girls. It all fitted in so well. She had stayed with the Crawleys in Singapore and now owed them return hospitality. They needed somewhere to live in London while looking for a flat and they were far too mean to pay for an hotel. It would be killing many birds with one stone. 'What do they think they're going to live on? The Eliott girls, I mean.'

'They intend to find employment.'

'I have no intention of being the aunt of a pair of shopgirls.'

'It would probably only be one shopgirl. Evangeline is bound to get married.' Arthur smiled foolishly. 'She's such a dear girl.'

This wasn't the first time he'd revealed an unfortunate interest in the girl, but it was out of the question. Lydia looked at her son sharply. It was no good him getting ideas in that direction, for many reasons.

CHAPTER TWO

'The *Lady*.' Evangeline scowled. 'There ought to be a newspaper called the *Worker*.'

'You sound like a Bolshevik.'

'I think I might be one,' Evangeline said daringly. 'Anyway, we're neither ladies nor workers.'

Beatrice looked up from the *Sketch* and laughed. The situation vacant column had proved disappointing. Although nannies and governesses were needed, they all specified the condition of living in.

Beatrice had reluctantly rejected 'Cook and gardener wanted', being unwilling to accept that the ability to make sardines on toast and to dead-head roses was sufficient qualification. 'What little work there is always goes to men now.'

'Why always?' Evangeline was scowling again.

'Evie, there are two million people unemployed.'

'Two million and two. Women are people, too, and now, because of the war, they have no work and no men.'

'Assistant to laboratory technician — our Miss Pilkington hardly trained us for that.'

'No indeed,' Evangeline said in a precise pinched tone. 'Painting, music and embroidery for young ladies. She even thought French was improper.'

'That's because she didn't speak it correctly. She would certainly have thought "Manicurist for gentlemen's barber shop" improper.' Evangeline was again examining the despised *Lady*. 'I wonder, though . . . Bea, give me your hands — let me try.'

'No, even *I* think that's improper.' Beatrice remembered her father speaking dismissively of Aunt Lydia, who had once been a manicurist. 'You don't marry women like that, you give them your hands. You don't ask for their hands in marriage.' Evie flung down the *Lady* with exasperation and moved her chair closer to the kitchen stove. It was the warmest room in the house but still not warm enough.

' "The Danielli Dancing Academy requires young ladies as dancing partners." ' Beatrice looked up from the paper. 'Evie, you could do that.'

Evangeline jumped to her feet excitedly. 'Yes, but I'm not doing it on my own.'

'But I've got three left feet and it does say

young ladies.' Bea could often be ironic about her advanced age.

'You can fox-trot. Try.' She pulled Beatrice to her feet, singing 'Marjie, I'm always dreaming of you, Marjie'. Evangeline danced around the room leading a reluctant Beatrice.

'Are ye having a party or what?' Molly popped her head round the door.

'I'm teaching Miss Bea how to fox-trot.'

'That'll take you a month of Sundays. What time do you want your dinners?'

'Come on, Molly, let's show her.' Evangeline was glowing and emboldened by this rare, tiny excitement.

'All right, then, Miss Evie. I'd best be the gentleman.' The young servant took the hands of her young mistress and they executed a perfect fox-trot across the grey flagstones of the kitchen floor. ' 'Tis just like the old days in the nursery.'

Signor Danielli was short, plump and very dapper, his dark hair oiled to perfection so that even now, whirling around the floor in a waltz, the tails of his black jacket flying, his hair remained immaculately in place.

He looks like a waiter, Beatrice thought. But he doesn't dance like one.

'One, two, three, up on the toes, one, two, three and dip, head up, not to look at the

34

feet, you are a swan, please. Glide, glide.'

'I hope he's not going to be gliding all afternoon with her. I'm due at the Trocadero at six.' Beatrice looked at the thin, feverish face of the girl standing next to her. She was looking anxiously at Evangeline. 'She's good,' said the flushed girl bitterly. 'And quite pretty.'

'Why did Signor Danielli send the other girls away?' asked Beatrice, still watching Evangeline who was now doing the rather complicated steps of the 'Twinkle'. 'Some of them were very nice-looking.'

'Wrong accent. Danielli's no fool, he advertised for young ladies and that's what he wants. Better for business if they have, you know, the right vowels.'

'*Grazie, grazie,* charming, and now for the other Miss Eliott.' Signor Danielli bowed to Evangeline and signalled for the gramophone record to be changed to the strains of 'Avalon'. He attempted to sweep Beatrice onto the floor in a quick-step; this wasn't possible because Beatrice was intent on doing the fox-trot which she did with a grim face paying no regard to either the music or Signor Danielli's feet. 'No-ow!' A cry of pain and despair escaped him as Beatrice placed one foot firmly on his. 'No, no, no.' The pain had somewhat changed his accent. He may have had Italian

35

parentage but he was probably brought up in Clerkenwell, thought Beatrice.

'Dear madam, I think it better you come for lessons.'

'I agree,' said Beatrice with relief. 'You need swans, not elephants.'

'But I am most happy to engage the young Miss Eliott. Practise the new dances if you please, the Jog-trot, the Twinkle, and to wear the pretty dance frock, yes?'

'Yes, yes, Signor Danielli, thank you.'

Signor Danielli approached the last applicant.

'Er, may I?' Beatrice took him aside. 'The gentlemen who come to your academy,' she said tentatively, 'they are . . .'

'Gentlemen,' he said decisively.

Beatrice's bedroom was like no other room in the house. The walls and ceiling were painted white and even the bare wood floors had been bleached and scattered with rag rugs. The walls were covered haphazardly with her own unframed drawings, water-colours painted by her mother and collages made by Evangeline from scraps of silk and tweed, and remnants of satins and velvets. There was a predominance of blue and yellow, which revealed the influence of Monet, and the room was flooded with light. In one corner was a wicker garden table which Beatrice had painstakingly painted with blue and white to look like gingham. The room was her sanctuary, the more so since she knew her father had never set foot in it, had never known it was there, tucked away in the attic.

'Stop moving,' came barely from her mouth, full of pins.

'Stop talking,' said Evangeline, 'when your mouth is full of pins.' She twisted to see herself in the long looking-glass.

Beatrice had cut and draped one of the cornflower blue curtains from her windows as a skirt and was now pinning an embroidered cream silk waistcoat.

'Bea, don't I look wonderful? I mean, you've done it wonderfully. But what shall I do about the sleeves of the shirt? They're far too long and we have no time.'

Beatrice rose from her knees and picked up two steel expanding arm-bands. 'I found these in Father's room.'

'Horrible!'

'Not when I've wrapped them in ribbon. You'll look like a Morris dancer.'

'That's one dance I won't be doing.' She laughed. 'I'm going to be a working woman, Bea, earning my own living.'

'Not a very big living.'

'No, not enough to keep the wolf from the door.'

'Not enough to keep the lodgers from the door. Where do you suppose he wore these things?' Beatrice said, abruptly picking up a frilled-front shirt. 'At his *medical conferences* in Leamington Spa, I suppose,' she answered herself with heavy irony.

They heard the chime of a bell downstairs. 'Bea, isn't that the front door?' Evangeline looked anxiously at her sister. The bell jangled insistently in the distance.

'Oh, yes, it is. Well, Molly will get it.' Beatrice looked at her sister, seeing only the clothes. 'No wonder I wasn't allowed in the room when they packed.' She spoke to herself.

'They?'

'Molly's mother, then Molly.'

'Get the child out of here.' That sentence from her father punctuated every unwanted appearance made by Beatrice, whether it was in the drawing room, consulting room or his dressing room. She could recall it now and the sound of his trunk being slammed shut as Kathleen looked guiltily over her shoulder at the child standing in the doorway. Beatrice never argued, she just turned on her heel and sped away, biting her mouth until it bled. By the time Kathleen had returned to Ireland and Molly had taken over the packing she no

38

longer wanted or needed her father, she had become self-sufficient, and Evangeline was growing up and beginning to give her much-needed companionship. She also knew that her only crime was to have been a girl and not the longed-for and much tried-for son and heir . . . Evangeline waited for an explanation that didn't come.

There was the sound of two sets of feet mounting the stairs, a firm swift step and a scurrying patter and Molly cut the odd silence as she opened the door breathlessly. 'It's Miss —'

'Maddox,' completed Penelope, striding in. 'I have good news for you, I think. My goodness!' She stood in the room spellbound. 'How extraordinary. Beautiful, beautiful room — lost for words, not like me. Did it yourself?' She looked enquiringly at both of them.

'Yes,' said Beatrice, elated at her reaction.

'All of it?'

'Yes, all.'

Penelope examined the wicker table. *'Trompe l'oeil,'* she said. 'Deception of the eye, very witty.'

'Deception of the eye,' repeated Beatrice. 'You can go, Molly,' she said coldly.

'You said good news?' Evangeline smiled shyly.

'Ah yes, hope so. My brother, only son.

Spoilt, frightful war, society photographer.'
Penelope paused and snorted derisively. 'Rather
successful, needs a general dogsbody, I've
been doing it. Not doing it any more, more
important things to do.' She looked at them
both closely and then rattled on in her odd
shorthand. 'Taking a job from an unemployed
person, told him I know an unemployed person who'd be perfect for it. You,' she said,
pointing at Beatrice and turning to Evangeline,
'not you. Far too young and pretty. That's
settled, then, tomorrow morning. One seven
seven Green Street, Mayfair. Got to go, busy,
got a lying-in, and a laying-out.' She looked
around the room again. 'Bloody marvellous,'
and left.

Lydia read the telegram again. The
Crawleys, the creepy Crawleys, would arrive
on Tuesday, a little earlier than she had hoped
but it would give Beatrice less time to think
about it and refuse. She accepted a glass of
sherry from Arthur, noting with distaste that
he was pouring himself an even larger whisky
than usual. 'I've got a splitting headache,' he
said, as he caught her flinty gaze.

'Oh, perfect cure.'

'I've had a bad day. The market's collaps-
ing.'

'It always is, and you always think that a

40

larger than usual intake of Johnnie Walker will solve the problem.' Lydia was in an unusually censorious mood with her son.

Arthur loved his mother — or, to be more exact, loved her loving him and didn't want the unqualified love to change or be withdrawn. He guessed that she was more anxious than she showed about the Crawleys' visit: for some reason, dealing with Beatrice always made his mother nervous.

'If it really worries you I won't finish it.' He took her hands and stepped back to examine her. 'I love you in that gown — rose, it's the perfect colour for you.' He cupped her face in his hands in a gesture that was not entirely filial. 'Are you never going to age? It's getting embarrassing introducing you as my mother.'

Lydia smiled indulgently. She knew she looked good for her age but she had enough remnants of self-knowledge to know that she didn't look *that* good. All this was a ploy to stop her nagging and it worked. This was a minuet they danced around each other, and she knew he would soon go to his club and continue drinking.

She flushed. 'I'm glad you like it. Matter of fact, I'm having this jacket copied by Beatrice. It will give me the opportunity to give her a little money.' Lydia took Arthur's hand from her face and squeezed it.

Very little, Arthur thought. 'And you will lay down the law?'

'No, Arthur, I will not lay down the law. I will persuade her that it is in her best interests.'

Beatrice watched from the front door as Evangeline walked down the street. Her sister looked beautiful and elegant and had been proud and happy. If she was nervous she was concealing it well. When Beatrice had warned her to be careful Evangeline had laughed and said, 'What of? Why should I be scared?' And indeed, Beatrice thought, What of?

It had been difficult to dissuade Evangeline from walking to Tottenham Court Road to save the bus fare from Highgate. Only the reasoning that it would take hours and tire her out before work had persuaded her not to. Beatrice turned back into the house. Molly was carrying coal into the drawing room. She heard her shovelling it onto the fire; this would have to stop.

Molly saw Beatrice and put her head round the door. 'You're off to the photography man, are ye? Ye look a right picture yourself.'

'I hope Mr Maddox thinks so.' She paused. 'We ought to be more careful with the coal, Molly.'

'Pity you don't have peat over here, I've never heard of a peat strike.' She looked at Beatrice's worried face and stood up.

'It isn't the strike, Molly, or the coal. There won't be enough for other things —' She broke off, embarrassed.

'If it's about me wages, no need to concern yourself, I've been here all me life and I'll not leave you, like rats when the ship's going down. If the Good Lord see fit I'll go to the workhouse with you.'

Beatrice was silenced for a moment and was not sure whether she wanted to laugh or cry. 'Thank you, Molly. Thank you. But none of us is going to drown, you know.'

'Do you have a morning job?' the young man asked. He was a callow youth, Evangeline decided. At last she knew what that meant, she had read it often without quite understanding.

'No. Why?'

'I thought perhaps you hadn't time to change.'

She looked around the dance floor: the other young ladies were wearing floaty pastel tea-gowns. The young man led her past the long mirror in a rather daring reverse, admiring his dashing reflection, and stepped heavily on her foot. 'Don't apologize,' he said airily. Evangeline was hard pressed not to scream but remembering Signor Danielli's instructions, 'You are always happy and the kick on the foot is always your fault,' she smiled sweetly and let herself be led or rather pushed into a series of complicated steps which finished with her other foot being stamped on. This time her smile was not so sweet. When the music stopped she hoped he would prefer to dance with someone who didn't look as if they had a morning job but after he had scanned the sea of sweet-pea muslin, he turned to claim her again. However, within a second of his having relinquished her to survey the opposition, another young man had rather masterfully led her away.

'Are you in absolute agony?' he said with a sympathy which was rather spoilt by a huge grin. 'He got both feet, didn't he? I'll try to be an improvement.' Evangeline forgot her bruised feet as they waltzed easily round the room, and relaxed into his arms as he held her lightly but firmly.

This is it, she thought. I'm dancing with a young man for the first time and he is a young man, not a callow youth. Grey eyes, like warm pebbles, and thick brown wavy hair, not oiled like Arthur's and Signor Danielli's, natural and a little untidy. 'You're

44

looking at me rather severely. What are you thinking?'

'Well, thinking you don't need the help of Mr Danielli's Academy.'

'Not in the waltz, perhaps, but I like to keep up with the new dances and I see you like to keep up with the new fashions.' He looked at her clothes with undisguised approval. 'Miss Eliott, you look absolutely stunning.' He said it warmly with obvious sincerity. Evangeline smiled. I'm happy, she thought, how odd, I know I'm happy.

Late autumn, what a wonderful time of year, she thought. Even in London the air was full of harvest-time and the smell of apples. Beatrice was walking through Camden Town and it was sunny and crispy cold. She was doing what she had persuaded Evangeline not to do: she was walking to Mayfair. Oh, what a goose I am. Of course there's a smell of apples, this is a market. She laughed and, picked her way carefully over the cobblestones avoiding the debris cast by stallholders trimming leeks, carrots and cabbages.

'D'you wanna cucumber, darlin'?' a cheeky young costermonger yelled.

'No, thanks,' said the pretty young shopper, eyeing everything before she made up her mind. 'I've already got one.'

'Not as big as mine,' he shouted back.

'Big enough for me, ta.'

Beatrice hurried on, smiling. Should she have been shocked? She wasn't. Life was going to be all right. If they both had jobs they could manage without Aunt Lydia's lodgers. Why did she call them 'paying guests'? It was so genteel. Anyway it didn't matter what you called them, it would turn their home into a boarding house.

The house in Green Street had three bells beside the door but only the lower was marked: GRAY'S RELIGIOUS PUBLICATIONS. If it's a studio it should be the top floor, Beatrice reasoned.

She looked through the windows of the ground floor. A portly middle-aged man was sitting at a large desk covered with manuscripts, smoking a pipe and day-dreaming. She signalled to him. He turned and smiled enquiringly. 'Jack Maddox,' she mouthed. He looked disappointed, but gestured to the ceiling very emphatically. She was right, the top floor. The portly man then gestured to her to push the door. It wasn't locked.

Beatrice walked up the stairs, her confidence evaporating. What had Penelope told her brother? Very little, she supposed, there was very little to tell. Well, this was the top floor. There was a door but again no name. She knocked, but this one, too, was open.

'Good morning,' she said brightly as she entered what was obviously an empty reception room.

'Who the hell is that?' A door was flung open and Jack Maddox appeared. He was wearing very rumpled evening clothes which matched his rumpled hair — even his face looked rumpled, Beatrice thought.

'Oh, er, sorry,' he said. 'I thought you were somebody else, a man, of course.' After this vague apology he snapped, 'What do you want?'

'I'm Beatrice Eliott. Didn't your sister . . .'

'Oh, the unemployed. I told her late this morning.'

'Mr Maddox, it is twelve o'clock. That's about as late as morning gets.'

He made a sound half-way between a snort and a laugh and opened the studio door. 'Sit down. Glass of champagne?'

'No, thank you.' She looked around the room for somewhere to sit. Every surface was covered with materials, books, magazines; the only chair was occupied by a saucepan filled with ice and water containing a bottle of champagne.

'Here.' He took a pile of negatives from a *chaise-longue* that had almost collapsed in the middle. Beatrice sat carefully on it but not carefully enough: she sank slowly to the floor. Should I stay here? she thought. Should I laugh? Should I hit him?

He looked at her with surprise. 'What are you doing down there? I didn't mean, here, sit down, I meant here, look at this.' He gave her a negative.

'Very nice,' she said doubtfully, standing up, examining the likeness of a middle-aged woman with as many double chins as ropes of pearls around her neck.

'You'll have to do better than that,' he said. ' "Very nice", good Lord. Are you a good liar?'

'I haven't done a great deal.'

'What have you done and what can you do?'

'I worked for my late father as his receptionist and bookkeeper.'

'So you can make appointments reliably?'

'I suppose so.'

'Suppose or know?' he snapped.

'Know.'

'Type?'

'Yes,' she replied, thinking, only two fingers, but if he approved of lying this was practice.

'Shorthand?'

'No,' and in a sudden rush of guilt, 'I only type with two fingers.'

'Know anything about cameras?'

'No.'

'Not many people do, so to sum up you type with two fingers and once worked for "Daddy",' he laid heavy derisive emphasis on Daddy.

'Yes,' she said, with great effort. 'And now I would like to work for you.'

He looked at her with amusement, his strong, angular features distorted in a sneer. 'I thought you said you didn't lie.'

He went into what Beatrice took to be a darkroom and returned with a large photograph. 'Here, and I mean look at this, don't sit on the floor again.' She took the photograph, it was the same as the negative but now the woman looked years younger, all the double chins were gone and the pearls glistened on a creamy white slender throat. 'That's where the lying comes in, you would have to convince her that it's a perfect likeness and never mention the word retouching. If this offends your sensibilities, Miss, er . . .'

'Eliott.'

'. . . then I suggest you seek work elsewhere, though what someone with your qualifications could expect to be paid for I really don't know.'

He picked up a glass from the floor, 'Sure you wouldn't like a glass of champagne?'

'I'm sure, Mr Maddox, I'm also sure that you are quite the most arrogant and ill-mannered man I have ever met.'

Had Jack Maddox known Beatrice Eliott for any length of time the two red patches on her cheeks would have warned him that he was playing with fire, but unknowing he said, 'That may well be, Miss Eliott, but I doubt you've met many men arrogant or otherwise.' He saw her hand clutch the saucepan of iced water and stepped back quickly to the *chaise-longue*. Beatrice's last picture of him, trapped between the two halves of the *chaise* covered in water, went a long way to soothe her ruffled dignity.

Even as a child Beatrice had had the ability to make her feel uncomfortable: that little fox-like face would stare at or through her, and Lydia felt that she knew something. Of course she couldn't, but that cold stare seemed to indicate that she could be as cruel as her father. She was staring now, looking with ill-concealed disdain at her aunt's hair. Lydia parted it, she knew it was all right, it had been done by Monsieur Alexandre. He had been so clever in concealing the thinning and greying that it looked as rich and russet as it ever had.

'Beatrice, you'd enjoy having the Crawleys. They've led such interesting lives, their travels alone . . . You've been so cloistered, my dear, this is your chance to make new acquaintances.' Beatrice hadn't been looking at her aunt's hair, she had been thinking about her final picture of Jack Maddox. She laughed. Lydia, now utterly discomfited, looked at herself in the mirror.

'They will be lodgers,' Beatrice said severely and examined the long silk jacket she was holding. 'If you want this copied in panne velvet it won't hang as well.'

Turning back from the mirror, Lydia smiled condescendingly. 'They are friends of mine who will be your guests, paying guests, and the jacket was shown in the collection in both silk and panne velvet.'

'Then I suggest you order it from Monsieur Worth who, although expensive, will clearly get it to hang properly.' Beatrice knew she was being more than brusque but having to accept the possibility of lodgers as being necessary had removed the traces of her morning's good humour that had survived her encounter with Jack Maddox.

Lydia played her trump card. 'You must think of Evangeline as well as yourself. She is a lovely girl and will certainly marry soon and well. When that happens I'm sure you would prefer to be self-sufficient and not a burden on your sister.' Her ploy succeeded

51

all too well. Beatrice, her face now pinched and tired, rose and put the jacket carefully on her chair. 'I won't wait for tea, Aunt Lydia, and I will certainly think about your "paying guests".' She put as much emphasis on this as Jack Maddox had on 'Daddy'. What would his camera have done with her aunt? she thought, and looked at her closely. Those funny fat bits by her mouth that made her look like a guinea-pig, they would go, and about five inches off her hips. She laughed again. 'Goodbye, Aunt Lydia, I'll let you know.'

Evangeline's nose poked over the warm soft rug with which Edward had covered her. She turned to look at him, but the wind whistling past the car wrapped her hair around her face so she looked at the road again. The car smelled of leather and saddle-soap; it was very well cared for. She had been pleased when Edward had told her rather sheepishly that it meant more to him than anything in the world. And anybody, she hoped. He was very nice, no, that wasn't right, more than nice, considerate. He had been so careful and clever at the academy: not wanting to annoy Signor Danielli and jeopardize her job, he had only danced every other dance with her and in between had danced with the plainest girl in the room. At the end of the long afternoon she had thought he had gone without saying good-bye and, looking around the emptying room, she felt like a sad dance-hall hostess and her feet in their flimsy slippers began to ache. The work had only been bearable because of him. She had turned left out of the academy, hoping he might be there waiting, but Tottenham Court Road was full of ordinary men and women leaving shops and offices and there was no sign of extraordinary Edward.

She trudged towards the bus-stop, her previous energy and happiness gone. She was just a working woman like others in the street, and romance and friendship were not for her.

'I say, cheer up, Miss Eliott.' He was there in a motor car by her side. 'I'd most awfully like to drive you home — you must be exhausted.' He handed her carefully into the car and wrapped the rug round her. Evangeline saw a young woman at the bus-stop looking at her with undisguised envy. She was thin and pale and her clothes were too light for the cold autumn air.

Oh, I'm so lucky! she had thought. Work and a new friend. She had smiled at the young woman trying to convey that it could happen to her, too.

Edward slowed down to let a stream of solemn-looking children cross the road by the pond at Jack Straw's Castle and looked at

Evangeline. The wind had whipped her cheeks enhancing the colour and her eyes were bright and sparkling. 'You ought to be worn out,' he said, 'but you look as though you could dance all night.'

She looked at him in mock horror. 'Oh, no, Mr Banks, anything but that.'

'Well,' he said hesitantly, 'I hope you won't think this forward of me, but I feel I've known you much longer than one afternoon, I —'

'Yes,' she said with surprise, 'exactly, so do I.'

'I wondered . . .' The crocodile included one not so solemn-looking little boy who ran to the car making inarticulate sounds of enthusiastic admiration.

Evangeline and Edward laughed, and Edward, translating, said, 'Yes, it is a De Deon Boutton 21, and thank you, old chap, I think it's ripping, too.' The boy grinned hugely and ran to join the crocodile. Edward drove along the tree-lined stretch of road which intercepted the Heath towards the toll gate and the Spaniards Inn. What does he wonder? Evie thought.

'You see,' he said, 'some of us, some friends, are going to see a moving picture this evening, *Those Glorious Years*, and it would be absolutely marvellous if you could come with us.'

Evangeline sat up excitedly. 'Oh, I would love to,' she began, but her enthusiasm faded away as she thought of Beatrice. 'No, I couldn't possibly, my sister is waiting for me.'

'Couldn't we tell her, ask her?'

'It wouldn't be fair on Beatrice, this is my first day at my first job and she's not just my sister — you see, she's always looked after me.'

Edward took his defeat gallantly. 'I like the sound of Beatrice. Perhaps we can do it another time.'

Beatrice, unaware that she was being admired, jabbed her needle sharply in and out of the white pique waistcoat she was embroidering; that it had belonged to her father made the vicious jabs more pleasurable. 'Damn Aunt Lydia,' she said aloud. 'And damn Cousin Arthur and damn the Crawleys and double damn Mr Jack Maddox.' She heard a car draw up and looked out of the large attic window: a flushed and high-spirited Evangeline was being helped solicitously out of the car by a tall, attractive, tousle-headed young man. They shook hands and paused, their heads close together, then Evangeline broke away, ran to the top of the steps and stopped, the young man gazing at her with obvious admiration. She waved and, tearing himself away from her, he jumped into his car and sped away.

'Bea, Bea, oh, come to me,' Evangeline sang as she mounted the stairs.

'She's in her room, Miss Evie.' Molly put her head out of the kitchen and called up to her.

Suddenly the house felt alive again, Beatrice thought, and, smiling, she laid down her sewing as her sister burst into the room.

'Did you see the car? Isn't it deevy? It's something called a Dian Button, I think, and Edward says it's very special.'

'And who is Edward?' Beatrice said anxiously.

'His name's Edward Banks, he danced with me most of the time, ooh, my poor feet, not him — I mean, not his fault my poor feet, he's a wonderful dancer. He wants to take me to a moving picture.' All this tumbled out of Evangeline as she removed her coat and, sitting down, eased her feet out of her shoes. 'With some others,' she added.

'With some other what?' Beatrice asked.

'With some other people, to the moving picture. You will let me go, won't you? I'm exhausted, it's so tiring, some of the men are so . . . Oh, Bea, I'm sorry.' She stopped and looked at Beatrice with guilty concern. 'How did you get on with Mr Maddox?'

'I didn't.' Beatrice's reply was short and sharp and Evie knew there was no point in questioning further.

'Oh, dear, poor Bea.' She hesitated. 'And Aunt Lydia?'

Beatrice rose and looked out of the window. The end of the day was as fine as the beginning; pink and yellow leaves lay in a drift across the grass lawns and a neighbour's bonfire was sending up a column of acrid blue smoke. She turned back to her sister, the melancholy of autumn imprinted on her face. 'I'm sorry, Evie, but it doesn't look as if I'm employable and so we may have to accept paying guests.'

'Paying pests, I'm going to call them,' said Evangeline.

I suppose I *have* got a job, Beatrice thought, as she wiped a wisp of damp hair off her red and shiny face: head laundress. The kitchen was full of steam from the copper boiling their washing, and wooden drying racks, hanging from the ceiling, were festooned with damp clothes. She looked over at Molly, who was passing heavy dripping sheets through the mangle. She, too, had a shiny red face — manual labour was a great equalizer. Even Evangeline was a manual labourer in a way: she might go to work wearing pretty clothes with her hair dressed beautifully but after four hours' dancing she was probably hot and had damp wisps of hair — although she certainly didn't dance wearing a large calico apron. Beatrice smiled at the thought and spat on her iron; it didn't sizzle. She had hated the laundress doing that but now she knew it saved time: if it didn't sizzle it wasn't hot enough. 'Is the other iron ready yet, Molly?'

'Indeed it is, Miss Bea.'

'Oh, it takes a brain to come up with an idea of that sort — it would never have occurred to Mrs Gaskin in a month of Sundays to use the two irons, she just sat there drinking her tea, waiting for the one to heat up. I thought I'd hate having to do all this when we let her go,' Beatrice said. 'But I get a certain satisfaction out of seeing it all washed, ironed and folded.'

'A job well done,' said Molly. 'Only it seems a shame to spoil it by using them.'

The front-door bell jangled on the wooden board, its brass not quite as gleaming as it used to be. Molly and Beatrice looked at each other. Neither of them was suitably dressed for answering the door. 'Were you expecting anybody, Miss Bea?'

'No, and there's nobody I want to see looking like this.'

Beatrice smiled again at Molly: the front of

her dress was wet from the sheets she had pulled from the copper. 'But I think I'd better be the one to go.' She laughed, went out of the kitchen, glanced in the hall mirror, smoothed her hair, straightened her belt and opened the front door.

'Miss Eliott?' The woman seemed a little nervous.

'Yes,' Beatrice said. 'Can I help you?'

'I'm Mrs Henshaw.'

Bea was puzzled. The woman seemed to think she'd know who she was. 'I'm sorry but . . .'

'I was a friend of your father's.' Beatrice looked at her coldly. 'I know we've never met but I would like to speak to you.'

'Speak to me about what?' Beatrice hadn't meant to be rude but her sharp tone warned Mrs Henshaw that she could be very rude indeed.

'It would be easier if — may I come in?'

Beatrice stood back reluctantly and held open the door. 'If you wish.' The woman was attractive, she thought, about forty perhaps, very well dressed but not ostentatiously so. They sat facing each other in the cold drawing room, the fire unlit. 'What did you want to speak to me about, Mrs Henshaw?'

'Well, it was about your father.'

59

'Yes, you said.' Again Beatrice was short and cold.

'I wanted to say how sorry I am and —'

'Thank you,' Beatrice interrupted and looked at Mrs Henshaw closely. 'Were you a patient of his?'

'No.'

'No, of course you weren't. I would remember.'

Mrs Henshaw got up and walked across the room, rubbing her cold hands. 'Your father and I were friends, personal friends. He spoke about you and Evangeline.'

Beatrice winced with distaste. 'Are you a friend from Leamington Spa?' she said suddenly.

'Ah.' Mrs Henshaw breathed a sigh of relief. 'So he did mention —'

'No.'

'Oh dear.' Mrs Henshaw smiled ruefully. 'This is going to be more awkward than I thought.'

Beatrice looked at her gently curved elegant figure; she was really very attractive, short straight nose, wide grey eyes and slightly fading chestnut hair. Not unlike Mama — obviously Papa's type, she thought bitterly. 'Awkward. *You* feel awkward. I am sorry.'

Ignoring the irony, Mrs Henshaw explained, 'I was fond of him and grateful. Now

60

I'd like to help you.'

'Help? What kind of help?'

Molly knocked at the door and entered. 'Did you ring for tea, Miss Bea?'

'No, I did not,' Beatrice snapped.

'Would you be liking some tea, Miss Beatrice?' Molly said with an unfamiliar deference.

'No, I would not.' Molly stood there, looking at the strange woman curiously. I wonder if there's a lot of chickens coming home to roost, she thought. Beatrice dismissed her: 'Thank you, Molly, you may go.'

Mrs Henshaw turned to Beatrice. 'I understand from your Cousin Arthur that your situation is quite serious.'

'Cousin Arthur?' Beatrice said angrily. 'Cousin Arthur said that? Is Cousin Arthur another "friend" from Leamington Spa?'

'He is a friend,' Mrs Henshaw said with some dignity. 'Your father and I often dined with him, not always in Leamington Spa.' She paused and said kindly, 'Miss Eliott, I came here out of concern for your welfare. I can see how difficult it is for you, it is difficult for me, but I came here only wanting to be of assistance,' she took a deep breath, 'I have been left comfortably off and I would like to give you —'

'Some money,' Beatrice said quietly.

61

'Yes,' Mrs Henshaw said.

Beatrice stood up. 'Your offer of money is not acceptable. My sister and I are perfectly capable of taking care of ourselves.'

Mrs Henshaw gathered her gloves and handbag, she was very pale: Beatrice had managed to make her feel tawdry. 'Of course you are, a mistake, I'm sorry.'

Having shown the woman out, Beatrice returned slowly to the kitchen. I wonder how old she was when Father met her. About my age, perhaps, or younger? Twenty? No, that would mean that Mama . . . No, mustn't think about that. I mustn't cry, I mustn't cry, anger is better than . . . and Evie will be home soon. I'll tell her she can go to the moving pictures with that young man, good for her to have friends. How odd it was that not to love your father made you feel lonely.

The organ-grinder was still playing old favourites from the war. She supposed the scars on his face were a result of his wounds. Lydia turned away with distaste. Victoria station took its usual pull on her heartstrings. If only I was going to Paris and not to Highgate, she thought, but who would I be going with? Stephen was married — well, he was married then, but not as married as he was now, three children and a sick wife. Who else, then?

Henry was dead and Richard, too. She thought guiltily of her husband.

The sour-smelling vapour from the engines evaporated a little and then Lydia saw the Crawleys. A porter led the way, trundling a push-cart which contained an enormous pile of luggage. 'Vera, how lovely, and Chips, so good to see you.' She kissed them both, observing that Vera was still very slim, too slim for a woman of her age, positively stringy. 'I have a cab waiting outside, I suppose it will take all that,' she said, eyeing a cabin trunk, four suitcases, three hat-boxes, golf clubs, a gun case and tennis and badminton rackets.

'No, no, my man, you've got to use your head,' Chips Crawley barked. 'A bit of logic is what's needed — the trunk first, then the large suitcase.'

'Darling, tell the man to be careful of my hat-boxes, I don't want them crushed,' Vera piped.

Still the same little-girl-lost voice and fifty if she's a day, thought Lydia. 'Vera, don't worry about your boxes, I doubt you'll find those hats suitable in London.'

'Lydia, dear, I can assure you my hats will be more than suitable for London. After all, they were made in Paris.' Lydia charitably forbore from asking her when exactly.

'Come along, ladies, chop, chop, Major

Crawley's party forward.' They climbed into the cab, Lydia in the back with Chips, the pleasure of the advantageous position spoilt by Vera's remark, 'You two jumbos can sit in the back and little me will face you.'

'Such a pity Kensington Square is too small for guests. Of course, with Stanton House it's all we need in London, and Hertfordshire is so easy to get to, and with Arthur at home . . .'

'When are you going to get rid of that great hulking son of yours? I'd have thought you'd have married him off by now.' Vera leaned forward sympathetically. The sun hadn't been good for her complexion, Lydia noted. All those broken veins, and the dirty yellow colour made her skin look like chamois leather.

'Arthur could have his pick,' she said curtly.

Major Crawley laughed. 'No gel good enough for your Arthur, eh?' He patted Lydia's knee. She saw Vera freeze and turn away. Silly woman, she was barking up a very wrong tree indeed. She couldn't know her husband well. Lydia was aware that she was too old for him. She'd always been too old for him. 'Traffic is terrible in London now,' she said. 'It will be much better when all the horse-drawn stuff is off the street. You'll find Highgate much quieter and convenient for your house-hunting. My nieces are charming girls.'

'If they are your nieces, my dear, they must be charming,' Chips said with heavy-handed gallantry.

'It's the house and its comfort I'm interested in,' Vera snapped. 'Their charm is immaterial.'

If only her husband wasn't so bloody miserly, she thought — and with her money too — they'd be staying in a service flat in Curzon Street, where she'd be near her dressmaker and he'd be far from the danger of Lydia's young nieces.

Beatrice faced Arthur across the drawing room. Her anger was such that she was shaking. He backed away. The craven coward, she thought contemptuously. 'They are on their way?'

'Oh, come on, Beatrice, Mother said you'd agreed.'

'I suppose I did in a way.' She felt cornered. 'But she gave me to understand that it wouldn't be for a week or two. I'd rather hoped there would be time to find something else,' she finished lamely.

'Like what?' Arthur was exasperated. 'This is a respectable way to make money, you should be grateful to Mother.'

'How respectable, Cousin Arthur, was the way my father lost money?'

'Now then, Beatrice, calm down. We only want to help you and Evangeline.'

'It seems that everybody wants to help us today,' she said in an undertone. 'You know, Arthur, I prefer you pompous to placatory.'

What the hell was the woman talking about? It had turned out much worse than he'd imagined — he'd only agreed to break the news himself in the hope of seeing Evangeline. 'Where is she?' Arthur asked suddenly.

'Where's who?'

'Evangeline. I expected her to be here.'

'She had to see some people,' Beatrice said vaguely.

'What people?'

'People you don't know.' The sound of a car drawing up outside forestalled further questioning.

'Ah, that must be the Crawleys' cab.' Arthur strode to the windows and looked out. 'My God,' he shouted. 'Eddie Banks, you stupid woman,' he roared at a bemused Beatrice as he charged out of the room.

Evangeline looked up, surprised, as she shut the front door.

'What is it, Arthur? What's the matter?' He grabbed her arm tightly and pulled her towards the drawing room. 'How long have you

66

known him? Where did you meet him?' he hissed.

Molly ran up the basement stairs calling, 'What's going on up there?'

'None of your business, girl. Get back to the kitchen,' Arthur yelled and, pulling Evangeline behind him into the drawing room, he kicked the door shut.

'You're hurting me,' Evangeline cried. You're also making me feel sick, she thought. He had taken her by the top of her arm and his hand was pressing against her breast.

'Leave her alone,' Beatrice said firmly. 'She met him at a very respectable dance academy.'

'There's no such thing,' Arthur said, releasing Evangeline, who was crying and rubbing her arm.

'It *is* respectable, I work there — I'm a dancing partner.'

'With a dancing partner like Eddie Banks it can't be respectable.'

'Edward has always behaved very properly to me,' Evangeline said, looking at him with loathing. Arthur could see that she knew he had touched her deliberately.

'Let me tell you, silly girl,' he moderated his tone, 'about Eddie Banks. He is a known philanderer, he takes little girls like you, Evangeline, uses them then throws them in the gutter.'

'How interesting,' Beatrice said slowly. 'And how, as a matter of fact, do you know so much about him?'

'How do I know? It's his sport, he boasts about it. He should have married the Markham girl but he wouldn't, he chucked her. That's why she was shipped off to Australia, where I presume a Baby Banks is thriving in the outback.'

Evangeline curled up like a ball in the big armchair, crying quietly. Arthur looked at her dotingly: she was adorable. Catching his glance she sat up straight and looked at him fiercely, remembering his odious touch. But as ferocity hardly altered her gentle features and in that armchair her feet barely touched the ground she continued to look adorable and Arthur continued to simper at her. Only an 'Ugh' of disgust from her distracted him and he turned his attention to her plain and angular sister.

'Really, Beatrice, I blame you. How could you be so irresponsible? Your behaviour is appalling. What kind of marriage do you think Evangeline will make if she's seen with cads like Eddie Banks? No wonder Uncle Henry made her my ward, he was certainly right not to trust you.'

'If we are talking about trust,' Beatrice said quietly, 'don't use the word in conjunction with my father. It's all right, is it, to philander in Leamington Spa and introduce your nephew to your mistress? And, incidentally, how dare you discuss our private affairs with her? It shows at the very least a lack of taste.'

Arthur was shaken. How did she know about Leamington Spa? Was it Jane Simmis? No, he hadn't seen her lately. Perhaps Lily Henshaw? He brazened it out.

'That has absolutely nothing to do with it. Don't you understand, woman? He's known as Eddie the cherrypicker.'

'What?' Evangeline stood up. 'What does that mean?'

Thank God, thought Arthur, as he heard the doorbell ring. They're here, Mother and the Crawleys. How could I have said that? Mustn't let Beatrice rattle me. 'Ah, the Crawleys.' His relief was evident.

'Tell me, Arthur,' Beatrice said bitterly. 'Are your friend Mrs Henshaw's pearls real? And is that one of the reasons we have to take in "paying guests"?'

From the hall they could hear Molly's surprised voice. 'Sure and wasn't I told nothing at all about visitors, missus, your ladyship.' Surprise always made Molly's brogue more pronounced.

'Now look here, Beatrice, I wasn't privy to every arrangement your father made.' Arthur made for the door but was stopped in his tracks by the dangerous calm of Beatrice's voice.

'No indeed, for there must have been many of them. For him to have spent his entire income and that of our mother must have entailed a life full of luxury, if not uxury, as Byron said, for most of his adult life.'

Oh, God, Arthur thought, what is the bloody woman talking about? 'Yes, well, no point in dwelling in the past,' he blustered.

'You are quite right, Arthur,' Beatrice said briskly. 'We must think about the future, and in the future I have no intention of letting you run our lives, you or Aunt Lydia. You have given us no choice but to receive the Crawleys, I accept that, but make no mistake, Arthur, they will not be staying long. We shall find a way of taking care of ourselves without your help. We will make ourselves independent, I have to believe that. Come, Evie,' she took her sister gently by the arm, 'no more tears, we have to greet our guests.'

Arthur put his head in his hands as they left the drawing room. He could hear them graciously greeting his mother and her friends.

'How do you do, Mrs Crawley? How do you do, Major Crawley? Good afternoon, Aunt Lydia. Molly, will you take the trunk to Father's bedroom and put the rest in his dressing room.'

Evangeline opened her eyes, she was obviously not going to sleep. Had she somehow always known about Edward, she wondered. Perhaps.

It had always been clear that he didn't need lessons and it explained why Signor Danielli was so careful with her, kind, really, steering her away from Edward whenever he could. And his veiled warnings, too veiled for her to understand — but, of course, she hadn't wanted to understand. She had wanted Edward to like her in that way, the way she liked him. His nearness when they danced, the way he led her off the floor holding her arm, his touch as he folded the rug around her in the car. She didn't want to end up in Australia with a Baby Banks, but as they had no money she was more likely to end up in Esher. She certainly didn't want to marry him either; he was attractive, but not really interesting. He didn't seem to care about painting, or Ireland, or the coal shortage — he hadn't even known that the miners were on strike. She didn't want to marry anybody, although it seemed that that was the only future everyone envisaged for her.

The thought of marriage reminded her of the Crawleys. What a creepy pair they were. She was so nervous and spiky with her lined yellow skin and emaciated body, and that powder blue and pink linen costume, too cold for the weather, too tight for comfort and too young for a woman of her age. Any age. And him, slightly fat with a damp brick-red face, nicotine stained moustache and yellow teeth — she laughed, they matched his wife's skin.

Would Edward be like that in twenty or thirty years' time? No point thinking about it, no point in thinking about Edward; it was all over and she wasn't going back to the Danielli Dancing Academy. Bea had given in to Arthur about that. What would she do tomorrow? Looking at her bedside clock she realized it was already tomorrow.

CHAPTER THREE

Beatrice watched the Crawleys turn the corner of the street: Vera was teetering in a hobble skirt and insubstantial shoes. It wasn't raining any more, but the pavement was still wet and slippery with fallen leaves.

Beatrice turned back into the house and slammed the door. Since the arrival of the Crawleys she was always bad-tempered — no, correction, since the discovery of her father's high life and their resultant low means she was always bad-tempered. How dare they? she thought. How dare they demand that she go to Highgate village to fetch them a taxi-cab? It would go a little way, they had suggested, to compensate for the Eliotts not having a telephone.

'If you want a telephone and a porter,' she'd said, 'I suggest you take rooms in Mayfair where both can be obtained for twelve guineas a week, not including board.'

'Have they gone?' Evie shouted from the top of the stairs.

Molly echoed her question, bounding up

from the kitchen. 'Have they gone, the blighters? Three eggs each and half a pound of bacon.'

'And they used the chamber pot,' Evie wailed. 'I can't bear it. Why don't they use Papa's bathroom?'

'Probably not used to them, coming from the jungle, and if they both eat three eggs a day they won't be needing one.' With that Molly started downstairs back to the kitchen but returned immediately saying, 'I'm sorry about that, Miss Bea, Miss Evie, but my blood's boiling, which reminds me, if they want their laundry inclusive you won't get much change out of that three pounds.' She descended back to the kitchen.

The sisters looked at each other and laughed but the front doorbell rang and their faces dropped. Molly appeared again, red-faced and panting.

'It's all right, Molly, we'll get it.' Beatrice sighed. 'I can't believe it, I thought we'd got rid of them for the day.' She opened the door dejectedly.

'Hello there, not much time, came for the rest of the clothes.' It was a breathless Penelope Maddox, clad in a long brown leather flying-coat and helmet both of which would have fitted a man twice her size. The severity of her piercing eyes and her long jaw should

74

have made her unattractive but her appearance was softened by the surprising fullness of her mouth.

'When can you start?' she barked at Beatrice. 'Like to help in Stepney today?' she asked Evangeline. 'May I come in?'

'Yes, yes, of course. Do come in.'

'Start what? Stepney?'

'Must try to concentrate,' Penelope said breezily. 'Got my motor, take the rest of the clothes, right? Brother Jack frightfully impressed with you, Miss Eliott, when can you start? Today? And you?' She turned to Evangeline. 'I'm visiting a family, sick mother, in the East End, like to come — help?'

'I don't understand,' Beatrice said. 'Mr Maddox, your brother, is offering me the job?'

'Yes, really took to you. Very gutsy, lot of grit, he said, or was it very gritty, lots of guts? Anyway, grit and guts got you the job. What about it?'

Evangeline looked at Beatrice, amazed. 'In spite of the iced water you threw at him?'

'Did you?' said Penelope. 'Good for you. This afternoon all right?'

'This afternoon is fine,' said Beatrice emphatically.

Evangeline, still astonished, was stammering, 'But, Bea, but Bea —'

'Two pounds a week to start off with and bus fares all right?'

'Two pounds a week and bus fares is just fine.'

'But, Bea,' said Evangeline, 'you loathed him — oh — sorry, Penelope.'

Beatrice smiled. 'Oh, not loathed exactly.' How wonderful, she thought, to get out of the house, to get away from the Crawleys, to earn a little money. No, I didn't loathe him, he enraged me, probably will again, but he's interesting. If I could cope with Father, I can cope with him.

'Right,' said Penelope. 'I'll drive you to my brother's studio and then we'll go on to Stepney.'

A hasty collection of their coats and their father's clothes, a shouted explanation to Molly, 'No, don't come up, we'll be back later,' and they were off.

The three women and the car were attracting a lot of attention as they drove down the Archway Road, not least because of the way Penelope was driving, squeezing between a horse-drawn delivery van coming towards them and a bright scarlet motor bus ahead and only just making it.

Beatrice, who was sitting in the dickey seat at the back, thought what a see-saw life was, exhaustion last night, gloom this morning, and now, freedom! She rearranged the Paisley cashmere scarf she had wound around her head like a Russian peasant. Hadn't Father's clothes come in handy! They'd been the means of introducing them to Penelope Maddox and made wonderful additions to their own wardrobe. Evie, too, was wearing something of Father's, a dark grey alpaca cardigan belted loosely at the hips with two of his ties interwoven as a sash. What would he have thought! Interesting how the mannish clothes made Evie look more feminine.

At Marble Arch the car was held up by a crowd of silent demonstrators. About two hundred men and women surrounded by police on horseback were marching slowly towards Speakers' Corner.

Beatrice leant forward. 'What is it? Supporting the miners?'

'No,' said Penelope. 'One of the Irish hunger-strikers died last night.'

'Oh, no, how dreadful,' exclaimed Evangeline. 'Which one?'

'Michael Fitzgerald.'

'You know,' Evangeline said, 'Molly our maid is Irish, she lost a cousin in the Troubles. I'm so confused about it all, I don't know who's right or wrong.'

'Nobody is,' said Penelope confidently, but with a touch of sadness. 'Ireland's one cause

I don't get involved with because I can't wholeheartedly endorse either one side or the other. Some things I *know* — the miners must get a living wage, Mrs Pankhurst shouldn't be in prison, and Marie Stopes should be compulsory reading for women of child-bearing age. But Ireland . . . Even my parents, whose opinions are usually unshakeable, straddle the fence there.'

'Your parents?' Beatrice was eager to hear more about the begetters of this unusual woman and her brother. 'Do you live with them?'

'Not really, they're in Borneo at the moment — always are somewhere else, rarely here . . .'

Beatrice heard no more as a mounted policeman waved them on and Penelope drove down Park Lane where the gas lamps were already lit relieving the foggy gloom of the November day. The lane was full of motorized vehicles expelling their fumes, their drivers shouting at the horse-drawn traffic that was expelling something more natural. Penelope turned left off Park Lane into a quieter Green Street and stopped outside Jack's studio.

'Not coming up, want to keep the motor going, takes so long to crank it up — all right?'

Beatrice climbed out as gracefully as she could, scrambling over a pile of clothes, dozens of pamphlets and the rolled-up hood. 'You really aren't coming up?' she said a little sadly.

'No, but good luck!' said Penelope, and began to pull away.

'Your sister looked as if she was going to enter the lion's den,' she remarked.

Evangeline laughed, 'Well, he was rather fierce when she went for the interview.'

'Yes, he can be,' said Penelope thoughtfully, 'but there's more to him than that. The war left him very rattled and, then, he despises his work.'

'But isn't he a huge success?' said Evangeline.

'If you call getting paid to photograph old trouts so they look like . . . er . . . like . . .'

'Young soles?' suggested Evangeline with a grin.

Beatrice watched the car drive down the street. Then she gathered her courage and rang the top door bell. More as a warning really, she thought, knowing from her previous experience that he wouldn't come down. She pushed the door, which was open as before, and tried to calm her nerves as she walked firmly and quickly up the stairs. On the second flight she ran into someone descending as rapidly as she was climbing up.

'You're late,' Jack Maddox said as he

grasped her arm to stop her from falling. 'Bad way to begin.'

'Late? Bad way to begin?' Beatrice was furious. 'Last time I was too early at twelve o'clock, now I'm too late at one — and why were you hurtling downstairs? I had to find my own way before.'

'I wanted to make a good impression,' he said, still holding her arm.

'You wanted *what?*' Beatrice was speechless.

She looks like a very angry fox, Jack thought. Interesting, those narrow slanting eyes — I'd like to photograph her. Suddenly Beatrice laughed and, losing her balance, sat on the stairs. Jack sat down next to her. 'I'm glad there's no iced water to hand, Miss Eliott.'

'Tell me,' she said, still laughing, 'what do you do when you don't want to make a good impression, Mr Maddox?'

'I know I can be pretty impossible, or so Penny says.'

'Your sister obviously speaks from experience.'

Jack ignored that. 'Let's get down to facts. Do you want the job? Are the terms all right?' They stood up and Beatrice followed him up the stairs.

'Yes, I want the job and, yes, the terms are all right. For now,' she added bravely. They reached the reception room, which was even more untidy than she remembered. Every surface was covered in magazines, newspaper clippings, photographs, negatives, and pieces of wood and glass which, Beatrice guessed, when assembled might make a camera. The telephone was ringing although she could see no sign of it.

Jack pointed vaguely towards the desk. 'Get it, will you?' Beatrice put down her handbag and discovered the telephone underneath a large, moth-eaten cardigan. She picked it up and unhooked the mouthpiece.

'Good afternoon.' Jack disappeared into the studio.

A thin piping voice said, 'I'm calling Mr Maddox. We want him to photograph the family at home, in the country, y'know.'

'Yes, Madam.' She started to search for an appointment book.

'It's the Duchess of Southchester.'

Beatrice amended her reply. 'Yes, Duchess. When did you have in mind?'

'Is he there? I need to speak to him, actually.'

'I'll look, Duchess,' said Beatrice carrying the telephone into the studio. She stood in the doorway, as far as the cord would stretch. 'The Duchess of Southchester,' she hissed, 'wants you to photograph the family, in the

81

country, wants to talk to you.' Jack shook his head. 'You must,' she hissed again and lifting the mouthpiece she said, 'Here he is, Duchess,' and handed the instrument firmly to Jack.

'Lavinia, what a pleasure,' he said darting a look of venom at Beatrice, who shrugged and returned to the reception room.

She listened to the one-sided conversation as she started to put the room in order. It seemed Jack Maddox was invited for the weekend. Would he still get paid? How awkward, she thought, to have to mix money and friends.

Having separated photographs from negatives, made a neat pile of the clippings and discovered an appointment book, she turned to today's date. Scrawled across the page she saw 'LUNCH — D — 12.30. LADY BONNER 2.0 P.M'.

He brought the telephone back to her. 'Never do that again.'

'I won't, when I know where I am and who is who. I've found an appointment book. You're late for lunch with D and Lady Bonner will be here at two. It's nearly that now.'

'Oh, yes,' he said absent-mindedly, ruffling his already well-ruffled hair. 'It looks as if Daphne won't get her lunch. What are you going to do with all this?' he asked then, looking round the room.

'Except for the camera —' she said, gesturing to the pieces of wood, 'I assume that *does* all add up to a camera?' He nodded. 'I shall file it,' she ventured.

Jack beamed. 'File it? How absolutely splendid. You do filing?'

'Of course,' she said.

'Then you are underpaid!' The doorbell rang. 'Damn it, she's early.' He strode to the window, opened it and looked out. 'Top floor,' he called, 'door's open. Push, you fool.' Beatrice looked stunned. Jack laughed. 'It's the boy from Madame Rochelle's with her dress.' He turned to close the window. 'Oh, here's Elizabeth Bonner.'

'Right,' said Beatrice, 'I've done what I can in here for now. How's the studio?' The studio was in a more acceptable mess, an artistic mess, strewn with huge bales of velvets and brocades, lighting equipment, dirty glasses and a tray with half-filled cups of cold coffee on it. She picked up the tray calling, 'Mr Maddox, do you have a kitchen?' and carried it into the reception room. No Mr Maddox. He's obviously gone down to meet Lady Bonner, she thought, putting the tray on the desk.

A young lad, smartly dressed as a page, appeared on the landing carrying a huge cardboard box emblazoned with MADAME

ROCHELLE — HAUTE COUTURE. 'Oh, put it on the couch here, will you?' She went back into the studio and, drawing aside some black velvet curtains hanging on a brass rod, discovered a sink full of dirty wine glasses and more coffee cups. 'I am being underpaid,' she said to herself as she went back for the tray.

'What, Miss?' the boy said.

'Oh, nothing. Thank you, you may go.'

' 'E usually gives me sumfink, Miss.'

'Oh, does he?' Beatrice said suspiciously. 'How much?'

'Thruppenny bit.'

'How much?' she said threateningly.

' 'A' pence.'

'Halfpenny, that's more like it.' She took one out of her purse and handed it to him. He smiled broadly. 'Cor fanks, Miss.'

She looked at him coolly. 'I gather, from your expression, that the something is usually a farthing.'

'Naah,' he said, and ran down the stairs. She picked up the tray as Jack and Lady Bonner appeared.

'Oh, have you made coffee, Miss Eliott? Splendid.'

Beatrice and Evangeline sat huddled around the dying embers of a wood fire in Beatrice's bedroom, which was also lit by an oil-lamp

84

and two candles. Their light was throwing a large shadow of Evangeline's profile on the wall. Her curved mouth and elegant short straight nose showed clearly but the wildly gesticulating hands made her look as if she were being manipulated by a puppeteer.

'Isn't it a good idea?' she said, moving a small twig on the fire with a brass poker. 'I'm going to the Heath every day now to collect wood, like Cinderella.'

'But, Evie, you haven't got Penelope's car now. How will you manage?' Beatrice regretted deflating her sister's enthusiasm and it had been a good idea of Penelope's to collect wood, not only because of their lack of money but because the coal strike was now taking effect.

'Well, perhaps not every day, Bea. But the exercise will be good for me. She's an extraordinary woman, you know, the way she helps people, not like someone all dressed up delivering soups and sermons. She took the woman something for her bronchitis that she'd made herself from herbs and things and it was Penelope who got the eldest daughter her job in service.' Evangeline sighed. 'Imagine, only fourteen, and she's keeping the family.'

'How much does she earn, then?' said Beatrice doubtfully.

'Six shillings and sixpence a week, and she only keeps ninepence for herself. Of course,

she lives in so she's kept, but all the same
. . .' Evangeline jumped up. 'It's terrible, absolutely terrible,' she said.

Her shadow loomed on the wall behind her
like a witch and Beatrice laughed. 'What is
absolutely terrible? Oh, I'm sorry to laugh,
but it's your shadow. When you were sitting
down you looked like Punch and Judy and
now you look like something from Grimms'
Fairy Tales.'

Evangeline turned and smiled. 'Oh, yes, I
see, but it is terrible. The daughter came in
while we were there. The landlady at the public house where she works had given her a
piece of pie and four eggs to take home and
they had to hide it because the means test man
was coming. Apparently they wouldn't have
been allowed to keep even that little bit of
food *and* have any assistance.' She sat down
again warming her hands at the fire muttering,
'No fire for them, no hot water.'

'That's the one thing Father did that makes
me think of him kindly,' Beatrice said. 'I smile
every time I look at our copper geyser. It
atones for him not putting the electricity up
here, although I doubt if he knew there was
an up here.' They both stared into the dying
fire and one candle sputtered and went out.
Although the room was dimly lit it was never
really dark: the white paintwork and the

bleached floors gave it a permanent lightness.

'I wonder if you could photograph in this light? It's very flattering — electricity is so harsh. That woman at the studio today —'

'Oh, Bea, I'm so sorry, I interrupted you before. Why does she want us to make her a suit? I don't understand.'

'Because she liked my clothes.'

Evangeline looked at her sister's long black cashmere jacket which had been cut from their father's overcoat. Round the button-holes she had sewn tiny pearl shirt buttons so that they circled the large black buttons, her high-necked blouse had been made from some of his silk evening scarves; she looked chic and original.

'I'm not surprised she liked your clothes, you look absolutely . . . it!'

'And because,' Beatrice added, 'I helped her.'

Lady Bonner stood in front of the full-length mirror in the dressing room examining herself. She was wearing a long straight dress made of cream duchesse satin embroidered with gold thread and amber-coloured beading. She looked good: the straight neckline displayed her yellow topaz necklace well; her hair, knotted at the nape of her neck, accentuated the whole clean line. But there was something wrong. What was it? She looked in the mirror at Beatrice standing behind her. 'What do you think?' she asked.

Beatrice thought it a little too tight but said, 'Charming, lovely, Lady Bonner.'

She doesn't think so, thought Elizabeth Bonner.

Jack called them into the studio where he had arranged the lighting to concentrate on the throne-like chair placed in the centre of the room.

Oh dear, she shouldn't sit down in that, thought Beatrice, but Jack beckoned and Lady Bonner sat. It was immediately apparent what was wrong with the dress; it creased like a concertina across her hips and stomach and made her look rather fat and coarse. 'Oh, look, Jack, this is frightful. Can you help, Miss Eliott?' Beatrice pulled the dress up at the waist and tried to pleat it but it made no difference. 'Perhaps it would be better if I stood.' She got up smoothing the dress down. 'No, it's worse — it needs pressing or something. I look frightful.' She was very distressed.

Jack stepped forward and took her hands. 'Elizabeth, you are a beautiful woman.' She smiled gratefully. 'Let me take some portraits of you, to hell with the dress.'

'No, Jack, thank you, I'm too old. I have lines on my face as well as my dress.'

'May I help?' said Beatrice quietly. 'I could

steam the dress with the kettle to lose the creases and if you would permit it, Lady Bonner, I could unpick the back seam so that when you are seated it will drape into an A-line shape which would be more flattering.'

Jack felt like hugging her. 'You're a genius.'

When Elizabeth was seated in the chair again, looking attractive and confident, Beatrice went back to the reception room and continued her organizing. The telephone rang frequently: Mr Maddox's presence was wanted for lunch, dinner and weekends; photographic sittings were desired for portraits, both *Tatler* and the *Sketch* needed work from him and Daphne wanted to kill him.

'Is that Daphne with a D?' Beatrice said.

'What the hell else would it be with? And who are you?'

'Miss Eliott, the receptionist.'

'Well, give him that message, Miss Eliott.'

'I will,' Beatrice said, but to an empty line. D had hung up.

The door bell rang and, copying Jack, Beatrice opened the window and looked out. A large car was waiting outside. The uniformed chauffeur waved. 'I'll tell Lady Bonner you're here,' she shouted and shut the window quickly — it was cold and windy.

She popped her head round the corner of

the studio. 'Your motor car is here, Lady Bonner.'

'Well, we're through. You were wonderful, Elizabeth,' Jack pronounced. She stood up and Beatrice darted forward. 'Let me help, I'll put this piece of velvet round you.' The women left the studio and Beatrice helped Elizabeth change in the dressing room.

'Thank you again, Miss Eliott, you turned a nightmare into a dream. Now, what am I going to do with this?' She held up the offending dress.

'I suggest you ask Madame Rochelle to insert two tapering narrow panels each side, then you will be more comfortable. Even if you don't sit down.' They both laughed.

'Do you make your own clothes, Miss Eliott?'

'Yes, my sister and I make all our clothes.'

'Then, Miss Eliott, I have a suggestion. You insert the panels and I would absolutely love a copy of the suit you're wearing.'

When Lady Bonner left Jack came out of the studio. 'All that sewing, you're to do it in your own time, you know.'

'Naturally, Mr Maddox, I intend to give you value for your money.'

He grinned. 'You're frightfully easy to tease, you know.'

Little red patches appeared on Beatrice's

90

cheeks and her eyes narrowed, a signal that Jack now recognized. He took her gently by the shoulders. 'I'm sorry, don't get ratty, you were bloody marvellous!' She turned away to recover from the shock of the 'bloody', or was it something else?

'Here are your telephone calls, Mr Maddox.' Beatrice handed him a list. 'And Daphne rang three times, basically with the same message.'

He looked apprehensive, 'What was it?'

'She'd like to kill you.'

'That's all?' He looked relieved. 'She usually mentions torture.'

Evangeline hugged her sister and laughed. Beatrice always told her stories so well. 'How exciting, Bea. Will she pay us, do you think?'

'I don't think, I know. Nothing if she doesn't like it, seven guineas if she does. We're to see her on Thursday at six o'clock.'

Evangeline went quietly to her bedroom not wanting to disturb the Crawleys. Life without Father was quite exciting. They'd met new people: an adventurous young woman, a philanderer or a romantic young man depending on how you looked at it — not very romantic really, as he hadn't tried to see her since Arthur's sharp letter — an eccentric photographer and two old fogeys. She made a face

91

at the old fogeys' door as she crept past. Beatrice hadn't said what Jack looked like but he'd be quite attractive if he had Penelope's bones and strong features. She opened the door of her room relieved to be in her bright bedroom after the gloom of the hall.

Why was she feeling so happy? The Crawleys had to be faced again tomorrow and now with no Beatrice to help. Nevertheless, she thought, life is full of possibilities.

The house was still dark when Molly woke, dark and cold. She pulled the blankets up to her neck and gave herself the indulgence of an extra five minutes in bed. Lying there listening to the noises of the street she could tell what time it was without looking at the clock. The clatter of the horses' hooves drawing the milk cart told her it was nearly seven. The next sound was the clink of milk bottles at the kitchen door followed by a screech of brakes from the paper boy's bicycle and his tuneless whistle; he was always whistling and you could never tell what song it was. Better get up now and race him to the front door or the letterbox would close with an almighty clang and wake up the whole house. 'Don't want that, I need every minute of the hour if I'm to have their breakfast ready at eight as well as rake the embers of the range and get it built up, and get meself ready, too. Oh, Lord!' And hadn't she forgotten? She'd left dishes from Miss Bea and Miss Evie's supper. She put on yesterday's woollen dress over her long drawers and camisole and pattered bare-foot up the stairs to the hall.

CLANG. The letterbox snapped shut after disgorging the morning newspaper. She'd just missed it. Picking up the paper she gave it a quick glance as she placed it on the hall table. Her pleasure and relief at seeing that the coal strike might be over was tempered by the news that the new Irish Republican Army had killed four soldiers and a policeman. Not that she was surprised — it seemed to be a weekly, if not a daily occurrence, but she would never get used to it. She had 'di-vided loyalties', Miss Evie said. Although she had spent most of her life in England, her looks, her accent and her heart were Irish, and the thought of her large and beloved fam-ily in danger there worried her.

'Good morning, Molly. Aren't your little feet cold?' She yelped. Major Crawley had padded down the stairs in his slippers so qui-etly she had not heard him.

'Yes, sir, they are, sir, here's your news-paper, sir.' She passed it to him, snatching her hand away as he tried to pat it. 'I'll be having your breakfast ready at eight o'clock, sir.' She smiled at him. 'It's the kedgeree, sir, like you spoke of.' He was an awful old goat, she thought, but it didn't hurt to please him — didn't he give her a florin just the other day?

'I shall look forward to that, Molly, my dear. I'm pleased, yes, very pleased you thought of it — of me.' Molly felt a little guilty: he had actually flushed with pleasure, which was hard for him seeing as how his face was always red, anyway. She pushed the green baize door and ran down to the kitchen. One of the reasons she sometimes made the kedgeree was that it was cheaper than the eggs and bacon every day.

She put the poker between the bars of the range and riddled the ash through — still well lit, what a relief. Although the kitchen was warm her feet were cold on the stone floor, so quickly fetching the kedgeree from the larder and putting it in the slow oven, she sat on the edge of her bed and put on her clean woollen stockings. As she rolled them up her legs, securing them with elastic garters, she paused to admire the shape of her calves and her narrow ankles. That old goat admired them too, she knew — she'd caught him looking at her bending over the fire and running upstairs with her skirt hitched up. It was uncomfortable having a man like that in the house, much better having a man like the master — maybe not better for his wife, but he hadn't been interested in young girls or servants.

'Molly Murphy,' she said aloud, 'all this idle dreaming won't get the baby washed, or the work done.' She took a flannel, towel and bar of soap to the kitchen, filled the sink, took off her dress and camisole and washed herself, towelling herself dry vigorously. Then, using a corner of the flannel, she rubbed her teeth with a mixture of soot and salt.

Another clang was heard upstairs as the postman made his first delivery. 'Twenty-five past seven, me hair not done and no tea taken, I'll never catch up with meself. I'll make a pot for me and Miss Evie, and she can help me taking the trays up.' While the tea was brewing to its favoured dark brown she performed the time-consuming chore of setting the heavy mahogany breakfast trays with linen, silver and plate. Then, taking a huge gulp out of a liberally sugared mug of tea, she set off upstairs with another mug.

'Oh, you're up and about then, Miss Evie?'

'Yes, Molly,' Evangeline said yawning. 'I had to get up early to finish Lady Bonner's dress.'

'Here's your tea, and if you could give me a hand in a minute or two with the breakfasts,

95

and it's coal that I've got to be fetching if they're staying in. Should I light the drawing-room fire? And I must sort the laundry and get some of the ironing done or I won't be able to change the beds — and will they want their lunch here? And it looks like the coal strike might be over.'

Evangeline looked helpless. 'Oh, Molly, I'm sorry there's too much for you to do. How many trays?'

'Three, Miss Evie.'

'You go down and get them ready and I'll ask Bea to help us.'

Beatrice was choosing her clothes for the day. She looked animated and happy.

'Oh, Evie, you're up, good. Do you think it's too cold for my navy blue gaberdine?'

'I really don't know, Bea,' Evangeline said with some asperity, 'but you're needed — we're both needed downstairs. Molly can't cope with all the breakfasts, the range, the laundry, the coal . . .'

Beatrice turned away from the wardrobe. 'Evie, I can't. We have a sitting at half past ten today. I can't even wait for breakfast.'

'Just as well,' Evangeline snapped, 'because there won't be any.'

Beatrice looked surprised, 'Don't forget to be at the studio at about five o'clock. Lady Bonner expects us at six.'

Oh, why did I say that? Evangeline thought, as she ran down the stairs. It's not her fault. I'm jealous, I suppose, stuck in the house working like a skivvy while she puts on her best clothes and goes up to Mayfair. But, she reminded herself, when Bea was stuck in the house and she had been working at Danielli's Dancing Academy her sister didn't display any jealousy . . . but she didn't have the Crawleys to cope with.

CHAPTER FOUR

Beatrice stood outside the house in Green Street and pushed the door again. It was definitely shut. Did that mean Jack hadn't arrived? It was ten minutes past ten, barely enough time to get the studio ready. She peered through the downstairs window: no sign of Mr Reed-Smith, the publisher. She pressed both bells and waited.

'Good morning, Miss Eliott. I see you are early and I am late.' Harry Reed-Smith paid his hansom cab, doffed his hat and opened the door.

'Yes,' she said, 'I am earlier than usual, too early it seems for Mr Maddox.'

'I'll be making coffee. Would you like some?'

'Another time,' Beatrice called as she ran up the stairs, 'but thank you.'

At least the reception room was unlocked and she could prepare the studio. Opening the door, she noticed the smell of cigarettes and in the half-light could just see a shape stirring. 'Oh, forgive me,' she gasped, 'I had no idea —'

Jack was half-asleep, sprawling on a couch wrapped in a velvet curtain, he lifted himself on to his elbow drawing the curtain around him. 'What time is it?'

'Ten minutes past ten,' Beatrice stammered.

'And are you Saint Beatrice?' The low husky voice came from a body that was disentangling itself from another velvet curtain. 'My dear, don't look so shocked.' A little white face appeared above the curtain, then white shoulders and a white body naked to the waist. 'I'm Daphne. Make us some coffee, would you?' The make-up on her face had run so that she looked like a rather beautiful clown. The lipstick had spread to her nose, the jet black mascara had reached her cheekbones and her bobbed, fiercely platinum hair stood on end.

'Certainly, I'll make you coffee, but, Jack,' she turned to him, 'the Gregsons will be here at half past ten.'

He put his head in his hands and groaned. 'The giggling Gregsons, the terrible twins, I forgot. Daphne darling, you'll have to do without coffee, you must go.'

Daphne stood up, Beatrice was relieved to see that her bottom half was clothed and in a way her top didn't matter: her breasts were so small she looked rather like a boy. 'And if I refuse, my love?'

Jack jumped up, suddenly awake and se-

99

rious. 'Just go, Daphne, and for God's sake cover yourself up.'

She looked mutinous but took the pale grey fur coat he flung at her and put it on. 'You, Jack Maddox, are no gentleman,' she snapped, picking up a torn and crumpled blouse.

'No, indeed,' he said, 'and that is why you like me. Here is your bag, your shoes. You'll find a taxi easily enough in Grosvenor Square.'

She put on her shoes and walked very slowly out of the studio. 'I won't, you know. I'll go to Worth's, they'll give me coffee, lend me something to wear . . .'

'Not when they see what you've done with *that*,' he muttered.

'. . . and call me a cab. Byee.' She waved, and Beatrice watched her descending the stairs unsteadily.

'Will she be all right, Jack?'

'Yes.' He'd pulled a jumper on over his evening shirt and trousers and was making coffee. 'Don't look so prim and disapproving, Beatrice, it doesn't suit you. Daphne Haycock uses me as much as I use her. Help me tidy up, will you?'

'Of course.' She picked up the full ashtrays, cigarettes and an empty champagne bottle. 'Anyway,' she said, trying not to look prim, 'it's none of my business.'

'Yes, it is,' he said with one of his startling

about-faces. 'If I expose you to a scene like that it is your business. I don't suppose you've seen many half-naked high-class trollops, have you, Beatrice?' He grinned as he handed her a cup of coffee but there was a curious sadness in his smile. 'I'll put a record on to cheer us up.'

She folded the curtains expecting to hear a dance tune, a quickstep perhaps, but instead the slow melancholy sound of a Bach partita was playing. She turned and found him looking at her gravely. Neither of them spoke until the door-bell rang.

'Saved by the bell,' he said softly.

Mrs Ashleigh smiled coyly, a grotesque sight from one so old, and waved Frou-Frou's paw. 'Say goodbye to nice Mr Maddox, you naughty little boy.' She turned to Beatrice. 'Thank you, Miss Eliott, you were wonderful with Frou-Frou, you obviously have an affinity with long-haired terriers.' She left still chattering in her baby-girl voice. 'Naughty, naughty, don't eat Mummy's gloves.'

Jack groaned. 'What a day — giggling young women and an incontinent dog. I don't know about you, Beatrice, but your costume certainly has an affinity for long-haired terriers.'

'I know, I'm covered in grey hairs, but at least he didn't use me as a lamp-post.'

'No,' he laughed, 'he saved that for her umbrella.' He looked out of the window. 'Her chauffeur's just taken the little monster as if it were a piece of Sèvres porcelain . . . My word!'

'What? What has he done now?' Beatrice ran to the window.

'No, not the dog. Look.' He pointed down the street. 'Look. That's one of the most beautiful girls I've ever seen.'

She looked. 'That, my dear Jack, is my sister.'

Evangeline looked at the two faces leaning out of the window. So that was Jack. Better than she'd thought. A strong face, same strong bones as his sister Penelope's but bigger eyes, brown, perhaps, and rich brown hair, a lot of it, not oiled and slicked back but untidy and blowing in the breeze. She could just hear Bea calling. What was it? Come up? No, don't come up. Really, Bea was a spoilsport, keeping him to herself. Suddenly the door opened and both Jack and Beatrice appeared.

'Jack, this is my sister Evangeline, Evie, this is Jack.'

Evangeline put her hand towards him saying, 'How do you do?' Jack ignored it and leant forward as if to kiss her but instead took off her hat and stared as if appraising her. Then, replacing her hat, he said coolly, 'You

102

really are very beautiful, the real thing.'

Evangeline felt a little discomfited, it sounded like a compliment but she knew it wasn't — it was just a statement of fact, like saying she had two legs. She noticed a tiny spasm of pain cross Beatrice's face as she said, 'And so she is. Let me take one of those bags, Evie, we must get a bus or we'll be late.'

'No,' said Jack with great command, 'that won't do, I'll drop you at Chester Square and come back and pick you up. How long will you be? An hour?' Not waiting for a reply he hailed a taxi, gave the driver directions and helped them in. Sitting opposite them he said, 'So if I'm back at eight o'clock, say, we could be at the Blue Bear by eight thirty. I'll bring Piggy Trenton.' He looked at Beatrice. 'You need a treat after this frightful day, all right?'

'No, Jack, it isn't all right.'

'It *is* all right,' Evangeline chimed in excitedly.

Beatrice went on, ignoring her, 'Why you should think that dinner with you and your fat friend a treat once again reveals your astounding and misconceived conceit,' she paused, 'and anyway Molly is expecting us home for —'

'Leftovers from the Crawleys,' Evangeline said gloomily.

'Of course it's a treat,' Jack said briskly.

'The food at the Blue Bear is very good, Piggy may be fat but he's also very nice and very funny, and I shall be charming and attentive, as is my wont.' He shouted over his shoulder, 'This is it, cabby, stop at the house at the corner.'

'What about our clothes?' Evangeline said. 'We're not wearing the —'

'Your clothes?' Jack looked surprised. 'Beatrice is the most chic, the most elegant, the most originally dressed woman to enter my studio, my life! Your clothes would be perfect wherever you went.' He then ruined the compliment by saying, 'And nobody dresses much at the Blue Bear, anyway. Go on, an hour.' They got out hurriedly and the taxi sped away. A butler appeared at the front door of the cream stucco house preventing further discussion between the sisters but in answer to Evangeline's pleading smile Beatrice nodded, 'All right.'

Lady Bonner's bedroom, like the rest of the house, hadn't been modernized: it was furnished with pieces of walnut, warm and gleaming with polish in the light of the gas mantles. The bedcover and curtains were the only sign of the twentieth century, made of richly coloured fabrics in deep golds and rust copied by Liberty's from Bérain's designs for the Ballet Russes.

Elizabeth examined herself in the long cheval mirror, the heavy cream satin dress with the extra panels now suited her, she could see that, but she pushed the top of the mirror disconsolately.

'I look better with the mirror swung away from me.'

'Better maybe, Mama, but that isn't the truth.' Her daughter, an exact replica of the mother, but half her age and half her weight, was ruthless. She jumped off the bed and rearranged the mirror. 'It's the Honourable Fred's fault.'

Beatrice and Evangeline laughed. 'Whose fault?'

'My brother's — that thing, in that thing.' She pointed to a baby sleeping peacefully in a cradle.

'Oh, darling, don't call him "that thing". Frederick is your brother, and you all contributed to my weight, starting with you.' She smiled at Sybil.

'Yes, Mama. If only I'd been a boy you need never have done it again. As it is, it took five goes to get it right.'

The Eliott sisters looked up from removing tacking stitches in the hem.

'Don't look shocked, Miss Eliott. Sybil is trying very hard to be a "bright young thing", but failing miserably. She hates smoking, doesn't like powder and lipstick and is, in fact, a wonderful daughter whom I love.' She embraced Sybil. 'I love all my girls.'

'All four of us, it's true, but not as much as you love the Honourable Fred.'

Elizabeth shrugged. 'I'm so pleased with the dress and the costume I'd like to order something else, if you have the time.'

'Yes, we have the time, Lady Bonner. What do you have in mind?'

Elizabeth pointed to the blouse Evangeline was wearing. 'That,' she said. 'I'd like you to copy that for Sybil.'

'Oh, Mama, thank you, thank you.' Sybil turned to Evangeline. 'Would you mind, copying it, I mean? I love it! That high-necked lace collar, how does it stay up?'

Evangeline showed her. 'You see I hate starch, it itches so. I use men's shirt stiffeners — in fact the whole blouse is modelled on a man's shirt worn back to front.'

'Mmm, I see,' Sybil said, examining it. 'I think I'd like it in white silk or maybe fine yellow cotton, I don't know, what do you think?'

Her mother smiled indulgently. 'If you promise to stop calling Frederick "that thing", you may have them both.'

'Wonderful!' came from each of the three

girls in turn, interrupted by a parlourmaid announcing the arrival of Mr Maddox.

'You're not going back to work, I hope,' said Elizabeth, discreetly giving Beatrice an envelope, adding softly, 'Seven guineas as agreed, and thank you again.'

'Mr Maddox is taking us to the Blue Bear. Do you know it?' Evangeline asked Sybil, who looked deeply envious.

'I know about it, very Bohemian, artists go there, but it's all right for people like us, I mean, people like you — no, that sounds frightful. I mean, I'm not "out" yet so I can't go out but if I could — and, oh, I will be next year.' She spun around the room joyously. 'Then I'll be allowed to go there.' Sybil led Beatrice and Evangeline out of the room in great high spirits but gave a sour backward glance at her mother lifting the baby out of the cradle.

The butler opened the front door and Beatrice walked out to the taxi. Evangeline waved once more to Sybil standing at the top of the stairs, then, changing her mind, ran up the stairs and said hurriedly to her in a low voice, 'I know how you feel about your brother. My mother kept trying to have another baby after Beatrice was born, even though it was dangerous for her, because Papa wanted a son. She died having me and I've always felt . . .' The butler coughed reprovingly, he was still holding the door open and the cool night air was filling the hall.

Sybil's eyes were full of tears. 'And at least I still have my mother. Thank you for telling me — I'm a selfish pig.'

Jack appeared in the doorway shouting, 'Hello, little Sybs. Are you coming, Evangeline?'

'Yes.' Evangeline sped down the stairs again.

'Tell me all about the Blue Bear at my fitting,' Sybil called as the door closed.

The Blue Bear was, in fact, quite simple, bare wood floors, scrubbed pine tables and chairs and benches, none of them matching. It was lit by candles in every conceivable form of holder — bottles, saucers, tins, flower pots, jam jars, every conceivable form of holder, that is, except candlesticks. To the Eliott sisters' untrained eyes there were no signs of artists, though. Jack had ordered champagne, two bottles of Bollinger, and 'dinner'. When questioned by Beatrice what 'dinner' would consist of, he had explained there was no choice. Their waiter had tried to describe what it was but as he spoke no English he had had to rely on gestures. Evangeline interpreted his mime as 'boiled something', Beatrice as a soufflé, Piggy as steak and kidney pudding (though perhaps that was wishful thinking) and Jack thought it was fish.

'Those movements with his arms looked as if he was swimming,' he said.

'Why do they have a waiter who can't speak English?' Evangeline asked.

'He's a White Russian escaped from the revolution — speaks French, of course.'

'Yes, but why . . . ?'

'Cheaper,' Jack said. 'I'm not ordering wine until we know what we're eating. Now then, Evie, I want to know the story of your life.' Jack gave her his full attention, excluding his companions.

Beatrice was annoyed to find herself hurt and for the first time in her life feeling a vague sort of jealousy of her sister. She looked at Piggy and smiled. 'I don't understand, why do they call you Piggy?'

Tom 'Piggy' Trenton smiled back at her. 'This, Miss Eliott, is love at first sight.' The reason he was called Piggy was self-evident: he was round. A round body topped by a round face with a round slightly pink nose.

Jack looked at her, surprised — she had never flirted or displayed feminine wiles with him. 'He's called Piggy because he looks and behaves like one, whereas you should be called Foxy.'

'Foxes are sly,' said Beatrice.

'Yes, indeed. They also have wonderful red hair, narrow slanting eyes and cheekbones a Cossack would be proud of.' The waiter appeared burdened with a huge tray containing plates, cutlery, napkins and a large dish containing something covered in a pastry case. He lowered the tray heavily on the table and left.

'Even our Molly serves better than that.' Evangeline laughed.

'Yes, but she's Black Irish, not White Russian.'

Piggy picked up two spoons and examined the contents of the dish. 'Fish pie,' he announced, beaming.

Evangeline and Beatrice crept quietly down the back stairs to the kitchen. Molly had left them a note on the table with their supper.

It's cold chicken so no harm done, hope the Lady gave you something to tide you over. THEY asked for dinner tomorrow night. MY NIGHT OFF. I'll leave a stew. Help in morning please, MOLLY

They crept out of the kitchen and upstairs. On the first landing Beatrice stopped and

110

looked at Evangeline. 'Evie, darling, don't take Jack too seriously, he's . . .'

'Yes?'

'He's very unreliable. He has — oh dear.' Beatrice looked uncomfortable.

'You mean he has relationships with women? Like Eddie Banks?'

'Oh, no, not like that.' Beatrice having attacked Jack, now wanted to defend him.

'No, I thought not.' Evangeline started up the stairs. 'I knew, Penelope told me. He's just part of the new generation, like me.' Beatrice gasped, she felt quite sick. Had Evie meant to be so cruel?

It was Molly's turn to empty the chamber pot this morning. At least they took it in turns, she thought, which was very good of them. Not many employers would share a job like that, but not many employers would pay her so little for so much work. Molly wondered why, seeing as how they'd had a night out and all, they'd been so offhand with each other — maybe just the money worry getting to them, just as well they'd got more sewing jobs. Even with Miss Bea's work and *Them,* they could barely manage. She carried the chamber pot carefully into the bathroom. You'd think having a proper water closet they'd use it. The front doorbell rang. She shouted down the stairs, 'Can you answer it, Miss Evie? Me hands are full.' Just *Their* bedroom and sitting room to finish, the fire, make the stew, do the stairs, thank the Lord for the carpet sweeper, wonderful newly fangled invention, the master hadn't been all bad, and if Miss Evie helps with the dusting . . .

'Molly, can I have a word?' Evangeline came bounding up the stairs. 'Would you mind if I went out?' The sight of Molly's despairing face checked her enthusiasm. 'Of course, I won't if you need me but I thought if I'm back this afternoon I can do the dusting then and anything else —'

'So long as I can be off by five, Miss Evie. I'm seeing me cousin, she's giving me my tea and then we're going to a moving picture show.'

'Yes, yes, Molly, I promise. I'm going to help Miss Maddox again. A family in Shoreditch, Gunpowder Alley.'

'Have a good time, Miss.'

Evangeline looked shocked, 'That's not the idea, Molly.'

Daphne Haycock folded her long thin legs under her. Curled in the corner of the sofa she looked like a cat about to pounce, Beatrice thought. She sighed as she started to write yet another letter asking for a bill to be paid, couching it in language designed to touch the debtor's heart-strings but not to seem like begging . . . 'Her husband is an earl, they have three estates but they've owed Jack money for five months,' she suddenly said, exasperated.

'The arrogance of the aristos, my dear St Bea. The richer they are the less likely they are to pay their bills.'

'So it seems,' Beatrice returned to the letters.

'Well, if you are going to work, I am going to sleep.' Daphne turned to the wall pulling her white fox cape around her. She had obviously used it as a blanket before: there was a patchwork of make-up stains where she had pulled it up to her face. Beatrice looked at the recumbent figure with sympathy: she had learned from Jack a little about Daphne's life. The favourite child of her father, Sir Peter Haycock, she had led a blissful childhood on their large estate in Dorset until the war when all three of her brothers were killed at Passchendaele and Ypres. After that her father had become a recluse staying in his beloved house in Dorset, which, being entailed, would pass on his death to a distant and disliked cousin. His attitude to Daphne had changed, and he treated her now with indifference, giving her an allowance perhaps sufficient for the country but certainly not for London, and woefully inadequate for Daphne's taste in stimulants. Beatrice had presumed he meant champagne, but Jack had laughed and said, 'Not champagne, cocaine.' Her mother, a discreet alcoholic who sipped dry sherry from waking to sleeping 'for her nerves', barely remembered her daughter's existence. Daphne was homeless at the moment, having let her flat for two weeks, and was sleeping wherever a friend or a casual acquaintance would let her.

The Gordon children would be here quite soon. Should she wake her? Beatrice knocked at the door of the dark room and heard muffled swearing.

Jack opened the door. 'Bloody hell, Beatrice, what do you want? Sorry, I shouldn't swear like that.'

She looked at him with a grin. ' "Bloody hell" is hardly going to disturb me after the few words I heard from the dark room.'

He looked abashed. 'Oh, could you hear?'

'It doesn't matter,' she said innocently, 'because, of course, I don't know what they mean. Look, Jack, the thing is I don't know what to do about Daphne. The Gordon children will be here and —'

'I'll send her down to Harry Reed-Smith,' he said striding out of the studio. 'Daffie,'

114

shaking her, 'Daffie, you've got to go, I have a sitting soon with the Gordon children.'

Daphne uncurled and sat up sleepily. 'Will Nanny Gordon be bringing them? She used to be my nanny, Nanny Haycock. I was her favourite child, she told me, I'll stay and say hello.' Jack and Beatrice looked aghast. 'She might lend me some money,' Daphne muttered, trying to light a cigarette.

Jack took the cigarette out of her mouth, lit it and replaced it in her mouth. 'Er, no, Daffie. The governess and their mother are coming with them,' he improvised, 'so why don't you go down to Harry Reed-Smith?'

'Might as well, he'll give me coffee.' She walked slowly down the stairs, carrying her shoes and trailing the grubby fox cape, which was now further embellished by singe-marks from her cigarette.

'How does she live, Jack? What does she live on?' Beatrice forgot her disturbed feelings at the casual and intimate way he had lit Daphne's cigarette in his own mouth. 'How does she manage?'

He looked at her seriously, kissed her gently on the cheek and said, 'You wouldn't like to know, Beatrice, you really wouldn't.'

Beatrice was hungry and cold. No, she amended that. She was hungry, cold and tired.

115

It had been a long, difficult day, Evie so sharp in the morning and then all the trouble with Daphne. She was looking forward to the braised beef that Molly would have cooked. Braised beef sounded so much more appetizing than stew, but even that was better than a boil-up, Molly's previous description of any dish that included meat or chicken and liquid.

She let herself into the house and headed for the kitchen. She had seen a light in the basement and presumed Evie would be there. 'Sorry I'm late,' she called, descending the back stairs. 'Both buses were late.' Mmm, she could smell the beef. Heaven. She paused on the bottom stair, she could hear somebody singing rather flatly in what was undoubtedly an Irish accent. 'Molly, what are you doing here? Where's Evie?'

'That's what I'd like to know, Miss Bea, I'm here because Miss Evie isn't.' Molly took a large plate out of the warming oven and banged it angrily on the wooden counter. 'She never come back from where she went with that Miss Maddox, and I promised to me cousin's for me tea and the picture show and Miss Evie promising, cross my heart, back by four.' She slapped some beef and potatoes messily on the plate. 'Here's your boil-up then. *They*'ve been served but no afters and I'm all done in.' Molly set the full plate on the kitchen table.

'Oh, Molly, I'm sorry. It's terrible. Very thoughtless of her. And your night off, I'll deal with the Creepies' dishes and take them their pudding and tomorrow you must have the whole day off as well as the evening.' She took off her coat and flung it with her handbag over the back of a chair and sighed.

'No, Miss Bea, you can eat first. *They*'ve only just got theirs and you look tired too.' She sat and watched Beatrice eat. 'I had me own while I was cooking. Me mother used to call it "tasting and testing", and I had to send little Davey from next door with a note to me cousin, and he wouldn't go without a sixpence. Is that all right, the beef?'

'It's more than that, it's delicious, Molly, and I'll give you the sixpence, don't you worry.' She finished her meal quickly, watched by a disgruntled Molly. 'Did Evie say where she was going? Give me the apple pie and the custard and I'll put the whole lot on warm plates.'

Molly stacked the large tray and opened the door. 'She did, too, but I can't remember. Some alley down in the city somewhere, helping the poor, it was.'

Tired and angry, Beatrice stumped up the stairs. Helping the poor indeed. They were the poor. Her help was needed here. Perhaps she should speak to Jack. His sister was a bad influence on Evie.

'He'd like some cheese for his apple pie.'

'But I asked them if they wanted cheese and "no" they said.'

'Give it to me,' Beatrice said wearily. 'I'll run up with it.'

In spite of Molly's protestations, she thought it wiser. The Crawleys had been quite clear about their disapproval of Molly's manner, accusing her of slamming it on the table and not wanting to serve it. They preferred to be served by Evangeline, they had said, and where was she? Beatrice had retorted that Evangeline was training to be a missionary and was nursing a child sick with scarlet fever. She got some small satisfaction from their frightened faces.

Turning back her linen cuffs and putting on a long apron over her costume, she plunged all the dishes in hot soapy water and flung in a handful of soda to cut the grease. She rubbed the plates with a cloth, rinsed them in cold water and stacked them in the wooden plate rack. There was a tentative knock at the back door.

'Bea, it's me.'

Beatrice unlocked and opened it.

'I saw you at the sink so I came down here to avoid . . .' Evangeline's voice faded away.

118

There was no disguising Beatrice in a rage. The hot red marks on her cheeks. The narrowed eyes looking greener than ever.

'I'm sorry, let me explain,' she said, in a faltering voice as she edged into the kitchen.

'The only explanation that would count would be that you'd had an accident, which you clearly haven't.'

'Please, Bea, it was awful, you've no idea how poor people live.'

'I've no idea, Evie, how we are going to live. And what about poor Molly? It was her night off. Not only did you ruin that but I had to help her serve the Crawleys' dinner and wash up and you should have been working on Sybil Bonner's blouses.'

Evie looked at her enraged sister. No, she wouldn't understand. What was the point?

'If you're not going to listen to me, I'm going to bed. I'm tired.'

That did it. There were various levels to Beatrice's temper: tonight the top level had been reached comparatively quickly. '*You*'re tired?' She pushed Evangeline to the sink and flung the wet cloth at her. 'Finish the washing up, dry up, apologize to Molly and get some coal in.'

But Beatrice had forgotten that Evangeline, too, had a temper and from the sink she pulled a wet plate and hurled it at her sister. 'You're

119

not my mother, not my guardian.' The plate missed its target and hit the large round clock, whose quiet rhythmical tick had sounded uninterrupted for all of Beatrice's thirty years. The glass broke, the clock stopped.

'No, I'm not your mother. Not your guardian. Would you prefer to live with Arthur?' Beatrice spoke quietly but with an underlying threat.

Evangeline was unnerved. 'There are more important things than blouses and lodgers and nights off. Where I've just come from people are cold and starving.'

Beatrice regarded her sister with contempt. 'You are a very conceited and silly little girl. There's nothing you can do to help such people. You're not a nurse or a Lady Bountiful. You're playing at it because you've got a crush on Penelope Maddox as a substitute for her brother.'

The next plate hit its target but Evangeline fled from the room before she could see its effect.

Molly waited until the kitchen was quiet and the light switched off before she slipped out of bed in her bedsocks and padded into the kitchen. Miss Bea had done a good job. All the dishes washed and dried and put away, the broken china and glass swept up and put in the dustbin. The only sign of the row was the silent clock. They may be fine ladies, but the brawl she'd just heard was no better nor worse than her cousin's kitchen on a Saturday night. And them with not a drop taken.

She pulled the curtains aside and looked up at the sky. There was a bright sickle moon and the evening star. She made a wish, a rather complicated one, involving her mother, the Eliott sisters, money and Rudolph Valentino.

Beatrice finished writing the note and picked up the oil lamp. It was smoking, the wick needed trimming, but the light shed was still sufficient for her to see her way. She crept down to the next landing where she slid the note under Evie's door. Returning to her bedroom she turned down the lamp and drew the curtains. She also made a wish on the evening star. But her wish involved only one person.

Evangeline waited until she was sure Beatrice was back in her bedroom, then silently retrieved the note that had appeared under her door.

I'M SORRY. EXPECT YOU ARE TOO.
I'LL GET UP EARLY AND HELP.
LOVE, BEA

Yes, she did feel sorry she supposed, but most of her feelings were still in Gunpowder

Alley. The bronchitic mother hastily concealing the baby at her breast, barely able to sus-
tain herself let alone a new-born baby. The
father's shame at being unable to provide for
his family since he had broken a hip in an
accident at work. His wife explaining so
proudly that he was a master painter, that he
had painted the dome of the Dominion The-
atre and that in spite of great pain he went
out early every morning to stand in line with
dozens of men waiting for daily jobbing work.
The little girl in the corner sewing who had
bandy legs, which told the story of rickets,
obviously from malnutrition. Evangeline had
looked at her work, she was embroidering tiny
crystal beads onto a velvet jacket and doing
it beautifully. As Penelope had pointed out,
the price of the jacket would keep the Allen
family for a year but Tilly, the little girl, who
had turned out to be eighteen, made it clear
she was thankful to get the job — piece-work
was hard to come by.

After giving them wood and coal for the
fire and groceries, Penelope had written
down all the details of Mr Allen's accident,
promising to help him apply for compensation. They left, both of them embarrassed
by Mrs Allen's gratitude for the tea and
bacon hock, as if it was champagne and caviare.

They had tried to call on people further down the street but the thin, drab, red-eyed woman had refused to let them in. They heard a man's voice shouting abuse and the woman had shaken her head nervously and slammed the door. Penelope had hoped he would be at work. A neighbour had reported the man for beating his wife and children and, almost as an afterthought, incest. Penelope hadn't been surprised, they all slept in one room, she explained, seven of them in two beds. The neighbour had only reported him because of the noise.

Evangeline looked out of her window: no noise here in leafy Highgate. She looked across the garden to the backs of the large Victorian houses. Nobody slept four to a bed here and no rickets either. Her gaze travelled up and caught the moon and the evening star now joined by other stars: Orion was very clear — and the Plough. That's lucky, she thought, I'll make a wish. Evangeline's wish started with the residents of Gunpowder Alley, and expanded to include the whole city of London, then finally encompassed the downtrodden population of the entire world. Exhausted, she slept the sleep of the just.

Molly had gone off to her cousin's early but not before she had started the clock.

123

'How did you do it, Molly?' Beatrice was thrilled.

'I just gave it a shake, that's all. It was a shock what stopped it. It was a shock what started it.'

'You're wonderful. Stay out all day and enjoy yourself.' Beatrice gave Molly a coin. 'That's for yesterday — well, every day, really.' Molly examined it. 'Oh, Miss Bea, this is half a guinea, not a sixpence.' She laughed and handed it back.

'I know,' Beatrice said, returning it. 'Don't worry, Mr Maddox increased my wages for work above and beyond the call of duty and I'm increasing yours for the same reason.'

Molly's face shone. 'Go on,' Beatrice added, 'or I'll make you empty the chamber pot.' Molly ran up the basement stairs and into the street pulling her scarf tightly round her neck against the cold.

Beatrice turned back to the kitchen and swiftly washed up the Crawleys' breakfast dishes after putting the last of the coal in the boiler. She hadn't woken Evie, thinking it wiser to have their talk when Molly had gone. Perhaps she should take her up a cup of tea and they could chat while she was changing for work. She felt the little bruise on her shoulder where Evie's plate had landed. What a vixen! And Jack had called *her* a fox. 'Oh.'

She looked up, surprised, as Evangeline entered the kitchen, dressed haphazardly and with her hair tied back rather roughly.

'Why didn't you wake me?' she demanded. 'Let's get on with their breakfast. Has Molly gone?'

'It's all right, calm down. The Crawleys have been fed and watered. I've washed up the dishes and Molly has gone.'

Evangeline looked at her aggressively. 'So, once again, you've been the best sister.'

'Oh, Evie, don't. I woke early and just wanted to make sure Molly had the whole day free and you've got enough to do, anyway.'

'What, exactly?' Evie was not going to be calmed down.

'Oh, the usual. You know. The coal must be brought in, their beds done, the living-room fire, dusting . . . you know.'

'Yes, I do know. I know very well because when I'm not off with Penelope being a silly conceited girl, that's what I do every day while you are in Mayfair working for . . .' She looked at the clock. 'You'll be late. You'd better go.' And picking up the heavy metal coke-hod, she went out to the basement area.

Beatrice realized she had been wrong not to wake her. She had put Evangeline at a disadvantage. Well, there was nothing she could do now. Perhaps this evening at supper they

125

would talk. Upstairs, she pinned on the black astrakhan hat she had made from the collar of one of her father's coats. Evie's temper was very like her father's. It took a long time to smoulder and burn out whereas her own happened suddenly; it burned fiercely and died as quickly. She called down to the kitchen from the hall stairs on her way out, 'Evie, 'bye. I won't be late.' Only a grunt came in reply from below stairs and, feeling sad and a little guilty at leaving her sister alone to cope with the house and the lodgers, Beatrice let herself out of the front door.

Hearing the front door close, Evie sat down at the kitchen table. Why, why, why had she been so mean to Bea? She didn't feel it inside. She had meant to hug her and tell her how sorry she was. It was like being a child crying and the more you're told to stop the less you are able to. What a day ahead. But if she started now and worked hard, and if the Crawleys went out, she would be able to work on the Bonners' clothes this afternoon and then she would make something nice for Bea's supper. She took the lid off the top of the boiler with a poker and, lifting the heavy hod, poured coke into it. The jangling of one of the servants' bells distracted her and some of the coke dust fell on her feet. 'Rats,' she muttered. 'What do they want?'

'More tea, Evangeline dear, Beatrice was in such a rush she snatched the tea away before we could stop her.' Vera Crawley's tinkly laugh matched her looks. Dressed this morning in a baby blue peignoir trimmed with maribou, the feathers of which fluttered upwards concealing one of her chins, Evangeline thought, She never looks right. Her clothes wouldn't be appropriate for me, let alone a woman of her age, whatever that was. How pathetic she was with her slack breasts and cavernous face. Keeping thin did not result in keeping your youth.

'I'll get it for you now.' She turned to go.

'Evangeline, I think I ought to bring to your attention that your hair has fallen down, you have soot on your skirt and your hands are unclean.'

Evangeline didn't turn but snapped as she left the room, 'My hair has not fallen down because it was never put up and when you fetch coal and coke from a dark bunker and stoke the boiler it is inevitable that your hands and clothes get dirty.'

'The impertinence of that little miss. To appear like that. No self-respect.'

But her husband wasn't listening. The image of Evangeline with her cloudy mass of uncontrolled dark hair surrounding the creamy oval of her face, the perfect skin

127

marred only by an endearing smudge on her cheek, was still imprinted on his mind. The little dear, he thought, the perfect little dear. 'Shall I help her, Vera? It's a heavy tray for a child like that.'

She looked at his silly wet smile, as he stared out of the room long after the girl had gone. Not answering him, she crossed the small sitting room and examined herself peevishly in the long mirror set into the front of the heavy mahogany armoire. She was younger than Chips, she'd kept her figure, her income greatly supplemented his army pension and yet . . .

'What did you say, old girl?'

'Help her?' Vera said flatly. 'No, Chips, I don't think so.'

Evangeline looked down at herself, at the dark smudges on her skirt, the dusty shoes, the damp patches on her blouse where the water from washing the hall floor had gone through her apron. I look like a skivvy, she thought, and let's face it, I am a skivvy.

All thoughts of Gunpowder Alley had left her mind as she wallowed in self-pity, thinking of the difference between her life and that of her sister. She idly kicked the rubbish pail, which overturned spilling its contents. No, don't wail, she admonished herself, don't give in to it, clear this up, take the rubbish out and then you can wash and change, make your bed and work on Sybil Bonner's blouses.

Lifting the dustbin lid, she carelessly threw the rubbish in and pushed it down with a newspaper. Squealing, she withdrew her hand. It was bleeding. Of course — last night's quarrel with Bea, the broken glass and plates. Not for the first time she regretted her temper, her lack of consideration. She could have hurt Bea. She had been less than fair, she knew, and, after all, she had her whole life ahead of her, unlike Bea who at thirty was middle-aged.

Passing the coal bunker she saw the brass scuttle waiting to be filled for the drawing-room fire. She had forgotten it. She filled it and carried it carefully into the kitchen. Then, after running cold water on the jagged cut on her wrist, she put iodine on it and wrapped it up in a piece of clean rag. Heaving a sigh, she carried the heavy coal scuttle up the back stairs to the hall.

The floor wasn't dry yet and, slipping on a damp patch, Evangeline dropped the scuttle, the coals and dust scattering across the clean tiles. 'No, no, no,' she cried. 'No, I can't bear it.' She scrabbled around on the floor picking up the coals and dropping them in the bucket.

'Oh the little one, poor little one.' Chips Crawley came down the stairs. 'Here, let me

129

help you.' He put his arm around her waist to help her up but Evangeline had already started to lift the coal scuttle, which came between them.

'I'm fine,' she panted.

'Oh, girlie, girlie,' he said softly as he slid his hand below her waist, caressing her gentle curves. 'My little girlie.'

'Don't. Don't!' she cried, pushing him away and dropping the scuttle with a loud clang, and coal once again skittering noisily across the tiles. 'Leave me alone — you're disgusting!' she sobbed.

Vera Crawley surveyed the scene from the top of the stairs. 'My husband was trying to help you.' She paused. 'I shall have to speak to your aunt about both your behaviour and your appearance, and,' a parting shot, 'our chamber pot hasn't been dealt with.'

Evangeline looked with loathing at both the Crawleys, and, unable to speak, wrenched open the front door and ran out of the house.

Chips Crawley slowly looked up at his wife, still dressed in that baby blue feathery thing. 'Sorry, old girl,' he said hoarsely.

As she turned the corner and knew she was out of sight of the house Evangeline slowed down. She was breathless and still crying. Aware that people were observing her, she smoothed her hair, looking at herself in a shop window. Reflected in the window were two taxi-cabs across the road. She turned and ran recklessly across.

The driver lowered his window cautiously, Evangeline did not look like a likely customer in her stained dress and tousled hair, and her lack of coat and bag did not add to his confidence in her.

'Green Street, Mayfair, please,' she said haughtily, hoping her manner would compensate for her appearance.

'Orright, Miss,' he said reluctantly. ' 'Op in.'

Once inside the taxi her hauteur vanished. She was cold and frightened. What if they weren't there? And what would Beatrice say? She tried to push from her mind the horrible thoughts of the Major's weak, pink face, his mouth slightly open, his pale blue eyes bulging as he had fondled her, his pudgy fingers probing her flesh.

'No,' she said suddenly.

'What, Miss?' the driver shouted.

He was manoeuvring the cab round a large brewer's dray, drawn by four equally large shire horses.

Evangeline pulled herself together and realized that she had almost reached her destination.

'I shall have to ask you to wait when we get there, driver. My sister will come down and pay you.' They were now turning into Green Street. 'There, yes, it's there. Next to the house with the blue door.'

The taxi stopped, the driver got out very quickly, opening her door. He looked mistrustfully at her.

'Three shillings, Miss,' he said.

Evangeline pressed the top bell hard, leaving her finger on it for a count of seventeen, her lucky number. Stepping back suddenly to look at the top-floor windows she bumped into the driver, anxiously standing behind her.

'Sorry, Miss,' he said, as she jumped away like a scalded cat. There's something up with her, he thought. Maybe she's one of them dope fiends. He had observed her shaking in the back of the cab. That was one of the signs.

The top-floor window shot open and Jack's head appeared. 'Who the hell is it?' he shouted.

The driver looked shocked. 'Not very nice, if you ask me, language in front of a lady,' he said pompously.

Jack withdrew his head. Evangeline couldn't tell if he had seen or recognized her and, trying to stifle her sobs, which had started uncontrollably again, with a hand over her mouth, she went to ring the bell again when both Jack and Beatrice appeared at the door.

'What is it?'

'What's the matter?'

'What are you doing here?'

Their questions tumbled over each other and Evangeline, now sobbing openly, unable to stop, held out her arms to Beatrice who took her gently.

'Ssh, ssh, my love, try to tell what happened.' She looked over Evangeline's shoulder and raised an enquiring eye at the taxi driver.

'Dunno, Miss, she jus' run across the road, no coat, no nuffin', obvious upset, and said to bring 'er 'ere. And that's three shillings, Miss, sir.' He looked at Jack being the one most likely to come up with the cash. 'Ackcherly, three and six more like by now.'

Jack took some change out of his pocket. 'Here's a crown, keep the change.'

The driver pocketed the money, got back into the taxi and drove away smartly before the gent could change his mind.

'Let's get her upstairs and get some tea or brandy down her.' Bea nodded and helped the still sobbing Evangeline up to the studio. By the time they had reached the top of the stairs, Evangeline's sobs had turned into hiccups.

'Please, Evie.' Beatrice examined her sister. She didn't seem hurt but why was she covered in soot? 'Please try to tell me what happened. Was it at home?'

Evie nodded, her hiccups convulsing her.

Jack spoke to her sharply. 'Come here. Put out your arms.' She opened them obediently. Jack opened his own arms and clasped her suddenly and fiercely, then released her.

'Oh, look,' she said amazed, 'it worked, they've gone.'

'Of course. Now I'm going to get us all a brandy.'

Evangeline looked round the studio. There were half-eaten plates of smoked salmon, thinly cut brown bread and butter and lemons on a rickety old coffee table. 'Were you having a picnic?' she said enviously.

'Sort of. Here,' Beatrice said, taking the brandy from Jack, 'drink this and then tell us.'

'Mm, nice,' said Evangeline, drinking it down in one gulp, 'all sort of burny.'

Jack laughed. 'To the manner born. Would you like to be alone, the two of you?'

He folded up some smoked salmon in a piece of bread, put it into his mouth and went into the dark room. He could hear the gentle rise and fall of Evie's voice, punctuated by Beatrice's lower tones. She sounded angry. He grinned to himself. Just as well that whoever was responsible for Evangeline's

134

distress wasn't to hand.

He took the negative out of the metol quinol and held it up. Blast, he thought, I've over-exposed it. Oh, well, it wouldn't be the first time Kitty Ashleigh had been over-exposed.

'Jack, could I have a word with you?' Beatrice was tapping gently at the door. He opened it immediately.

'Could you manage without me this afternoon?' Beatrice was clearly upset. 'I have to go home with Evie.'

Evangeline jumped up from the sofa. 'Bea, you're wonderful. I don't deserve you.' She turned to Jack looking ashamed. 'I threw a plate at her yesterday.'

'You Eliott women. Your sister once threw a bucket of cold water at me. Sit down. I want to talk to you both.'

He looked at them sitting together on the low sofa. Both so attractive, so interesting and so innocent. He crouched in front of them.

'I don't want to pry, but it was the lodgers, or lodger, wasn't it?'

Evangeline nodded dumbly. Jack stood up and made himself another smoked salmon sandwich.

'They're a waste of time. A waste of energy,' he said brusquely. 'For two talented bright women, you've been remarkably dumb about what you could do with your lives.'

'Just a second, Jack.' Beatrice rose angrily.

'Sit down. Hear me out. You have two assets which you don't use. Your house and your talent. Sell the house, rent a flat and set up a dressmaking business. I've never seen women better dressed than you and that includes the *haut monde* of Paris dressed by Chanel.'

Evangeline's large brown eyes opened even wider. 'Do you think we could?' she said slowly, a smile appearing on her face. 'Oh, Bea, do you think we could?'

'Of course you could.' Jack stood up impatiently and strode about the room. 'The Bonners love your work. Every woman who has been to this studio admires Beatrice's clothes. Piggy's mother would come to you. And his sister. He'd see to that. And you wouldn't need staff to start with. You both know how to do it all — buttons — edges,' he hesitated, 'all that stuff.'

Beatrice smiled sadly at him. 'What about Cousin Arthur? He'd never let us. He's Evie's guardian,' she explained.

'Evie, go and clean your face and tidy your hair. The dressing room is out there.' When she had gone he took Beatrice's hands. 'Listen to me and don't ask questions. If your cousin Arthur Eliott attempts to stop you selling your house, just mention Janey from Cadogan

136

Mews.' Beatrice started to speak. 'No, don't say anything. I guarantee it is not what you think. It is much more unpleasant.'

Beatrice was stunned. 'How do you know?' she managed at last.

Jack turned away, his face scarlet. 'Let's just say I know.'

Beatrice paid the taxi driver and, fishing in her bag for the key, approached the front door of 125 Temple Gardens, Highgate, her home for thirty years, but perhaps not much longer. The dour mock-Gothic façade with its pretentious crenellations had always filled her with gloom.

'Come on, Evie, let's get it over with.'

Evangeline was looking at the car parked outside the house. 'Bea,' she groaned, 'isn't that Arthur's car?'

Beatrice looked. Yes, it was. No matter, she thought, get it over in one go, while she was still angry and still filled with the enthusiasm that Jack had instilled in her. She opened the door, took Evangeline's hand and said, 'This is our house and they are uninvited visitors.'

The coal scuttle was still where Evangeline had dropped it with the coal still scattered across the hall floor. The hall was cold as well as dirty: its high ceiling had always made it impossible to heat.

The drawing-room door opened. The Crawleys? No, Arthur.

'Hello, Arthur. How did you get in? It's Molly's day off.' Beatrice spoke calmly, controlling her anger.

'I let myself in, Beatrice. With the Crawleys' keys.'

'Ah, of course, Major and Mrs Crawley's keys. Then I imagine they won't be coming back. Be good enough to return them to me.' She held out her hand commandingly. He felt inside the pocket of the heavy coat he was wearing, took out the keys and gave them to her.

'Now, look here, both of you.' Arthur was worried by Beatrice's attitude. It was somehow too self-assured. Insolent, almost. He looked at Evangeline and lost the thread of what he was about to say. With her masses of dark hair demurely tied at the nape of her long creamy neck and her face showing signs of recent tears, she looked vulnerable and even younger than her years.

Beatrice coughed. 'Yes, Arthur? You were about to say?'

'I think we should sit down before we go any further.'

'By all means.' Beatrice graciously ushered him into the drawing-room, followed by Evangeline. 'Aunt Lydia, what a surprise!'

138

But then the day had been full of surprises. Not all of them pleasant.

Arthur stood in front of the unlit fire. 'You can come off your high horse, Beatrice,' he said. 'The Crawleys, your main source of income, have gone and I expect you know why.' Not waiting for a reply he ploughed on. 'The attitude of everyone in this house has been slapdash in the extreme, late meals, surly behaviour from your maid and then this morning a temper tantrum from Evangeline, who should never have been left in charge.' He hoped that would mollify dearest Evie.

'It's all been very awkward for us, you must see, Beatrice.' Lydia looked ill-at-ease as she spoke. 'The Crawleys have been good friends of mine for years.'

'So I understand, Aunt Lydia, and as such I presume you must be aware of Major Crawley's proclivities, and you, Arthur, "man of the world" ', Beatrice spoke with heavy irony, 'you were privy to my father's peccadillos and instantly aware of Eddie Banks's notoriety, you must surely have recognized a similar character.'

Evangeline regarded her sister with admiration; there was no stopping Beatrice when she was in full flight.

Arthur looked shiftily at his mother, who glanced away. What cowards, Beatrice thought with contempt.

'Chips Crawley, my dear Beatrice, has never to my knowledge had a reputation as a lady's man.' Lydia fiddled with her gloves, avoiding her niece's gaze. Beatrice lowered her voice and, speaking slowly, she said, 'So the disrespectful and ungentlemanly behaviour shown by Major Crawley this morning was a temporary aberration brought on by the lure of my sister's beauty and the erotic atmosphere of Highgate?' Evangeline snorted. Beatrice gave her a look of reproof, but behind the reproof was a twinkle. 'I see no use in discussing it further, Aunt Lydia. No doubt you meant well, but you were guilty of a lapse in judgement, to say the least.'

Lydia lowered her eyes. I'd like to smack the little madam's face, she thought, I could tell her a tale or two that would take the wind out of her sails. That door in the corner led to Henry's consulting room, always locked, of course — the child might burst in. Or the child's mother. Lydia smiled maliciously.

'Sit down, do, Arthur. Evangeline and I want to discuss more important things with you.' Beatrice indicated the armchair opposite her.

'Oh, yes?' He perched on the edge of the large sofa: sitting above them made him feel more in command.

Beatrice hesitated but, remembering Jack's advice, she said, 'We've decided, Evangeline and I . . .' She looked at her sister for support.

Evangeline nodded, 'That's right, we've decided.' They both looked very firm.

Lydia laughed, relieved to be off the subject of the Crawleys. 'My dears, you both sound very sure, but of what, one may ask?' Her condescending tone galvanized Beatrice who stood and spoke rapidly in her normal voice forgetting her assumed lofty dignity. 'We've decided to sell the house after all, Arthur.' He opened his mouth to speak but she silenced him. 'Please let me finish. We are going to rent rooms, a flat, and start a dressmaking business. In a small way to begin with, naturally, but we already have clients.'

Arthur smiled and raised his eyebrows at his mother. 'I have told you before, Beatrice,' he said wearily, 'I forbid it. As Evangeline's guardian —'

'As Evangeline's guardian you're not doing very well. Anyway, I own half this house and if you push me to it I'll get legal advice.'

Why was the boy making such a fuss? Lydia thought. They were frightfully good at dressmaking — the cream satin thing that Elizabeth Bonner was wearing at Faversham House the other night was ravishing, she wanted to ask the girls to copy it for her.

141

'You needn't bother about advice, Beatrice, legal or otherwise.' Arthur spoke with his usual pomposity but this time it covered feelings of rising panic. How much would he have to reveal? 'There's very little of the house to sell. Your father mortgaged eighty per cent of it to the bank.'

The high colour drained from Beatrice's face. 'It's not possible,' she stammered. 'It wasn't his. Mama left it in trust to us.' Mustn't cry, she thought, don't cry.

She was saved by Evangeline who shouted at Arthur, 'Who is paying the mortgage, then, I'd like to know?' She turned to include Lydia. 'Not you, not either of you, I can't imagine that.'

'Actually,' Arthur cleared his throat, 'I have been paying it since your father died.'

Beatrice pulled herself together. 'And I suppose you think that gives you a little more power over us, Arthur, but I think we'll stick to our own plan, we will sell the house, pay the bank its eighty per cent and —'

'No, Beatrice, no, you won't. Your ten per cent will not be sufficient. If when Evangeline is married you wish to discuss this again —'

'I don't think that will be necessary, Arthur,' and with a sophistication she was far from feeling, she added, 'By the way, Janey from Cadogan Mews sends her good wishes.'

It was Arthur's turn to be shocked into silence. He dropped heavily into the sofa, his face a dull brick red.

'Janey, from Cadogan Mews?' Lydia dropped into the silence.

'Shut up, Mother.'

What was the matter with him? Such a fuss, about what was probably just a little tart. Arthur looked up, examining Beatrice's face. How much did she know? Enough, it seemed. He'd have to play along with her. 'You're a fool, Beatrice, but if you want to burn your boats go ahead. Come on,' he said impatiently to his mother.

Could they have won so easily? Beatrice let Evangeline show out their unwelcome guests; she could hear their goodbyes as she sat in the same armchair that Aunt Lydia had used. Beatrice shivered. It wasn't just the cold: that unpleasant smile when Lydia had looked at Papa's consulting room had reminded her of something. A trace of sadness from her childhood. Was it Mama? Mama's tears? Papa shouting? But he often shouted, especially if she tried the handle of the door when a patient . . . She put a hand to her face, remembering a bruise . . . No, best not to think about Mama and sad things. She heard the door slam and Evangeline calling, 'They've gone, they've gone, they've gone.' Beatrice joined her and, clasping each other, they danced joyously round the hall scattering the coal even further. When the doorbell rang they froze. Could it be Arthur? A change of mind? The Crawleys? The very young man who stood outside the door holding a telegram was quite over-whelmed by the two beautiful girls before him smiling and laughing and effusive with their thanks. Not often that happened, he thought, as he cycled away, telegrams usually frightened people, hope it's good news for them.

Beatrice opened the envelope. 'I'm scared to look, Evie.'

'It can't be bad news, we're already or-phans.' Evangeline snatched it away and read it aloud. ' "ARRIVING 8 O'CLOCK STOP FOR SUPPER STOP WITH SUPPER STOP JACK AND PIGGY." ' Evangeline's smile spread from ear to ear. 'Bea, I can't believe it, a day that started so foully is ending as one of the best.'

'What a mess.' Beatrice looked at the hall. 'Pity Molly isn't here.'

'No, that's not fair,' Evangeline said. 'I made it, I'll clear it up.'

Down in the kitchen they looked at the clock. 'One hour,' Beatrice said. 'You know, Evie, if we need more money, you could al-ways get a job in a circus.'

'What do you mean?' Evangeline was fetch-

144

ing a dustpan and brush.

'Plate-throwing, you're very good, very accurate.'

'Oh, Bea, I'm sorry.' She dropped the brush and hugged her sister. 'Did it hit you? How awful.'

'It's all right. Just throw a tin one next time.'

Beatrice poured coke into the boiler, which was nearly out, and held a sheet of newspaper in front of the bars to encourage the fire to draw. 'When you've swept up the coal take it upstairs to my room, we'll eat up there.'

'Perfect.' Evangeline ran upstairs to the hall singing,

'After you've gone there'll be no crying,
After you've gone, there's no denying.'

Smiling, Beatrice took the newspaper away from the bars where it was turning brown: the fire had caught well. She sighed. That little nagging memory of Mama wouldn't go away. What had happened that day? Was it one day? Or a memory of many days? She remembered a ride in a hansom cab through the park, two parks, Mama holding her hand tightly, her head turned away looking out of the window at the drifts of wet fallen leaves.

'Bea,' Evangeline's voice floated down from the top floor, 'I can't find the matches and

145

shouldn't you get ready?'

Yes, she should get ready. For tonight, tomorrow and all the tomorrows — how poetical — how practical! Beatrice raced up the stairs. 'What do you think they'll bring?' she shouted.

Jack eased the cork gently out of the bottle. It gave a slight pop and before it could fizz out of the neck he poured it into four glasses. 'Well done, Jack, didn't waste a drop, admirable.'

'It isn't admirable at all, Tom.' Beatrice seemed quite stern. 'It simply showed a lifetime of practice.'

She looked around her room and smiled at them all. This was probably the first time champagne had been drunk here and certainly the first time two men had dined here. Jack took her hand. 'Everything I do, Bea, I do well, believe me.' He walked round the room holding her hand examining the prints and sketches on the walls. 'And so do you. This room is remarkable. It's utterly original, every individual touch — you could design houses as well as clothes. And your father didn't know it was here.' He lightly stroked her cheek. 'I admire you, you're a survivor.' They stood in a shadowy corner watching Evangeline and Piggy unpacking the hamper. In the firelight

146

they looked like children with their Christmas presents. 'What's this, Jack?' Evangeline held up a dish.

'It's a chicken stuffed with a partridge stuffed with a quail.' Jack and Beatrice joined the others on the carpet in front of the fire.

'How interesting,' Evangeline said uncertainly.

Beatrice handed round knives, forks, plates and napkins. 'Everything is in here,' she said, 'everything, even salt and pepper.'

'And everything goes back, that's the beauty of it.' Jack helped himself to cucumber salad. 'No clearing up, no washing up.'

'Is there enough?' Piggy spoke through a mouthful of potted salmon.

'There should be, I ordered enough for six — Bea, Evie, me and three for you.' Jack started to carve the stuffed chicken.

'Don't tease Tom, it isn't fair, you're eating more than he is, anyway.' Piggy blushed with pleasure — he hadn't been called by his real name since he was about seven.

Jack glanced at Beatrice; her red-gold hair looked like part of the fire. 'Candlelight suits you two, you know,' he said, gesturing at Evangeline as well. 'You've both got very good heads.'

'I say, old chap,' Piggy shook a stick of celery at him, 'you make them sound like horses.'

Jack ignored him and gave them all plates of chicken. 'There's some apricot chutney in there and a sort of rice salad thing. Throw me the corkscrew, we're having a very fine Montrachet, courtesy of Piggy.'

'Is that cheese?' Evangeline asked innocently.

Piggy hooted with laughter. 'Hardly, Evie, you don't need a corkscrew for cheese.'

She joined in the laughter. 'Oh, another wine, I see, delicious.'

Jack swirled the golden-amber liquid in his glass and tasted it. 'Mm, very good — oh, Piggy, it's very good indeed, thank you. Now,' he said briskly, 'I want to discuss the future. You've won the battle to sell your house. It won't be much money, after all, but what will you do with it? Where will you go?'

'We thought, Jack, of looking in Bloomsbury.'

Beatrice's tentative suggestion was immediately squashed. 'No good, Bea, no good at all. Women who dress at couturières wouldn't go to Bloomsbury.'

'We're not going to be couturières just dressmakers, and we'll get more for our money in Bloomsbury.' Beatrice looked at her chicken: the outlines of the three birds were clear.

'You may start off as dressmakers —'

Jack was interrupted by Beatrice still examining her chicken. 'What an odd idea.'

He continued impatiently, 'But my money's on it, you'll become as successful as Jeanne Lanvin.'

'My money too,' Piggy added eagerly.

Evangeline stopped eating and starry-eyed drank her white burgundy. It was nectar, she thought, and I'm in heaven. 'Why odd, Bea?'

Her sister was still squinting at the chicken. 'Stuffing these birds inside each other. Could you do it with a lamb, a goat and a piglet?'

Jack leaned back against the armchair. 'My plan is this . . .' Catching an angry glint in Beatrice's eye he paused. 'My suggestion is this, old Harry Reed-Smith's giving up his office, he's going to work from home.'

Beatrice put down her glass. 'And you think we could . . .'

'Mayfair! A flat in Mayfair.' Evangeline jumped up. 'My cup runneth over.'

'So will mine if you're not careful,' Piggy retrieved his glass from the floor.

'May I go on?' Jack didn't wait for an answer. 'He'll let you have the rest of the lease, three and a half years, very reasonably, and there's plenty of room for the two of you.'

'Three, don't forget Molly,' Evangeline added.

'Three then, and your dressmaking. And

you,' he said turning to Beatrice, 'won't have far to travel to work.' He looked very pleased with himself and reaching into the hamper said, 'I'm going to have a brandy.'

'You conceited pompous pig. You self-satisfied overbearing bully.' Beatrice flung a half-eaten roll at him.

'Nevertheless?' he said.

Evangeline stopped dancing and looked at her. 'Nevertheless,' Beatrice said quietly, 'we'll do it.'

CHAPTER FIVE

Jack Maddox looked at the large tins of paint
and brushes sitting in turpentine and inspected
the room. Harry Reed-Smith's office was unrecognizable. All the bits and pieces of book-
shelves, cupboards and office files that had
been amassed over years had been stripped
away leaving a finely proportioned room,
much larger than it had seemed. Beatrice and
Evangeline had removed the green and brown
curtains, the green and brown wallpaper and
the green and brown paint and washed down
the walls and ceiling with sugar soap. A small
army of volunteers was dressed for work.
Piggy, looking like a gardener in his brown
overalls with a handkerchief knotted at the
corners on his head, was about to start on the
ceiling. Penelope, enveloped in what looked
like a shroud but was really a dust sheet with
a hole cut out for her neck, had already begun
to paint a wall, and Beatrice, wearing one of
her father's old shirts with her hair tucked
into a tweed cap, was delicately painting the
woodwork round the window. She had chosen

her usual colour scheme of blue and white, with the walls a matt blue like a dark sky and glossy white on all the woodwork. The only other colour in the room would be yellow for the curtains. That material had been obtained for nothing. They had collected samples of yellow fabric from every draper's in London and were gradually sewing it into a huge patchwork.

'How can you all work at the same time?' Jack said. 'You'll drip paint on each other.'

'No dripping allowed,' Beatrice said firmly. 'And we have to work together, everybody's got other things to do. Wind up the gramophone, please, my staff work faster to music.' Jack wound the gramophone and inspected the record. ' "Toreador" from *Carmen*. Let's see if it works.'

Piggy, who was now balanced precariously on a plank supported by two ladders, started painting in time to the music but nearly lost his balance and flicked some white paint on Jack. 'Piggy!' he yelled. 'Be careful of my clothes, and your body.'

'Trust you to put your clothes before Piggy's body,' Penelope said tartly.

'It would be quicker if you got it done professionally, you know,' Jack said as he inspected Penelope's work. 'Have you ever done this before, Pen? It doesn't look right to me.'

152

'I've done it many times before,' she snapped. 'After tenements have been fumigated and at the East End Mission.'

'I see, a perfect way to practice.'

'Oh, shut up, Jack.' Beatrice was now lying on the floor applying paint to the skirting board. 'We can't afford to get it done professionally, I know we sold the house but twenty per cent of very little isn't very much.' She looked up at him and smiled.

He knelt and bent over her as if about to kiss her. 'You've missed a bit,' he said, dipping his finger in her paint tin and dabbing the end of her nose.

'Jesus, Mary and Joseph.' A crash was heard from next door and Molly's voice, 'Oh, Miss Evie. Oh, I'm that sorry. Are they all broken then?'

'It's hopeless.' Evangeline burst into the room closely followed by a contrite Molly.

'Neither of us are any good at beading, we've ruined Lady Bonner's material and now Molly has spilt all the beads.'

'And trodden on them as well,' Molly added. 'I'm useless, that's what I am, can't do beading and can't paint walls even worse.'

'I know something you can do.' Jack felt in his pocket for some money. 'Here, Molly, go up the road to the pub, the Pig and Whistle on the corner, and get us some lunch. They'll fill a jug of shandy for you and get some bread and cheese for us all.'

'I'd better come with you, you won't be able to manage.' Evangeline looked at Beatrice. 'All right?'

'Don't be silly, Evie, you can't go into a public house.'

'But Molly can?' Penelope said softly, but not so softly that Beatrice couldn't hear.

'Can you manage, Molly? Do you mind?'

'Pleasure to get out, Miss Bea, don't worry, I'll get my coat.'

'Have you thought about Tilly Allen, Evie, the girl from Gunpowder Alley?' Molly heard Miss Maddox say as she left the house. Surely be to God she couldn't be suggesting they get a new maid. Her beading was bad, she knew, and her painting even worse, but she was good at basic sewing and she'd cleaned the new flat and workrooms till it was spotless. Much easier to look after than that old house in Highgate. No, they wouldn't get rid of her for a bit of beading. Molly loved being in the centre of things. The Underground at Marble Arch, and all the buses you could wish for, grand for visiting her cousin. Just as well — no room for having callers in Green Street. And the shops, their windows as good as a show, gleaming, lit with the electric, full of things you didn't know existed and now you wanted very much. Oh, Lord, there was that poor young man again, dressed in his khaki, one empty trouser leg pinned up showing he's been crippled. Amputated, it was. People walked past quickly, they didn't want to look at him or the card he had propped against the wall.

KITCHENER NEEDED ME NOW I NEED YOU.

So many of them, you can't give to all. I'll get him some bread and cheese, she thought. Mr Jack had given her enough for that.

She pushed open the door of the saloon bar and was greeted by a warm, smoky fug. Not too busy, not quite lunchtime, good. It could be awkward, a girl on her own in a crowded pub. The barmaid caught her eye and frowned. What's she doing, on her own, a little slip of a thing? Looks respectable but you can't tell these days. 'Yes,' she said, 'What can I get you?'

'It's for Mr Maddox, please, and I'll need a tray.'

The barmaid softened. 'Ah, I see, dearie, and what does he want put on it?'

'A jug of shandy and bread and cheese for six, please — no, seven, sorry.' She remembered the beggar.

The barmaid put the jug under the tap and

pulled the lever. 'Is he broke again, then, love? It's feast or famine with him. Champagne or shandy.' She added ginger-beer to the jug and sorted out a pile of thick sandwiches. 'I'll put a pot of mustard on the tray and a bit of cress and some pickled onions.'

In the large mirror, ornately engraved with vines and bunches of grapes, that hung above the bar, Molly was aware of a man eyeing her from a table where he was drinking what looked to Molly's experienced eye like a pint of Guinness. Nice-looking, he was, thin, straight hair, light brown almost blond pushed off his face, wire-rim spectacles on a bony nose. Must be some kind of house painter, she thought, in that white cotton coat all covered in reds and yellows, like those back at Green Street, though more likely professional.

'Here you are, love. Can you manage?'

Molly handed the barmaid the money. 'Not far to go. If you can open the door . . .'

The painter man appeared at her side. 'You open the door,' he said, 'I'll take the tray.' Molly didn't answer. She was flabbergasted. He was even better-looking close up, but it wasn't that. No ordinary painter he was. No, he was a gentleman. From his voice, anyhow. 'What's the matter?' He was laughing at her.

'It's just that you're not, well, I thought . . .' She gave up and opened the door.

'You finished with that Guinness, Mr Bunting?' the barmaid called.

'Thank you, Poppy, yes, I'll see you tomorrow, no doubt.' The saloon bar banged behind them.

'So you're a regular?' Molly enquired.

'Temporary regular, I'm working on a house in Grosvenor Square. Where to, Miss . . . ?'

'Murphy. It's half-way down Green Street, and thank you.'

'Ridiculous,' he said, 'to send a slender young lady like you to carry all this.' He meant it, she could tell, he was admiring her but gentle, like.

They passed the crippled soldier and Molly remembered the bread and cheese. 'Could you wait here for a moment? I want to give that fellow something to eat.' She took a sandwich from the tray.

'Would you like me to come with you?' He started to walk back.

'No, it wouldn't be good for his dignity.' She ran back with the sandwich. 'I don't have any money but would you like some bread and cheese?' she said, offering it to him. He nodded and opening his mouth made a harsh strangled sound. Molly stepped back a little frightened, 'What — what is it?' He leant heavily on his crutch and pointed to his throat, the same grating sound happened. He was dumb, she realized, not just the leg, but dumb too. Smiling crookedly he fluttered his right hand against his heart, that must mean thank you, she thought. In the cap that lay at his feet were a few coppers.

Hugo Bunting waited for Molly to return. Nice, the consideration about the chap's dignity, and what a difference the voice made, a gentle Irish lilt rather than the raucous sound of the average cockney girl.

'Sorry to keep you waiting. I know people say you shouldn't encourage them but I'm not used to it. In Highgate, you see, there weren't any.'

Molly chatted on and within the distance of a few yards Hugo had heard the story of her life and that of her nearest and dearest, the Eliott sisters, her cousin in Kilburn and how to clean furniture with vinegar before polishing it with beeswax.

'Here we are, then.' She opened the front door and led Hugo into the big front room where all five were now working: Jack, with a rag dipped in turpentine, was cleaning blue drips from white paintwork, and Evangeline, in her painting smock, was on a kitchen chair scraping white paint off the windows. The gramophone was now playing the 'Nuns' Chorus' from *Aida*, which had slowed Piggy down considerably. Molly shouted above the noise, 'This is Hugo Bunting and he's a painter and decorator too.' Hugo was surprised; he hadn't volunteered this information. He presumed it was his paint-spattered coat that had given her a false clue.

He looked at them all as they dropped their brushes into the turps. 'Is it a fancy-dress luncheon?' he enquired.

Jack took the tray from him, 'Thank you for helping, no, it's a charity luncheon. Get some glasses, Molly. I'm Jack Maddox. Piggy Trenton,' he gestured at Piggy descending the ladder, 'my sister, Penelope.'

'How do you do?' She took a hand from underneath her shroud and shook his hand firmly.

'Beatrice Eliott, my amanuensis.'

'Excuse me,' she said, 'my hands are covered in paint.'

'And this,' Jack added, 'is Evangeline Eliott.'

Molly, who had returned with the glasses, saw all chance of a romance dashed as Hugo shook hands with Evangeline. It was like the pictures: they looked at each other and didn't say a word. Not that she minded so much, Hugo Bunting was obviously a gentleman and therefore not suitable really, not for her, Molly Murphy. Now that footman she'd talked to in Jackson's, Piccadilly, half Irish he was, much more suitable. She sat on the floor eating her bread and cheese, listening to them all talking away.

So, Mr Bunting was an architect, was he, building houses and changing houses into flats, like this one. Miss Maddox was hell bent on having a barney with him. Pull down the slums, she says, and build new for the poor. Miss Evie was in a tricky position trying to please both. 'Couldn't we conserve the old and build new ones, Penny? Mr Bunting is right. The old are more pleasing to look at.'

'To look at from the outside, maybe, but walls running with condensation, kitchens infested with cockroaches and wall plaster concealing nests of bugs are less than pleasing to the eye.'

'Of course I want new housing built, I'm an architect, after all. I just can't stand the derivative trash that they do build.'

Jack jumped to his feet, 'Time we went up to the studio, Bea, we have a sitting at half past two.' He put his hand out and, pulling Beatrice to her feet, took off her tweed cap and ruffled her hair. 'You're like a golden Medusa.'

'Yes, I must go too.' Hugo took a brush from the jar of turps. 'Piggy, if you paint like this,' he angled the brush to demonstrate, 'the paint won't drip, or not quite as much, any-

160

way. If there's anything I can do to help. Not painting,' he added hastily.

'We do need advice, we want to knock a wall down.' Evangeline spoke impetuously. 'Our workroom is too small, we want to extend through Molly's room.'

'Mine?' Molly wailed. 'And where am I to sleep?' Hugo looked at her bright little face. Difficult position for her, he thought. Friend and servant. Careless of them, really.

'Don't worry, Molly.' He patted her arm. 'I'll find somewhere for you.'

Molly gazed up into his eyes, trusting him. 'Thank you . . . er . . .' Hugo or Mr Bunting, she wondered. 'Mr Bunting.'

'Why don't you show me the whole flat and I'll work out the logistics?'

'You'd better do that, Evie, we have to go.'

'Thank you, Hugo. You all right, Tom, for a couple of hours?'

Piggy looked down from his ladder. 'Yes, two hours will see me finished, then I have to go.'

The room was silent, only Piggy and Penelope still working.

'They didn't say anything about the beading, Miss Maddox. Should I be getting on with . . . ?'

'Not to worry, Molly, there's a girl I know —'

161

'In Gunpowder Alley, Miss?'

'Right. Excellent beadwork and all-round needlewoman. Needs the job. The Eliotts have enough work to use her part-time, and now that you are looking after Jack's studio as well, you have enough to do.'

Molly shifted restlessly. 'You don't think then . . . well, that I'm not needed at all?'

Piggy peered round to look at her. Molly was twisting her apron strings in her fingers. 'Miss Murphy,' he said gently, 'both Miss Beatrice and Miss Evangeline have told me that they couldn't manage without you, and if they ever let you go it would be at your request and then only if you were to be married.'

'Is that so?' Molly brightened in an instant and she took off her apron. 'It's the shopping I'd better do. Will you tell them where I've gone, Mr Trenton?'

'Where are you going?'

'Jackson's, Piccadilly,' she said triumphantly. They did need some shopping, too, though strictly speaking it wasn't necessary to go all the way to Jackson's, but the quality was worth the extra distance, and so was the chance of seeing her footman. Maybe not as interesting as Mr Bunting but — now that's a funny thing. He was Hugo till he met Miss Evie and now he's Mr Bunting. He liked her enough, though, in spite of Miss Evie. That wouldn't suit me, she thought, a man like that, giving the eye to two girls in one day.

She paused at Hampden House, the best, or at least the biggest, house in the street. A little group of people was waiting outside, some of them with Union Jacks.

'What is it? Is it the Prime Minister or the King?' she questioned a girl of her own age.

'Not your king, anyway. Bugger off. Ireland for the Irish. England for the English. Taking the bread out of —'

Molly rushed on. She was shaking. Oh, Lord, she thought, that's those police stations being bombed yesterday. She kept running till she had turned the corner into Grosvenor Square.

A young girl like that, swearing at her. She paused to regain her breath and walked through the gardens in the centre of the square where children were bowling hoops round and round watched by their nursemaids. A little girl sent hers right at Molly who stopped it and sent it spinning back. The little girl jumped up and down, delighted.

'More, more,' she cried, and catching her nanny's eye, 'Please,' the little girl spun the hoop again.

Molly caught it and returned it, this time with a backward twist so that the hoop stopped on the way and came back to her.

'How do you do that? How did you do that?'

Molly just smiled and sent it skittering back. Waving, she hurried across the square and down into Mount Street.

There, now, I didn't speak to her so's she didn't know I was Irish. I'm a fool. But at least Mr Bunting didn't mind, nor, come to that, did anyone she knew. It was people she didn't know who did. Forget it, Molly Murphy, spring is on the way, you've still got a job and two men have paid you court in one week. How long would the job last, though? She felt life was like a jack-in-the-box in the Eliott household since the master had died. Little bits of the past kept coming up, and how long would it be before the lid blew off and everything was known? They wouldn't like it that she'd always known, specially Miss Bea. But it was Mr Eliott who'd paid her and, though being nice and friendly was all very well, she was still only a servant and in those days his servant. Still, as her mother used to say, 'Don't lie down till you've been hit.'

She decided to walk down Burlington Arcade even though the Beadle scared her. He was so imposing in his black and green uniform and brass buttons, and he was tall enough without his black top hat to add to it. He was there at the entrance, barring the way to a cyclist who was demanding rights he didn't have. No cycling, no hoops, no bouncing balls, no large parcels, no running.

Molly walked sedately down the Arcade lit by gas torchères examining the shop windows intently. Did she prefer the triple pearl necklace or the diamond spray brooch? Perhaps those emerald earrings? The value of any one of them would have kept her for the rest of her life. She came out into Piccadilly opposite Fortnum and Mason. Was that him? There was a footman in the same sort of livery leaning against a very grand car. It looked like him. That thick black wavy hair and those broad shoulders. If it was, it was an omen. Crossing the busy road, avoiding buses, taxicabs, delivery vans and bicycles, all honking horns and ringing bells, she walked in front of the car without looking at him.

'Molly,' she turned, 'it's me, Michael.'

Feigning surprise she walked up to him. 'What are you doing here?'

'Her ladyship's in there.' He gestured towards Fortnum and Mason. 'I'd like to see you. I was such a fool last time not to ask where you lived.' He looked anxiously at the door of the shop. 'Look, can I see you tonight? I have three hours off. I can't talk to you here. They don't like it.'

'What about him?' Molly pointed to the chauffeur. 'Won't he tell?'

Michael shook his head. 'Not him. So can you?'

'I'll try. What time?'

'Eight o'clock.'

'All right. If I'm not outside it means I can't.' She started to move off. ' 'Bye now.'

'Molly,' Michael grabbed her arm, 'where?'

'Oh, aren't I stupid? A hundred and seventy-seven Green Street.'

'Good. You know, I didn't know you were an O'Malley.'

'I'm not,' she said curtly. 'I'm a Murphy.'

'Don't worry. I'll not be telling anybody. I'll see you at eight.'

She walked down to Jackson's to get some cheese and more tea. There was plenty of cold lamb left. How did he know she was related to the O'Malleys? Pray to God he wasn't involved in the new army. Would Miss Bea want to meet him before letting her go out? She pushed the swing doors of Jackson's as if she had done it all her life.

Beatrice ran down the stairs, anxious to see the finished room. Tomorrow when it was dry they would pin all their sketches and designs with swatches of material on the walls and move in Father's desk, once dark heavy mahogany now painted white, and the furniture from her room in Highgate. Her bedroom here was too small for it.

'Evie, it's wonderful, you've finished.' She looked around the room, cleaned, tidied and swept. 'Tom, thank you, oh, thank you.' She put her arms round him and kissed his cheek. 'And, Penny, I don't know what to say but you've all been marvellous and I'm so grateful.'

Penelope had removed her dust sheet and was putting on her coat. 'Pleasure. Evie, we must go.' She turned to Piggy. 'So you're going to drop us at Gunpowder Alley to see Tilly Allen. Then Hugo picks us up there, takes me to the Mission and Evie to . . . wherever.'

'Chilton's. It's in Bury Street,' Evangeline looked anxiously at her sister. 'Do you mind, Bea? He's going to bring some plans for the flat. He's got good ideas which won't cost very much.'

Beatrice sighed. 'Yes. I think so. Oh, everything is so different now. Before the war you could never have dined alone with a man and now . . .'

'Now . . .' prompted Evangeline.

Beatrice smiled. 'Now you can. But, please, Evie, come home immediately after. Yes?'

'Yes.'

'I'm going to crank up my motor.' Piggy put on his cap and goggles. 'Where's Jack? We ought to be off.'

167

'Off?' Beatrice was startled. 'Where are you going? After Gunpowder Alley, I mean.'

Piggy tried to avoid her question. 'Friday to Monday,' he said heartily. 'See the parents.'

'And Jack?' Piggy adjusted his goggles.

'Is Jack going with you?' Beatrice said impatiently.

The appearance of Jack in his outdoor clothes saved Piggy an awkward reply. 'I'll have to move my suitcase if you two are sitting in the dickey, and heaven knows where Daffie's going to sit.'

'Will you be all right, Bea?' Evangeline suddenly felt like the older sister.

'Of course. I'm going to start cutting out the Gregsons' dresses. Goodbye. Have a good time. Thank you again, all of you.'

She stood at the front door: the car was taking a long time to start and her smile was wearing thin. Suddenly she felt lonely. Their high spirits had set them apart. She shivered.

'It's cold. I'm going in.' She waved and went into the house. With her back to the door she waited till she heard the car start and move away, then, wrapping her arms around herself, she began to cry.

Beatrice looked at the watch pinned to her jacket. Nine o'clock. Time to eat her supper. She put aside the navy blue silk dress she was

168

hemming and stretched her arms. She was stiff, but what a lot she'd got done. Both the dresses cut out for the Gregson twins, Sybil Bonner's jacket nearly finished, just the pockets left for Evie who would do them so much better, and when she had finished hemming the silk dress for Aunt Lydia she would see what she could rescue from Molly's débâcle with Lady Bonner's material.

When she stopped working that fluttering-bird feeling in her chest returned. Maybe food would help. Molly had left her cold lamb and beetroot prettily arranged on a plate with a linen napkin and a glass. She had seen that Molly clearly felt guilty about going out. Funny, because nobody else had. Her young man had been charming. Quite a day for her. Not only Michael the footman but clearly Hugo Bunting, until he'd seen Evie, had been taken with her too.

She let herself think about Jack again. That seemed to be safe now. No more tears. She was thirty, for goodness' sake, those things were past. He had reminded her of another Jack, Jack Bisham, a patient of her father's, was it six — no, seven years ago? He had managed Papa very well, deferential, yes, sir, oh, indeed, sir, but with her when Papa wasn't there he had been freer, funny and kind, interested in her opinions. She hadn't seen him after he had enlisted and been posted to France. His farewell when he came to collect his morphine had been rather formal.

'How awful for you,' she had said rather tearfully, 'I hope you won't need that.'

'If I do, Miss Eliott, it will be during the execution of my duty to my country.'

He hadn't died in the war as she had thought: she had seen him in Hampstead once with a pretty young woman pushing a perambulator. He had been a passing acquaintance, it was nothing serious. Like her relationship with Jack Maddox. He was fond of her, as she was of him, but it was a brotherly affection. Teasing fun, not serious. In fact just what she wanted because her work, her career, was going to come first. Only two weeks in their new flat and everything was going so well. Seven clients already, and when they paid, it would be enough to live on for at least three months. She laughed, remembering Arthur's face when she had told him that the house was sold. 'Not legal,' he had said. But as the mortgage wasn't legal either, she had retorted, two wrongs in this case did make a right.

He had questioned her in a rather circuitous way about what she knew about Cadogan Mews but she had been mysterious and deflected his questions, rather hoping that he would give something away. Anyway, it was easy to be mysterious because she knew nothing. Jack had not been forthcoming either.

She heard the front door opening. Was that Evie or Molly? If it was Molly, better hide her supper. She had hardly eaten anything.

'Bea? Bea? Where are you?' It was Evangeline bounding up the stairs. 'How are you, Bea? I'm so excited.' She burst into the kitchen. 'So many first times in one day.'

Beatrice stopped scraping her supper into the rubbish pail and froze. Then slowly she straightened up and faced Evangeline. 'What, Evie? What were they?' Evangeline looked radiant, glorious. Her usually pale face was slightly flushed and gleaming. Beatrice looked away. She didn't want to know.

'Bea?' Evangeline put her hand out and gently pulled her sister's face towards her. 'Bea? You don't think . . . ?' She started laughing. 'Bea, it's a quarter to ten. We met him at Tilly's at seven o'clock. We arrived at the restaurant at eight o'clock. I'm not an expert on such matters, but surely a seduction would take longer than that?'

'I'm a fool. I'm sorry, Evie. But this is the first time you've —'

'Yes. That's what I was going to say . . . Oh, I've got to tell you all his plans.' Beatrice raised an eyebrow quizzically. 'For the flat,

171

Bea! And then Tilly . . .'

'What did she say?'

'She said yes. But better than that. She'll work for us doing piece-work to start off so until we really get going we don't have to give her a regular salary. And it isn't just beading. All her work is beautiful. She showed me. Phew, I'm exhausted.' She sat down, then leapt up again. 'Shall I make us some cocoa?'

'In a minute. Evie, I've been thinking hard.'

'Sorry to rush on. Are you all right, Bea?' Evangeline pressed her hand against Beatrice's cheek. 'It was awful leaving you alone. It was all so surprising, Jack and Piggy taking Daphne away. Both Piggy and Penelope were angry in the car.'

'Evie, it's none of my business or yours. Jack and Piggy are friends and Jack is my employer, that's all. Who they invite for a weekend is really nothing to do with us. Now let me tell you what I've planned.'

'Please let me go first, Bea. I've got to persuade you.'

'All right.' Beatrice smiled indulgently. 'Go first. I'm excited, too, but I can wait.'

'Well.' Evangeline took a deep breath. Then in a rush, 'We're wasting space, Hugo says, and we've got to have the basement.'

'That would be wonderful, but that's Jack's, isn't it?'

'We went down and had a look. There's quite a lot of junk there. Probably Jack's. And millions of books just mouldering. Definitely not Jack's. Definitely Mr Reed-Smith's because they're all religious. But Hugo said . . .' She paused, Hugo had said so much. In the taxi from Gunpowder Alley he had held her hand, first taking off the kid glove slowly. The feeling had been quite shocking as if he were removing a more intimate garment. He had talked through the whole journey, describing the architecture, telling her stories about the building of St Paul's Cathedral, what the Great Fire of London had destroyed, pointing out the tiny church of St Ethelburga-the-Virgin, a fifteenth-century church which had survived the Fire, one of his favourite churches in London and the smallest, with a secret garden tucked away behind; the origins of Milk Street, Bread Lane and Blackfriars, and how the fashionable had gradually moved from the City to the West End. In the restaurant he had ordered for her, in very good French, a *mousseline* of sole, *veau en feuilletons* and a *petit pot au chocolat*.

When they arrived he had told the head waiter, 'Bunting. Table for four,' explaining to her when they were seated that tables for two were too small. He had drawn some rough plans and talked about them with great an-

173

imation all through dinner.

Nothing personal was said. No 'You've got lovely eyes' or 'What beautiful hair' yet occasionally he would gaze intently at her, not smiling and again, like removing her glove, his gaze was more disturbing, she felt, than even a kiss might be.

The basement, he said, was vital. It would be a kitchen, and a big bedsitting room for Molly. It would free her room to be expanded into the workroom and give them all privacy.

While he was explaining this, she remembered that it was Molly who had brought him home. Was she jealous of her maid? The evening had ended abruptly. He was going away for the weekend and had to catch a train. He had taken her home, waited until she had opened the door and then, almost as an afterthought, said he would telephone her.

'The walls that have to be knocked through are all false partitions, he said, and easy to do. And if we do it now we can use his builders very reasonably and he will supervise and not charge — well, we can make his mother something, he said. What do you think, Bea?'

Beatrice looked around the kitchen. 'So this would be a little sitting room for us and the whole of the ground floor would be for work, including a fitting room.'

'Yes. It makes sense, doesn't it?'

174

'Yes, it does,' Beatrice said emphatically. 'And it absolutely agrees with the ideas I've been thinking about. We've been quite brave so far — as Cousin Arthur said, we've burnt our boats. But, Evie, I don't think it's enough. We don't want to be dressmakers, that isn't what we do best. Plenty of people can cut and sew as well as us. It's our ideas, our designs, that set us apart. Look at you now, Evie. Did you see any woman in the restaurant as well dressed?'

Evangeline thought, and looked down at her dress. It was a two-piece navy blue crêpe with a slightly flared skirt that stopped two inches above the ankle, and a top that they had copied from a man's cricket sweater long to her hips, with a V on the front outlined in white and maroon worn over a white *gilet*.

'You know, Bea, I don't remember anyone else in the restaurant. Or even the restaurant.'

Beatrice smiled at her. 'You must have had a very good time.'

Evangeline obviously didn't want to add anything more to her thoughtful 'Yes'.

Beatrice continued, 'What should we try to offer, apart from our talent, I mean?'

'Is there anything else?' Evangeline asked seriously.

'Yes, there is. Three of our commissions came because the clients needed or wanted

175

things in a hurry and their dressmakers couldn't do it. If we have Tilly permanently and possibly someone else and if we're prepared to work any hours . . .'

'Yes, yes.' Evangeline added, 'You're right, we will create a need. All women want their clothes immediately. I always do.'

'And I think we should advertise.'

'Oh, Bea. What about the money? Do we have enough?'

'The rent on the flat is there in the bank. Enough for four years. We have the tiny income Arthur doles out and my money from Jack. All that's enough to live on especially as we're making money already, but we need a lump sum for everything else.'

Evangeline's excitement vanished. 'I think I'll make the cocoa.'

'Didn't you have enough to eat with Hugo? What did you have?'

As she fetched a pan, the cocoa and milk, Evangeline said, 'Sole, veal and chocolate.'

'All at the same time?'

'No. You're in a funny mood, Bea. You really think we can do it, don't you?' She put a mixture of milk and water on to heat and mixed the cocoa powder to a paste in the mugs. 'What are you planning? You look all foxy. As if you knew where the hole in the chicken run was.'

'I don't know, but I'm having a guess.'

Beatrice regarded her sister carefully. She was only twenty. Should she tell Evangeline her suspicions? Would it hurt her? Would it take away her trust? And they were only suspicions. Perhaps it was better for her to know about men. Or some men.

'It's about Arthur. And maybe Papa.'

Evangeline gave Beatrice her cocoa and sat down. 'Yes.'

'All right. Here goes. Why do you think Arthur, one of the meanest people ever, paid our mortgage, which was a huge amount? There was no gain for him and, if he was doing it to impress us, why didn't he tell us? And why, at just the mention of Cadogan Mews, did he capitulate and let us sell the house?'

Evangeline's excited eyes appeared over the rim of her mug. 'Why?' she breathed.

'I don't know.'

'Bea!' Evangeline banged her mug down. 'You are a terrible tease, like a child. I think I'll pull your hair.'

'I said I don't know. But I'm going to try to find out.'

The front door banged. 'I'm back,' Molly called up the stairs. 'Shall I lock up, Miss Bea? Is Miss Evie back?' She went into her tiny bedroom and took off her coat. Tiny as it was even that might be taken away from her.

Have they decided to put me out, she wondered. I could go back to Armagh. Live with my mother. But what about Michael? She ran upstairs.

'Oh, Miss Evie, you're back. And what did you want to say, Miss Bea?' She was both curious and worried and didn't know which feeling to indulge first. Where had Miss Evie gone with Mr Bunting? And what about her bedroom? What time did she get back and where was she supposed to sleep if they took her room for sewing?

'We've got good news for you, Molly.' Beatrice paused. 'Or at least we hope you think it's good news.'

Evie burst in, 'Of course you will. Where did you go, Molly? Mr Bunting took me to a restaurant — Chilton's — and I ate sole, veal and chocolate. He says we're to take over the basement then you can have a much bigger room next to the kitchen down there. Like in Highgate.'

Molly gave Evangeline a huge grin. That was easy enough. Both questions answered in one go. 'It's wonderful news, Miss Evie, Miss Bea.'

'And you'll be too busy with an extra floor so you'll only have to help us with the dressmaking if we're very busy.'

'And I won't have to do any of the painting down there?'

'Certainly not.'

Molly sat down, relieved, all her worries taken away. Well, not all, but enough for to-night.

'My friend Michael took me to Collins' Music Hall in Islington. Lots of singers, comics, men and women, Harry Lauder and a sing-along and I knew all the words. I was very good.'

'I'm sure you were,' and Beatrice was sure. She had been listening to Molly singing as she went about her work for years. That was how she kept up with popular songs.

'And what about Harry Lauder? Was he good, too?'

'Now that I couldn't say.' Molly spoke with some disapointment. 'We had to leave before he came on. Michael had to be back before eleven o'clock to let in the young master and give him his whisky and draw his bath. He's not just a footman, you see. He's under-butler.'

'So he has prospects, then? That's good.'

Evangeline nodded encouragingly. 'Especially today with so many people out of work.'

'Yes, that's true.' Molly got up and yawned. 'But not much freedom in service.' Her hand flew to her mouth. 'Oh, I'm sorry — I didn't mean — not that I don't have freedom. And you giving me the evening off like that, Miss Bea . . .'

'I don't mind you having the evening off when there's nothing to do, Molly, just as long as I know who you're with and when you'll be home. Both of you.' Beatrice included Evangeline in that hint of warning. 'I'm glad that you both had a good time. I'm happy that you were both home at a reasonable hour.' She laughed. 'Oh dear, I sound like an old maiden aunt. Come on, it's time we all went to bed.'

As she went downstairs Molly thought about Hugo Bunting. Would he have taken her, Molly, to a restaurant if Miss Evie hadn't been there this morning? She thought so.

Tilly sat at the long kitchen table in the basement squinting at the grey chiffon top she was stitching. It would be good when the rooms upstairs were finished — more light.

'Don't tack the bottom of that, Tilly.' Beatrice looked up from the belt she was making for the same dress. 'We won't finish it until Mrs Trenton's had another fitting.'

'What shall I get on with next, then?'

'Let me think.' Beatrice wasn't sure that there was anything to be getting on with until

Evangeline had been to Liberty's to get some more material.

'Miss Beatrice, I'd like to say something.' Tilly gathered her courage.

'Yes, Tilly, go on.'

'This isn't just because I want to work but you ought to make some things before they're ordered. The popular things. Miss Evie's high-necked blouse, for instance, and your black cashmere jacket with the double buttons. That's what a lot of houses do and you ought not to get your materials at the retail price, you should buy it wholesale, in quantities.'

Beatrice put down the belt. 'That's good, Tilly. And I know you're right about buying in quantity, wholesale. It's a question of being brave and the outlay of money.'

'Well, you don't have to pay for the material straight away any more than your ladies pay for their frocks straight away.'

'Mm, if only they did. Just a minute.' Beatrice shouted up the back stairs, 'Evie, Evie,' and again, more loudly to drown the noise of the builders: 'Evie! Can someone send Evie down, please? Thank goodness they did this first. It's an oasis of calm. I almost envy Molly sleeping down here.'

Thinking of her own family's two rooms crowded with six people Tilly was sure she did.

181

'What is it, Bea?' Evangeline poked her head round the door. 'I'm just off to Liberty's.'

'We don't think you should go to Liberty's, at least Tilly doesn't.'

'I just think you should get more at a time and get it wholesale. I could take you to Digby and Gordon in Hallatt Street. Beautiful stuff and a big range.'

'All right, come with me now. Don't you think, Bea? And we'll get the chiffons we need and I'll see if they have anything interesting in cotton and piqué. What about money?'

'According to Tilly we don't have to pay immediately, and get Tilly to tell you her other idea. Off you go. Hurry!'

When the bills did come in she would have to deal with Arthur. If only people paid them on time, they would be able to pay their bills. But they didn't.

'Miss Bea, I've got a message for you long as my arm from Mr Jack.' Molly was twisting a rag in her hands, not from anxiety, but in an attempt to clean off the paint. 'He's on the telephone and he's very ill.'

Jumping up, Beatrice started to run upstairs.

'No, no, Miss Bea, he's not on now.'

Beatrice stopped and came back down the stairs. 'Molly, I wish you'd get your tenses right.'

'So do I, Miss. Now, here goes. He's been

very ill, he says, though I don't think he is, not by a long chalk, just got a bad chest if you ask me and that's all from that gas in the war, mark my words.'

Beatrice was startled. 'Gas in the war? I didn't know that.'

'No, Miss Maddox says he doesn't talk about it but in any way and in any case, about his chest. I says, take some pig lard and sulphur, put it on his chest, and then some brown paper.'

'Oh, Molly, you're wonderful. You do make me laugh.' Then, seeing her confused face, Beatrice added hastily, 'I mean, can you imagine Jack Maddox letting anybody wrap him up in pig fat, sulphur and brown paper?'

'Perhaps not, Miss Bea, put like that I can't. Also you're to telephone all these people and tell them not to come and you are to go to his house and take him some soup.' She handed Beatrice a list of barely decipherable names.

'Thank you, Molly. Soup. What a cheek.'

Looking up from the basement window, she could see a chauffeur helping two women out of a long, highly polished, dark green car. Too late to telephone Kitty Ashleigh and her friend. Blast. And she had that damned Frou-Frou with her. Beatrice ran up the basement steps. 'Mrs Ashleigh. Good morning. It's Miss

Eliott. Don't go up. I'm so sorry that you have wasted your time but Mr Maddox has been taken ill. Pneumonia. Double pneumonia with complications.'

'I should have thought double pneumonia was quite complicated enough. Look, Frou-Frou wants to be held.'

Her sweet smile belying her sour feelings, Beatrice took the hairy little dog.

'This is my niece, Olivia Stett-Gittins.'

'How do you do, Miss Eliott? Give me that dog, he's moulting all over that beautiful jacket. Here, Simpson, you take it, will you?'

Beatrice smiled with gratitude.

'May we come in, Miss Eliott? My aunt was telling me how helpful you were the other week with her evening gown and now I see for myself that you really have great style. I would like to ask your help.'

Seated at the table the two women examined more sketches and designs and were clearly impressed.

'We do copy clothes, if that's what the client wants, but we would like to extend our own line as well.'

'Naturally.' Mrs Stett-Gittins put down the designs. 'What I'm interested in immediately is something for a fancy dress party. Would you mind?'

184

'Not at all.' Beatrice was disappointed but tried to conceal it. 'Fancy dress. That would be fun. What's the theme?'

'Rural England.'

'What do you mean? Milkmaids? Shepherdesses? That sort of thing?'

'I suppose so. But won't everyone do that? I'd like to think of something original.'

Beatrice looked at her intently, examining her slender body and square shoulders. 'I might have an idea. I would love it myself. But you might not. You said outside you liked my jacket. It's quite mannish . . .'

'Yes. That's one of the reasons I like it. What is your idea?'

Beatrice hesitated. 'It seems rude but . . . very well, then. A scarecrow.' She hurried on. 'You're so slim, we could make you a mannish suit with trousers, braces, all in different materials and different colours and create a straw wig for your head.' She waited apprehensively.

'Brilliant. I love it. What fun. I need it by Friday. Can you do it?'

Beatrice, quiet but triumphant, said, 'Of course we can.'

'I think you should see a doctor, Jack. That's bronchitis, that cough.'

'This cough is because you're making me

185

laugh. Pig fat, sulphur and scarecrows.' He coughed again.

'I'll heat up that soup. Where's your kitchen?'

Jack was now coughing too much to speak and pointed down to the floor indicating the basement.

Beatrice poured the soup into a saucepan and lit the gas. What an odd house. Bare. Without character. Neither his parents, Penelope nor Jack had made any impression there at all. It was a lovely house, probably late Georgian, but seemed purely functional. The parents were usually away but even so you would think that somebody at some time would have made an attempt to make it their own. Maybe Fabians or Socialists, whatever they were, didn't believe in decoration, ornament. She'd never met a Fabian, or if she had, she didn't know. The kitchen hardly seemed used. Just the bare essentials.

She looked out of the window at the garden. Only grass. Not a flower to be seen — funny for botanists, but then she'd had no experience of them either. There didn't appear to be a tray. The soup would have to go on a bread board. Laughing, she wrapped the toast in a napkin and put it in one pocket with the salt and pepper in another and carried it all upstairs.

'I'm only surprised, Bea, you didn't carry

186

it on your beautiful head.' He balanced the bread board on his knees. 'It's delicious. Who made it?'

'Molly, of course, and there's enough for tomorrow.'

'No. Tomorrow I'll be back at work. This is nothing.'

'Absolutely not.' Beatrice pulled a chair to the bed and faced Jack. 'Look here, Jack, Molly told me you'd been gassed during the war and I happen to know, because of my father, that it leaves the lungs permanently damaged.'

'Your father?' Jack was surprised. 'Was he in the war?'

'He was a doctor, remember?'

'Oh, yes. Hard to reconcile that with —'

'With?' Beatrice saw her chance to elicit more information. 'What you said that time about Cadogan Mews? Was it anything to do with my father as well?'

'Difficult to say. Is there any more toast?'

How wily he was. He had avoided two subjects without actually refusing to answer. 'I can make some more.'

'No, stay here with me.' He put his hand out and took hers. 'Thank you for coming over.'

'So my father and the war are two taboo subjects?'

'Not at all, my love.' He gently stroked her hand. 'My war experience is the same as many others'. All of which, no doubt, you've heard about. In a sense I had a good war because I was at the front in the forefront of things and in another sense I had a bad war because I was at the front in the forefront of things.'

'Mmm. I understand.'

'That must be Daffie.' Someone was ringing the doorbell insistently, as if they were leaning on it.

'Oh, I must go.' She stood up and tried to remove her hand from his clasp but he held it firmly, pulling her.

'Why? She'd be disappointed if you did. It's you she's come to see.' He released her hand suddenly and she fell back.

'You're a child, Jack. An irritating, nasty little boy.'

'You must make allowances for my war, you know.' He coughed pathetically.

'Sod your war.'

'Beatrice!' He was genuinely shocked. 'I've never, ever —' His real cough took over, leaving him speechless.

'Very good. You should be an actor.'

The doorbell was still ringing when she opened the door.

'Good. Just the person I wanted to see. My God, is that him coughing?'

188

Daphne Haycock walked into the small hall and headed up the stairs. She obviously knew where she was going. 'Better get him some water, don't you think?'

Beatrice turned to go back downstairs to the kitchen.

'Get it from the bathroom opposite his bedroom.' Well, Beatrice thought, as she followed Daphne up the stairs admitting a little stab of jealousy, she obviously knows where the bedroom is and it follows she'd also know the whereabouts of the bathroom. She's likely to have spent more time there than in the kitchen. 'Hello, poor old thing, you sound ghastly. Is it as bad as usual? Mind if I have a ciggy?'

Beatrice rushed into the bedroom with the water in a tooth mug.

'Don't smoke, Daphne. That's a really stupid thing to do. Sit up. Lean forward, Jack, and drink this water.'

'Take no notice of her, Daffie.' Jack spoke hoarsely between coughs. 'She arrived as a ministering angel but she's turned into a gorgon.'

'No, I won't smoke. Sorry.'

Daphne dropped into a big sagging armchair, after pushing some clothes off it, and watched Beatrice massaging Jack's back. 'You can massage me when you've finished. It looks good.'

'It isn't massage,' Beatrice said shortly. 'I'm rubbing his back. It helps shift phlegm.'

'How romantic, my love.'

'I'm not romantic and I'm not your love.' She took her index finger and scratched his spine, none too gently.

He gasped. 'You little cat.'

Observing the red mark she had left, she ran the pad of her finger down soothing it and felt an intense desire to kiss the nape of his neck.

'I'm going to take these things downstairs,' she said, collecting the bowl, spoon and bread board, 'and then I must go.'

Her face was hot, she couldn't look at him. What was the matter with her? She was a spinster of thirty. 'I'll come with you and have a cigarette.' Turning at the door, Daphne gave Jack a cynical smile. 'Your self-imposed abstinence isn't going to last very long.'

'Now, my idea is this.' Daphne perched on the kitchen table. 'We can help each other. I want you to design me a dress and make it for me for nothing.'

Beatrice turned round from the sink. 'So far, I can see how that helps you but I can't quite fathom how it helps me.'

'I'll explain.' Daphne swung her elegant legs. 'I've been asked to do something. Sing, actually, at the Munfords' big charity do.'

'Lady Munford's ball at the Ritz?' Beatrice wiped her hands. This might be interesting.

'She's not doing it at the Ritz this year. It's going to be at a night club, I think the Lark and the Owl, and there's going to be a jazz band and a cabaret with a mixture of amateurs and professionals.'

'And you will be one of the amateurs?'

'I could be professional, of course, I'm good enough.'

'You know, I believe you.' Beatrice smiled; she really did believe her.

'But life's too short to take that seriously.'

'I've got to go, Daphne. I must get back to Green Street. Could you tell me all about it in a taxi?'

'Good. Yes, I'll come with you and talk to Evangeline as well, I need it by Friday week.'

Beatrice went back into the bedroom. Jack was nearly asleep, still breathing hoarsely but a little better than when she had arrived. She started to scribble a note to him but he opened his eyes.

'Bea?'

'Yes. I'm just leaving. I'll be back this evening.'

'I'm sorry.' He closed his eyes and pulled the sheet up round his neck.

'What for?'

'I can't remember.'

'See you this evening, then.'

The taxi pulled out of Campden Hill Square and edged into the traffic driving up Notting Hill Gate. Beatrice looked back. 'Very odd that house. How long have they lived there?'

'Nobody lives there. They just stay there. They're all the same. Can't put down roots. The parents are always off. Always were. Jack and Penelope were brought up by nannies and governesses then both sent off to schools.' Daphne lolled back in the cab. 'So if I pay for the material, you do see it would be a great showcase for you?'

Beatrice looked at the thin figure sitting next to her. Her short spiky hair was blonder than ever and her pallor extreme. The pinky brown eyeliner was echoed under her cheekbones and on the thin but curved mouth. She was extraordinarily attractive. Dazzling and different.

'Yes, it would be,' she admitted. 'You make a wonderful clothes horse, I'd love to dress you.'

The pink flush that suffused Daphne's face made her look less extraordinary and more real.

'Can you afford the material, though?'

'Yes, now Jack's fixed it up with my father. Don't look so surprised. He told him he's got to increase my allowance or I would go to the bad. Although, as everyone knows, I've already gone.'

Beatrice frowned. 'Couldn't you come back?'

'It might be too late. Don't nag me, Beatrice. You're like Jack. He doesn't like some of the things I do and hates others, he acts like all of my brothers rolled into one.'

'Your brothers were killed in the war, weren't they?' Beatrice said gently.

'Yes. Worse luck. And Jack thinks he should make up for them all.'

Looking out of the window as they drove through the park, Beatrice noted how crowded Rotten Row was. Riders in immaculate tweed hacking jackets and cavalry twill jodhpurs were cantering under the trees, accompanied by women on side saddles wearing black skirts and jackets, white stocks and bowlers with veils. They looked as if they were having a rather gentle race.

'We're not lovers, you know, Beatrice. Jack and I. Well, once, when we were drunk aeons ago. Never to be repeated.'

'It's none of my business.'

'Isn't it?'

Tilly walked out of the stuffy, fetid air of the Underground station and took huge breaths of fresh air. The Underground was faster but the bus was much cleaner and nicer. To sit on top of a double-decker omnibus and travel from one end of London to another was like a holiday. Her favourite was starting at the Elephant and Castle where her gran lived, going through the City past Lambeth Palace, her favourite building with its pink brick towers, over the bridge, looking down the Thames on both sides at the brightly painted barges and grimy freighters bringing coal down from the north, then curving round through Victoria by the station, the excitement always tinged with sadness because that was the last time she saw her older brother before he went off to France, to Wipers. After Victoria the bus headed for Park Lane. You could see from the top deck all across the park to Kensington Palace.

The sound of people shouting stopped her day-dreaming. It was coming from the direction of Grosvenor Square, she thought, or nearby, perhaps South Audley Street. She tried to quicken her step, but rickets had damaged the strength of her legs. She could hear now a regular chanting. 'More jobs, more jobs, more jobs,' alternated with 'We want work, we want work.'

That was me, she thought, only a few weeks ago. Not marching, but certainly out of work. And now not just working but appreciated.

They listened to her, often took her advice, and Miss Evie had even said she was an artist.

The marchers were now heading up Green Street. They were obviously going to have a meeting in the park at Speakers' Corner near Marble Arch. She would wait till they were well out of the way. Not wise to get involved.

Beatrice walked into the kitchen carrying a roll of black chiffon. The long scrubbed table was covered in cotton reels, fragments of material, cardboard boxes containing pins and needles and large boxes of pearl and crystal beads. Evangeline, working with a paper pattern, was cutting out a trouser leg.

'You've started the scarecrow. Good. I'm going to work on the straw wig and I've brought the black chiffon down for Kitty Ashleigh's dress.' She looked up at the basement window. 'That noise is getting nearer. Sounds like a drum and people shouting. It's going to drive me mad.'

Evangeline took some pins out of her mouth. 'It's the unemployment march. They're going to be addressed by George Lansbury.'

Beatrice went to the window and banged it shut.

'You can shut out the noise, Bea, but you can't shut out the problem.'

Picking up a silk stocking Beatrice cut off the foot just above the ankle and stretched it. 'There is work if people looked for it. The streets are filthy, for instance.'

'Two million people cleaning the streets? Don't be ridiculous. Penelope says —'

'Penelope says a lot of things. She can afford to be charitable.'

Evangeline ignored this. It was wiser where Beatrice was concerned not to defend Penelope. It was clear she envied both Penelope's freedom and Evangeline's growing friendship with her.

'How are you going to do that wig, Bea?'

'I'm going to pull the stocking on my head to stretch it a bit more.' She did so and, seeing herself in the mirror, roared with laughter in which Evangeline joined.

Hearing them outside Tilly started to laugh too, although she didn't know why until she peered in at the kitchen window. Beatrice saw her and beckoned her in. 'Thank goodness for you, Tilly. We've got a lovely dress to make, sadly not for a lovely woman, all because she saw your beading on that long chiffon scarf.'

'And Bea was so clever she invented a dress on the spot.' Evangeline examined her own work. 'And I've been relegated to fancy dress.'

'What's the dress, Miss Beatrice?'

'A plain silver tissue taffeta tube with an

196

overdress of black chiffon embroidered with pearls. I think that's one of the dresses we could always have prepared, Tilly, following your idea. Only the loose overdress, though. Pearls on black chiffon and crystal on grey.'

Tilly took off her jacket and washed her hands at the kitchen sink. 'And jet bugling on white chiffon?'

'Yes. Good.'

'Lovely. I am going to be busy. Do you have any cream for my hands? Don't want to snag delicate materials.'

She sat at the long table, clearly happy. 'Nice to be busy, nice day . . . well . . .' remembering the unemployment marchers, 'nice for some.'

'Nicer still if people paid their bills.' Beatrice wove straw in and out of the stocking cap she had made.

'Shall I start the black chiffon, Miss Bea, or finish the grey silk? Once the first bills start to be paid, you catch up with yourself. You're at the beginning now but you'll be all right.' Tilly spoke firmly but with great confidence. 'I know you will.'

From the stairs the gruff voice of one of the workmen called, 'There's a Miss Bennett on the telephone for a Miss Eliott about the advertisement.'

'How exciting, more work. Shall I go, Bea?'

Not waiting for a reply, Evangeline sped upstairs hoping that she might bump into Hugo. He was so unpredictable. She had only seen him alone twice and each time he had had to leave early. When he was in their flat instructing the builders he spoke to Bea about the design and costs, and although he was gentle and sweet with Molly, he didn't speak to Evangeline, just stared at her occasionally.

After talking to Miss Bennett she looked into the newly extended workroom.

'Nearly finished, Miss, end of tomorrow should do it, shouldn't it, Mr Bunting?'

Hugo turned from the joist he was examining. 'So I should think, Bert. I want you back up the road with me.' He didn't smile. He didn't say hello. Evangeline felt uncomfortable.

'I must go back to my work. Sorry you had to answer the telephone.'

'Not used to the telephone, Miss, and never will be. Don't see how it works, don't rightly get the hang of it.'

She smiled. 'I don't try to get the hang of it. I just use it.'

Hugo crossed the room suddenly and, taking her arm, piloted her across the hall into the empty reception room.

Kicking the door shut he pushed her very deliberately against the wall without saying a word. His face was arrogant, Evangeline thought, yet it also had the appearance of pain. He pushed his hand up through the hair at the nape of her neck and pulled her head sharply towards him, kissing her so hard she gasped and opened her mouth, which was obviously what he wanted.

It was so surprising, so strange, but she liked the feeling of his mouth almost eating hers, his tongue exploring, and the warm ache at the pit of her stomach.

He stopped as unexpectedly as he had started but didn't release her. 'I want you, you know,' he said, quite flatly.

She recovered her breath and said lightly, 'I think you've made that clear.'

'Don't be facetious. Think about it.'

He left her leaning against the wall, trembling. The front door banged. He had gone. She touched her wet mouth with shaking fingers and explored it as he had with his tongue.

'Evie, Evie.' She heard her sister calling. Quickly she looked at herself in the long mirror. She was flushed. Her eyes looked as if she had taken belladonna but no one would guess. Guess what, though?

'Where have you been? Why have you been so long?' Beatrice had finished the straw wig and was wearing it.

'Oh, just talking to the workmen. They'll be finished tomorrow. Isn't that good?'

'Well?' Beatrice waited expectantly.

'Well, what?' Evangeline sat down and picked up the bright cyclamen wool trouser leg.

'My scarecrow wig. Really, Evie, do I always look like this?'

'Sorry, Bea. It's wonderful. It suits you. You should make one for yourself.'

Beatrice punched her arm playfully. 'Little monster. I'm going to damp the straw so it looks a bit softer. What did Miss Bennett want?'

Tilly sat up expectantly. More work, maybe.

'Peculiar, really. She's coming round straight away but she had a very . . .' Her voice trailed away.

'A very what?'

Evangeline thought quickly. She could hardly say 'a very common accent' in front of Tilly. 'A very bad cough,' she said lamely.

Walking through Kensington Gardens, Evangeline stopped at one of the rose beds. The smell was strong but discreet. You could sleep in a room full of roses, the smell was never overpowering. Not like hyacinth or narcissi. They smelt as if they were over-ripe the minute they bloomed. Much better in a garden than in a house.

She remembered the Maddoxes' garden last night. Bare. Empty, except for a few wild flowers that had escaped the gardener's mowing machine. Penelope had been dismissive about the suggestions of flowers. Far better to have vegetables, she had said, more practical.

She had also been practical and far from sentimental about Hugo. Had Beatrice known, or Arthur, what they had been talking about, she would be put in a home for wayward girls!

Her laugh attracted the attention of an old man, a gardener. He looked up from the plants he was tending and smiled. 'Lovely day, Miss.'

'It is lovely. You look like a gnome down there!'

'And you look like a fairy up there.'

'Thank you. And thank you for the beautiful roses.'

His smile increased to reveal all four of his remaining teeth.

Penelope had been so blunt about her own life. She had been engaged twice during the war and both times had 'anticipated marriage', as she had put it. Both of the men had been killed in action, and if the war hadn't ended she would probably have been engaged again. She had spoken about sex as if it was therapeutic for the men at least.

Evangeline had tried to talk to her about her feelings but had been rebuffed. The physical side wasn't to be discussed, or emotions. She had simply said in a matter of fact way, that as Evangeline had strong natural desires and in Hugo an outlet for them, she should behave responsibly. Behaving responsibly didn't seem to include marriage or even an engagement. Just a visit to the Marie Stopes clinic in Holloway, although she had been adamant about her dislike of promiscuity and its dangers. It was all rather confusing. How many anticipated marriages constituted promiscuity? She shivered. Had a goose walked over her grave? No, she was a goose — a cloud had passed over the sun.

She must hurry back. They were all working so hard. Thank goodness for the new girl, Letty Bennett, the Miss Bennett from the telephone call — she had been looking for work not clothes — especially now there was another commission from Lady Bonner. Both the Honourable Sybil and her mother had been pleased with their clothes, and Lady Bonner had told her in secret that Sybil was getting married and that the Eliott sisters would be making the dress for the bride's mother. It showed great trust. Sybil's dress, of course, was being made by Madame Rochelle. Best of all, Lady Bonner had paid her. Bea would be so relieved.

Her mind drifted back to Hugo. This was the first time, Evangeline thought, that she had had a real secret from her sister. It would remain a secret, too. As she didn't understand her feelings herself, how could she expect Beatrice to understand? It would only worry her and she had enough to worry about. Their success had brought problems: the more clients they had the more they had to spend on materials and now wages. If they could *only* keep going until everybody paid their bills. But Bea would manage. Last night, going home, she'd been rather subdued but, just before they went to bed, she had unexpectedly announced that she was going to see Arthur. 'I'll have to have money for wages,' she'd said. 'Maybe we can't afford Letty Bennett, although she's very good.'

Letty was indeed very good, Evangeline thought, and she had wonderful references from such good houses. Fortuny and Paquin. Both she and Bea had been impressed by her honesty. It seemed that she had lost her last position because she had tried to form a union. In spite of her bravado in admitting this, Evangeline remembered the desperate look in Letty's eyes. Even Bea had been understanding. 'Difficult to have principles when you're hungry,' she had said.

Evangeline looked through the railings at the basement. Everybody was working. Bales of material, the pearls and crystals glittering in shafts of sunlight, their dressmaking dummy from Highgate dressed in the scarecrow outfit and the straw wig sitting on the china biscuit barrel. She went to the front door. A tiny brass plate had replaced GRAY'S RELIGIOUS PUBLICATIONS. It now said ELIOTT. It was all too exciting — life, work, everything. She bounded down the basement steps and threw open the door. 'Good news,' she sang.

Beatrice continued darting her needle in and out of the lengths of silvery taffeta. 'It had better be good news. You've been ages. I bet you walked. Molly has started cleaning up in the workroom. We needed you.'

'Sorry. Sorry, everyone. I did walk. The sun seduced me.'

'As long as it was only the son and not his father.'

Tilly was surprised to see Evangeline blush deeply at her modest little joke.

'Here's the good news — part of it, anyway.' She handed Beatrice the envelope containing the money. 'The other part is, but this is a secret, Sybil is getting married and we are to do her mother's dress and she wants the black jacket with the odd button-holes copied in coffee-coloured tussore as well.'

Letty and Tilly exchanged glances. More work!

'That's marvellous! Evie, would you take over Kitty Ashleigh's silver taffeta? I'm going to help Molly upstairs. I want to get the desk into our office.'

'No, Bea, that's not fair. I'll help Molly clean up. After all, I've had the treat of going out.'

Beatrice picked up her sewing again. 'Good. I didn't want to ask you in case you threw a plate at me.'

CHAPTER SIX

Molly stood with her mop and bucket at the door of the workroom. 'All done in here, Miss Evie. Just got to get the furniture in. Mr Bunting said he'd come back to help with that. If you help me clean the office they can get the desk in there too.'

'Let's do it now, then.' Evangeline took the bucket of soapy water. 'Very nice of Mr Bunting to help like that.'

Molly followed Evangeline into the office.

'I'll do the floor, Miss Evie. You do the paintwork. Here's a cloth.' She squeezed a clean wet cloth and gave it to Evie.

'He is nice, Mr Bunting, the way he treats you is special. On Sunday after mass Michael and I were standing outside the church in Mount Street and I saw him, Mr Bunting, coming along with a young lady. They were going for their lunch to that hotel. Well, he stopped . . . are you all right, Miss Evie?'

Evangeline dipped her cloth in the soapy water. Her heart was racing. 'Yes, yes, I'm fine. I'm tired, that's all. I walked back home from the Bonners'.' She started wiping the pane on the large folding doors that divided the office from the reception room.

'All the way from Chester Square? No wonder you're tired. Why don't you leave this to me? I'll manage.' Molly felt she should do all the cleaning as a penance. She knew she had mentioned the young lady deliberately — wasn't jealousy awful? More than just a sin.

'No, don't fuss.' Evie tried to control the quaver in her voice. 'Go on. What were you saying?'

I'm ashamed of meself, Molly thought. I'll put her to rights, and I'll stop hankering after him too.

'Only that when Mr Bunting saw me he stopped and said hello just as polite as could be and introduced me very properly to his sister. Now, not many gentlemen would do that. Not real gentlemen.'

Even in her relief at the news that the young lady was his sister the irony of Molly's words wasn't lost on Evangeline. She was saying, in fact, that a real gentleman wouldn't behave like a gentleman.

'How is your friend Michael? Do you have an understanding with him yet, Molly?'

Molly smiled. The colour had returned to Evangeline's face. 'No, Miss Evie. And I'm not sure I want to.' She took a hard-bristled brush and scrubbed vigorously at a stubborn stain. 'You see, I like him fine and he's very suitable but . . .'

'Yes, Molly? But? You can speak to me. You can trust me.'

'Yes, I know, well my *but* is he talks about politics all the time and expects me to feel the same as him because we're both Irish.'

'But, Molly, that's natural. Think of what is happening right now. The future of Ireland will be decided soon and all the terrible Troubles will be over.'

'He says they'll never be over till . . . Oh, it isn't because it's Ireland — I'd feel the same if it was Iceland. I don't want to talk about politics all the time. Do you reckon, Miss Evie, that when you're married they forget about the politics and get on with it? Because, otherwise, half the time I'd as soon be at the pictures with me cousin.'

'I'm sorry, Molly. I'm not laughing at you,' but she couldn't stop laughing. 'You've always had a funny way of putting things.' Evie stood back to admire her work. 'After dinner I'm going to help Bea put up the curtains in here.'

'No, you're not.' Hugo stood in the doorway. 'You're having dinner with me.'

Later that evening, listening to Beatrice and Piggy arguing with Hugo about expressionism, Evangeline wondered why he was so puzzling. Why had he suggested that they all have dinner together? Piggy and Beatrice were happy enough alone. 'Tommyrot! It's absolute twaddle. Just like Picasso,' Piggy was nearly shouting.

'You can't have an opinion when it's based on two or three reproductions.' Hugo was quite calm. 'You should go to Vienna, that's where his best stuff is.' Although this was addressed to the whole table, his glance rested on Evangeline.

'Who? Sorry, I wasn't listening.'

Beatrice looked at Evangeline. Was she all right? She seemed in a day-dream.

'Egon Schiele.'

'Oh, yes, I like his work,' she said with enthusiasm, 'and Nolde and Klimt. Especially Klimt, I'd like to use his painting in designing material. I'd love to go to Vienna.'

'And so you shall.' Hugo raised his glass. 'I'm going there for a symposium on architecture. I'll take you with me.'

That was how it would happen. How glamorous, to become his mistress in Vienna. Anybody else would have suggested Paris, so conventional, or worse, Brighton. Evangeline stole a glance at Beatrice. She was laughing, not taking it seriously.

'You've been to Vienna, then, Hugo?'

'Yes, before the war, with my family and

then last year on the way to Salzburg.'

'For the music?' Beatrice asked with envy. 'Mozart?'

'Yes, partly that. My family is, well, was very musical. They all played something.'

Beatrice noted Hugo change the is to was. How sad. 'You say "was"?'

'Yes, my brothers were killed in the war and since then neither of my parents have been interested in music and they will never to go Germany or Austria again.'

Piggy shifted uncomfortably. 'Bad show. Sorry about that. Your brothers, I mean. No sisters?'

'No. No sisters. Fortunately I'm short-sighted, couldn't fight. So there's one little Bunting left.' He sounded bitter.

'I'd like a brandy, please.' Evangeline had drained the wine from her glass. 'Don't look so surprised, Bea. It's after dinner, isn't it? That's when you have brandy. Jack gave it to me once. Remember? I liked it then, I'd like it now.'

'Good luck, Bea. I don't envy you Arthur at nine o'clock in the morning.' Evangeline stood at the front door groaning and put her hand to her head. 'I'm never going to drink brandy again.'

'Good. That's why I let you drink so much.

210

I knew it would put you off. I did the same thing when I was seven.' Remembering the occasion Beatrice winced and put her hand to her face. She had drunk Papa's port, sweet and delicious, but absolutely forbidden to everybody including Mama. But it was what she had done afterwards that was worse. The port had emboldened her to look into Bluebeard's den, as she thought of it, Papa's consulting room. Through the keyhole she had seen that peculiar thing, that contraption . . . What was Evie saying? 'Molly and I will get on with everything, don't worry.'

Evangeline shut the door. What a relief it was to have so much work to do. It would distract from the hammering in her brain and the pain in her heart. Bea had been so considerate and kind last night. Gently teasing, but concerned.

'What is the matter, Evie? You have tears in your eyes. Something happened, didn't it, in the restaurant?'

Evangeline had wanted to tell her but underneath her pain and anger she knew she might still go to Vienna with Hugo and it wouldn't be wise to turn Bea against him. And what about Molly? Had Hugo lied to her to cover up or, Evangeline thought, did Molly lie to me? If so, it was absolutely humiliating and now she had to face her. They were going to finish taking everything from the kitchen to the workroom.

The doorbell rang, intruding on her daydreaming. Good. Tilly or Letty were early, that would help distract her. How splendid of them to be so keen. Work. That was the answer to everything.

But it wasn't either of the seamstresses, it was Hugo.

'It's only half past eight,' Evangeline stammered. 'What is it? What do you want? Did you leave something here?'

He regarded her steadily. 'I want to speak to you. Has your sister gone?' He came in and shut the door without waiting for a reply. 'Let's go to your room.'

Once inside the room he faced her. 'All right. Tell me. What was wrong last night? Why did you behave so stupidly and drink so much?'

A part of me feels so angry and hurt I want to hit him, she thought, but it's a small part. Looking at his face so near to hers and remembering his mouth so insistent and exciting . . .

'I was hurt and angry.'

He put a hand on her shoulders and gazing directly into her face he put his other hand under her chin and started slowly to unbutton her high-necked blouse.

'Why, Evangeline?' He continued to unbutton her blouse until he reached her camisole. 'Why were you hurt and angry?'

It was impossible to speak — she could hardly breathe. He slid his fingers between the buttons of the camisole and found her erect nipple, touching it firmly but gently. 'Why?' he said again softly as he bent his head and, parting the camisole, took her nipple in his mouth. She could hear, as if at a great distance, her little moans and cries, but as suddenly as he had stopped kissing her, he took his mouth away from her breast. He regarded her with the same impassive gaze as he closed her camisole and rebuttoned her blouse.

'Because,' she gasped, 'you haven't got a sister.'

'Do you want to explain that?' For the first time since she had met him, Hugo was disconcerted. Embarrassed now, Evangeline told him awkwardly about Molly's story.

'How dear of her to protect you, how kind. She's a good girl, isn't she, and that pretty piquant face.'

He had never called her pretty, or piquant or dear.

'Yes. I was taking a woman friend to lunch at the Connaught. A woman to whom I had to explain, or rather remind, that a relationship with me, however close, wouldn't necessarily lead to the altar. Do you understand?'

Evangeline regained her equilibrium. 'I understand that you're warning me.'

'Perhaps.' His fingers lightly brushed her mouth. 'We'll finish this in Vienna.'

Beatrice sat across from Arthur at the large mahogany partner's desk. As usual his gloomy office oppressed her and the pompous way he was sitting in his chair, tilting it back and twirling a fountain pen in his fingers, was utterly infuriating.

'Well, Beatrice, just as I thought. Money going out. Nothing coming in.'

I'd like to push him off that chair and hit him with the paperweight, she thought, but he's not worth swinging for. Besides, she wanted to win. She must stick to her decision to be charming and reasonable.

'Yes,' she said ruefully, 'you were right, Arthur, but we do feel that we could have a good business and with a little help and a little time —'

'And a little money, I suppose,' he interrupted.

'Yes. A little money. You see, we have some excellent clients now, people who come back to us, but they take their time to pay their bills.'

'As Evangeline's guardian —'

'I know it's difficult for you.' Beatrice smiled across the desk with understanding. 'We both want the best for her but we disagree about what the best would be. I think that until she gets married —'

Arthur sat up sharply. 'Gets married? Has she met someone?'

He's really worried, Beatrice thought, the little toad. Does he think he stands a chance? What a fool.

'Oh, no. I was speaking hypothetically. Until she gets married, I think using her talents as a dressmaker is both respectable and lucrative.'

'I am not releasing any more money for a venture I don't approve of.' Why was the woman being so calm and reasonable? Not like her. Arthur got up and looked out of the window longingly at the Star and Garter opposite. Only half past nine. If the blasted government hadn't introduced licensing hours during the war he'd have slipped out for a quick whisky. How much does she know about Cadogan Mews? Shall I call her bluff? Where does she get it from — one of the men? Maybe one of the women is a client of theirs. I'd better go to Green Street, look at the books.

Beatrice controlled herself — bad to lose her temper. Silly when she had her trump card. Although it would be nice, give her more confidence, to know if it was an ace or a Jack.

'Look, Arthur, I know you've got our security at heart, but you could think of it as an advance. Let me have six months' rent now and then don't give me any more until January 1922.'

Arthur looked out of the window. 'I find your attitude to fiscal matters rather feckless, Beatrice.'

A note of ice crept into her voice. 'Alliterative, Arthur! Well done. Not like you. Perhaps it's in my genes. Perhaps I inherited it from my feckless father who squandered both his earnings and my mother's inheritance. Is it feckless, the use to which you put Cadogan Mews? Make no mistake, Arthur,' Beatrice abandoned all attempts to be conciliatory, 'I have no illusions about what goes on there. It is no mere love-nest for a mistress and I know it was something to do with my father.'

So she didn't know the whole story. Arthur sighed with relief. I'll tell her the truth, he thought, or a small part of it. He turned to face her. 'Your father was being blackmailed.'

She felt choked with her rage. Blackmailed. 'What other filthy thing was he involved in that he could be . . . blackmailed?' She spat out the word with disgust. He turned back to the window. 'Answer me,' she demanded.

I'll explode. I can't bear it.

There was a silence.

'Answer me!' she shouted again.

'I don't know,' he said simply. And she knew it was true.

Beatrice stood outside 177 Green Street looking down into the basement. The kitchen was empty. They had finished moving upstairs. How they must have worked! A subdued chatter was coming from the workroom as she opened the front door. 'There she is, there's Bea. Come in, Bea. Look!'

They were all working, even Molly. Letty was putting the finishing touches to the scarecrow costume, now draped on the dummy; Tilly, who had finished the pearl beading, was bent over the bodice of a guipure lace dress which she was embroidering for one of the Gregson twins, while Molly was basting the hem of another guipure lace dress for the other twin, and Evie sewing on the buttons of Lydia's navy blue silk.

'I don't know what to say, I'm so grateful. I'm —' Beatrice tried to stop the tears. 'I wish I could give you all a bonus or something. I will one day.' She took out her handkerchief and blew her nose. 'Sorry, I've had a horrible morning, with somebody horrible, and now to see that you've done all the work

. . . Thank you. All of you.'

'And they've put up all the mirrors in the fitting room, so when Daphne Haycock comes this afternoon, she can see herself as others see her.' Evangeline spoke gaily but she was worried. Clearly Arthur hadn't agreed about the money.

'Is this a good time to stop for lunch? Tilly? Letty? Would you like to go down to the kitchen? Take your lunches. Half an hour, say.' The girls trooped down to the kitchen looking forward to the baked potatoes Molly had put on. Cheaper, she'd said, than bringing sandwiches, and they could have dripping in them from the Sunday joint.

'What is it, Bea? Arthur said no?' Beatrice nodded.

'Don't want to barge in,' Molly put her head round the door, 'but if it's money again, don't worry about me. You can put me right when the money comes rolling in. It will, you know. Tilly's right. You're just as good as Channel.'

Before they could protest, she had slammed the door. 'Do you think she's referring to Coco Chanel or the Irish Channel?' Evangeline laughed. 'She's exaggerating, but I feel confident, too.'

'So do I. This morning was rather a shock, that's all.' How big a shock she wasn't going to tell her sister. 'To be practical, Evie, we

218

have enough to pay Letty and Tilly this week from Elizabeth Bonner's money. Jack pays me on Friday which will keep us for a week, being very frugal, and when Aunt Lydia collects her dress, if she doesn't pay she won't get it! I think Olivia Stett-Gittins can be persuaded to pay for her scarecrow immediately. After all, we did it in three days . . .'

'And then?'

'And then it's in the lap of the gods. If the builders will wait and everybody else pays up and we get new clients . . .' Beatrice smiled wanly. 'I know. Too many ifs. How are you, Evie? I forgot your poor head.'

'My head? Oh, I'd forgotten. It's been such a busy morning.' Evangeline put her hand on her left breast suddenly suffused with longing to feel his mouth there again.

'What is it? Have you got a pain?' Anxiously Beatrice examined her sister's face. 'You look all right. In fact, you look beautiful.' She touched Evangeline's face. 'I forget sometimes how lovely you are.'

'Don't be silly, I'm not beautiful and I've got indigestion, that's all.'

'Good idea, those potatoes. If I make a big pasty one day, Molly could heat it up for us.'

'I'd like that, Letty. I've never been much of a cook.' Tilly swiftly threaded a pearl bead and delicately attached it to the black chiffon.

'There'd only be onions and potatoes in it, my pasty, but it's tasty.'

Beatrice returned from the telephone. 'It was Aunt Lydia. She's coming tomorrow afternoon, which is good, but so is Arthur, which is bad. But, amazingly, when I told her she had to pay immediately, she agreed.'

'Don't forget what I told you.' Tilly was setting in a sleeve on a voluminous pale blue grosgrain coat meant for Piggy's mother. She had already had one in apricot and was so pleased with it she had ordered another.

'What did you tell Bea?' Evie glanced at the heap of pale blue material. 'Gosh, Tilly, that coat would fit Piggy as well.'

Beatrice shook her finger. 'Don't be rude about Tom. I love him.'

'And he loves you, too, Bea. Only, poor man, he really loves you. So,' she persisted, 'what did Tilly tell?'

'Aunt Lydia was all sly and cadging. Said would we give her a special price?'

'And I said you should put twenty per cent on all the prices because they all say that, even the richest. Then you say, "I'll take twenty per cent off just for you, but don't tell anyone", and you're back to the starting price.'

'It's true,' Letty added, 'they do it everywhere.'

There was a screech of brakes outside and a slamming of car doors. Beatrice looked out of the window and saw an enormous highly polished black car with a liveried footman on the running board. 'It's Daphne Haycock. My goodness!' She sounded so shocked, they all stopped working. 'She's with a . . . a dark girl a — an African. Absolutely stunning. I'll open the door.'

'Take them into the reception room.' Evangeline folded her work away. 'And we'll show her our sketches, but Letty should see her, too, for the measurements. She'll be cutting it.'

Daphne was sprawled in a deep armchair. She waved her arm vaguely in the direction of her companion. 'This is Renée. We're going to be black and white like negative.'

Renée laughed. A low lazy sound. *'Ça c'est parce que nous sommes noire et blanche mais pas negative.'* She regarded the astonished faces of the Eliott sisters. *'Oui, je suis française.* What do you think I am — a Zulu? I live in Paris. I was born in Martinique.'

'Yes, so we're singing together. I'll be in black. Renée will be in white.' Daphne took the sketches from Evangeline. 'What do you think, Renée? God, I'm tired. We were at the Bee Hive till dawn.' She closed her eyes. 'Have you got a bathroom I can use?'

'Yes. I'll show you upstairs.'

'Don't show. Just tell.'

'Upstairs, almost facing you to the right.'

Daphne took her bag and slouched out of the room. Renée watched her go. She was obviously worried.

'These are good. *Oui.* But how does it remove?'

Beatrice showed her a sketch of the back. 'It will be cut so that untying the ribbon between the shoulders releases it.'

'Parfait, parfait.' She smiled at the sisters, and walked round the room examining the sketches that lined the walls. 'You are what Jack says. Artists.'

'Of course they are.' Daphne appeared at the doorway, her fatigue apparently, completely gone. 'Are you going to measure us? You go into the fitting room, Renée. I have to speak to Beatrice.'

Renée approached Daphne and lightly brushing a little powder from her lip said, *'Tu es complètement folle, chérie.'*

'The thing is, Beatrice,' Daphne said when she was out of earshot, 'I know I said it was only me, but when Renée turned up I thought it would be too deevy, so I must give you something,' she fiddled in her purse, 'specially as you're doing it so quickly. Did you see that divine motor? It was waiting outside

Claridge's and the most frightfully sozzled old goat was about to get in.' She took two five-pound notes from a purse stuffed untidily with money. 'Here's ten pounds. All right? And I said, "Have pity on a poor god-daughter, sir." I'd just been at luncheon with my god-father and he said, breathing whisky all over me, "Are you my god-daughter?" and I said yes and he said you can keep the car all afternoon after you've dropped me at Lancaster Gate and I did and I will.' She paused for breath, her eyes glittering.

Beatrice held the ten pounds. 'It's very good of you but your increased allowance won't last long at this rate.'

'Allowance?' Daphne gave a short laugh and waved her purse in the air. 'This isn't from my allowance.'

Beatrice looked at her tenderly. 'You know, Daphne, you really are *complètement folle.*'

Evangeline observed the figure of Mrs Stett-Gittins displayed in the three-sided looking glass. It had been a bold idea but it had worked. She looked droll but very attractive. The mannish suit in different and multi-coloured materials fitted gently over her bosom and hips revealing their curves discreetly, and the wig was a triumph, its stiffness modified by an uneven fringe and tendrils

223

curling at the nape of the neck.

'You look wonderful, Olivia. I thought it was a terrible idea but it makes you look so young and more feminine than you do in a dress.' Kitty Ashleigh, being fitted by Letty into her silver and black chiffon, eyed her niece enviously. 'You look twenty again.'

'I was wicked, an imp, when I was twenty.' Olivia looked at the far from impish Evangeline. 'Are you a wicked twenty-year-old?'

Evangeline examined them both in the looking-glass. She could imagine this woman behaving unconventionally.

'Not yet,' she said. 'But I plan to be.' And so she did, but when? How would she get away? Would Bea let her? What excuses could she make? Should she go to that clinic in Holloway? Would it be soon? She was conscious of him all the time. Every action made her think of him. Bathing, dressing, undressing, cleaning her teeth.

Olivia observed her in the looking-glass. Beneath that exquisite madonna-esque face there was certainly a strongly developed sensuality. Hope the child can deal with that, she thought.

Evangeline became aware that a silence had developed, that her last remark had remained hovering in the air, and decided to change the subject. 'It's Miss Bennett, our head cutter, who is responsible for making my sister's idea work.'

Letty smiled. 'Thank you, Miss. It was interesting and a challenge and I'm glad it worked,' and turning back to Mrs Ashleigh with great diplomacy added, 'I always knew *this* would work. The contrast of black against your pale skin.'

Leaving Letty with a very satisfied Kitty Ashleigh, Evangeline took Olivia Stett-Gittins into the office, ostensibly to show her some designs for the autumn season, but once there began awkwardly to present the bill. 'You see, the service we supply is a high standard of work at a reasonable cost and, being so quickly executed, means that our staff —'

'Must be paid. I quite understand. I'll give you a cheque right now.'

Evangeline was so surprised that she lost her dignified manner and blurted out, 'Gosh! Thanks. That's terribly good of you.'

Olivia thumbed through some of the sketches. 'Honestly, I can never make up my mind months ahead. I'll think about it.' She put down the sketches and smiled candidly at Evangeline. 'But there is something I want. Rather naughty, I'm afraid.'

'Naughty?' Evangeline grinned. 'How naughty? A very low back? A very low front?'

225

'Not a bad idea, but no. That chiffon and pearl thing you're doing for my aunt. Could you copy it for me in another colour? We rarely go to the same things in the evening.'

Evangeline thought for a moment. 'What about black and very pale grey? The grey chiffon embroidered with jet beads?'

She paused, working it out. 'And I've got a wonderful idea. The under-dress black satin — only reversed so that the matt side shows and the satiny part is next to your skin. The effect would be sort of misty and it would feel — I don't know . . . sumptuous.'

'Brilliant.' You really are very sensual, Olivia thought. I know because I am.

Sorting through the bills Beatrice could hear Jack's voice from the studio, alternately soothing and sarcastic. He wasn't well enough to be back at work and his weakness was making him bad-tempered. She could hear that poor Lady Smythson was paying for it. At least she was a friend so she should be used to him. I don't think I ever will be, Beatrice thought. He had been so despairing this morning, hating his work.

'Useless,' he'd said. 'I'm ashamed. I do no good for man or beast!'

He had disappeared into his studio when she had suggested that he try something else if he was tired of photography. Moving pictures, perhaps?

'So you agree that what I do is worthless?' he had shouted. Then, reappearing, asked her quite gaily what she was going to wear at Daphne's party next week. They were all to go, Tom, Evangeline and Penelope. He was going to take a table. They would have a good time. Then as suddenly his mood had changed again. 'Cancel the Blue Bear for tonight, will you? I'm not well enough. I can't go out. Sorry.' She had been bewildered, not knowing that he had intended going out. And why should he say he was sorry? 'Another time,' he went on. 'You don't mind, do you?'

Hesitantly she had explained that he had never asked her out, so, with a little smile, she had added, 'How could I be sorry?'

'No? My God, I'm an ass.'

He had seemed really disturbed. Embracing him she had said, 'You aren't well yet. Bronchitis is very taxing, very tiring.'

He had returned her embrace, holding her closely, his head buried in her hair. 'You mean so much to me. I'm very, very . . . comfortable with you.'

Laughing, she had pushed him away. 'Would you like me to bring something for you to eat this evening?'

'I'd rather be alone,' he had said, returning to the studio.

'You're wobbling, Joan,' Beatrice heard him say now. 'Every time you wobble, everything is going to be out of focus.'

Oh, the poor woman, he was going too far. Beatrice knocked on the studio door and entered. 'Would you like tea or coffee?'

'I'd like a large drink, my dear. Jack's artistic temperament has made me a nervous wreck!'

Beatrice could see that Jack was right. She did wobble, even when she spoke. And there was so much of her to wobble. 'We only have champagne, Lady Smythson, will that do?'

'No. I need a large whisky. Jack, haven't you done enough?'

He shrugged.

'Well, I've had enough. I'm going home for my luncheon. I hope you're in a better mood when you come up to Wellthorpe. Bring Miss Eliott.' She turned to Beatrice. 'You're a clever gel, managing this monster and running your little business. I'm sending my granddaughter to you. Goodbye, Jack. I'll see you on the twelfth. No,' she held up her hand, 'don't bother to see me out. I'll wobble down on my own, thank you.'

The studio was quiet. Beatrice wondered if she should leave him alone or suggest he went home. Jack put his head in his hands. Was he shaking? 'Do you have a headache?' She spoke so quietly he could barely hear her.

'Don't go,' he said, his shoulders shaking. 'I trust you.'

He was crying, she realized. Sobbing. 'I would like you,' he spoke haltingly, 'to lie down with me — hold on to me — without speaking.'

Gently she led him to the large sofa where she removed the usual pile of curtains, magazines and photographs and lay down with him. He held her tightly, his sobs gradually decreasing until he fell asleep. He turned slightly away from her and once again she had an overwhelming desire to kiss the nape of his neck but she reminded herself of the words he had used. Trust. Comfortable. Very brotherly. She moved her arm carefully. It was getting cramp. He stirred and turned away from her taking her hand and folding her arm around him.

'I love you, Bea.'

She held her breath, but nothing more was said. 'I love you' could mean as a brother, and how typical of him that he couldn't face her to say it. Gradually she relaxed and she, too, fell asleep, her head on his shoulder. Her hand clasped in his against his chest. The jangle of the telephone woke them both.

'I'll answer it. Do you want to speak to any-body?' She ran to the telephone.

'Nobody.' He sat up, rubbing his eyes. How sweet, he thought, to sleep with my little vixen. She came back into the studio pinning up the hair that had tumbled about her shoulders.

'It was Elizabeth Bonner. Will you do the wedding portrait of Sybil?'

'Why not?'

'Good. I said yes. Jack, I have to see my Aunt Lydia. She's collecting a dress. Will you be all right?'

He jumped up briskly. 'I will be fine. Tell you what I'd like to do. Stay here working — I've got lots of retouching to do — and then have dinner with all of you in the kitchen. May I? Will Molly mind?'

'What a relief.' She smiled at him. 'I'd have worried if you had gone home alone. Come down whenever you like. Of course Molly won't mind.'

She stood awkwardly for a moment and then turned with a little wave. 'See you later.'

The workroom was busy with Evie, Tilly and Letty all working and Molly carefully wrapping a dress in white tissue paper and folding it into a cardboard box.

Evangeline looked up with pleasure at her

sister. 'Have you finished with Jack? Because I want to know if I should deliver the Gregsons' clothes — and don't forget Aunt Lydia.'

Beatrice looked out of the window at the hot dusty street. If she let Evangeline go she would be tempted to walk through the park and dawdle and there was too much work to do. 'Sorry, Evie. I think Molly should go.'

'Oh, I'd love to, Miss Bea.'

'And you can shop on the way back. Mr Maddox is staying for dinner.'

'Huh. Cauliflower cheese won't do, then. Men don't count that sort of thing as dinner.' Evangeline remembered her father's refusal to accept omelettes or cauliflower cheese or macaroni as anything but 'little savouries'.

Beatrice laughed. 'You're thinking of Father. But maybe you're right.'

'Ducks,' Molly suggested, 'and peas and new potatoes?'

'Ooh, don't, Molly, you're making my mouth water,' Letty said enviously.

'I don't think so, Molly, that would be rather expensive.'

Evangeline dropped her scissors with a clatter on the table. 'Oh, I forgot, Bea. Mrs Stettwhatsit paid. Gave me a cheque and, what's more, ordered an evening dress.'

Beatrice bit her lower lip. This was all too

vexing. 'Good, that's very good,' she said. 'The ducks will be splendid, Molly,' and, indicating that Evangeline was to follow her, Beatrice left the room.

'I've never 'ad duck,' Tilly murmured as Evangeline followed her sister and shut the door behind her.

'What's the matter, Bea?'

Beatrice seemed upset. 'Come into the reception room where we can talk.'

Once they were there she turned to her sister. 'It's all wrong, Evie. All this talk about our money and our food and our private lives in front of Letty and Tilly. We should have a table in the office where we can work. There's plenty of room.'

Evangeline was shocked and eyed her sister with dismay. 'But it's all going so well in there. They're helpful and understanding. It would seem so rude.'

Beatrice thought for a while. 'It needn't be done all at once. Every day we get more work. It would help them to have more room. And they need privacy, too, to talk about us.'

'Yes, I understand, at least,' Evangeline said reluctantly, 'I think I do. But that's just it. I *think* you're right, but I don't *feel* you're right.'

'Oh, no. We'll have to talk about it later.'

Beatrice turned from the window. 'Aunt Lydia is here. With Cousin Arthur . . .'

'Don't forget. Twenty per cent,' Tilly mouthed as Beatrice and Evangeline led Lydia into the fitting room.

'Would you like to try it on with one of our bust bodices, Aunt Lydia?' Evangeline handed her a cotton broadcloth garment. 'It's designed to minimize the bosom without squashing it uncomfortably.'

She eyed her aunt's large and still quite shapely breasts. There was quite a lot to minimize. Had Uncle Richard done to her what Hugo did to me, she wondered. And smiled. Lydia eyed herself. Why should they be disguised? They were a full womanly shape. 'I'll try. But there is nothing the matter with a full bosom.'

Beatrice looked away, the sight of her aunt's unclothed body made her feel uneasy.

Lydia did up the bust bodice and stepped into the simple navy blue silk dress. They were right. She looked much thinner, more elegant, modern — younger, even. She smiled complacently at her image in the three-cornered looking-glass.

'Yes, navy blue does suit me. It always has.'

Evangeline glanced quickly at Beatrice who raised her eyebrows. Nothing about the bust bodice reducing her bulk, nothing about the design, nothing about the cut skimming her hips, flattering her, making her look lighter and younger. 'Navy blue patent pumps, I think, don't you?'

With a businesslike air Beatrice examined her. 'No, I would prefer old rose with a small heel.'

Lydia considered this. After all, they both had great style. 'Wouldn't I need another touch of old rose somewhere? A scarf? A hat?'

'What about,' Evangeline walked round Lydia slowly and winked discreetly at Beatrice, 'a coat of rose slub silk lined with the navy?'

'That's it. Splendid.' Lydia was very enthusiastic. 'I could wear it at the royal garden party next week. Could you do it in time?'

'I think we could, Aunt, but . . .'

'But?' Lydia waited impatiently.

'The trouble is that as we have a lot of work, we now employ, as you saw, two excellent seamstresses. They have to be paid, the material has to be paid for —'

'Yes. Yes. I see what you're getting at. Money. Well, if I pay you now as I said for this and give you half for the coat . . .'

Beatrice looked at Evangeline. 'In that case, Aunt, we would put you first and buy the material and start immediately.' That they already had some old rose slub silk and plenty of navy blue left over was none of her business.

'About your bill, then.' Lydia put her head coyly on one side. 'You're not going to be cruel, are you? You're going to make a *prix d'amis?*'

'Of course, Aunt Lydia. Evangeline and I have discussed it and we are going to take twenty per cent off so your dress is now nine guineas and your coat will be about sixteen guineas, and may I say that we are proud to see you in our clothes. You wear them beautifully and give us great credit.'

I can't look at Bea, Evangeline thought. I may be sick.

Arthur sat at the desk thumbing through the ledger. As Beatrice had said, nothing much of interest there. If things went on as they were, they were likely to have a successful business. Only thing needed was payment of accounts and that would happen. Time for him to stop feeling guilty. But nothing useful in the ledger about Cadogan Mews. The little Gregson twins, Lady Bonner, the Ashleigh woman. Nobody who could have talked to Beatrice. Where did she get the information from? How much did she know? He opened a desk drawer. Receipts, bills, letters — very flattering letters, too, from clients — nothing there, though, either. Had she discovered something in Uncle Henry's papers in his consulting room? He thought he had been through everything in there but he hadn't had much time. Picking up the appointment book he skimmed through it quickly. The same names basically and two or three new ones. They had had a busy day today. He flicked a page back, to yesterday. Yesterday! There it was. Daphne Haycock. The little bitch. Had to be her. Probably under the influence. Stuff enough cocaine up her nose and she would blab to anybody.

He closed the appointment book and replaced it on the desk. Now that he knew, what could he do about it? And he still didn't know exactly how much Daphne Haycock had told them. Enough, anyway, to make life very uncomfortable — but, one saving grace, Beatrice hadn't told Evangeline everything. His face softened as he thought about his young cousin. She would be worth giving up all that for. She was more beautiful each time he saw her. He would take her out to dinner. A guardian's duty, he would say. Away from Beatrice's presence, he'd be more himself, entertain her, treat her like a woman.

'Where are you, Arthur?' His mother opened the door, followed by Beatrice. 'I'm extremely pleased. I'm going to wear it at the garden party at the Palace.'

'What?' Arthur said. 'What are you going to wear?'

'My new dress and you'll be very proud of me.'

'I'm always proud of you, Mother.' He pecked her cheek.

'Do you approve of my bookkeeping, Arthur?' Beatrice rearranged the top of her desk, aligning the appointment book with the blotter and straightening the pens and ruler. 'As you can see, business is building every day.'

'Yes, indeed, Beatrice. I may have been a little lacking in belief in your talent but I am willing to change my mind. Not that I could release any more money,' he added hastily, 'but if you cut your coat according to your cloth you should have a useful little business.' He smirked, pleased with his little quip and Lydia obliged him with a smile but Beatrice didn't. 'A little business,' he continued, 'that you can manage on your own when Evangeline —'

'When Evangeline marries?' Beatrice asked. 'That's not likely to happen yet. She is very happy living here and working.'

Arthur was relieved that there was no sign of a potential husband. 'Where is she? I'd like to say goodbye.'

'Sorry, Arthur, she's working.' Beatrice

nodded to Lydia. 'If we're to get your mother's coat ready for her visit to the Palace, it's all hands on deck.'

He looked crestfallen. 'Come along, then, Mother. Tell her I will telephone her. I ought to see her, you know, perhaps dinner, a guardian's duty.'

Beatrice closed the door on them sighing with relief. Seventeen guineas. And cash, too. And another order. Poor Evangeline, though, having to have dinner with Arthur. What piffle, she thought, saying it was a guardian's duty. He had always had a pash on Evie.

From the workroom she could hear Jack's voice talking with great animation. He must be feeling better.

He certainly looked better.

'You've come down. Good. How are you feeling now?'

'I'm feeling fine.' Jack looked at her with surprise. 'Just fine. What are we having for dinner? I must get some wine.'

'Ducks.' Both Tilly and Letty spoke in unison without looking up from their work. 'Ducks, green peas and new potatoes, and lucky to get it,' Letty added, her silky black hair cut in the latest bob, falling across her face. Pushing it aside she noticed a look of irritation on Beatrice's face. Seen that there before, she thought. Better mind my Ps and Qs.

'Miss Beatrice, could you check that the back ribbons are in the right place on Miss Haycock's dress so that it's the same as her friend's?'

Beatrice took the black satin sheath and compared it with the white one. 'Yes, that's perfect. I just hope it works.'

'Should do. She says she's going to do a wriggle.'

Tilly put down her sewing and laughed. 'She really is one of the Bright Young Things, isn't she?'

'Not very bright, I wouldn't call it,' Letty spoke with severity, 'being a dope taker.'

Beatrice flushed angrily. 'You don't know what you're talking about, Letty.'

'Sorry, Miss Beatrice, but I do. There was one or two used to go to Paquin when I was there. I can tell.'

'How terrible. Why would they do it? What for?' Evangeline felt it was hard enough learning about alcohol.

'I know why Daphne does . . . well, let's say, might do it. Her brothers were killed in the war and it made her father turn away from her.' Jack got up and peered at the dummy draped in coffee-coloured tussore. 'Bloody awful war. Took the cream of England's families. The brightest and the best.'

'Just a second.' Letty pushed her chair away

239

from the table. 'Why? Why are they the brightest and the best? Eh? My father was killed at Passion Dale 'owever you pronounce it, me two cousins on the Somme, Tilly's brother. All English. All lost their lives in the same war. So who's the cream, I'd like to know?' Her voice broke and she started to cry. 'Do you 'ave to go to Oxford, talk with a plum in your mouth and have a nanny before dying counts?' She stopped, appalled at herself. She'd thrown away her job. Covering her eyes with a shaking hand she said, 'Sorry. Leastways I'm not sorry for what I said, but 'ow I said it.'

There was a silence in the room.

'Would you like me to go?' She took her hand away from her red eyes and addressed Beatrice.

'No, Letty, but I'd like to think it wouldn't happen again.' Beatrice's voice was calm but she was visibly shaken.

'You're right, anyway. It was crass of me. I'm an insensitive idiot.' Jack slumped back in his chair. 'Every one of the millions of men who died had lives of equal value.'

'It's like this, Tilly.' The two young women walked up Park Lane towards Marble Arch. 'Granted, they're good employers. Granted, she was very fair with me today, but they

240

could change and we have no rights 'cos we don't have any union.'

Tilly thought about it. 'I don't see how a union with just you and me would do any good. And look at how thoughtful they are. Miss Evie knew I couldn't come to work in my old clothes and she give me all the linen and cotton for this outfit and me other dress.'

She looked down at herself, the beige linen skirt and long hound's-tooth check jacket in brown and white were the best she'd ever had. While she was making it she had to keep reminding herself it wasn't for some lady, it was hers.

'Remnants, though. Not that generous,' Letty pointed out.

'Yes, but they wear remnants, too. What ladies do you know who wear their father's clothes cut down? And their evening dresses for the night-club do are going to be made with leftover bits.'

'True. And I'll say this for them, they've got good ideas. I like doing the work.'

They held hands and scurried across the busy road to the Underground station.

'What are you doing tonight, Tilly? Want to come to a meeting? The socialist party discussing the rates and poor relief. I'm going with my Charlie.'

'Can't, Letty. Got to get back.' Tilly felt

a bit guilty. 'It's not that I don't agree about that, I think it's awful. Fancy that government bloke saying three pound thirteen and six is too much for a family on relief. Let him try and live on it.'

'Why don't you come, then? You might meet someone, too?'

'No. My mum and dad expect me, and I'm giving them a treat tonight. I'm shopping at the market and getting stewed eels and mash.' And even if she did not have to get home, a socialist party meeting was not her idea of a night out.

They disappeared down into the bowels of the earth where their train would take them under London, following the subterranean route of the river Fleet, under Hyde Park Corner, Sloane Square, skirting the Embankment and down along to Shoreditch and Hackney Fields till it finally deposited them in London's East End.

'Can you see all right, Jack?'

The kitchen looked better by candlelight but it might not be easy for Jack who was carving the ducks.

'Mm, just. I've nearly finished. You can put the vegetables out.'

'Evie,' Beatrice banged on the window to attract her attention, 'Evie, it's ready.'

What were they doing out there, gossiping? It was hot in the kitchen but no hotter than in the street. If it had been anyone but Penelope she would have presumed that they were talking about men in general and Hugo in particular. But she couldn't imagine Penelope ever being interested in romantic possibilities. A pity, really. It would have been natural, she smiled at the thought, young men and women on a lovely summer evening. Molly had gone off to meet her young man at the bandstand in the park. She looked at Jack serving the roasted ducks. Even he had said, 'I love you,' this morning, although he'd forgotten about it ever since. She caught Piggy looking at her.

He took her hand and kissed it. 'The world is out of joint, dear Bea.'

'This duck is out of joint now.' Jack put the platter on the kitchen table. Taking a cloth, Beatrice put out the hot dishes of peas and potatoes.

'What a lovely smell.' Evangeline sniffed appreciatively as she opened the door. 'Mint and something else? You sit here, Penny.'

'Mint on the potatoes and I added Madeira to the gravy. What do you think?' Jack asked anxiously.

'I think it's absolutely delicious.'

'You don't count, Piggy. You think everything is delicious. Anybody else?'

Jack looked round the table.

'Tom is right. It *is* delicious.' Beatrice paused between mouthfuls.

'You *do* count, so thank you.' Jack blew her a kiss. 'What are you wearing to Daff's do on Friday?'

'Patchwork.' Evangeline frowned. 'Bea won't let us buy any material so we have to make do with oddments.'

Jack looked at Beatrice. 'Aren't you doing well? You seem to be very busy.'

'It's not that.' She sighed and reached for her glass. 'We're doing very well but people take so long to pay. The Gregsons, for instance, the material was frightfully expensive and then the embroidery took days but we can't expect to be paid for ages.'

Piggy looked embarrassed. 'I say, did my mother . . . ?'

'Please, Tom, let's not talk about it. Too awkward. Actually, we're celebrating. Two people did pay us today.' Beatrice took a large sip of red burgundy. 'This is delicious, too. Do you two never buy cheap wine?'

'Never,' they replied as one. Beatrice listened to the hubbub of conversation around her. This sort of evening was quite normal for most people in their position, but her life had been abnormal till she was thirty. Worth

244

waiting for, though.

'Is Hugo taking you to the party?' Piggy turned to Evangeline.

'If he can. He's working on a house in Berkshire, on the river, and staying down there. I'll come with all of you and he'll join us if he can. Is that all right, Jack?'

'Yes, of course. Are you coming, Pen old thing?'

'Certainly not. Waste of time. And you two may be in patchwork but I'd be in rags. Moths have eaten what's left of my evening dresses.'

'It *is* for charity, Penny.' Evangeline felt defensive.

'Charity? Huh!' she snorted. 'Distressed gentlefolk, not my idea of the deserving poor.'

Beatrice got up to start clearing away but turned back to Penelope from the sink. 'We were distressed gentlefolk until we met you and then Jack,' she said quietly. 'You helped us change our lives.'

Penelope blushed but was clearly touched. 'You've helped yourselves. Damned hard, considering. Admire you. Let me do this.' She stood up and started to stack the plates.

'Molly will wash up when she comes in if we just clear away.'

'Still hot.' Evangeline stretched her arms above her head. 'I've got a good idea. Why don't we walk home with you across the park and then we'll walk back again? We need some air. Don't we, Bea?' She also needed to continue her talk with Penelope. They could walk ahead out of earshot. 'Please, Bea?'

'We do need some air and I need some exercise. Yes, I'd love to.'

They said goodbye to Piggy at the corner of Green Street, crossed Park Lane and entered Hyde Park.

The sun had brought out the smell of the grass and flowers. It was quiet here away from the traffic. Jack stopped and looked back. 'All those people going out for a good time, nightclubbing, partying, they seemed so pathetic, middle-aged, the streets and cars dusty. But from here, now they've lit the gas lamps, it looks rather beautiful. As you do.'

Evangeline and Penelope had gone ahead and were just out of sight. They were alone on the edge of the riding path, Rotten Row. He took her hand and crossed his fingers in hers. 'We'd better catch them up.'

Walking briskly hand in hand across the park towards Kensington Palace they soon caught sight of the figures of Evangeline and Penelope. Penelope's long stride was forcing the shorter Evangeline to vary her normal pace into a hop, skip and a run.

'She looks like a puppy.' Beatrice laughed. 'I wonder what they're gossiping about?'

'The East End Mission. Unemployment. Poor Relief, the League of Nations, I suppose,' and changing tack in his usual surprising way Jack said, 'How old were you when your mother died?'

'Ten. Why do you ask?'

He squeezed her fingers and paused briefly to kiss her cheek. Or at least she thought that's what he did. His mouth brushed her skin fleetingly. She supposed that could pass for a kiss.

'You're quite an extraordinary person, Bea, and your mother must have been too. You made a life for yourself and Evie with no help from your monstrous father.'

She held her breath. Was he going to tell her any more? But they walked on in silence.

'Mother gave me any worthwhile things I know. She took me to museums and galleries. She made me feel like a friend.'

'And then she died and you passed all that on to your sister.'

Beatrice was frightened of breaking the mood and spoiling things but she couldn't control herself. 'Jack, did you know my father was being blackmailed?'

He released her hand and pushed his hair off his brow. 'Not surprised. He was playing a dangerous game.'

She waited for some explanation. 'A dangerous game?'

They were nearly abreast of Penelope and Evangeline.

'Yes. He also dealt in drugs.'

Returning home in the taxi, which Jack had insisted they take, the sisters were silent, both absorbed in their separate worlds.

Evangeline had been disappointed in her conversation with Penelope. She wouldn't accompany her to the Marie Stopes clinic, feeling it would be wrong of her to go behind Beatrice's back and come between the sisters. Yet she thought it was correct for Evangeline to go to a family planning clinic. Nor would she endorse her decision to take a lover, although she thought it was healthy! It was all very confusing and it wasn't possible to talk to Bea about it. That was the problem. She had always talked everything out with her sister.

'What are you thinking about, Bea?'

Beatrice frowned at her sister. 'This is all wrong,' she said, 'I'm treating you like a child. Protecting you. It's not fair on you. I should share things with you like I used to.'

'Er . . . yes, Bea,' Evangeline said guiltily.

'I was thinking about Papa.' Beatrice paused but only for a moment. 'Arthur told me he was being blackmailed.'

Evangeline gasped. 'Papa? But why? What had he done?'

'It could have been something to do with drugs.' But Jack had said 'also' as if there was something else. 'Easy for him to get them. A doctor.'

Evangeline screwed up her face with disgust. The cabby shouted back through the partition. ' 'Undred and seventy-seven, was it?'

Beatrice leant forward. 'Yes. The one next to the house with the blue door.' She sat back in the comfortable leather seat. 'Hope they never paint it. Evie! I didn't bring my bag. We haven't any money.'

As they got out of the cab the driver grinned at them. 'No need, Miss. The gentleman paid.'

Beatrice put the key in the lock of the door. 'Look, Evie,' she pointed to the small brass plate which said 'Eliott', 'that's us. You know, I'm going to forget about Papa.' She spoke with passion. 'We're living in the present, which is pretty wonderful. We have good friends and a successful start to our business. I'm going to enjoy my life. Not worry about his grubby past.'

'And the future, Bea. The future is exciting too.'

The Lark and the Owl was lit by electricity but for all the light that was shed it could have been lit by oil. There was no overhead illumination, only small pottery lamps on each table in the shape of an owl with the light emerging from the eyes. Wreaths of cigarette smoke added to the gloom. Couples were moving on the small dance floor to the music of a Negro band. They were playing in syncopation, almost unrecognizably, the music from 'Maid of the Mountains'. The dancing was also unrecognizable, probably loosely based on a quickstep. Most of the dancers were shuffling in time to the music, some leaning heavily on their partners. Every table in the room seemed occupied so where the dancers would sit in the intervals was difficult to see. Perhaps that was why they were leaning on each other.

A young waiter led Jack and his party to a table in the centre of the long narrow room and after exchanging heated words with a group sitting there ejected them and drew back chairs for Evangeline and Beatrice.

'A magnum of Bollinger? Yes, sir. Now, sir, don't leave your table unattended at any time. The table will be taken and your champagne. And don't leave the young ladies either or they might disappear too.'

He left, threading his way through the tables. Jack watched him go. 'I wonder if we'll ever see him again. Or my ten pounds.'

Evangeline slipped her wrap from her

shoulders and looked expectantly round the room.

'If you'd done that before, Evie, he'd be certain to return.' Piggy was used to her beauty but not to seeing quite so much of it. The dress, though high at the front, dipped below her waist at the back; were it not for the narrow piece of violet silk buttoned at the back of her neck, Evangeline's dress would fall off.

'Is it too much?' she said anxiously. 'That's all there was left of the material. Shall I put my wrap on?'

Jack regarded her seriously. 'No, you look perfect. It could look too much on somebody else but your kind of beauty has great dignity.'

'What a wonderful thing to say.' Impulsively she kissed him. 'Thank you. That gives me great confidence.'

Piggy stood up. His white tie and tails suited him, making him look more dashing than usual. 'Would you like to show your pretty back to the rest of the world by dancing with me?' He took her hand and led her on to the floor.

Beatrice and Jack could tell they were laughing, Piggy didn't know where to put his hand. He tried one finger on the narrow strip of silk on her neck then put his hand on her waist and finally settled for holding both her hands as if they were dancing a cotillion.

'You will have to take it in turns to dance with her. I'm undanceable with and, according to that waiter, if you leave me alone you'll lose me to the White Slave Traffic.'

'I'm not going to risk losing you, Beatrice, ever, and anyway here comes our champagne.'

He has a way of saying the most serious things lightly and being serious about something utterly frivolous, she thought. He gives equal importance to me and champagne.

'We'll have another magnum of this before the cabaret.'

'Yes, sir. But it won't be starting till everybody's here.'

'How will you get any more in?'

Beatrice looked at the tables. In a restaurant there would hardly be room for four but there were at least ten people crowded round each one. Except for one at the edge of the dance floor at which a middle-aged couple sat with two pretty young women. Standing to attention on either side were two footmen in livery. 'Who is that, Jack, sitting over there with the footmen?'

Carefully pouring the champagne, the waiter replied, without looking up, 'Lord and Lady Munford, Madam. He's the munitions millionaire — his millions barely dented by the hundred thousand or so his viscountcy cost.'

Jack roared with laugher. 'He's quite right, Bea. Filling the coffers of the Liberal Party for Lloyd George.'

The waiter straightened. 'I'll return with the other magnum of Bolly, sir.'

Jack looked at him curiously. 'Odd sort of chap. Ah, there's Evie and Piggy. He must have seen the champagne arrive.'

'He looks very nice in his tails. I was surprised.' Beatrice watched them battle their way through the throng of people, some now sitting on the edge of the dance floor.

'You haven't noticed, then?'

'Noticed what?'

'Piggy has been on a diet, ever since the first time you called him Tom he's been losing weight.'

'Oh, Jack,' she put her hand to her mouth, 'I feel so guilty. He's such a dear. I'm very fond of him but . . .'

Jack looked at her with disapproval. 'But you were only flirting. Women!' He stood up to pull out Evangeline's chair.

'It's all right. He knows that you're in love with me.' He saw her eye the champagne bucket.

'Don't, Bea. You can't throw iced water on me every time you lose your temper. Where's

253

Evie?' he demanded as Piggy arrived at the table alone.

'Powder her nose. Or maybe her back. Marvellous music. Are you sure you don't want to dance, Bea?'

'Sure, thank you, Tom. Is the music good? There's so much noise I can hardly hear it. I hope they're quiet for Daphne and Renée.'

The music stopped with a clash of cymbals and, to a drum roll, a thin elegant figure stepped on to the floor.

'It's Jack Buchanan,' Piggy whispered. 'He's the master of ceremonies.'

Dancers milled around looking for chairs, some eventually settling for the floor. Beatrice looked anxiously for Evangeline but Jack had already seen her. 'Evie's over there.' He pointed to a figure held firmly by their waiter being steered towards them. Beatrice wasn't sure whether to be pleased or not. Evie wouldn't get through the crowd on her own but it was rather familiar of the waiter to take her over like that.

'Here she is, safe and sound, and your champagne, sir.' The waiter pulled out Evie's chair, refilled all the champagne glasses and put the new magnum on the table.

'Thank you, I'd never have got back without you.' Evangeline smiled up at the waiter and took her champagne.

'A pleasure, Miss Eliott.'

'How do you know my name?'

'It's my duty to know. You see I'm Tittle.' He looked at the blank faces. 'Tittle, from Tittle-Tattle on the *Orb*. That's Tattle over there, the fat woman in maroon brocade wearing spectacles.'

'Oh I see.' Jack laughed, delighted. 'I should have guessed you were no ordinary waiter.'

Suddenly, people were saying, 'Ssh,' making more noise than the talkers.

'It's Buzzy Fitzgerald doing his magic act.' Jack pulled his chair behind Beatrice. 'He's very good but I've seen him so often I know all his tricks. Don't be so angry, Bea,' he whispered in her ear, 'we'll get used to it.'

'Used to what?' Turning round she glowered at him.

'Being in love. It's hard for me, too. Not at all what I'd planned. I thought I'd be a debonair bachelor till I was forty at least, not fall in love with a red-headed, green-eyed bad-tempered career woman.'

Shrieks and squeals came from the women sitting at the next table. 'Oh, no, how foul!'

'Mice! He's taken mice out of his topper.'

'Supposed to be a rabbit, isn't it?'

'Perhaps the mice ate the rabbit.'

'Don't be an absolute fool, Milly.'

Evangeline turned to look at the next table.

255

'Bea, Bea, look! Look who it is.' In a sibilant whisper she hissed, 'Eddie Banks.' He was sitting with three young women who were shrieking and giggling, feigning terror of the mice.

'Keep calm, Evie, you're with us, just watch the cabaret. Remember what Jack said — you are a dignified beauty.'

'I don't feel like it.'

'What's going on?' Jack leant forward. 'Who are you looking at, Bea?'

'Nobody,' she whispered. 'I'll tell you later.'

He put his arms round her and brushing tendrils of hair aside kissed the nape of her neck. I don't think I will ever get used to it, she said to herself.

A sudden burst of applause from those sitting near enough to see and hear signalled the end of the magic act. The applause was as much for relief as appreciation. On the stage the lights dimmed and Jack Buchanan announced, 'Daphne Haycock and Renée Rivière accompanied by Lennie Hayton.'

When the lights went up a little, Daphne and Renée were leaning with their backs against the piano, Daphne in a high-necked black satin dress cut on the bias that stopped above her ankles but clung all the way down and Renée dressed identically in white; neither was wearing any jewellery. A pinkish spotlight pinpointed their heads, accentuating the glossy black of Renée's short hair and the brilliant white peroxide of Daphne's. The pianist started to play 'For Me and My Gal', normally a song sung quickly and happily. Slowly and sensuously Daphne's low, husky tones blended with Renée's lighter, purer voice. The song was given a totally different value in their rendition. A sad note crept in as they sang, hardly moving except to look at each other on the words 'For Me and My Gal'.

The room was quiet for the first time that night. Suddenly the rhythm changed: a drummer had turned it into a tango. Leaving the piano, Lennie Hayton, a tall broad-shouldered handsome Negro, stood between the two women and untied a ribbon at the top of each dress. With a little wriggle from each woman the front part of the dress fell to the floor revealing dresses in the same material but now stopping at the knee and cut low with tiny straps. The dresses also revealed that neither of them was wearing underwear.

There was a gasp from the audience as Lennie returned to the piano and, still singing 'Me and My Gal', Daphne and Renée moved into a very dramatic tango.

'What do you think?' Beatrice whispered to Evangeline.

257

But Evangeline was aware that Eddie Banks had seen her and was staring at her. 'Ssh, later.'

The number came to an end with Daphne swinging Renée into a deep back bend and, almost as an afterthought, kissing her casually on the mouth. The audience applauded and shouted, banging their glasses and bottles on the tables.

'Wonder what Lady Munford thought,' Piggy said, clapping enthusiastically.

Evangeline saw Eddie stand up and walk towards her. She pretended she hadn't noticed and joined in the shouts of 'Encore'. Eddie stopped and frowned, looking beyond her. A finger lightly drew an X on her back.

'Sorry I'm late.' It was Hugo. 'I got here just as they were starting so I stood by the door to watch.' He took her hand and helped her up. 'Beatrice, I'd like to say how much I admire your dress.'

'Hugo! I didn't see you arrive. Thank you.'

Because of the fuss about Evangeline's back and the anxiety about the cabaret clothes, nobody else had mentioned Beatrice's dress, a Grecian column in pink and gold lamé stripes tied under the bust with the same pink and gold ribbons that held her thick, wavy, golden-red hair off her face and caught it up on top of her head.

'We're going, Beatrice. Do you mind?' Hugo took Evangeline's wrap and placed it round her shoulders. 'I'm hungry. We're going to the cab stand at Hyde Park Corner for terrible coffee but wonderful bacon rolls.'

'Well . . .' Beatrice looked doubtful.

'I'll get her home probably before you do.'

Tittle appeared with a tray bearing a note. 'Miss Eliott, this is from the gentleman at the next table, Mr Edward Banks.'

'Eddie Banks? How dare he?' Beatrice darted a furious glance at him. 'What does it say, Evie?'

Evangeline unfolded it and read it. 'May I see you?'

'No,' Beatrice said emphatically.

Taking a fountain pen from inside his tailcoat, Hugo took the note and wrote 'No' on it and returned it to Tittle.

'You go, the two of you. Take her away and have a good time.'

Beatrice could see that they were arguing as they crossed the room. Evie was probably angry that Hugo had taken charge of the note.

'Jack, quite a lot of people are leaving. See, the Munfords have gone.' Beatrice scanned the room. 'Did Daphne go too far?' That kiss. And then the pianist almost undressing them.

Piggy leant forward and patted her arm. 'Dearest Bea, all the people leaving are old, at

259

least forty or more, and few people here would be shocked at anything Daphne did.'

'Especially with a woman,' Jack added.

They walked down Piccadilly, Hugo's arm round Evangeline, his hand resting lightly on her shoulder. He had apologized for being authoritarian about the note and explained gently, when questioned angrily about the merits of their clothes, that hers was a pretty dress but was a little like a show-girl's, that Daphne's and Renée's were exquisitely cut and very erotic, not something she wanted to hear, but that Beatrice's was the wittiest and very daring, most redheads hadn't the courage to wear pink, and he knew it was overbearing of him to presume that she wanted to leave the party and be alone with him . . . But at this she had laughed and forgiven him. He was right on every point. The back was too low, she had been going to say no to Eddie Banks, and she certainly wanted to be alone with Hugo.

The night was still very warm even though it was well past midnight and the only traffic was a hansom cab slowly clip-clopping past the Ritz Hotel and being overtaken by a bicyclist with packed baskets on both the front and the back, balancing yet another basket full of lettuces on his head.

'He must have come from Covent Garden, poor chap.'

'Why poor chap, Hugo?'

'He's buying for a greengrocer's shop, a small one I should think, and can't afford the stock. Not like here.' He pointed to the large well-filled windows with the sign Jackson's of Piccadilly written above them.

'Jackson's. It's Molly's favourite shop. It's where she met her footman.'

Evangeline stood in the sheltered doorway peering through the glass. 'Look, caviare.'

He stood close behind her. She waited for him to touch her expecting him to put his hand into her dress at the back and touch her breast. But he kissed her back and let his tongue travel down her spine, then, kneeling, he lifted the back of her dress a little, unhooked her stocking from her suspender belt and ran his tongue across the back of her knee.

She trembled. He was always so unexpected. She knew that she desired him in the strict sense of the word. She had looked it up in the dictionary and discovered that it described her feelings exactly: 'That emotion which is directed to the attainment of some object from which pleasure or satisfaction is expected; longing; craving; physical appetite; lust'.

She turned to face him as he stood up and pulling his head down to hers she removed his glasses and kissed him.

'When?' she whispered.

'Soon,' he said, folding her in his arms.

At the coffee stall on the corner of Hyde Park next to the Duke of Wellington's house, they had what Hugo had accurately described as wonderful bacon rolls, and milky coffee served in thick white china cups without saucers. It was cooler now, but the taxi driver who was going to take them home let them sit in the back of the taxi while he chatted to the other drivers until they were ready to go.

They didn't kiss or even hold hands. Hugo described the house he had designed on the Thames, against his artistic wishes but for his financial needs. The owners wanted an Elizabethan oak-beamed inside with a Georgian brick and flint exterior and sloping clapboard wings as if they had just been added. The swimming pool was to be disguised as a lake with the changing rooms made from old garden privies, and the garages, of which there would be two, were to be built like a converted coach-house and a granary.

She laughed dutifully, sensing that it was expected of her, but secretly thought it sounded much nicer than the severe straight lines of the one he wanted to build.

Eventually he took her home. Keeping the

taxi, he waited till she had let herself in. 'Good-night.' He kissed her forehead. 'Your sister and Jack are going to Wellthorpe for a week-end in August. I think I'll take you to Vienna.'

He closed the door and she heard the taxi drive away.

'Evie, Evie, lock the door before you come up.' Beatrice's voice floated down from her bedroom.

Evangeline rushed up the stairs. 'Sorry I'm so late, Bea. We were talking. We sat in a taxi with our coffee and talked and talked.'

'It's all right.' Beatrice smiled. 'I've only just got home anyway. What did you talk and talk about?'

'Life, religion, Ireland, architecture — What is a humanitarian, Bea? I was trying to describe what Papa thought about religion and Hugo said it sounded as if that was what he was — or a humanist.'

'You did have a serious talk.' Beatrice pulled off a shoe and wiggled her toes. 'No, Papa thought he was a freethinker, which was un-usually honest of him, and Mama was an ag-nostic, which is why we only go to church at Christmas and Easter.'

'Yes, I sort of know. I've just never thought much about it. I mean, I know Molly's a Cath-olic but I don't think I've ever really thought about my own beliefs.'

'I somehow can't imagine Hugo talking about religion.' Beatrice kicked off her other shoe. 'I'm not too sure that I'd be up to it at this hour. I'm still so excited by this evening.' She untied the ribbons holding up her hair and shook her head till it fell down around her shoulders. 'The party, our new clothes . . . Daphne being so extraordinary.'

Evangline went into her bedroom and took one last look at her beautiful dress before she slipped out of it. She would definitely have to fill in part of the back. She wandered into Beatrice's bedroom yawning. 'I forgot to tell you I spoke to Celia Munford in the cloakroom. She loved my dress and said her mother wouldn't let her wear a backless one so I suggested that we made her one with hooks and eyes that could be folded back when necessary.'

Beatrice looked dubious. 'Rather sneaky to her mother. But wonderful if she comes to us.' She banged her hairbrush down on her gingham-painted table. 'Why does everything happen at the same time? All this work and all this . . .'

'What?' said Evangeline smiling slyly.

'All this . . . friends.'

Evangeline lay staring at the shadows on the ceiling.

How could she go to Vienna? Bea and Jack were only going away for three days and two nights, and, anyway, Bea hadn't decided definitely to go. It would depend on work, she'd said. Evangeline gave up trying to sleep and sat up. Hugo always questioned her about so many things, most of which she didn't know the answer to. Not just religion but her feelings about her work, the future. Would it be fashion, or social work like Penelope? If she added it all up she could see he was probing, finding out if she knew her own mind, whether she could take responsibility for herself. Did that mean he wasn't a cad? Unlike Eddie Banks. Bea's right, she thought, there's too much happening all at the same time. Penelope had said, be logical if you're in a muddle. Right. She knew that she was in love with Hugo and that she wanted him desperately. Therefore she must go to the clinic, because she also knew that she couldn't get pregnant. Neither of them would want that. There was no doubt that Hugo did not want to get married, to her or to anyone, so there would be no problem about continuing her work, which she wanted to do. Although, she thought sleepily, I wish he did want to marry me and I wish I could talk to Bea about it.

Evangeline was still asleep when Molly took

in her tea at eight thirty but Beatrice was up early and working in the office dealing with the post. It was bills as usual. There was a letter from Digby and Gordon, quite polite considering, to say that they couldn't supply any more material until their bill was paid. The irony was, Beatrice knew, that if they were a large and famous business with no need of credit, they would be able to get all the credit they needed.

There was a nice letter from Mrs Stett-Gittins to introduce a friend who intended to order something from the Eliotts and confirming her fitting, and a cheque from Mrs Trenton!

Beatrice sat back in her chair and breathed a sigh of relief. It would pay Digby and Gordon. She heard a door. Was that Letty? She listened to the sound of heavy footsteps coming up from the basement. It must be Letty. Tilly had a lighter tread.

'It's me, Miss Bea! Just to let you know that I'm here.' Letty knocked on the door.

'Come in, Letty. You're early.'

'Not much. Just a few minutes. More like you're late after last night. Go all right, did it?' She didn't wait for a reply. 'Here's the work-plan I've made, like I said.'

Beatrice took a neatly made chart from her. 'This is excellent, Letty. I can see that you've worked out the priorities very well.'

'And one more thing, Miss Bea. A bit awkward this.' She hesitated.

'Go ahead.'

'It's about Molly. She isn't really good enough except for basting and tacking but when we're busy it'd be helpful if she could thread needles. In all the dressmakers' that I've worked there's been a needle-threader, though usually just a young girl.'

Beatrice thought about it. Letty was right. Molly wasn't good enough but she wanted very much to be part of the workroom with girls of her own age. 'I'll ask her, Letty. I'll have to make it sound important. We don't want to hurt her feelings.'

'Right, Miss Bea. I'll get on with my work, then.'

At the door she paused and flung over her shoulder 'Nice bit about you in the *Orb* this morning. It's a terrible paper. Very Tory. But people read it.'

Beatrice rushed out into the corridor shouting, 'Letty! What did they say? What did it say?'

'Haven't you seen it? I read all the papers at the station kiosk. I don't buy them, mind. Wouldn't put money into their pockets. Exploiters of the working class —'

'Letty!' Beatrice shouted again. 'What did

267

it say? Why didn't you buy it for us?'

'I only buy *Socialist Weekly* — leastways Charlie, my young man, does. It said something about you being best dressed.'

Evangeline walked down the stairs, sleepily calling, 'What's going on?'

Molly met her in the hall. 'Don't know, Miss Evie. It's Miss Bea shouting at Letty, but what for I don't know.'

Beatrice burst out of the workroom. 'We've been written about in the newspaper the *Orb* but Letty didn't —'

Molly and Evangeline rushed out of the front door. 'We'll get it at the corner.' But hardly were they out of the house when they returned. 'Money,' Evangeline said breathlessly. 'Forgot money.'

'Here,' Beatrice said pulling two silver threepenny bits from her pocket. 'Hurry.'

When they returned panting and red-faced with their hair falling down, Beatrice calmly announced, 'It's very good.'

There, spread out on the main workroom table, was the society page of the *Orb*. An excited Tilly had brought it in. 'Bloke sitting next to me on the Underground only looked at the racing, left it on the seat. Oooh, the telephone'll start ringing now with lots of orders.'

'Not yet it won't.' Letty was being phlegmatic about the whole thing and far more practical. 'Ladies won't be up yet.'

Evangeline bent over the table and read it aloud. ' "One of the most striking women in the room, Miss Beatrice Eliott, dressed in pink and gold, a brave clash with her Titian hair . . ." Golly, Bea,' Evangeline looked up wide-eyed, 'that's you.'

'Go on, go on, Miss Evie.' Molly nudged her impatiently.

' ". . . her Titian hair," ' Evangeline picked up the paper and read aloud, ' "was accompanied by society photographer Jack Maddox. He who has the elixir of youth in his studio. For what else would explain the loss of chins, frown-lines and poundage undergone by his matronly sitters? Miss Eliott's sister, the ravishing Evangeline, who was wearing one of the new backless dresses in violet silk and purple charmeuse (the talented sisters designed and made their own clothes) arrived with Tom "Piggy" Trenton, son of Vice-Admiral Sir Peter Trenton, exchanged smouldering glances and notes with young racing driver Edward Banks and then left with the saturnine architect Hugo Bonner. Tittle predicts a string of broken hearts for Miss Eliott." ' Evangeline dropped the newspaper in dismay. 'It's not true, it wasn't true. It makes me sound like a flirt.'

269

'I dunno, Miss Evie,' Tilly piped up. 'Nice to have someone to flirt with.'

'Doesn't say anything about Daphne and Renée either.' Evangeline was thinking of Hugo. If he read it, would he mind?

'Don't worry, Evie, everybody takes gossip writers with a pinch of salt.' Beatrice picked up the paper and reread it. 'It does mention Daphne under Tattle. She goes on about Lord Fitzgerald's magic and the Greek dancing of the three Sykes sisters but says . . .' Beatrice paused and started to laugh, 'sorry . . . er . . . let's see. "But the unusual Sapphic interpretation of 'Me and My Gal' by Miss Daphne Haycock and partner was the hit of the evening." '

'That's all? Nothing about their dresses?' Evangeline was outraged. 'We did it all for nothing. All that work and nobody noticed.'

'I think you'll find that all they wrote about you and Miss Beatrice will do you more good than getting credit for a cabaret artist's costume.' Letty collected her work and sat down. 'And would everybody look at the notice on the board, please. I've made a plan for distributing work.'

Molly, who was quite overwhelmed at the honour of seeing the name Eliott in the newspaper and felt keenly the reflected glory, glanced at the plan. 'What about me, then,

270

Letty? It doesn't say a word about me. Won't you be needing me when I've finished the bed-rooms?' Anxiously looking back and forth between Letty and Beatrice, she said, 'I don't mind doing what I can. I like to help.'

'Yes, Molly, we know.' Beatrice tried to think of a polite way of putting it. 'You see, we need you for a special job.'

Molly brightened up. 'Yes, Miss Bea?'

'But it's up to you. If you don't want to do it just say so. You have such good eyesight and such steady hands, would you consider threading needles for everybody? Especially when we're busy.'

'Oh, Miss Bea, Miss Evie, that's just the ticket. I'll be here, in the workroom with my own special job. Don't worry, any of you,' smiling confidently, she took in everybody, 'your needles will be always ready.'

'Good, we're all very grateful.' Beatrice shot a glance at Letty. 'Aren't we?'

Letty was already holding up a needle. 'Every high-class establishment has an exclusive needle-threader.'

The telephone did ring that day once 'the ladies' were up but it wasn't only potential clients who called. The first call of the day was from an irate Arthur raging about Evangeline behaving like a Bright Young Thing.

271

A backless dress? What could Beatrice be thinking of? And 'Who were those men?' She managed to make Hugo sound old and Piggy a figure of fun and pointed out that it was hardly their fault that Eddie Banks was at the next table and Evangeline had certainly not smouldered at him she had shunned him. This last, at least, was true. Nevertheless, Evangeline had to agree to dine with him next week. Celia Munford arrived with her sister, both wanting non-backless backless dresses and then on seeing Tilly beading the chiffon ordered versions of that as well.

During lunch when her fellow workers were downstairs in the kitchen eating Molly's famous cold apple and curry soup, a favourite of Dr Eliott's who had taught it to her, and homemade soda bread, Jack arrived early for his afternoon sitting. He was in total despair.

'Bea, I can't go on.' He flung himself into the armchair. 'I feel such a fool. "The elixir of life". Everyone will be laughing at me and my poor old trouts will never believe in me again.'

'Or themselves,' Beatrice murmured. 'I'm sure they know that you retouched them a little.'

'Yes, but if they did know, they didn't want everyone else knowing.' He leapt up again.

'Come and have lunch. I need to talk. I've got an idea.'

'Just a minute.' Beatrice answered the telephone. 'Hello. This is Miss Eliott speaking.' She paused, listening. 'Yes, Madame Roncard, thank you . . . Oh, I am pleased, how kind of you to say so . . . Yes, we can do that . . . Tuesday. Eleven A.M.? That will give us enough time to show you our autumn designs as well. Thank you. Goodbye.' She hung up the receiver slowly. 'Jack, that was Madame Roncard, the Belgian ambassador's wife. She is one of the most chic women in London.'

'Then we must have lunch to celebrate.'

He had gone off rather forlornly on his own to the pub when she had explained that she was seeing the bank manager at two o'clock. After their usual argument about him lending them the money, he had accepted that they wanted to be independent, but rather than let the business founder, she would borrow the money from him if all else failed.

The bank manager had been less than helpful. They had no collateral and could therefore have no overdraft, and he agreed with Mr Arthur Eliott that their best interests would not be served by saddling themselves with a debt. He had managed to make her feel both young

273

and foolishly naïve, and middle-aged and tired.

At Digby and Gordon she paid the bill and proudly showed them the piece in the *Orb*. If they were impressed they concealed it and insisted on a limit of fifty pounds' credit which would accrue interest monthly. Oh, yes, they understood only too well how dilatory clients were in paying off their bills. Why, Savile Row tailors often waited for a year or more. Burdened with yards of chiffon, pale grey cashmere and oyster white mousseline she took a bus home from Hallatt Street down an Oxford Street so crowded and noisy that she thought with longing of a quiet restaurant with Jack.

'It's not a question of setting rates.' When Letty was angry, her voice was shrill and she became incoherent. 'It's a question of whether the rate set is possible for people in the position to pay or not to do it, Tilly.'

'You mean,' Evangeline tried to help her, 'what is the point of setting a rate that nobody can pay?'

'That's what I said. So Poplar council is right by not doing one, see, and you ought to back them up by going to the meetings.'

Tilly sighed. Meetings were all she was short of. She helped her mum in the morning with the baby, did a full day's work here, shopped on the way home and then did the kids' tea and there was always the washing to do, nappies and everything.

'She's right, Tilly.' Evangeline spoke with some authority. 'Miss Maddox supports the councillors, Letty, but she thinks they might have real trouble on their hands. I'm sorry. I can't come to the meeting tonight. I'm helping at the soup kitchen at St Saviour's.'

'My Charlie says charity is demeaning and if the government did what they ought to it wouldn't be necessary.' Letty sounded even more belligerent.

Molly concentrated on threading the pale pink silk through her needle and placed it ready for Tilly. This was as bad as being with Michael, except Poplar didn't interest him as much as Dublin. She wanted to talk about Rudolph Valentino, whose face she often substituted for Michael's when he kissed her. Sitting in the park last week listening to the military band playing 'The Fishermen of England' she thought she'd rather hear 'The Four Horsemen of the Whatsit' and when Michael had finished asking her if she would wait till he was a butler before being married, which might take seven years, she felt as if she was engaged to Rudolph Valentino. Not

275

that she was really engaged. No ring. He said it was a waste of money.

'I'll be ready for the cream, Molly.' Evangeline bent over the shantung tunic she was pleating. Beatrice would be back soon; perhaps she could ask her if she was going to Wellthorpe with Jack, persuade her she needed a rest.

'Ooh, my eyes.' Tilly rubbed her head.

'If your eyes are giving you gyp, stop the beading and get on with the lapels on the black cashmere.'

Letty was being a little too officious, Evangeline thought, but she was a wonderful organizer.

'Or would you rather rest for a while? We have been working non-stop except for twenty minutes at lunch. Oh, there's Bea, we could stop for a cup of tea.'

Beatrice pushed open the workroom door, laden with her parcels. She was hot and tired and her arms were aching.

'It's frightfully stuffy in here. Why don't you open a window?'

'Dust, Miss Bea,' Molly said. 'It would get all over the beautiful materials.'

Beatrice looked for somewhere on the crowded table to put her parcels.

'Molly, you know that old trestle table that's in the broom cupboard in the kitchen. Would

276

you set it up in the office when you've got time?'

'Good idea, Miss Bea. I'll do it now. We're stopping for some tea.'

'Tea? Have you caught up, then?'

A groan came from everybody. 'Nooo.'

'Well,' she said, with a forced brightness, 'don't worry, Evie and I will finish everything that's to be collected tomorrow after dinner.'

Evangeline looked uncomfortable. 'Sorry, Bea. I can't. I've promised Penelope to help —'

'Unpromise her then. Charity begins at home.

'St Saviour's isn't on the telephone, Bea. I have to go.'

Beatrice dropped her parcels on the table. 'Get the table, Molly,' she snapped. 'Have you got time now, Evangeline? I'd like to give you the list of future appointments.' She left the room banging the door.

Evangeline placed the shantung tunic carefully on a padded hanger and followed her. Letty raised her eyebrows and whistled softly.

'It's hard on them.' Molly felt protective towards her employers. 'This is all new and a lot of hard work.'

'Hard work isn't new to me,' Letty started to say but they were all silenced by Evangeline shouting, 'I'm not a liar.'

Facing each other across the desk, Evangeline was responding to Beatrice's suspicions that it wasn't Penelope she was seeing that evening but Hugo.

Evangeline knew that she was blushing. She wasn't lying about tonight but she soon would be. 'Come with me if you don't believe me.'

'What I find difficult to believe is you putting your responsibility to Penelope Maddox before me. No, not me. Our work. And especially today when there's so much to discuss.'

'What happened at the bank, Bea? No good? Is that why you're in such a paddy?'

Beatrice regarded her sister coldly. 'Right now, I haven't time to discuss our finances, the bank manager, the overdraft or the humiliating request for credit at Digby's because I have another job, the money from which helps support you.'

Beatrice was barely out of the room before Evangeline hurled a portfolio of sketches at her.

Beatrice was still shaking when she reached the studio.

'My darling, there you are.' Jack embraced her. 'I missed you at lunch. Very frugal it was too, smoked salmon and only one glass of champagne.'

'Not as frugal as mine. Nothing. Not that I was hungry,' she added hastily. 'Quick, tell me your idea before Mrs Grover arrives.'

'Sit here with me, you look rattled. You're working too hard,' he said pulling her on to the sofa and cradling her in his arms. 'I wouldn't make as much money but I would have more respect from others as well as myself.' He stroked her cheek and turned her face towards him, 'Green, green eyes.' Closing them with the tips of his fingers, he kissed her eyelids and then her mouth. 'My beautiful Beatrice.'

'Jack, Mrs Grover will be here.'

'Yes, you're right.' He kissed her again more passionately.

'Jack, I do love you but . . . I don't want to share it with your clients,' she murmured, and 'What is your idea?' she managed to say before he again took her face and covered it in tiny kisses murmuring, 'Do you love me, do you love me?'

Thinking, to hell with Mrs Grover, she relaxed against his body and languorously put her arms around him. 'Yes, my beloved, I do love you.'

When the bell announcing Mrs Grover's arrival was heard, Jack helped her off the sofa.

279

'Molly will send her up, won't she?' he said absently. As she was leaving the studio he called, 'Beatrice.'

She turned. 'Yes?'

'Do you think it possible to combine a career and marriage?'

Mrs Grover appeared, leaving no time for a reply. She had been a very demanding woman, arriving with six outfits and a lady's maid whose requirements included irons, pins, needles and cotton, clothes brushes, shoe polish, comb, hairpins, a manicure set and endless cups of coffee. They were both exhausted when she left but Beatrice began to tidy the studio hurriedly.

'Dont do that, Bea.' He stood at the open door. A silence and stillness fell in the room and neither spoke till Jack closed the door. 'I want to marry you, Beatrice. I want to know that you will always be in my life. I don't want ours to be a relationship where we fumble and tumble on sofas. And I don't want to change you. I love you and part of you is your work which I accept,' he smiled, 'even if you can't have lunch with me.'

He paused, looking at the slender figure of the woman he felt would make his life complete. She was wearing a pale grey and white cotton dress enlivened by a startling tomato red collar. It echoed her personality, he thought, both reserved and vibrant.

'I can't have dinner with you, either.'

'You monster!' He grasped her shoulders. 'Answer me.'

The answer had been easy, she thought, marriage to Jack seemed absolutely natural. It was simple, uncomplicated. They loved each other and knew each other. There would be no surprises. She was aware of his fluctuating moods and would be ready for them, and he was prepared, he said, for the occasional bucket of iced water to be flung at him. And there was to be no settling down, he had been quite firm about that. Domestic bliss would be punctuated by trips to Paris, dinner at the Blue Bear and lunches on the river. When they would be married and where they would live would be decided when things were calmer. Finally Jack had described what he hoped would be his new career. Photo-journalism. Photographing real incidents and events for newspapers and magazines. Realistic pictures, unretouched, telling the stories of death, love and war. Photographs would be more important than words — after all, moving pictures didn't need them, they were silent because a picture said a thousand words. Would she mind? He would earn much less money. Cachet not cash, he had said.

Beatrice yawned. She was nearly finished, about half an hour would do it. Perhaps it would be better to do those cuffs in the morning. Get up a bit earlier.

There was a scratching sound at the office door. 'Who is it?'

'It's Molly, Miss Bea. Can you open the door, please?'

Molly stood there carrying a tray with a plate of delicately cut sandwiches on it, half a bottle of champagne and a white rose in a narrow glass vase. 'It's Mr Jack,' she said beaming. 'He said as how I was to bring this up prompt at half past ten and you was to stop work.' She placed the tray carefully on a side table next to the large comfortable armchair. 'And then you're to go to bed, he said.' She looked with consternation at her mistress. 'Don't cry, Miss Bea, don't upset yourself. He meant it for the best.'

Beatrice nodded. 'I'm tired, that's all. It's a surprise. A lovely surprise. You go. I'll be fine.'

When Molly returned to collect the tray Beatrice had gone and so had the white rose. He must have declared himself, she thought. No waiting seven years to be a butler for him.

There was an uneasy truce between the two

sisters the next day. Evangeline had finished the sewing when she got home and pressed everything, but Beatrice had merely acknowledged it, not thanked her and, worse, she hadn't mentioned Jack. So now they both had secrets from each other. Molly had chattered to Evangeline the night before and described Jack's loving concern and Beatrice's tears. She had voiced her opinion that they must have an understanding. At breakfast Beatrice explained briefly about her failure at the bank and partial success at Digby and Gordon, suggested that Evangeline deal with Mrs Stett-Gittins and she would see Lady Bonner.

'Oh, in future, Evie, I think it preferable that we discuss anything private in private. I mean personal arrangements, money et cetera.'

Molly hovered by the stove feeling very awkward.

'Er, Miss Bea, should I leave the room?'

Beatrice looked surprised. 'Sorry, Molly, I don't mean you. You're different. We've both been lax in the workroom, Evie. It's undignified and sets a bad example.'

She can't have had a proposal, a declaration of love, Evangeline thought. She's behaving like a dried-up spinster. 'Are you and Jack going to Wellthorpe? Have you decided?'

Beatrice was surprised by the directness of

her question. 'Well, no, we decided not to.'

Then Molly is definitely wrong. It would be a perfect opportunity for people in love to have a weekend together. Evangeline got up from the table and put her cup and saucer in the sink, running water on it to rinse it. 'Why not?' she said casually.

Molly busied herself wiping down the kitchen table, alert to the hidden meaning underlying everything that the sisters were saying.

'Because we are going to spend the day driving around London and the Kent coast. Jack wants to photograph all the bomb-sites made during the war and then do the same thing in northern France later in the year.' She was flushed now and full of enthusiasm and pride. 'He's going to do a series of photographs showing the aftermath of war for ordinary innocent people.'

'That's wonderful, Bea. He could get something like that in a magazine.'

'Or do it on a moving camera to be shown next to a Charlie Chaplin piece,' Molly volunteered.

Now, she thought as they went upstairs excitedly talking about Mr Jack's new career, the breach was healed. Both were happy. She'd certainly been right about Miss Bea, and Miss Evie was up to something, too. She must have a plan afoot for the day, and I'll go to the big ceilidh, she thought, with Michael. Maybe dancing will loosen him up. He can't talk about the troubles while he's doing a jig, not if he does it properly. Sometimes she felt his affection for her was based on the fact that her step-father's brother was in prison for shooting a policeman. He was an O'Malley, she was a Murphy. If only Michael was a Valentino. She put the pan in which she had scrambled the eggs to soak. The photo of him on the posters as the Sheikh filled her with longing as she lay in bed at night. It would mean making another confession about impure thoughts on Sunday.

CHAPTER SEVEN

The Honourable Sybil had arrived with her mother, chartering like an exotic bird, swooping round the reception room, her sentences barely decipherable. She wanted to approve of what 'the mother of the bride' would wear and was anxious to report on her own dress made by Madame Rochelle.

'He's designed me something totally, utterly original. It's all mine and it's a secret from everybody.'

'He?' Beatrice questioned, laughing.

'Mr Ronald. He's the head designer,' Sybil explained. 'All I can say is that it's floaty from top to bottom. I will look wonderful. And I'll have six adorable pages dressed as shepherd boys.'

Beatrice showed Elizabeth Bonner the swatches of yellow shantung and very lightweight grey cashmere. Sybil gave it a cursory glance and a nod of approval then suddenly squealed, 'The grey cashmere. Oh, Mama, could I have an afternoon coat made of that?'

'With a yellow leather collar,' Beatrice suggested.

'Yes. Yes. Where's Evangeline? I want to ask her.'

Beatrice nodded towards the folding doors. 'In there with . . .'

Sybil didn't wait but opened the doors and darted through.

'Sorry. I say, you're not alone.' Smiling at Evangeline she put out her hand to Olivia Stett-Gittins. 'How do you do. I'm Sybil Bonner. I'm getting married in three weeks' time. We're to live in Leicestershire. For the hunting, and my fiancé is giving me two hunters and I'm so excited I think I'll explode.'

Olivia Stett-Gittins shook her hand smiling quizzically. 'I hope you'll be very happy.'

Evangeline agreed that the grey cashmere and yellow leather would be a good idea and Sybil darted back to her mother.

'Same age as you, I'd guess?' Olivia looked at Evangeline, amused. 'But not at all alike. She's more interested in her horse than her husband whereas you . . .'

'Don't believe what you read in the *Orb*.' Evangeline made a deft tuck and pinned it.

'I believe that you're ravishing and I believe that you could break hearts but I also believe from our short acquaintance that you would not be careful of your own heart. Neither was

I. I was "passion's slave" as I think you might be.' She laughed lightly. 'And I wouldn't have it otherwise.'

Evangeline sat in her bedroom with the pale grey silk spread out before her; she was avoiding lunch with everybody in the kitchen. She wanted to think. Everything was going to be all right. Olivia was going to help her. You didn't have to go to the clinic in Holloway, you could see a doctor and Olivia had a woman doctor and she would go with her. She carefully drew the needle through the delicate material thinking of Sybil. Fancy being more excited by two hunters than her husband. Not that Hugo wanted to marry her, but he might one day. Olivia had been so wise, so understanding. 'Don't make an enemy of your sister,' she had said. 'The secret is to protect her, not to estrange her.'

A sudden rush of love for Bea flooded her. What a terrible life she had had since Mama died. Finally it seemed that there was a possibility of love and marriage for her, but at thirty! Thirty! To have to wait till middle age. Whereas she would be going to Vienna on Saturday. It was a code between them, a euphemism, Hugo said (she had had to look it up in the dictionary), but without stating it they knew that they would become lovers then.

288

She finished the fine seam and knotted the thread. The grey silk had been left over from a blouse ordered by Aunt Lydia. Nobody had noticed her taking it. She started to laugh. It was wonderfully funny to think of Aunt Lydia paying for the camisole and knickers in which she intended to be seduced.

Molly stood by the workroom table. It was covered in materials, trimmings, beads and pins. It looked a mess to her but Tilly and Letty appeared to know what they were doing.

'And you think we will go on, then?' she said anxiously. 'I know it's doing fine now but it could all change.'

'You're a gloomy Gladys, aren't you?' Letty took two pieces of red taffeta she had been cutting out. 'We're so busy I'm going to have to take you off needles and put you on tacking. Here,' she gave Molly the material, 'I want you to do this with long loose stitches. All right?'

'It's like I said, Molly,' Tilly looked up from the grey chiffon dress, the hem of which she was hand rolling, 'once they start paying, you catch up with yourself and they've started paying, haven't they?'

'I suppose so.' Molly didn't feel that she had the right to reveal the Eliotts' dealings since Beatrice had spoken about more discretion, but, after all, she had asked the seam-stresses what they thought.

'And not only that but new clients have come and, what's more important, old clients keep coming back.' Tilly stood up and stretched. 'I believe in them. They've got good ideas and we carry them out good and they don't run before they can walk. Mark my words, they're going to be as big as Worth and Chanel one day.'

'As long as we're here when it happens.' Letty narrowed her eyes with suspicion.

'Sure you will be.' Molly had cheered up. 'Weren't they saying this morning how wonderful the two of you were?'

Tilly stood thinking with her hands clasped behind her back. With her pre-pubescent figure and barely reaching five foot, she looked like an old child. 'You know,' she said solemnly, 'I'm happy. I like coming here. I like working with you. I like the work. I like getting out of the house.'

'And I'd like you to get on with your work,' Letty said, her grin belying her stern tone. 'Miss Evie will have finished that chiffon for you to bead.'

Tilly sat down again and picked up her needle. 'I'm not the only one who's happy. There's a sort of feeling here. All excitement like . . .'

★ ★ ★

Hugo arrived early in a cab and kept it waiting. The hall was full of Jack's photographic equipment which he was busy sorting out.

'Where are you two going?'

'Paddington station, I'm taking Evangeline to see my new house, or half a house so far, on the river at Wargrave.'

'Will you be late back?' Beatrice asked.

'Very late. We'll have dinner somewhere on the Thames,' he turned back from the door which he was holding open for Evangeline, 'if that's all right, Beatrice?'

'Of course,' she said gaily. 'Enjoy yourselves.'

They sat in opposite corners of the cab. Were they really just going to the country, Evangeline wondered. He didn't speak. He sat looking at her with that odd expression as if he were in pain. He leant forward picked up her ungloved hand and put her fingers in his mouth sucking them and then with his eyes half closed he put her wet fingers in her own mouth.

'We're here,' he said quietly, drying her fingers on his handkerchief.

She looked out of the window. 'Not Paddington?'

'No. But it's on the river, Hammersmith.'

HAMMERSMITH TERRACE, she read as he paid the cab driver.

The house was like a smaller version of their house in Highgate, or so it appeared from outside. Inside it was quite different. He held her hand and led her along a corridor past doors open into rooms in which she saw briefly white, grey, black, steel and glass. The whole house was filled with light. Windows had obviously been widened.

Reaching the foot of the stairs, they paused.

'The bedroom is upstairs.' He stood aside to let her go first.

So there was to be no pretence, she thought, no offer of tea or coffee, no 'Would you like to see the river?' Suddenly she felt weak, her legs were wobbly as if she had flu. She stumbled on the stairs. He put out a hand to steady her, placing it on her back, at the base of her spine.

'Don't be nervous, Evangeline.'

The bedroom had three large windows, partially obscured by half-open shutters, facing the river. The sun was shining on the water, and light was reflected into the room dappling the walls like a reflection of the river itself.

He took her face in both of his hands and tilting it a little he kissed under her chin, her neck, and gently touched her ear with his tongue. Then slowly he turned her round to face the long cheval mirror. Unhooking her dress to her waist and easing it off her shoulders and arms, he gazed at her intently in the mirror. He removed the pins that held up her hair. It fell below her shoulders and he could see the auburn lights revealed beneath the dark brown by the sun.

He lightly caressed her breasts, enfolded in the soft grey silk of the camisole, then facing her he took her nipple in his mouth through the silk. She felt the wonderful aching pleasure she remembered from before. He stood behind her again touching her breast and the hard nipple which showed through the wet where he had kissed her. Taking off her camisole, he cupped both her breasts in his hands.

She was aware that she had been holding her breath and exhaled, feeling a little dizzy. He sensed that, as she felt he sensed everything about her, and tenderly carried her to the bed. As he undressed her he touched and kissed every part, and undressed himself. He finally unbuttoned her glacé kid shoes and rolled down her stockings. He kissed her on the mouth for the first time as he entered her. There was pain, as she had read there would be, but a pain of exquisite pleasure. She arched her back and lifted her body to meet him. It was the only time he spoke as he shuddered inside her. 'Evangeline.' His eyes rolled back in his head.

He lay with her in his arms, smoothing the damp hair off her forehead. Softly he said, 'I knew you would be extraordinary.'

'You,' she said, running her hands down his strong back.

'Us, then.' He rolled on top of her. 'But you moved and . . . Oh, God, I should have been more careful . . . In future . . .'

'In future,' she said shyly, blushing, 'you won't have to be.'

When he realized what she was talking about, he was touched.

'You brave girl. You beautiful brave girl.'

And later when they had bathed and he was drying her body he gently inserted the cap himself as if it was part of the love-making.

The sun was starting to set when they woke, their arms and legs entwined. 'I think I should make us lunch and dinner, don't you?'

They sat in the tiny garden to eat their omelettes, a hurricane lamp spreading a pool of light on the wrought-iron table. The tide was in and some mallards, their metallic green heads just discernible in the dark, were bobbing in the water waiting anxiously for crusts. Evangeline crumbled some bread and threw it to them. 'Do they ever float into the garden?'

'Not yet but I've only been here a year.'

A year. Time, she thought. Suddenly feeling desperate she did something she had sworn to herself that she would never do. 'When will I see you again?'

He seemed surprised. 'Tomorrow, of course, if you can. You don't work on Sunday, do you?'

'If I have to I'll get up early.'

'No, work in the evening. The last train to Wargrave goes at eight thirty.'

She started to shiver.

'What is it? Are you all right?' He bent forward and took her hand. 'We will both be working hard next week but I'll come up to see you during the week.'

She nodded, looking at him dumbly.

He let go her hand and stood at the river's edge. His voice was cool and distant when he spoke. 'You like your work, don't you? You're having a great success, you know, and it will grow.'

She didn't reply and when he turned to look at her, he could just see that she was crying. 'I don't want to get married, as you know.' His voice was still cold and detached. He could have been discussing the merits of a mushroom as opposed to a cheese omelette, she thought. 'And I prefer to live on my own, but I want to be with you as much as possible. If you can't cope with me the way I am, if it causes you too much pain, we should not see each other again.'

She stood up, controlling her tears. 'Hugo, you are nine years older than I am. What happened here today was just one of many occasions for you. For me it was the first time.'

She went back into the house through the french windows. A fire was laid in the grate. She found matches on the overmantel and lit it. Sitting on the floor hugging her knees, she stared into the flames. I do like my work, she thought, my life is very interesting. I can cope with him as he is.

He entered the room closing the french windows and joined her at the fire. 'I hadn't planned to like you as much as I do, Evangeline. Forgive me for being so cold.'

She put her hands up and clasped them round his neck, pulling him down to her. 'I can't think of anything except wanting you.'

He pulled at her clothes, tearing the delicate grey silk of her knickers. As he pushed inside her, her eyes opened wide, looking like topaz in the light of the fire.

'You're not always cold,' she murmured.

Beatrice pointed to the sign nailed to the oak beam, 'MIND YOUR HEAD', as Jack rubbed his forehead.

'Where? I didn't see it.' He ducked back under the low beam.

'See?'

'Well, if I'd been reading that I would have fallen down the step.' He ducked under again, and again hit his head.

'I'm sorry to laugh but . . .'

'You're not sorry at all.' Jack was laughing himself.

'Come on, we need a drink. Ouch!'

Jack looked at Beatrice in amazement. 'You did it? A little shrimp like you? Poor girl.' He kissed the red mark on her forehead. 'Sit down there by the window and I'll order our drinks.'

A waiter came hurrying up. 'This table is reserved, sir.'

'Yes, it's reserved for me. Mr Maddox.'

The waiter consulted the pad he was carrying. 'Yes, sir. Mr Maddox,' he said reluctantly, clearly disappointed he wasn't to have the pleasure of embarrassing somebody.

'And we know what we want so don't go away. Two dry martini cocktails. Ham from the joint that is sitting on the bar, new potatoes, whatever salad you have, and bring me the wine list.'

'Yes, sir.' The waiter dropped the wine list disdainfully onto the table. Anybody who ordered ham salad without looking at the menu wasn't going to buy a good wine. From experience he knew the man would look at it and choose the second cheapest.

'All right, Bea? Your head, I mean.'

'All right everything.' She put her hand across the table. He took it and pressed it against his cheek. 'Pity the sun was shining.' He sighed. 'It made everything look so attractive, so pretty. All those wild flowers on the bomb-sites.' He examined the wine list. 'Would you like a Bonnes Mares? It's a bit young but should be good.'

'Jack, if you're going to give up your old trouts, shouldn't you —'

'I'm giving them up gradually,' he laughed, 'and meanwhile you must have good wine, and if your business continues to flourish you will be buying me Romanée-Conti.'

The waiter appeared with the cocktails. 'Has Sir decided? I could recommend a nice little claret.'

'Thank you, I prefer a burgundy. The Bonnes Mares.'

Impressed, the waiter bowed, 'Yes, sir,' and backed away.

'I preferred him uppity to 'umble. No, the best photograph of the day will be that child standing where his school had been, just grinning.' The child a raggedly dressed skinny little thing had appeared from behind a pile of masonry. 'Ahsoryerkisser,' he had said. 'Ahsoryerkisser.' When they had translated this into 'I saw you kiss her', the child had asked them to do his shoes for him. 'Dunno 'ow ter do knots, see.'

The shoes themselves hardly existed. The soles, which were mainly cardboard, were only attached to the uppers by two or three threads and the whole was joined together by string. Jack had found some stronger cardboard and cut and shaped it for the insole and Beatrice tied it all together using double bows instead of knots.

'Ta, Missus, that'll last me till tomorrer.' He had watched Jack suspiciously as he set up the tripod for his camera. 'Whassat for?'

'To hold my camera. Keep it steady.'

The boy thought about that. 'Right. You gonna photo 'er, are yer?' and, screaming with laughter, he had hidden himself behind the fallen walls of the bomb-site shouting, 'Ginger. Ginger nut.'

He hadn't come out till he had heard Beatrice laughing too. 'Don't worry. It's not the first time I've been called Ginger.'

'My school, this woz before it woz bombed.'

'Yours? But aren't you too young?' Beatrice thought that for his height and weight he looked about five or six.

'Nah. I'm ten, I fink. Anyways, about ten.

It was smashin' after the bomb. Nobody 'ad ter go to school. Not fer ages.'

Beatrice looked at Jack. 'Behind every cloud . . .' Ten children had been killed that day but this child only remembered the unexpected holiday.

Jack had photographed him standing like the King of the Castle on lumps of concrete covered with moss, roughly where he thought his classroom had been. They had given him a shilling at first, but it had been too much. It had confused him. 'Blimey, they'll orl fink I stole it,' so Beatrice had found him a shilling's-worth of coppers instead. But the biggest treat had been the chocolate. Beatrice had discovered a half-eaten bar in the car melting in the sun but to the boy it was like an untouched box from Fortnum and Mason. He wouldn't tell them his name and address. 'In case,' he said darkly. In case of what, he wouldn't say.

Across the marshes they could see the sun setting, sinking behind the estuary. 'If we went back, Jack, do you think we would find him?' She looked round the room at the dark oak beams, the flagstone floor and their fellow diners all eating food that they didn't really need. 'I want to buy him some shoes.'

'I don't know, my love, but we could try.'

The waiter had set their food in front of them and poured some wine for Jack to try. He sipped it and nodded and the waiter filled their glasses. They ignored the food and wine, contemplating each other across the table. 'When we're married, we'll come and stay here,' Jack said, breaking the silence.

'When we're married?'

The sadness in her voice disturbed him. 'Bea?'

Her head was turned to the window.

'Bea, look at me. Listen, darling Bea, let me explain.'

'Nothing to explain, Jack, don't worry.'

He pushed his plate aside and took both her hands.

'I don't want a tumble on the studio sofa or an illicit weekend with you. I want to marry you and try to live happily ever after. Ssh, wait,' his hand stopped her, 'I love you. I'm in love with you. I want you madly, crazily, but I'll wait until we're married.'

'People say today that it's dangerous to marry without knowing that side of somebody.' She spoke pensively.

'Rubbish. If it isn't perfect the first time we've got the rest of our lives to get it right. You haven't finished your martini.'

She pushed it across to him. 'You finish it.'

'Are you trying to get me drunk and then

301

seduce me?' He quickly tossed it down. 'Let's eat. It's late.'

After a few mouthfuls, Beatrice said, 'The ham is excellent, the potatoes good, the salad disgusting.'

Jack put down his knife and fork. 'Obviously we should get married as soon as possible, if only to prevent you running off with the newly pared-down Piggy.'

'I refuse to feel guilty about him, Jack. He may have done it for me but it's good for him, losing weight. Even Molly noticed the difference the other day. She said he looked like Douglas Fairbanks.'

'I mean it, Bea. If we wait till our lives are calm we might wait for ever. If you're not eating that ham, may I have it? I think we should marry in a small church either in Notting Hill Gate or Mayfair. Only Penny, Evie, Piggy and Molly, oh, and I suppose Hugo.'

'Where would we live?'

'Your eyes are greening in the candlelight.'

'Gleaming?'

'No, greening. I love you. Would you mind living in my house? You can do what you like with it, I know that there's room for improvement.'

She frowned. 'Your house? Is it yours?'

'Not mine, as such. Like the motor it belongs to my parents, but they've kept it for us. For Penny and me. They prefer, when they're here, to live in their little cottage in Hampshire.'

Beatrice put her head in her hands and made a low groan.

'What is it, Bea?'

'It all seems so difficult. You and me, Penelope, and what about Evie? I don't know.'

'This is hopeless.' He stood up. 'Get in the car, I'll pay the bill. We can't discuss the rest of our lives whispering in the corner of the Old Ferry Inn surrounded by people discussing their handicaps. Golf, I mean.' He paid the bill quickly and soon joined her in the car. 'I'm going to drive us towards London. We'll stop outside Peasmarsh. We can talk there.'

They drove on in silence, the roads almost empty. The moon had replaced the sun and the countryside, which had been bathed in a golden light, was now all shadows and silver. Jack took Beatrice's hand and held it on the steering wheel.

After some miles he turned off the main road onto a narrow lane and parked in an opening in the hedgerow: rough tracks showed where a plough and harrow had access. Taking her in his arms he held her close. 'It's your turn to speak but remember I love you.'

'I'll say practical things first. It's easier. I

agree with you about the church and only the five or six of us and yes, please, soon.' Smiling, she quickly kissed his cheek. 'But what if your parents want to stay in the house? Will Penelope stay there? And will she mind? And most important of all, Evie. She's still a child. Can I leave her with only Molly in Green Street and would Cousin Arthur let me? He's her guardian until she's twenty-five, you know.'

'Shall I try to answer all that before you start the impractical bit?' He opened the driver's door and stretched his legs. 'Let's sit outside on the running board. It's still warm.'

They sat facing a field of wheat, ripe, nearly ready for harvesting, studded here and there with brilliant red poppies.

'All right, in order, remind me if I forget something. My parents might, only might, stay one or two nights in a year. I don't think it would be good to live with anyone in the house, either Penny or Evie. I would ask my parents to give us the house legally and I would pay Penny for what would have been her half of it. She doesn't care about it at all, the house, I mean, and only uses her room. It doesn't have any associations for her, good or bad. Now Evie. She's not a child — no, Bea, let me finish. She's nearly twenty-one and not an average twenty-one. Neither of you has had a conventional upbringing and the effect on her has been to make her quite mature in some ways and quite selfish. I may be wrong but I also think she's very pragmatic. When she's twenty-one she's likely to lead her own life, anyway. Since we've been talking, though, I've had an idea. Penny and Evie get on so well that they might like to share the flat when we marry. It would help to keep your cousin Arthur quiet.'

That same look, Beatrice thought, whenever her cousin's name was mentioned, bitter and sad. Well, he would tell her one day. 'And as for his guardianship, after Evie becomes twenty-one, he is virtually only in control of what little money she has.'

'Let me think.' Beatrice stood up and walked a few yards until she was waist high in a field of wheat.

'Don't go any further,' he called. 'The man in the moon might turn you into a loaf of bread.'

'Yes, it all makes sense, and it's a wonderful idea, our sisters living together. I see that that's as far as we can plan . . .' Her voice trailed away.

'Come back, Bea, I can't hear you.'

But as she walked towards him he stood and turned his back towards her pushing his hands in his pockets and throwing back his head. 'Christ, I wish I could make you understand.'

'Try,' she asked gently. 'I want to understand. I don't want a friend, Jack. I want a lover. You hardly ever kiss me, and when you hold me you let me go suddenly as if you were frightened.'

'I am a little. Something happened. I'll try to tell you one day.' He spoke jerkily. 'I felt sick with myself and since then,' his voice was almost inaudible, 'I've led what's called a monastic life.'

She felt stubborn. She couldn't understand and didn't want to. 'You have a past. That's how you know what you want from your future and I want —'

He interrupted her, grabbing her shoulder. 'What do you want, Bea?' He kissed her mouth hard, bruising it. 'Is this what you want?' He took her small round breast roughly until she struggled. 'This? I'm an adult. I can't kiss you and stop politely. Do you want me to prove I want you? That I'm a man?' He snatched her hand and pressed it against his body then pushed her away. 'You wanted proof?'

'I'm sorry,' she was sobbing, 'forgive me. I'm stupid, I'm worse than a silly servant girl wanting kisses in the moonlight.'

'You're not silly, darling.' He had slumped

back on the running board. 'Do you understand a little now?'

'Yes, but let's meet early tomorrow morning and look for our church.'

He helped her into the car. 'I think we had better, it's obviously an emergency.'

'Eleven and tenpence?' Tilly couldn't take it in. 'Eleven and tenpence in the pound? Don't understand.' She concentrated on the pale blush pierrot frill she was making for the neck of Mrs Ashleigh's dress. It was supposed to conceal all her chins. Good idea, she thought.

'The councillors have gone to prison,' Letty spoke deliberately and slowly as if she was speaking to a child, 'rather than set the rate, see, 'cos it's too bleedin' much.'

'Orl right, orl right, and you want me to go to the town hall and complain with you. I'm ready for another blush pink, Molly.'

'There'll be thousands there now they're going to take the women councillors to prison, too.'

'If there's going to be thousands there, I won't be missed.'

Letty took the new needle and thread from Molly. 'I despair of you sometimes, Tilly. Are you coming, Molly?'

'Of course, specially if there's going to be

a band. The fife and drum always makes things a bit livelier.'

Letty scrumpled up all the paper patterns she had finished with and threw them at Molly with great accurary. 'I despair of both of you. There, now I'm hung up waiting for the sleeves. Would you ask Miss Bea if she's got Lady Smythson's sleeves ready? Even one would help.'

Molly crossed the corridor to the office. Better walk making a noise and knock loudly in case they're talking about 'it'. Daft to pretend she didn't know, but she hadn't been told so least said soonest mended.

'Miss Bea? Can I come in?'

Beatrice opened the office door. 'Of course, Molly. What do you want?'

'Letty needs sleeves, though she says one will do.' She wondered why they had stopped their sewing and were at those sketches again.

'White grosgrain would keep its shape best, and have the stock made of white chiffon.' Evangeline took another page from the sketch pad. 'It means that there'll be no contrast at the neck, though.'

'Is it a wedding dress you're planning for Miss Bea, then?' There now, thought Molly, it was out of her mouth and she had been so careful.

Evangeline and Beatrice exchanged glances.

'How did you know that I was getting married, Molly?'

'I didn't. I guessed you had an understanding with Mr Maddox and then the cook next door but one told me you'd had the banns read last Sunday at St Anne's. I hope you're not angry, Miss Bea, that your secret's out, and may I offer me congratulations?'

'Thank you, Molly.' Beatrice wasn't at all angry as she explained. She had not told Molly to protect her from the curiosity of Tilly and Letty. 'There will only be us, Mr Trenton and Mr Bunting at the ceremony. And, of course, you, Molly. But I don't want to tell everybody until the last minute.'

'I won't tell a living soul, not even Michael, and all they talk about in the workroom is the goings-on at Poplar.'

Evangeline hoped that Beatrice hadn't really taken in Molly's last remark. She intended going to the rally herself with Penelope, however much work there was.

'May I see?' Molly bent over the sketches.

Evangeline smiled. 'You may. But this isn't Bea's wedding dress, she's making that in the safety of her room and it's much simpler. No, this —' She broke off and turned to Beatrice. 'Do you think we're ready to discuss it with everyone, Bea?'

'Yes. Lets go in now.'

Molly hopped up and down eagerly. 'What's going on? Is it your wedding dress, Miss Evie?'

'No. And bring that sleeve.'

In the workroom Beatrice waited expectantly. 'Would you like us to leave the room so that you can discuss it?' she said.

The two girls looked at each other.

'I don't need to. What about you, Tilly?'

'No, work's work when all's said and done. I'd rather do overtime and work harder than you take on someone else and then we might all have to go on short time when the wedding dress is finished.'

Letty added seriously, 'This puts you on a different footing too. Wedding dress for the débutante of the year, and coming on top of Madame Roncard, the Belgian whatsit's wife.'

Beatrice moved materials on the long table and spread out five sketches. 'We had to think of something utterly different from Miss Bonner's previous dress, which was a delicate floaty chiffon and maribou. This is it.' She placed a copy of the *Tatler* open at a full-length photograph of a young woman in a wedding dress with a caption underneath: 'The Lady Elizabeth Harting on the occasion of her marriage to Captain the Hon. Dudley Wingley'. They all bent their heads over it.

'And it's exactly the same? No wonder she was angry, poor girl.' Tilly felt real sympathy for the Hon. Sybil. 'After all, you only get married once and to see your dress or exactly the same on someone else four days before . . .' She straightened up. 'Blimey! Oh, 'scuse me, please. Beg pardon, but — four days!'

'Yes, Rochelle's must have thought they would get away with it. The Wingleys' wedding was in Scotland. So now Evie will explain our design.'

Evangeline pointed to the main sketch. 'As you can see, it's based on a riding habit. A long, full skirt, a very tightly fitting top, cut to look like a jacket, revers, buttonholes, all copying the side-saddle design. The neck is filled in with a silk *faux* shirt and the stock will be made of pleated chiffon. The headdress will be a white matt satin bowler with white veiling, again exactly the same as if it was the real thing but all the veiling edged with seed pearls. We're hoping to get white glacé kid boots made in time and if so — and if she's got the nerve — little silver spurs.'

There was a stunned silence, broken by Letty. 'Likes horses, does she?'

Evangeline was exhausted. When Lady Bonner had telephoned this morning with her request, the conversation being punctuated by

311

grunts of fury from Sybil, she and Beatrice had agreed quite blithely to design and make a new wedding gown for Sybil. Now the reality had sunk in. Three and a half days precisely for the most important dress that they had ever made. All the materials were bought, trimmings, seed pearls and hat shape. Letty had a rough paper pattern and by midday tomorrow the toile would be ready. But tonight had to be got through first. Dinner with Arthur. Not as bad, though, as it might have been.

She dressed carefully. Her shortest dress, only just below the knee, a lilac blue pleated tunic cut like a tennis dress with only a thin white silk chemise and knickers underneath and her new flesh-coloured silk stockings. She had railed and complained when Beatrice had said she had to see him but Hugo, who had planned to come to London, had been amused.

'I'll take my mother out to dinner that night. Where are you dining?'

'Café de France.'

'And what time?'

'He's collecting me at seven. I told him that I had to be home early.'

'I'll see you there, then, with my mother.'

Beatrice regretted forcing her to go out now. She had suggested telephoning Arthur and postponing it.

'No. I'll get it over with,' Evangeline had said philosophically.

Beatrice was going to work with Letty on the toile for the skirt and then have a late supper with Jack.

The front doorbell rang. Arthur was early. Evangeline looked into the workroom where Letty and Beatrice were busily cutting and Tilly already sewing seed pearls on the veiling.

'You look ever so lovely, Miss Evie.'

'Yes. Nice of you to put on your favourite dress for Arthur.'

'Well, Bea, I don't suppose Arthur will be the only man in the restaurant.'

She smiled like a child with the run of a sweetshop.

'You are growing up to be a very pretty young woman, you know, Evangeline.'

Arthur had sped round the car when they arrived to help her out. He didn't want some doorman johnny touching her, looking at her legs.

'Growing up, Cousin Arthur? Surely, like Topsy, I'm growed.'

I wish she wouldn't call me cousin, Arthur thought. It spoils it all.

The waiter pulled out the table and helped Evangeline in. Hugo was already there at the next table facing her. Arthur sat down with

313

his back to Mrs Bunting. 'Champagne, Evangeline?'

'Wonderful, Arthur. I love champagne.'

They looked at their menus. Hugo was speaking to his mother, smiling fondly at her. Or was the smile for Evangeline? When his mother looked up to the waiter arriving with their first course, he did look directly at her but not with a smile. It was that look that she had begun to recognize. To others he might appear stern or in pain, but she knew it meant that he wanted her.

He had ordered an artichoke with Hollandaise sauce. She would have the same and if she could guess what he had chosen next it would be a good omen. 'After the artichoke, I'd like the *loup de mer en croûte,* Arthur.'

'Good girl.' He wasn't so much pleased about what she had ordered as the fact that she had dropped the 'cousin'.

'I want to talk to you not only in the position of your guardian, Evangeline, but as someone, a man, who has your best interests at heart and someone who indeed hopes that those interests can be furthered to the goodwill and satisfaction of both of us with regard to your future and what it holds and where it lies, bearing in mind your youth and the suitability of that future not being far away and holding more in it than a life of commerce, be it lucrative or not, in so far as a life without another person is not the life that can be lived without an emptiness of purpose and unfulfilment, given that in the natural course of time it is what everybody who cared for you would agree.'

What on earth is he talking about? Evangeline thought, as she gazed winningly at him between mouthfuls of artichoke.

'Er, I seem to have lost my thread.' Arthur ate his lobster cocktail hurriedly. Lord! He had never been any good with young women like this. That's why Cadogan Mews was such a godsend.

'Don't worry, Arthur.' Evangeline smiled sweetly. 'I think I understand.' Suddenly the sweet smile grew and lit up her face. The girl was obviously enjoying herself. He knew that she would be more responsive away from her spinster sister.

But Evangeline had just heard the Buntings' waiter say, 'And for Monsieur, the *loup de mer en croûte*.' Feiguing a deep interest in Arthur's further convolutions, she ran the tip of her forefinger along her upper lip, hoping to convince both Arthur of her thoughtful interest and Hugo of her memories of their intimacy.

Each time Arthur's baroque ramblings dried up, she would regale him with amusing stories of their clients' peculiarities. She was animated and entertaining.

'I am so enjoying my evening with you, Evangeline.' Arthur leant forward and patted her hand. She snatched it away as if bitten by a snake.

'Sorry,' she apologized, 'but my hands are tender from all the work. Yes, Arthur, I've enjoyed it, too. Thank you.'

'In that case it must be repeated as often as possible, don't you think?'

She could see Hugo paying the bill. He looked at her, pointed to his wristwatch and gestured to the door. She nodded, smiling. Did that mean he would meet her at Green Street? Arthur presumed her smiling nod was an agreement.

'That's settled, then, my dear.' This was more than he had hoped for. 'Raspberries or Diplomat Pudding? I know you ladies prefer to indulge your sweet tooths or teeth, or, er, tooth, rather than cheese.' He had drunk quite a lot of wine. The girl had only sipped hers and hadn't finished her champagne. Quite as it should be. He didn't want to be married to a heavy drinker. The thought of marriage brought a foolish smile to his flushed face. 'What do you say?'

Hugo had gone. Evangeline gave Arthur her full attention and with an air of grave responsibility said, 'No more for me, Cousin Arthur. I have work to finish when I get home. It was a little unfair of me to come out, anyway. Poor Beatrice will be slaving away without me.'

Damned 'cousin' again. It was thinking of her sister that did it. Rather ungraciously he asked the waiter for the bill. 'I can get coffee and brandy at my club if you can't wait for that.'

'Good idea,' Evangeline said, smiling brightly.

In the car home he was silent. He longed to hold her hand but her hands were clasped round her little handbag, out of reach. Funny that, didn't know that needlework hurt the hands.

'Goodnight, Arthur, and thank you again.' She pecked him on the cheek and, turning, opened the front door with her latch key. Was there a slight movement of a shadow in the basement steps? Smiling again at Arthur she walked in and closed the door.

Pretty, pretty little thing, Arthur smiled to himself. Now, what he needed was a large brandy and soda. Two large brandies and a good think.

Evangeline waited in the hall. It was only nine thirty. Beatrice wasn't in. She heard the sound of Arthur's car drive away and waited. Nothing. Disconsolately she opened the door and looked down the street. A policeman pushing a bicycle, two men in top hats and tails striding towards North Audley Street closely followed by two women almost running to keep up with them and a barrow boy pushing his barrow loaded with violets, roses and carnations. The policeman must have moved him on, she thought.

She turned to go back into the house. There was a sudden movement behind her and an arm came past her pushing the door open. She didn't need to look. She knew it was Hugo. He followed her in and closed the door. Taking her by the arm he opened the workroom door and pulled her in, shutting it behind them. She started to speak but he put his finger on her lips and led her into the fitting room. The gaslight from the street was shining through the unlit workroom, dispelling some of the shadows in the smaller fitting room. He took her handbag away from her, putting it on a large gilt chair. She was facing the three-cornered mirror. He put his hand under her skirt and gently removed her cream silk knickers, slipping them carefully over her shoes, then, tilting her slightly forward so that her hands had to clasp the back of the chair, he lifted her skirt at the back and pushed himself inside her. They seemed to be there forever. She could see him in the mirror as he moved in and out of her, slowly. Even in the near darkness of the room she knew he was looking at her face, as he always did. It was as if her reactions excited him as much as the physical act itself.

The sound of a key in the door startled her, then she heard Beatrice's muffled voice as she closed the front door. Jack was with her. Evangeline straightened her back involuntarily. Hugo took her firmly round the waist, pushing faster and faster. The incongruity of lovemaking while they were fully clothed and the danger of her sister's proximity excited her. She shook violently as he held on to her, releasing her only as her quivering subsided. He turned her slowly to face him and brushing her hair away from her ear whispered, 'Only wonderful.'

He left when she opened the front door pretending it was her arrival, then she turned and walked back into the house, knocked on the door of the sitting room and called, 'It's me. I'm just going to change into something comfortable.'

'No, no, come in.' Beatrice opened the door.

'Yes,' Jack called, 'if that's my favourite sister-in-law-to-be.'

She stood uneasily just inside the door, longing to go to her room. She was aware of her nakedness beneath her chemise and of the silk knickers crushed into her tiny handbag.

'You are wonderful, Evie, going out with Arthur. It's such a help.'

'It wasn't as bad as I thought it would be.' Evangeline hated being praised so generously by her sister. She didn't deserve it.

'He might even tell you more about Papa.' Beatrice regretted mentioning her father the minute she saw the reactions on both faces. Jack turned away and his face darkened while Evie's shoulders sagged as if with the weight of the world. She rapidly changed the subject. 'We've heard from Jack's parents, so sad, they can't get here in time for the wedding, but they'll be here for Christmas.'

'Must be a long journey.' Evangeline smiled.

'And Penny did something wonderful for us today. Oh, Evie, do sit down. Don't hover there.'

'No, Bea, I'm tired. Tell me about Penny and then I'm going to say goodnight.'

'Yes, darling, whatever you like. Well, you remember the little boy we came across on the bomb-site in Woolwich? The one with shoes like old cardboard boxes? Jack told Penny about him and said we'd like to find him and buy him some shoes. She took the

320

photograph Jack had done of him and went to three schools in the area and she found him!'

'Oh, Bea, Jack, that *is* wonderful. Did she get him the shoes?'

Jack got up out of the armchair and put his arm round Beatrice. 'She got him forty pairs of shoes.'

'What?'

'My sister bought a pair of shoes for every child in the class and do you know what she said? It's our wedding present.'

Evangeline lay spreadeagled on her bed covered only by a light cotton sheet. Her bedroom window was open and she had just heard midnight strike from the church in South Audley Street where Jack and Beatrice were to be married. In three weeks' time! The night was still warm and she kicked off the sheet. Even her cotton nightdress was too hot. Life was stupendous. In three weeks everything would change yet again. Beatrice would move to Jack's house and she would have this flat all to herself with Molly tucked away in the basement. She would have freedom without loneliness. Not that Beatrice knew this yet: she still thought that Penny would be moving in with Evangeline and this wasn't a total lie. Penny would come here until her own large flat in Bloomsbury Square was ready. She was going to share it with two people, one of them Miss Rogers, her friend from the Mission. Like the forty pairs of shoes, it was typical of Penny. Miss Rogers was a penniless forty-year-old spinster living in a cramped room in a boarding house that smelled of gas and overcooked cabbage. She addressed envelopes for a living and worked at the Mission for pleasure. Penny had used part of the money given to her by her parents as compensation for Jack now having the house to take a long lease on a flat in Bloomsbury big enough to rent a room to her friend at the same price as the boarding house, and big enough to accommodate Hilary. When Penny had first talked about Hilary, Evie had presumed that she was referring to a woman but gradually the fact that Hilary was a man became obvious. He was working for the Hogarth Press learning to be a printer and had printed some political pamphlets for Penny. What wasn't obvious was his position in Penny's life. Friend or lover? There was no point in asking her; she didn't discuss her private life; she would talk about facts but never intimacies. Once when visiting the Bloomsbury flat Penny had explained where the sitting room would be, the dining room, Miss Rogers's bedroom, her bedroom, the small study; but although she'd told Evangeline he would be staying there she didn't mention where. Then, looking out of one of the windows across Gordon Square, she had pointed to a house opposite, saying casually, 'Some writer friends of Hilary's live there.' Evangeline had been a little jealous of these friends once, but now that Hugo was in her life she felt gracious about the relationships of her nearest and dearest. Beatrice could get married, Penny could live with her friend and Molly was permitted her understanding with her footman.

It had been difficult to persuade Penny to be less than truthful about moving to Green Street. In fact it had been impossible. She had agreed only after a long talk with Beatrice and Jack about their plans. It was clear from Beatrice's anxiety about leaving Evangeline and Molly that the marriage would be delayed if her senses of guilt and responsibility were increased. Guilt and responsibility utterly misplaced in Penny's point of view. Though oddly Hugo had understood. 'She's been partly responsible for you since you were born, and if Molly's mother married and returned to Ireland when you and she were both fourteen, Beatrice has been wholly responsible for you both since then. She took the place of your mother and compensated for a less than adequate father.'

It was easy to discuss Papa with Hugo. He

listened attentively and gave advice when asked. 'Evangeline, don't pester Beatrice with questions about his past. He's dead. The blackmail died with him. She may not be able to bear knowing the reason for it and you don't need to know. Your sister needs to look after somebody. Jack needs somebody to look after him. When they're married she's likely to transfer her sense of duty to him and she might be able finally to accept what I would guess to be the pain and disloyalty inflicted on her mother.'

'My mother too.'

'Don't ask for the same sympathy, because it isn't the same situation.'

'You make Jack and Bea sound like a nurse and patient. Don't you think that they love each other?'

He had been shocked at her question. 'Of course they do. You can tell that they're in love, just as you can see that Molly and Michael are not. They *want* to be. It would be suitable. But they're not.'

They had been standing in the little sitting room in Green Street looking out of the long windows at two large marmalade cats stretched out on their backs in the sun in the tiny paved garden. Hugo had laughed.

'Look at them. Do you think they're sunbathing?'

'What about us?' she'd said after a while.

'Us? Oh, we're like those two marmalade cats. We have a place in the sun.'

Evangeline turned restlessly onto her stomach then pushed one of the overstuffed down pillows onto the floor. He never talked when they were making love and never discussed it after. He was like two people. A platonic friend and a passionate lover. I'll never sleep if I think about that. Arthur, I'll think about Arthur. That will put me to sleep.

The sisters were up at six thirty in the morning, organizing.

'Everything that isn't Sybil's dress leaves the workroom, Evie, do you agree?'

'Yes, but where will it all go? We'll still be working on a few other things, other essentials.'

Beatrice spoke with quick efficiency as she pinned her hair up. 'All the bales of material in the kitchen. Will you run down and tell Molly to scrub the floor and put an old sheet down in the corner where the rocking chair is, and Jack said we could have a table from his studio.' Beatrice put the last pin in her hair. 'I'll put that in our office.' She looked at Evangeline. 'What time did you get up? You're all ready.'

'I didn't sleep well, it's so hot, can't believe

it's September. I got up at five thirty, had a cold bath and made my bed. I'll go down to the kitchen now.' Half-way down the stairs she called up, 'I'm taking the grey cashmere with me, and shall I tell Molly to make tea and toast?'

Beatrice leant over the banister. 'Good idea. Then when we've got that done we can put everything else in the office.'

When Letty and Tilly arrived at eight thirty, the workroom was cleared of everything except the sketches of the wedding dress, yards of white grosgrain and veiling, needles, pins, scissors, reels of white silk thread, the bowler-hat shape in buckram and fine cotton for the toile.

Letty bustled in and took the old work-plan off the wall. 'You're ahead of yourselves, you must have been up with the lark.' She pinned another work-plan on the wall. 'If Miss Evie works with me on cutting the toile and Tilly starts the pearl beading that'll free you, Miss Bea, to get on with Lady Bonner's dress and we'll have them both ready for fittings at, what, eleven is it they're coming?'

Beatrice was amused. 'Yes, eleven. You could have been a sergeant major, Letty.'

'Begging your pardon, Miss, hope I haven't overstepped the mark. Only trying to be useful.'

'And so you are, we're very grateful.' Beatrice turned and smiled at Tilly who had already started the arduous and monotonous task of sewing tiny seed pearls to the edge of a full-length veil. 'Grateful to both of you.'

The quiet atmosphere of concentration in the workroom was broken by the appearance of the Bonners. Even the normally placid Elizabeth was bordering on hysteria, while for Sybil it was in full swing.

'Is this it? Is this all you've done? Where's the hat? What about the boots? Did you call Belissi's about my last?' She calmed down a little when Evangeline explained they had also cut the skirt, the hat was being covered by Beatrice, Tilly was beading and the shoemaker had promised that the white kid boots would be ready.

Lady Bonner had her fitting in the office with Beatrice while the Honourable Sybil was taken to the fitting room by Letty and Evangeline. She examined herself closely in the triple mirror as Letty, on her knees with a mouthful of pins, adjusted the kick pleat of the skirt. Evangeline rested her hand on the back of the gilt chair and looked at them both in the mirror. In her mind's eye she replaced the figure of Sybil with that of Hugo.

'Keep still, please, Miss,' Letty growled, as

Sybil twisted, flirting with her image in the mirror.

'It's going to be absolutely extraordinarily wonderful, Evie. Such a pity about the page boys.'

'Why?' Evangeline came out of her reverie. 'What's the matter with them?'

'Well, they're dressed as Watteau shepherd boys.'

'Ah, I see. They ought to be dressed as little huntsmen, in pink.'

The minute it was out of her mouth she regretted it. Sybil shrieked with approval. 'You are brilliant, Evie. It would be too, too sweet!' Evangeline's face showed complete dismay. 'Oh, I suppose not.' Sybil grimaced with disappointment. 'You wouldn't have enough time.'

Removing the pins from her mouth, Letty looked up at the Honourable Sybil. 'Yes, we would, Miss.'

'We would?' Evangeline eyed Letty with horror.

'Yes, Miss Evie,' she said firmly.

Tilly filled her glass from the large bottle of ginger beer on the kitchen table. 'It's like this, see, Letty's right, turn work down and they'll go to the person who *does* do it again. Better not take the chance.'

Beatrice pushed her plate aside. 'So Molly

will go to Gieves and buy a child's hacking jacket for us to use as a model, pick up the pink gaberdine and everything else at Digby and Gordon. Keep a taxi waiting everywhere, Molly, and come straight back.'

'That was lovely cheese, Molly.' Tilly got up from the table, and went to the sink to wash her hands.

'It's Irish cheddar, I got it at Jackson's.'

'Surprise, surprise.' Evangeline laughed. 'I think you'd like to be buried at Jackson's.'

'If you don't mind, I'll have a rest from the pearls and work on the chiffon stock, Miss Bea.'

'Good, yes, Tilly.'

As soon as everybody had finished their bread and cheese Beatrice summed up the work. 'When Molly returns, Letty will supervise her work on the loose tacking, I will continue with, and hope to finish, Lady Bonner's dress, and work on the bowler hat and maybe Aunt Lydia's garden party coat. Letty will complete cutting the wedding dress, Evie will start work on the sleeves which are already cut, and at Molly's return both Letty and Evie will take the little hacking jacket apart and make patterns. First I'll telephone Lady Bonner and tell her we'll be ready for the six little boys to fit at ten o'clock tomorrow morning.'

She leant back against her chair exhausted at the thought. Noticing Letty's stricken face, she sat up. 'What is it, Letty?'

'It's about tomorrow, Miss Bea, it's September the fifth.'

'And?'

'And it's the day they're arresting the women councillors at Poplar Town Hall.'

'And?' Beatrice's voice had taken on a note of acid.

'And I have to go to the demonstration. I must, Miss Bea, I'd be a traitor to my class if I didn't,' Letty said desperately.

'You'd rather let us down, would you?'

'No, Miss, no, I'll work ever so late tonight to make up and tomorrow, no charge.'

'I see. So we are to be kept up until midnight, are we, to assuage your Bolshevik conscience?'

'I couldn't have known we'd be so busy, Miss Bea.'

'We *are* so busy because it was *you* who rashly accepted more work. Tell me, Letty, approximately what time could you pop in tomorrow?'

Letty flinched at Beatrice's sarcasm. 'It should all be over by eleven the latest, Miss Bea. I'm ever so sorry, honestly, and I will make it up to you.' She hated grovelling but she knew that, strictly speaking, right

330

was not on her side.

'Then I presume it will be safe for me to inform Lady Bonner that you will be available at half past eleven tomorrow.' Beatrice said this with icy politeness as she left the kitchen.

There was silence in the room for a while, broken by Tilly. 'You must be daft or something, Letty. What difference are you going to make in three thousand?'

'If three thousand people think like that there'll be nobody,' Letty said defensively. 'I don't suppose you'll be going now, Miss Evie?' Evangeline shrugged; she had been resigned about not going since the advent of the Bonner wedding.

Molly was scandalized. 'Of course you can't go, Miss Evie.'

'No, of course I can't.'

The quiet of the workroom was punctuated only by the occasional request.

'Anyone seen my thimble?'

'Pass me those pins.'

Molly was heard from time to time asking for approval. 'This what you had in mind?'

Letty, who was determined to prove her worth, was working swiftly and methodically. Having finished cutting the grosgrain for the wedding dress she had unstitched the little hacking jacket and bravely cut into the very expensive fine pink gaberdine, muttering, 'I

331

hope those mothers got their little darlings' measurements right.' The trouble was, the more work that was done the more there seemed to do. Letty was relieved that Beatrice was working in the office now, although when she saw how well they were doing she ought to calm down.

At seven o'clock their concentration was broken by the unexpected arrival of Daphne Haycock. Molly wisely showed her into the office. Let Miss Bea deal with her, she thought.

'We both need new dresses, same colour, style and everything, but those old ones are falling apart.'

'What have you been doing with them?' Beatrice stitched the pleated satin to the bowler hat, barely glancing at her visitor, who kicked off her shoes and sat cross-legged on the table bearing Madame Roncard's half-finished evening dress and Aunt Lydia's coat.

'Please, Daphne, get off that table.'

'Sorry.' She slipped off it, managing to pull everything on the floor. 'Oh, bloody hell, I'd better go.' Bending, she picked it all up and replaced it untidily.

'Yes, I think you had. We'll make you and Renée new dresses but we can't start them for at least a week. Why do you want them?'

'Haven't you heard?' Daphne sounded outraged. 'We are the most popular cabaret singers in London. Since that party we've been working at Jill and Jill's. People stand on tables, we're full every night, women scream when we appear.'

'That's good, is it?' Beatrice said drily. 'It obviously suits you, I think you've put on weight.' Daphne looked aghast. 'Oh, only about half a pound, don't worry.'

'It's Renée, she makes me eat.' Daphne started rummaging through her handbag. 'Get Jack to bring you. Oh, damn,' she snapped the handbag shut looking distracted, 'got to go anyway, got to pick something up in Cadogan Mews. Bye-bye.'

Beatrice put the hat down. 'What sort of something?' she said, trying to keep her tone casual.

Daphne paused at the door. Stupid thing to say, she thought, under the circumstances. 'Just something I left somewhere,' she said brightly. 'See you soon.'

Lydia watched Arthur mix her drink; he was making her a Royal Smile — gin, grenadine and lemon juice with lots of crushed ice — and he was being charming about it. No bother, he'd said, it's the latest cocktail, good on a warm evening. He had come home early from the office in a good mood and was dining at home. Unusual behaviour; Lydia wondered what was behind it.

'Here you are, Mother. Tell me what you think.' He mixed his own usual whisky and soda, though Lydia noticed that the proportions were not balanced in favour of the whisky as was his normal practice. 'Delicious, I really like it, thank you, darling.'

He sat in the only comfortable chair in the room, an old armchair that had escaped the interior decorator's improving hand, the only chair that wasn't covered in slippery silk.

'Did you have a drink on the way home?'

'Why?' He looked genuinely surprised.

'Your whisky, you've put quite a lot of soda in it.'

He laughed self-consciously. 'Don't want to go to bed in a swinish stupor every night, getting too old for all that.'

She laughed with him. There was no doubt at all in her mind: something was up, but he would tell her when he felt like it, no use probing. She entertained him with the story of her day which included malicious gossip about her best friend, luncheon at Claridge's with the Crawleys, where she'd eaten oysters and grouse, depressing Chips who had to pay, and a massage from her new masseuse who had told her she still retained the body of a thirty-year-old. 'And you know, Arthur, I

334

told her I wasn't pleased. No, I said, I know women of thirty who look like elephants, both in size and quality of skin.'

Neither of them wanted another drink, and when dinner was announced Arthur took his mother by the arm and led her into the dining room. 'This is charming, I feel as if it were my birthday.'

The young footman pulled back her chair to seat her saying, 'Good evening, Lady Eliott,' then rushed to Arthur's side where he had already seated himself.

'Oops, sorry, missed you that time.' Arthur raised his eyebrows, but Lydia shook her head.

'Don't worry, Josiah, you'll get used to it. Give Mr Eliott the wine to taste and serve the soup.'

Josiah handed an open bottle of Corton Charlemagne to Arthur and when he had served the *consommé en gelée* he withdrew.

'Isn't he priceless? He's Mrs Pontings's son, just up from the country. This is his first evening serving.'

Arthur squeezed a little lemon juice on his soup and tried it. 'Cook's son? If he learns to buttle as well as she cooks you'll be all right.' He poured a little more wine for her and, after silently finishing the soup, said with studied casualness, 'About the country, Mother.'

Ah, at last, Lydia thought. So, it was something to do with Stanton House. 'Yes, my darling. Would you like a little more soup? If not, I'll ring for Josiah.'

'No. Very good, though.'

She rang the little silver bell that sat on the table. 'He must light the candles, too, it's getting dark. What about the country, Arthur? You were saying?'

Josiah entered carrying a long white dish which he placed on the hotplate on the sideboard. Removing the soup plates with a flourish and replenishing the wine with great formality, he served Lydia from the white dish.

'*Beignets* of sole, Madame,' he announced with gravity, spoiling the effect by adding, 'Lovely.'

When he had lit the candles and withdrawn, Lydia tried the sole. 'He's quite right, it is lovely.'

'Yes, yes,' Arthur said irritably. He had waited too long and now he was losing courage.

'Do go on. Poor love, you keep being interrupted.'

'I'd like you to ask Evangeline to Stanton for the weekend,' he said in a rush. 'We had an interesting time together last night, she clearly cares a lot about my opinions and things and er . . . and I'd like you to ask her to Stanton for the weekend.'

'As you've already said.' Lydia helped herself to some more sauce. 'Eat your *beignets* while they're still hot — they lose their lightness when they're cool, they turn into indigestible lumps.' Arthur dutifully ate his sole, waiting for a reply and fortifying his courage with the white burgundy.

'Both of them?' Lydia broke a roll into pieces and mopped up her sauce. 'I suppose we should. They're very busy at the moment, you know. Of course you know, you dined with Evangeline last night. They've got the Bonner girl's wedding, which is a great coup even though they were second choice, Jeanne Roncard is trying them out with a ballgown for a State dinner and Lady Smythson sent her granddaughter and liked the dress so much she's ordered from their autumn collection, and I hear she's asked them to Wellthorpe.'

Arthur waited for her to finish. How did she find all this out? His mother had always been amazingly up-to-date with gossip, some of which he was sure was either embellished or entirely manufactured.

'Not both of them, Mother, just Evangeline, it would give us an opportunity to get to know each other better, away from the influence of Beatrice.'

Lydia examined the white dish that had held the sole. 'I was going to offer you more, darling, but there isn't more. Mrs Pontings will be pleased with us.' She rang the bell and, wiping her mouth delicately with a white linen napkin, she said nonchalantly, 'Why do you want to get to know your little cousin better?' The slight emphasis she put on the word cousin warned Arthur where the resistance would lie.

'I like her, Mother, I've always had a soft spot for her, she's a dear girl. And she's . . . well . . . she's . . . unspoiled and . . .'

'And she is your cousin.' Lydia knew she could win this battle but hoped it would be possible without losing her dignity and his respect. If necessary, though, she was prepared to forfeit both. 'Ah, Josiah, what have you got for us now?' The young footman cleared away the remnants of the previous course aware of the tension in the room: just as he had entered a muffled 'damnation' had escaped from Mr Eliott's mouth. Presenting the claret, which the butler had decanted, he suddenly snatched it back and turning a red face to Lydia he said in a broad Suffolk accent, 'Should Oy've done the meat first, m'lady?'

'No, no. You're doing very well. Let Mr Eliott try the Cos-d'Estournel and then present the meat. What is it, Josiah? I've forgotten what I ordered.'

Arthur sipped the wine and nodded to Josiah to fill the glasses. Josiah cleared his throat, he was dreading this. His mother had coached him in the kitchen but it was a different thing saying all that in front of them. 'Lamb,' he announced, hoping that would do.

'Lamb?' Lydia repeated.

Yere goes then, he thought. 'Lamb noisettes Cussy.' He beamed from ear to ear, so far so good. Lydia gestured for him to continue. 'Lamb,' he said again, and then without pause or punctuation he rattled off, 'sautéedonfriedcroûtonsartichokeheartsfilledwithmushroompuréecock'skidneyssauceMadeira.'

'Delicious,' Lydia said with approval. Arthur could see his mother was anticipating it with relish — and, after grouse and oysters for luncheon, amazing. After serving the lamb and all its accoutrements, Josiah walked out of the room carrying a tray of dishes with his head held high. He'd done his mother proud.

'Exactly,' Arthur said suddenly. 'She's my cousin, which means there are no nasty surprises, I know all about her.'

Poised with a forkful of artichoke in her hand, Lydia regarded her son. 'Are we still talking about Evangeline?'

'You know we are, Mother. And there is

339

no need to worry about the blood tie of cousins —'

A loud crash was heard in the hall followed by a clearly articulated, 'Well, bugger me.' The footman's head had been held too high and the tray and its contents were strewn at the bottom of the stairs.

Arthur picked up his glass and finished the wine. 'This is ridiculous, it's impossible to speak for more than a few seconds without that buffoon interrupting.'

'Oh, ignore that,' Lydia said, waving her hand at the door. 'He'll learn and while he's learning he isn't costing anything and the plates are all oddments from different sets and the nursery.' She held out her empty wineglass to be filled. 'You say I'm not to worry about the blood tie of cousins, Arthur, why not?'

He filled both their glasses, noticing a slight tremor in his hand. Thank goodness he'd got his wits about him, that he'd held back from the whisky. 'Because,' he said triumphantly, 'neither the Church nor the law are against it, as proven by the Consanguinity and Affinity Act.' Now he'd said it, nothing she could say or do about that. He would enjoy his lamb. Very good, not too heavy. Wonder what the difference is between a cock and a hen's kidney.

Lydia placed her knife and fork carefully on her plate and pushed it away. Then she rang the little silver bell. Arthur looked up from his lamb, surprised, 'You've finished, Mother? Not like you.'

'This discovery of yours, Arthur, the Consanguinity and . . . ?'

'Affinity Act,' he completed for her with his mouth full.

'This discovery was necessary for you to be able to consider marrying your cousin Evangeline?' Lydia felt tired, she spoke flatly without emotion.

'Not a surprise to you, was it? I've dropped plenty of hints. But it was last night, Mother, I knew I stood a chance.' His face was happy and confident but Lydia knew she was about to destroy both his happiness and his confidence.

'Your pudding, m'lady.' Josiah stepped hesitantly into the room. The thin veneer of his self-esteem had been punctured by his mother's contempt, she had even boxed his ears. In the same flat voice Lydia told him to clear away and leave the pudding, they'd serve themselves.

As Josiah left the room he pointed to the pudding and mouthed timidly, *'Mont Blanc aux marrons.'*

Left alone with his mother, Arthur felt uneasy: her mood had changed. 'You'll get used to the idea and it's time I settled down.'

She turned her chair to face him. 'I'm sorry, Arthur, it's out of the question, you can't marry Evangeline.' She'd never thought this would be necessary; she'd been aware of her son's little pash on the girl, but thought it hadn't been reciprocated. Evangeline must have tired of work and knew a good marriage when she saw one.

'Don't make it difficult, Mother, she won't come between us. You'll always be my number one girl,' he said gallantly. 'And I won't be able to fall in love with anyone else after Evangeline,' he smiled at her, 'I know that.'

She stared at him for a while and then said simply, 'You can't marry Evangeline. She's your sister.'

Arthur pushed his chair away from the table. His face crumpled like a child's about to cry, he said stuttering, 'I don't understand.'

'I think you do.' Lydia's voice was firm and cold. 'I was Henry's mistress.'

'What do you mean? When?' he said helplessly.

'I was always Henry's mistress. I met him before I married your . . .' She had been going to say father but that pretence was no longer necessary. 'Before I met Richard.'

Arthur looked at her with loathing. 'You

fathered your illegitimate child on its father's brother?'

She shrugged. 'I had no choice. Richard and I had been married for three years, we were no longer . . .' she paused trying to express the situation delicately to her son, 'we were no longer sharing the same bedroom.'

'Then he knew.' Arthur laughed. 'He, my uncle, my uncle who was my father, he knew.' He leapt to his feet and, opening a door in the sideboard, took out a bottle of brandy, filled his wine-glass and took a large drink. His mother was speaking as if she were discussing an unfortunate incident.

'I tried to, well, cover things up. When I knew I was pregnant, I arranged things. Richard was still attracted to me even if we weren't on good terms so I, shall we say?, seduced him. But although we never discussed it, I knew he didn't believe he was your father. That was when he bought Stanton and what money he didn't spend on that went on his research.' She filled her glass with the remains of the claret. He'll get over it, she thought. It was rather a relief talking about it, there had never been anyone else she trusted. 'Of course, Richard was the better doctor and his research into tuberculosis —'

Arthur interrupted, 'Was that why he accepted a knighthood rather than a baronetcy

— because it was not hereditary?'

'I imagine that's the way he wanted it.'

He finished his brandy and poured another. His anger dissipating, he was left with self-pity. That stupid fat raddled woman sitting there had taken away in a matter of seconds his precious Evangeline and a father for whom he had had respect and admiration.

'Is that why Uncle Henry was being black-mailed?' he said, his voice thick and fuddled with alcohol and misery.

'Blackmailed? He wasn't being black-mailed.' She reached for the brandy. 'You've had enough, Arthur.'

'He was, I know, that's why he got involved with Cadogan Mews and mortgaged his house, he needed money. Saw his bank book. Lots of money taken out, no explanation. Give me back.' He lunged for the brandy bottle and nearly knocked it over but Lydia rescued it expertly. She filled his glass. He might as well pass out, she thought, Josiah could put him to bed.

'Not his only mistress, you.'

'I am well aware of that.'

'S'pose him not your only lover.' He ex-amined the pale amber liquid in his glass as if searching for the answers to life among the tea leaves at the bottom of a cup.

She smiled enigmatically. 'And you weren't

his only bastard, but you were his only son. Henry was a great believer in primogeniture, so all that unexplained money wasn't blackmail, it was for you, your education.'

'Ah, of course, explains why he gave me Cadogan Mews. He paid for Harrow, did he?' he mumbled to himself, and finished his brandy. Turning a red blotchy face to his mother he frowned and shook his head.

'Why, Mama, why?'

'Don't be ridiculous, Arthur. Why? He was a fascinating man. He knew women. Understood them.'

'Did he understand Aunt Sarah?' She had the grace to blush.

'And he was very handsome, you know that. Think of Evangeline, she gets all her looks from him.'

At the mention of Evangeline his head slumped to the table and his shoulders shook with sobs. She touched his arm but he jerked it away. Slowly she sipped her claret and thought about Henry. 'Why?' he'd asked. 'Why?' She'd had many lovers and Henry hadn't been the first but he was certainly the best. He could be cruel both in bed and out but that had been part of what intrigued her. She had no regrets about their rather volatile relationship, although a little flush of shame crossed her face when she thought about Sarah

Eliott and her pain. Henry had found it exciting, courting danger. Arthur's sobs had subsided and he was snoring. The swinish stupor he had intended to avoid had happened after all.

Although Tilly arrived early at Green Street — it was barely eight o'clock — Beatrice and Evangeline were already in the workroom. Both of them, using strong thimbles necessary for the thick material, were working on the jacket of the wedding dress, Evangeline making the collar and Beatrice the button-holes. At one end of the long table was a pile of pink gaberdine cut into shapes waiting to be fitted on the six little pageboys. The bowler hat, finished except for the pearl trimming, was sitting on top of the dressmaker's dummy.

'Oh, it's you, Tilly.' Beatrice looked up from her work. 'I heard a bell, I thought it was the telephone.'

'It was, Miss, well, it was both, me and the telephone. Molly said to say as how Nanny Bonner had rung up to say Miss Bonner would be here earlier, more like two than three and Lady Bonner would be later, more like four than three.'

'Huh.' Evangeline snorted. 'The Lord giveth and the Lord taketh away. Ouch, this material, ouch, it's difficult to work on.'

'Would you like me to take over, Miss?' Tilly settled herself in her usual chair with her back to the window: the light suited her better that way.

'No, you get on with the beading and when your eyes need a change, you can work on the cuffs.'

'And the hat is ready for trimming, too,' Beatrice added. 'I finished it last night.'

'You deserve all the success you get, you two, Miss Bea, Miss Evie, you work as hard or more as any labouring man I've ever known.'

'Thank you, Tilly.' Evangeline smiled across at the tiny figure bent over the yards of veiling. Tilly looked up and smiled back. Her smile filled the thin little face, revealing gaps in the row of crooked teeth. 'One doesn't always get what one deserves. Look at your father, for instance.'

'I know, but things is a bit better at home at the moment, what with me here full time and —'

'Overtime, Tilly,' Beatrice said firmly, 'and you'll be getting overtime money, too.'

'Lovely, Miss Bea, ta. And my dad e's been doing a bit better too. He usually gets a couple of half days a week, that's better nor what it was.' She spoke with such gratitude about such a small improvement in his lot that Beatrice, glancing at her sister, understood, perhaps for the first time, her involvement with Penelope Maddox and the East End Mission.

Molly heard the telephone ringing in the office as she was making Miss Evie's bed and hurled herself downstairs to answer it. She had to get there before it finished ringing three times. It had become a superstition with her: getting there on the third ring would bring good luck or at least stop bad luck, but she also had the mistaken belief that the charge started with the first ring. 'Hello,' she said, 'this is Mayfair four five three.' She heard the operator and then Mr Jack's voice.

'Molly? Get Miss Bea for me, will you?'

'No, I can't, sir, she's not to be disturbed, nobody is, not even me.' She heard him laughing.

'Working hard, are you? Well, remind her I'm working in Kensington Gore this morning and as I've got the motor, my sister's at some demonstration, I'll be there at lunch-time with lunch and will be her slave for the rest of the day.'

'That will be very useful, Mr Jack, the lunch and the motor.'

'And the slavery,' he said and hung up.

A car at your beck and call now, that would be nice, she thought. It would have been useful after the ceilidh the other night: they had missed the last bus home, had to walk most of the way and they'd been dancing most of the evening too. The driver of a hansom cab had taken pity on them half-way up the Edgware Road and driven them to Marble Arch for nothing.

'On his way home,' he had said. 'People not wanting the horse-drawn any more, they preferred the motor taxis.' She'd leaned against Michael in the comfortable old leather seat and he'd put his arm round her and given her a kiss, but his heart wasn't in it, she could tell, he was probably still thinking about that new army. Hadn't he talked all night, when he wasn't dancing, with that Patrick friend of his, talking about cells and battalions and units? Maybe he was planning to start a battalion of Irish footmen! She finished the bedrooms and started running downstairs to the basement. Clean apron, scrub her hands, then help out in the workroom. She liked that, liked the socialness of it.

'Who was on the telephone, Molly?' Evangeline called from the workroom

Molly put her head round the door. ' 'Twas Mr Jack to remind you, Miss Bea, he's working in Kensington but will be here in the motor car with your lunch and he's your slave all afternoon.' She cried to conceal her grin; she was only reporting the truth but Miss Bea looked quite uncomfortable.

Beatrice continued sewing but a blush spread across her face. 'Thank you, Molly, are you going to join us yet?'

'In two ticks.' She sped off down to the basement.

Really, Bea was silly, Evangeline thought, she might as well tell everybody about her engagement, it was quite clear, anyway, from their behaviour.

Beatrice looked at the clock. 'Quarter past eleven. I'd hoped Letty would be here by now to sort out those jackets.'

'Don't worry, Miss Bea, she won't let you down.' Tilly spoke with more confidence than she felt. She, too, had been looking anxiously at the clock since eleven.

'Let's prepare for the invasion of the pages.' Evangeline carefully draped the white top on the dummy.

'And the invasion of the nannies, they'll probably create more trouble than the children. Help me fix the skirt on the dummy, Evie, and Tilly, I think the veil will be safer in the office until they go.' The workroom was cleared and the little hunting jackets ready for fitting when sharp at half past eleven the first page and nanny arrived, but no Letty. Two hours later there was still no sign of her. Six little boys and six large nannies had been dealt with, tears had been mopped up and tempers had been cooled.

It had taken all four of them to sort out the errors of long sleeves on short arms, thin collars on fat necks and narrow waists on big tummies. Letty was supposed to have sorted each cut piece into individual piles for the boys. Only Molly's brilliant idea of taking all the nannies below stairs for a cup of tea enabled them to finish the fittings without also finishing the boys. There was one special little horror, the Honourable Rupert Jenks, who kept shouting, 'Pink is for girls. Pink is for sissies,' and nearly started a rebellion. That was stopped by an accurately aimed kick by the pint-sized Viscount Tighe of Tighe who followed it up with the calmly voiced threat, 'My father's an MFH and he's the bravest man in the field and he wears pinks. Take it back or I'll kill you.'

When the last nanny had left, Evangeline, Tilly and Molly had to deal with a Beatrice white-faced with fury. 'That took at least an hour longer than necessary. Not only has she' (Beatrice spat out 'she' as if it were a swear word), 'broken her promise to be here but she left all those pieces of jackets with no instructions and no clue as to whom they belonged and they're still in a total mess.'

'Something must've gone seriously wrong,

Miss, it ain't like Letty.' Tilly's gentle attempt to calm Beatrice was misguided: she didn't know her well enough to realize that any effort to quieten her produced the opposite effect.

'Wrong, Tilly, you're wrong, it's exactly like Letty, she's untrustworthy, unreliable. It's no wonder that such a talented worker should have needed to work in our little dressmaking business.' She pushed the dummy viciously, rocking it.

Evangeline stepped forward quickly and saved it. Catching Molly's eye, she felt a nervous giggle rising. 'Come on, Bea, it's not as bad as that, the jackets are pinned correctly now, one or two of them might need another fitting, that's all.'

'That's all? Sybil will be here in half an hour and the dress hasn't been assembled. The wedding is the day after tomorrow.' She picked up a box of pins. 'Well, we might as well start.' Her hands were shaking as she stabbed a pin into the waistband, and she dropped the box scattering pins across the floor. The doorbell rang at the same time, muffling her archaic curse, 'Hellfire and damnation.'

Molly, eager to escape before she laughed aloud, volunteered, 'I'll get it, might be her.'

Tilly dropped down on her hands and knees, reassuring Beatrice, 'Don't worry, the magnet will pick 'em all up.'

It wasn't Letty. They could hear the staccato delivery of Penelope followed by the low urgent tones of Jack. They burst into the workroom and with no preamble Penelope launched into the explanation of Letty's absence. 'Over three thousand there. Followed the women councillors when they left Poplar Town Hall to the parish boundary. Mounted police as well as police on foot controlling crowds, over-controlling in my opinion, crowd surged as women arrested, horses frightened. Saw Letty up near the front, policeman thrown, badly hurt, I'm afraid.'

'What about Letty?' Beatrice interrupted.

Jack could see she was containing her rage, but the pinched white face and trembling hands showed that the control might not last. 'Get on with it, Penny.'

'Shut up, Jack, and I will.' She continued, 'Anybody near the injured policeman was arrested, including Letty, and I believe her friend Charlie.' She took a breath and paused.

'How badly injured was the policeman?' Evangeline felt a little frisson of fear; she knew her friend didn't exaggerate.

'Very, may not live.'

'Oh, no, poor Letty — she could be charged with murder.'

'More likely manslaughter,' Penelope corrected Evangeline. 'But now, look here, don't

353

expect the worst, we've already —'

'Poor Letty?' Beatrice pushed her sister sharply. 'Poor Letty? Is that where your sympathy lies? Good God, Evangeline what about —'

'If the government hadn't demanded a grossly unfair rate,' Evangeline shouted, 'three thousand people wouldn't have had to demonstrate, over fifteen councillors wouldn't be in jail and no mounted policemen would be hurt.'

Penelope's voice rose above the sisters'. 'Waste of time, all this. After the riot, I went home. Jack telephoned the lawyer who's representing George Lansbury, friend of parents. He's gone to court, see if Letty's charged, put up bail. She'll probably be out some time today.'

'I'm going over there now,' Jack addressed this to Beatrice, 'and I'll bring her back here as soon as she's released.'

Penelope eyed the grand white dress draped on the dummy. 'Though the wedding dress of a spoilt débutante hardly seems an emergency in the circumstances.'

'Would you prefer us to join the two million unemployed, then, Penelope?'

Jack took Beatrice by the arm. 'I need to talk to you. Let's go to the office.' As he led her firmly away, he said quietly to Evangeline,

'There's lunch in the kitchen, Molly took the hamper down.'

Jack closed the door behind them, took Beatrice in his arms and held her tightly. 'My poor darling, you do suffer such rages.'

'Would you prefer I didn't?' She was still tense, her body rigid.

'No, I think you have to after a lifetime of controlling your feelings. It's part of you, and as I love every part of you I love that too.' She gradually relaxed in his embrace and kissed him. With his hand on the small of her back he held her to him. 'I want you so, my love.'

'I know,' she whispered.

When Beatrice, calm and with her colour returned, looked into the workroom she found three people industriously working.

'Oh, Bea, we decided not to have lunch yet, we'll have it after Sybil's fitting and before Elizabeth's. All right?' Evangeline meant all right in more senses than one.

'Yes, all right, in fact good idea.' Beatrice kissed her sister's cheek. 'With the three of you working on this I think I'll finish Elizabeth's dress and if nothing is wrong she can take it with her. Then if all goes well . . .' She sighed. All going well meant Letty being released and back at work today. They all knew that.

'We'll work till nine o'clock. If you can, Tilly?'

'Yes, Miss, I warned them at home, expect me when you sees me, I said.'

'Jack will drive you both home, if there is a both, and pick you up in the morning at seven o'clock.' Tilly's eyes widened with pleasure. A ride home and back, what a treat!

'Then tomorrow he'll drive Letty with the pages' costumes to all their houses where she can finish them off.' Beatrice smiled and added with a touch of humour, 'The costumes, not the pages. And we'll just work till we finish. Then Friday, Evie and I will cope with the wedding and get back as soon as we can while you three, pray God there are three, work on Madame Roncard's gown and Lady Eliott's garden party coat, and, oh, I can't think further than that.'

Just as well, Molly thought, she was tired even thinking about it. Lucky they was, though, that Mr Jack was in love with Miss Bea. She was back to normal now. He must have kissed her, she decided, slow and passionate. Like the Sheikh.

Tilly stared at the large hamper and its contents, which Molly was dishing out. 'I think I'd choose the little bouquet of flowers shaped like a winner's rosette if it was me, but nice to have a choice.'

'What made you think of the amaryllis, Miss Evie?' Molly put cold Bradenham ham and chicory and orange salad on everybody's plate and set the loaf and butter and cold rice salad on the table. 'Shall we save the salmon and cucumber for supper, Miss Bea?'

Beatrice nodded absent-mindedly. She was trying to work out alternative plans if Letty didn't come back. Evangeline sat at the table and cut the bread, handing some to Tilly.

'I thought of amaryllis when Sybil, Miss Bonner, was standing on the table while we were tacking the hem. I had a sort of picture of her in my head on the hunting field holding her crop and I absolutely knew she couldn't carry a conventional bride's bouquet wearing that dress, so . . .' she helped herself to more rice salad, 'this is delicious, it must have come from Jackson's,' she smiled at Molly, 'so, I wondered what flower would be the nearest to a crop or whip and I thought — amaryllis! It's long, quite thick, and straight,' she started to laugh, 'with a pink flower on the end.' The rice spluttered out of her mouth. 'Sorry, I'm getting hysterical.' She made an effort to control herself. 'And if the florist could attach a trail of silver ivy to the end . . .' She gave up and putting a napkin to her mouth she laughed uncontrollably. Beatrice hadn't been listening and regarded her sister with surprise, but Molly, who had a shrewd idea why she was laughing, joined in, then Tilly, who had no idea what the hilarity was about, laughed too out of relief and sympathy.

Jack heard them as he helped Letty out of the car. He peered down into the basement. Really, women were extraordinary, the young ones were helpless with laughter, and even Bea, though she seemed a bit bemused, was smiling.

'She's 'ere, she's 'ere.' Tilly looked up at the figure of Letty, pale and nervous, descending the basement steps. Molly rushed to the door and opened it.

'Are you all right, then?' Evangeline pulled out a chair. 'Sit down, Letty, have something to eat.'

'I'll be making you a cup of tea, hot and sweet, that's what you need.'

'Did — did Charlie, was he . . . ?' Tilly hesitated. 'Was he allowed out?'

The only person who didn't speak was Beatrice. Letty looked at her. 'Not much I can say, Miss Beatrice, but I'm truly sorry, and I'll work me fingers off to make up.' She held herself erect with a pathetic dignity. 'It's the class struggle, you see.' Then a shadow of doubt appeared, muting her voice, confusing her. 'Though the councillors, they've all gone on hunger strike. "We're starving in prison," George Lansbury said, bit of a toff really, "so you don't starve outside." '

'Nevertheless, Letty, I think Molly's right, something to eat and a cup of hot sweet tea.' Beatrice spoke gently.

Letty sat rigidly in her chair staring ahead. 'I've been bound over to keep the peace,' she said, 'but Charlie's been charged.'

Jack spoke quietly to Beatrice. 'I've got to go back to the court, my love, then I'll take Penny to the Mission, but I'll come straight back and be your errand boy.' He patted Letty's shoulder. 'Don't worry too much, the policeman is improving, they say.'

Letty lifted her face, 'Thank you, Mr Maddox. If it hadn't been for you and Miss Maddox . . . dunno what to say.'

Jack looked embarrassed. 'Drink your tea. I'll be back as soon as I can.'

Into the quiet after he left, as they finished their lunch, Letty said, 'He's a really decent bloke,' and looking round the table she added, 'And you're all decent blokes too.'

Her humble manner all but vanished when she saw the mess they had made of the pages' jackets. 'It's all up 'ere, up on me wall-chart, every measurement, every blinking one. I dunno, you lot need your brains examined.' Just as well Bea is fitting Elizabeth Bonner,

359

Evangeline thought.

'Strike me pink, Letty, we should've known better.' Tilly was relieved to see Letty nearly back on form.

'I can sort this lot out now, and tomorrow, if Mr Maddox is driving me, shouldn't take more than a couple of hours, so's I'll be back to finish the dress with you.' Eyeing Evangeline she said, 'You'll 'ave to undo that sleeve, Miss Evie, it'll be too tight with the lining in.'

Comparing her measurements with the jackets, she looked back on the morning's riot. What had she got out of it? What good had she done? For a start she'd got a police record now and a boyfriend who'd probably have to do time. And her job, where they'd given her responsibility and believed in her, well, she'd very nearly let them down completely. The jackets wouldn't have worked and as for the dress itself, she'd already had to straighten out one fault. She hoped nothing like it happened again, but if it did? She'd do the same, of course.

Molly finished packing Lady Bonner's dress in white tissue, put the lid carefully on the cardboard box and tied it with yellow ribbon. 'That's beautifully done, Molly, you must help me wrap my parcels at Christmas, I'm hopeless.'

Molly smiled. 'I'll take it out to your chauffeur, Lady Bonner.'

'I notice, Beatrice, that your boxes are always tied with the same colour ribbon as the dress, such a clever touch. I also notice you're looking very tired. This must have been a great strain for you. We both appreciate it very much. Sybil's thrilled, you know, much prefers it to Madame Rochelle's one.' She pressed an envelope into Beatrice's hand. 'Here, I'm settling the whole bill now, see you at nine o'clock Saturday morning. Pray for sun!'

Beatrice narrowed her eyes examining Molly, it would be a good idea, she was exactly the same size as Sybil except for her hips and that didn't matter. Not only would it save time but it would ensure no mistakes. 'Have you had a bath?' she said abruptly.

'Yes, Miss Bea.' Molly was hurt. 'Only yesterday, and today I had a good up and down with my flannel.'

'All right, all right,' Beatrice said hastily. 'We don't need the entire history of your ablutions. Put it on.' She indicated the wedding dress.

'Will I be needing me stays?'

'No, the bodice is boned.' Evangeline and Letty took Molly and the dress to the fitting room where oohs and ahs could be heard as

361

Molly gazed at herself with total approval, imagining herself on the arm of Rudolph Valentino.

Tilly was stitching what seemed to her the millionth little seed pearl to the long veil when Molly stepped shyly into the room. The dress fitted her perfectly. The tight boned bodice accentuated her narrow rib-cage and tiny waist and the chiffon stock knotted above the collar made her hold her head up and displayed her long neck. Tilly gasped. 'You look like Mary Pickford.' There was a tap-tap at the window.

'It's Hugo. Did you know he was coming, Evie?' Beatrice beckoned for him to come in. 'The door's open,' she mouthed.

'Course not. I told him I wasn't free till after the wedding.'

Hugo stopped as he entered the room, looking at Molly with undisguised admiration. 'Glorious,' he said softly. Evangeline saw him take in every detail of her: the narrow waist, small high round breasts, the tumble of glossy wavy hair above slightly flushed cheeks and dancing eyes. He hadn't even glanced at her once.

' 'Tis not mine,' Molly explained. 'It's the Honourable Sybil's, I'm only helping out with the fitting of it.'

'If there was any justice in the world, Molly,

it would be yours.' She dropped her eyes under his intense gaze. A little thrill of excitement had darted through her as she knew it had through him. 'But when you marry you won't need an elaborate dress, your own beauty will be sufficient adornment.' He tempered the high-flown compliment with a grin, which she returned, and the spell was broken. 'Sorry to disturb you all. I'm working nearby.' He turned to look at Evangeline for the first time. 'As you have to eat, Evangeline, will you eat with me? I could be here at eight o'clock, say, and promise to return you by eleven.' It was a statement, not a question. He expected her to say yes.

'No, Hugo, thank you, we're too busy.'

'You do have to eat, it will do you good to get out of the house.'

Beatrice thought she was being rather generous and was a little put out when Evangeline frowned at her and repeated, 'No. As I said, I would rather work.'

Hugo nodded. 'Of course, I understand.' He started to leave but as an afterthought, looked back. 'I'll come at eight o'clock anyway, in case you change your mind. I hope you do.'

'Right. Let's have a look at the back, Molly.' Letty turned her round. 'Look, Miss Evie, see the strain there? That centre bone should come out and those two seams be released a bit.

I think that's it, otherwise the whole thing can be finished off. What do you think?'

Evangeline made an effort to concentrate. 'I agree about the bone, Letty, but won't the material mark if we undo seams?'

'They're only tacked, won't show.'

'Good, what do you think, Bea?' She didn't hear her sister's reply. Had nobody noticed? Had she imagined it? She had felt humiliated. For her own maid to be so pointedly admired and in front of her and everybody else, too. Then for him to assume arrogantly that she was always available for him. No, she definitely would not go.

When Hugo arrived at eight, Evangeline was ready, dressed casually in a simple navy-blue and white cotton dress, which had taken some time for her mentally to choose. While sewing the cuffs on to Sybil's dress, she had alternated between her cream silk dress, which was so soft it fell against her body outlining every curve, and this one.

'I'm glad you changed your mind,' he said. 'I missed you.' She didn't reply, trying to work out how to tell him. 'You look like a schoolgirl in that dress.'

'That wasn't the idea.' They turned into South Audley Street in silence.

'Don't you want to know where we're going?'

'Not particularly.'

He stopped. 'I don't want to spend my evening with somebody who is sullen and clearly in a very bad mood. Do you want to tell me what's wrong?'

'What's wrong?' She looked at him examining his face carefully. What would she be giving up? 'I don't want to spend my evening with someone who ogles my maid in front of me.'

'Don't be vulgar, Evangeline, I didn't "ogle" Molly, and don't demean her by calling her your maid like that, she's also your friend.'

She blushed furiously: he had a knack of turning the tables on her, of finding her weaknesses. She would be frank and straightforward.

'I don't want to see you again. It was obvious this afternoon that you desire Molly. I felt angry and sad and used.'

He turned away from her, pushing his hands in his pockets. 'True, I do desire Molly a little. I can't imagine a time when I won't desire other women, but it doesn't mean I act on it. I choose you. My desire for you overwhelms any little lust I might feel for anyone else.'

An elderly couple hand in hand and deep in conversation walked slowly past them. 'You must keep your strength up, Georgie,' they heard in a quavery voice before the couple crossed the road, both treating the other as if they were blind.

Shrugging casually, he continued, 'And, of course, I love you.' He took his hands out of his pockets and removing his glasses polished them with the edge of his jacket. 'You, too, you desire other men. I can see, for instance, you still have a little residual sexual feeling for Jack, but I presume you don't intend to do anything about it. That you choose me.' He replaced his glasses and put his hand under her chin, lifting her face. 'I want you desperately, feel me, I'm hard just holding your exquisite face.'

He had taken a suite at the Curzon Hotel and ordered dinner, which had already been served in the sitting room. He led Evangeline silently to a large armchair and seating her gently he knelt and unbuttoned her dress to the waist. Removing her knickers and caressing the inside of her thighs he parted her legs and lifted her from the chair with her legs wrapped round his waist. He entered her suddenly and forcefully then carried her through to the bedroom. When lowered on the bed he moved rhythmically inside her looking at the lovely face with its half-closed eyes and slightly parted moist mouth, receiving as much from her pleasure as from his own.

'You still working, Bea?' Evangeline looked

at the heap of shot silk taffeta. 'Can I help? I'm not tired.'

'I am.' Beatrice looked at the small gilt carriage clock sitting on the mantelpiece. 'Quarter to eleven. Good girl, Hugo's so reliable. We all worked till ten o'clock then Jack took Letty and Tilly home.' She put her sewing down, yawning. 'Evie, I've just had rather an odd telephone call from Arthur. He was drunk, I think.'

'He does drink a lot.' Evangeline groaned. 'I don't have to see him again, do I?'

'No, that's what's odd, he wants to see me and you are not to be there. It's been such a difficult day, I couldn't be bothered to deal with him tactfully, I just snapped, "Oh God, what do you want?" '

Evangeline laughed. 'No, Bea, that wasn't very tactful. What did he say?'

'He was rather cryptic. You might think it good news, he said.'

'Oh, Bea, you don't think he's going to ask for my hand in marriage? Or would he have to ask himself, being my guardian?' They both laughed.

'No, he sounded too miserable for that. We'll see, I told him I'd see him next week.'

'Maybe he wants to ask for *your* hand in marriage!'

'Hardly likely.' Beatrice put aside Madame

Roncard's gown. 'Look, Evie, isn't that good news?' Beatrice handed her a cheque.

'Golly! Four hundred pounds! Pay Beatrice and Evangeline Eliott four hundred pounds.' Evangeline danced around the desk, waving the cheque. 'We've earned it, it isn't a gift.'

'Yes, but four hundred. Does that mean we're a little ahead?' Evangeline stopped her dance and stood in front of Beatrice earnestly, her hands behind her back.

'More than a little. We can pay all our bills, Tilly and Letty and Molly and still have some over. Incidentally, about Molly . . .'

'Bea, do you think I could . . .' Evangeline found it very difficult to continue. 'Bea, may I . . . ?'

Beatrice stood up, smiling, and kissed her sister. 'Yes, Evie, you can, you may. From now on, we'll pay ourselves a salary, probably tiny at first, and I'll open a separate bank account for you.'

Beaming, Evangeline hugged her. 'Soon?'

'Monday soon enough? Now about Molly, it's her twenty-first birthday next week. I think we should make something special for her, pretend it's for Sybil Bonner, and fit it on her, Letty and Tilly would help. What do you think?'

'Good idea.'

'She looked so sweet, lovely, in fact, in Sybil's dress, didn't she?'

Evangeline gave a wry smile. 'Yes, Bea, oh, yes, she did.'

CHAPTER EIGHT

Beatrice pushed both hands through her springy vivid hair. Her voice was low, barely discernible. 'What for? You watched other people . . .' She started to retch, holding her stomach. Jack took hold of her intending to lead her to the bathroom. 'Don't touch me.' She recoiled from him as if stung and started to shake.

'What does he mean?' she whispered in a light childlike tone. 'What does Papa mean?' She'd been discovered hiding under the thick red plush cloth that covered the round table. She was naughty. Was Mama naughty, too? Mama was crying. Somebody was in Papa's room where he played doctors. They were hiding and wouldn't let Mama play with them.

Beatrice's arms were hanging at her side, her eyes stared unfocused in the middle distance and incomprehensible sentences came from a mouth distorted with pain. Jack tried to speak calmly.

'My love, my love, I'm so sorry. Please listen. It was only that once. I was just back from France, the war over two months. It's no excuse, I know. When I saw it was poor Daphne I felt sick too . . . Oh, Christ, Bea, forgive me, try to understand.'

She was still shaking and piping in that thin empty voice, 'What does Papa mean?' Now Papa was holding Mama's wrists, hurting her. 'Stop it,' she yelled.

Jack looked at her in despair. 'What is it, Bea? What's happened to you?'

Kathleen was there now, kneeling, holding her hand. 'Come along now, we'll go to the kitchen, find you a cake.'

'What did Papa mean?'

'What is it, my pet, what did your papa say that ye don't understand?' Kathleen was trying to pull her out of the room.

'He said to Aunt Lydia . . . Oh, Mama, it's Aunt Lydia who's hiding.'

Her father stepped forward and raised his hand. She was frightened, she started to whimper. His hand slapped her face, so hard she fell over.

'Oh, my beloved one.' Jack knelt at her side. 'I had to hit you, you were almost having a fit.'

Beatrice looked up from the floor. 'Papa said, "Let the boy play with his sister." '

After he had forced some brandy between her chattering teeth and wrapped her in a

371

blanket, he sat with her folded in his arms in front of the fire, rocking and soothing her. 'Yes, Jack, I see now. That's something I've always known.' She had stopped crying, but her voice was still frail. 'I don't know exactly how long, twenty-five years or more.'

Jack held her closer, kissing the top of her head lightly. 'Only talk, sweetheart, if it helps.'

'I've remembered odd bits from time to time, but it wasn't bearable. I wasn't brave enough to bear it all.' She sighed deeply. 'Poor, poor Mama. She was so frail, after all her miscarriages.' Struggling out of his arms she turned to face him. 'I hated being my father's daughter and now I loathe being Arthur's sister.'

'Half-sister.'

'Still too much.'

'If you're a bit better, Bea, I'll heat up that pie. We can eat in here in front of the fire. Do you think you should come to the kitchen with me? I don't want you to be alone.'

'No, I am a bit better, I'll just sit here.' She rose from the floor and settled herself in the large armchair. 'Thank goodness we came to your house.'

'Our house,' he corrected her. 'Promise to call me if you feel . . . well, if you need me?' When he had gone she curled herself up into a ball, hugging her knees. These last two days had been so tense, so tiring, and yet when the wedding was over and everything had been a success, Sybil looking wonderful, the dress a perfect fit and her mother, beautiful, too, and very grateful to them, she had felt even more tense, not less. Returning here with Jack for supper on their own to discuss their wedding she had been overwhelmed with love for him. Without his help it wouldn't have been possible. Driving Letty with the pages' costumes, taking and collecting both the girls. Hiring the large car so that there would be plenty of room for the dress had been his idea and then rushing off to the haberdasher's to buy petersham ribbon. Exhausted, she had refused his offer of champagne to celebrate and out of the great feeling of love had come a need, as it were, to tidy up, to have this love uncluttered and she had asked him to tell her the truth about Cadogan Mews.

He had hesitated at first but he, too, seemed to know that it was necessary. He had told her simply, concealing nothing. Cadogan Mews wasn't only a brothel. It was a house where you could watch, through a two-way mirror, people making love. 'Making love', that was a pretty euphemism. He had gone there, Jack, two years ago, drunk, although

373

he said he wasn't excusing himself. The first woman he saw was Daphne — she was wearing a mask, but he knew immediately it was her. Feeling sick with himself he left. Shyly he told her he had been celibate ever since.

And then the extraordinary thing had happened: her father's voice had sort of exploded in her mind and she had felt like two people, each observing the other. That her father had been connected with Cadogan Mews, as was Arthur, and therefore indirectly with Jack, had triggered off a reaction she'd been unable to control.

'Tomorrow's Sunday, thank the Lord,' Jack said, as he came in carrying what looked like a large square tray covered with green felt with their chicken pie and a bottle of wine on it. 'Can you unfold the legs under this? It's an old card table I found.' She unwound herself and jumped up, helping him to set up the table. 'Smells good, Jack. I'll still have to work, though.'

'No, Bea, you won't. You will sleep late. I will collect you about eleven o'clock, we will go to church and hear our banns read. We will have a proper lunch and afterwards we will walk in the park.' He put a chair for her at the table and served her. 'Will you obey me? What do you say?'

'I will.'

On Monday morning Beatrice woke up very early plagued with thoughts of Aunt Lydia. More than anybody she had been responsible for her mother's sadness — more, even, than her father. Other mistresses Mama wouldn't necessarily have known about but Aunt Lydia, her own sister-in-law, and in her own house. Now that Beatrice was able to remember everything, or so she hoped, she knew that what she had seen that day she'd drunk Papa's port was Aunt Lydia in that horrible-looking examination thing and Papa had been — no, she couldn't term it 'making love'. He had heard her outside the door and opened it, brutally smashing the door in her face, and for years what she had recalled had been the physical pain masking the ugly picture she had seen. Then, leaping out of bed, she hurriedly washed and dressed. That garden party coat. She must finish it and get it out of the house. It was like an ill-omen sitting down there. She would send Molly off with it the minute she got up. There wasn't much to do to it: finish hemming the rose-coloured lining, make one large buttonhole and sew on one large button. It had been pressed when the lining was attached. She had finished it by half past seven when she heard the postman. At last, a cheque from the Gregson twins! Letter for Evie, looked like an invitation. Another cheque, this time from Kitty Ashleigh, and what a sweet note, her husband said it made her look like a girl again. Poor thing, she looked more like a stick with a meringue on top. That hair! And a reminder from Digby and Gordon. At the sight of the envelope she'd been perturbed but, remembering, she sighed happily. A bill? Who cares? She hurried back to the office, and fetching tissue paper and a large cardboard box, she packed the offending coat. A note must be added. 'Dear Aunt Lydia.' No, nothing dear about her. 'Aunt Lydia, we no longer wish to be either your nieces or . . .' No, too pompous, too self-conscious. Just be brief and to the point. She settled on, 'Aunt Lydia. We will not see you or make clothes for you again. Evangeline and Beatrice Eliott.' She put the lid on the box and was about to tie it up, as was their custom, with rose ribbon when she changed her mind. She took out a roll of black tape and looked at it. Perfect. She heard Molly humming as she passed the office door on the way up with their tea. She had obviously been listening to the brass band in Hyde Park. 'Chu Chin Chow' wasn't in her usual repertoire.

'Ooh, Miss Bea, I nearly dropped it. Didn't expect you to be working early now the wedding's over and done with.'

'Over and done with? That doesn't sound very romantic, Molly. For them it's just beginning.'

'Yes, be that as it may,' Molly said with great foreboding. 'But the wedding may have been the best bit.'

'I hope you're wrong,' Beatrice said softly.

'Look, I'd best get this tea up to Miss Evie before it gets cold.' Molly felt she'd put her foot in it, right enough.

'Wait a minute, Molly, I'll take it. I want you to run an important errand.'

'Yes, Miss?'

Beatrice took the tray from her. 'The box that's in the office is to go to Lady Eliott. Leave it with her butler and don't wait for a reply.'

'Now, Miss?'

'Yes, now.' Beatrice smiled. 'And, Molly, you can stop at Jackson's on the way back, I'm sure we need cheese or whatever.'

She knows something, Molly thought, as she picked up the parcel and took it down to the basement. Black ribbon, what did that mean, somebody dead? More like a joke, knowing Miss Bea. Funny if after all this time the chickens is coming home to roost. She had been fourteen when her mother had gone back to Ireland to marry Mr O'Malley. She had considered Molly old enough to be told a certain amount about Dr Eliott, and a lot more she had guessed. 'Look after Miss Bea,' she had said. 'She's highly strung,' and so she was, but now Mr Jack would have to look after her.

'You were asleep when I came in last night, Evie. What did you do after lunch?'

'Nothing much,' she said vaguely, taking a cup of tea from Beatrice. 'We all walked to the Victoria and Albert then Piggy brought me home. Can't call him Piggy any more, now he's slimmed. No wonder he was fat, he's a terrific cook.'

'It was a nice day. You were sweet to come to the church, Evie.'

'It was a lovely day, Bea. Like a proper family day, even though Piggy had to cook the Sunday lunch.' After lunch she and Penny had gone to Gunpowder Alley to see Tilly — well, really to see Mr Allen, her father. At lunch Bea had been excited and full of plans for the house. To begin with everything was to be painted white, everything, all the walls lined with white paper, and when she had lived there for a while she would know what she wanted unwhited. Like her bedroom in Highgate the floor was to be sanded and bleached. As Evangeline explained to Mr Allen, Bea and Jack were going to northern

France for three days after their wedding. Would that be long enough to do it? He had been very pleased and was sure it could be done in time if she would allow him to bring a couple of mates. 'It's my wedding present,' she had told them proudly.

Beatrice poured more tea. 'Evie, I've got something important to discuss with you and we ought to do it now, we have such a busy day.'

Evangeline sat further up in bed, a look of apprehension on her face. 'I've been dreading this, Bea, but I won't stand in your way. I understand being married makes a difference, but don't do it too quickly. Not now we've really got going.'

Beatrice put her cup down. 'What are you talking about?'

Evangeline's eyes filled with tears. 'It's all right. I won't be selfish.'

'Evie, shut up, please. I had a long talk with Jack about work, mine and his.'

'Yes, I know,' Evangeline said mournfully.

'You obviously don't know and if you don't listen, I'll . . . I'll . . .'

'I'll listen.' Evangeline didn't know what the threat would be but she thought she'd rather hear the bad news without delay.

'Jack has definitely sold his photographs of war damage in the East End and whatever

379

he takes in France when we go there to the American magazine *Alive*. That has settled his mind about the future, he's giving up the society photography and concentrating on journalism. Which means, Evie, he doesn't need the studio any more. He's giving us the rest of the lease so we can expand.'

Evangeline jumped out of bed spilling her tea.

'Wonderful, darling Bea, I thought you were going to say the reverse.'

'What, give it all up? Of course not. Jack knows I want to work and he wants me to — in fact he thinks I'll probably be able to keep him.' She laughed. 'Don't forget all this was his idea in the first place.'

Evangeline dabbed at the tea stain on her sheet. 'I'll move up to the studio then, and this,' she gestured expansively, knocking the tea over again, 'can be another fitting room or workroom.'

'No good dabbing at it, Evie, use some water from your jug.'

'So you agree? It's a risk, you know, and we'll probably have to take on another seamstress.'

'Why doesn't Molly answer the door?'

Beatrice noticed suddenly that the door bell had been ringing. 'Oh, Evie, I forgot. I sent Molly off with Aunt Lydia's coat, I'll explain later. I'd better let Tilly and Letty in.'

'Here she is.' Letty looked over her shoulder, distracted momentarily from her wall-chart, as Evangeline came in sticking the last pin in her hastily put-up hair.

'I think I'll have this bobbed or shingled.'

'Or bingled, Miss, don't know what it is but it's the latest.' Tilly was already seated and working, black chiffon and crystal beads having taken over from white veiling and pearls. 'Wouldn't mind being bingled meself, easier to wash,' she said, 'less chance of nits.'

'Well, how did it go?' Letty sat down at the table looking at the sisters expectantly. 'Though don't think I'll ever forget the looks on both your faces when Mr Maddox said, "What are you two wearing?" Quickest hats ever been made, I should think.'

'Don't remind me.' Beatrice groaned.

'Let's see. Nothing went wrong. The dress fitted perfectly. The pages behaved reasonably well, except for Lord Rupert.'

'No surprise,' Letty interrupted. 'What did he do?'

'He shouted, "Tally-ho", as they went up the aisle and —'

Tilly shrieked with laughter. 'I don't believe it, I'd've 'ad hystirics.'

Beatrice continued, 'And, "Gone to earth", as they left.'

'People say anything about the dress?' Letty asked with anxiety. 'You don't sound that pleased.'

'Well, Letty, it was odd.' Evangeline took over the story. 'Sybil was thrilled, everybody said the idea was original and that she looked beautiful, but the real success, what made people ask for our address — and lots did, don't worry, two women are coming today to look at our sketches —'

'That's more like it.' Letty cheered up.

'What most people were interested in were Lady Bonner's dress and our clothes.'

'It was just like the night-club party,' Beatrice butted in. 'When everybody admired Daphne and Renée but it was our clothes they wanted.'

'Quite right.' Letty nodded. 'The other will get you attention, but it's fancy dress, theatrical. It's your straightforward, everyday, that's your market. Because your everyday isn't everyday, know what I mean? Hope they don't all think they're going to look as good as you, though. It's not just your looks either, you've both got real style.' The sisters were overwhelmed by the unexpected compliment, till Letty added calmly, 'So have I.'

'Er, yes, you do, Letty.' Evangeline smiled with encouragement.

'Right, back to work. On my work-plan,

Madame Roncard gets priority closely followed by Lady Eliott and then Miss Haycock's copies, not forgetting —'

'Letty, Letty, stop.' Beatrice held up her hand, 'We've got two important things to discuss with you both, but first, I finished Lady Eliott's coat this morning and Molly is delivering it right now.'

'Oh, that's where she is.'

'Yes, and about Molly. It's her twenty-first birthday next week and we thought we'd like to make something for her as a surprise. We can fit it on her and pretend it's for Sybil Bonner — Sybil Cherrington, as she is now.'

'Lovely idea,' Tilly said, looking up. 'She'll be bowled over, Miss Bea. Before you go on, these crystals are too heavy for one layer of chiffon, I think I'll have to line it with another layer and use less crystals.'

'That's fine, Tilly.'

'And in future, for the see-through black chiffon mother-of-pearl *paillettes* would be better.'

'Honestly, Tilly, give over, will you? I want to hear the important news.' Letty had a sense that the news was going to be good. Cupping her bright, intelligent face in her hands, her elbows on the table, she said, 'Go on, Miss Bea.'

'About Molly, what should we make? What

would she like? You talk to her, you might have a better idea.'

Evangeline remembered Molly's reaction to a cream chiffon dress with floating panels and suggested that but Tilly put down her work firmly and said, 'Now, where would she wear it?'

'True, just an idea.' Evangeline thought again. 'I've got it. She loved the pale grey cashmere with the yellow collar. Let's make her a long tight skirt in that grey and white man's suiting we've got, a three-quarter length coat in the grey cashmere buttoning up to the throat, and a white piqué blouse with a collar that can come out of the jacket and stand above it.'

'Yes, yes, wonderful, Evie, and a little grey astrakhan neck piece she can tie on in the winter with black grosgrain ribbon.'

'Perfect! Ssh, ssh, here she is.' Letty gestured to the door.

Molly paused at the workroom door. Why was it so quiet? They'd been talking nineteen to the dozen when she'd been climbing the stairs. 'I'm back, Miss Bea, I give it to the butler like you said and didn't wait. And it was too early for Jackson's.' She looked at them all pathetically; they were silent, they'd been talking about her, she could tell. Now the wedding rush was over she was to be told she wasn't needed, that was it.

'Thank you, Molly. Have you got a minute?'

'Yes, Miss Bea,' she said glumly.

'We wondered if you could do us a favour.'

'Yes, Miss Bea.'

'Lady Bonner called to order an autumn suit for Sybil, but of course she's on honeymoon.'

'Yes, Miss Bea. Vienna, famous white horses.'

'Indeed. So, it would be a great help if you'd let us fit it on you.'

'Yes, Miss Bea.' She beamed. 'Let me know each time and I'll have a bath.'

'Thank you. No, don't go, we've got something to say which affects you all. Mr Maddox has decided to give up his studio on the top floor because, well, because . . .' She strolled to the window to avoid the scrutiny of three pairs of eyes. 'He is changing his career, and we,' she tossed a glance in Evangeline's direction, 'are taking it over.'

'Yes. We are going to expand.' Evangeline spoke with great determination. 'I, that is, we,' she corrected herself, 'will take over the studio and our floor will be adapted to another fitting room, workroom, whatever becomes necessary.'

'Storeroom,' Tilly suggested.

'That, too. Not immediately, and not all at once. It depends on money, but the extra space

385

will be available soon. We will also need . . .'
She paused: the hiring of another worker
would affect Tilly and Letty; she hoped there
would be no resistance.

'You ought to take on another seamstress,
Miss Evie.' Letty leant back in her chair tick-
ing requirements off on her hand. 'You've got
your *directrice*, you. You've got your *vendeuse*,
you. You've got your *première main qualifée*,
Tilly. You've got your main cutter, me.'

Beatrice was surprised. Letty used the correct terms and with the correct French accent.
'Exactly, thank you, Letty. I hope you all
agree that we're right to take this step?'

There was a chorus of, 'Ooh, yes,' 'Definitely,' 'Best thing you could be doing,'
'Nothing ventured, nothing gained.'

'Any questions before we examine Letty's
wall-chart and get back to work?'

'Yes, Miss Bea.' Tilly spoke with her head
bent over her sewing. 'When are you and Mr
Maddox getting married?'

Beatrice slumped back in the taxi taking her
to Arthur's office. She was exhausted and anxious. The day had started badly and got worse.
After the euphoria of yesterday's talk about
expansion and the arrival of five women during the day, all of whom ordered clothes after
looking at the sketches of the autumn collec-

tions, it had been a shock. Letty had arrived in the morning with the black news of Charlie's sentence. He had pleaded guilty on the advice of the lawyer, expecting a short one, but had been given seven years. Letty had worked hard at first, brushing off attempts at sympathy, but at lunch she pushed aside her plate, stood up and, gripping the back of her chair, started to cry silently. Evangeline had suggested she go home but Letty had turned on her shouting, 'Home? One room, with my mother sucking on a bottle of gin?'

Then, there had been the quarrel with Evangeline. 'You lied to me, Evie. What else have you lied about?'

'I lied for your sake, Bea. I worried that you might not get married if you knew I'd be here on my own.'

'I don't see how I can get married now.'

Evangeline had exploded. 'If Penny hadn't been so stupid and let it out to Jack you wouldn't have known till it was too late. What difference does it make, Bea? Whatever you're worried about could happen while you're living here. In a motor car, in the park, when you're out, at his house, morning, noon, or night.'

'And has it, Evie?' Beatrice's voice shook, she couldn't look at her sister.

'Perhaps. But it's none of your business, and

what you and Jack do is none of mine. I'm nearly twenty-one, Bea.' And inconsequentially, she added, 'The war is over.'

Beatrice shook off the memory of the unpleasant morning as the taxi drew up outside Arthur's office. She paid the driver and, straightening her shoulders, prepared to face her cousin.

She was shocked by the change in Arthur. He looked bloated, his face was an unhealthy red and his eyes were bloodshot. What could have happened to him? He had always been a heavy drinker but this was different.

'Please sit down, Beatrice. I asked you to come here immediately because my plans have changed, our plans, that is.'

'Our plans, Arthur, yours and mine?'

'No, no.' He was fiddling with a long buff envelope on his desk. 'Mother's and mine. We are going to Rhodesia on Sunday. I'm going to go into tea or tobacco or something,' he said vaguely. 'Mother is closing the London house for the winter and the Crawleys will take Stanton.'

'Closing the house for the season? What has come over Aunt Lydia?' He looked so ill and dejected that she regretted her sarcasm.

'The note you sent her, Beatrice, was that necessary? You frightened her, you see. She thinks she'll be cut if you tell people about your father. I suppose you do know, you have found out, about your father, that's why . . .' His voice trailed away. She felt sorry for him; he was a pathetic creature.

'Arthur, this meeting was requested by you, you said you had something to tell me, something I might consider good news. But before you tell me that news I'll answer your question. Yes, I know about my father and your mother having an affair which continued through my mother's marriage to him, her pregnancy with Evangeline and after her death. I also know you are my father's son and not Uncle Richard's.' Being unable to resist a further barb she added, 'As for telling anyone, don't worry, Arthur, I am far too ashamed to claim a further kinship with you.'

He winced at the insult but ignored it. 'And how much do you know about Cadogan Mews?' he asked her, hoping she knew enough so that he wouldn't have to explain and see the disgust on her face.

'If you haven't the courage to tell me, Arthur, I will tell you what I know and you can fill in the missing pieces.' She spoke with a composure she didn't feel. 'You and my father owned or rented Cadogan Mews and ran it, not just as a high-class brothel, though what is high class about any woman selling her body I don't know, but where people could watch sexual acts through a two-way mirror. It was also possible to buy drugs there, cocaine, very easy for my father to obtain.' She was twisting her fingers violently, he noticed, the only outward sign of her distress.

'There's little to add to that. Would you like a drink?' he said desperately, moving to a shiny walnut-veneered cocktail cabinet and taking out a cut-glass tumbler and a bottle of whisky.

That's a new addition, she thought. He can't wait for the pub to open. 'No, I'd like to finish this meeting and go.'

He poured himself a large whisky and drank half of it. 'There are extenuating circumstances.' He eyed her pleadingly.

'Go on.' She turned away from him. It was disgusting, he was begging like a dog.

'Uncle Henry knew the woman who owned the house. She was in trouble, her husband died suddenly and left her very little and he, well, he helped her out.'

She stood up. 'I can't bear any more. Please, just give me the facts.' She felt very faint and the smell of the whisky on his breath was making her feel sick.

'Righto, yes.' He took another swig at his drink. 'Uncle Henry bought the house quite cheaply and then let the woman do what, er, she did. Then, when he knew he was dying he gave the house to me, that and the bank account that went with it.'

She picked up the marble inkstand on his desk and threw it at him. 'Did he pay for your education?' she screamed. 'Did he give money to your whore of a mother for you?' She was trembling violently. 'Money that came from my mother.'

'Yes, yes,' he stammered. His cheekbone was bleeding badly where the inkstand had struck it. He dabbed it with his handkerchief and seemed surprised at the amount of blood. 'But I'm making it up to you, Beatrice. Here.' He handed her the envelope. 'I've sold Cadogan Mews back to Mrs Henshaw and transferred all the money to your bank account.'

'Mrs Henshaw,' was all she said as she left his office.

'What did he say? What was the good news? Does he want to marry me?'

'Not in the circumstances, I doubt it.'

'Leave her alone, Evie.' Jack led Beatrice to a chair. 'She's exhausted, can't you see? Sometimes you behave like a selfish little girl.'

'Sorry, Bea.' Evangeline was immediately contrite.

'I brought some champagne with me to celebrate the article.' He opened a Jackson's paper bag.

'I'd love some champagne, darling.'

'So would I, if I'm included.' Evangeline fetched three glasses.

'But what article, Jack? What are you talking about?'

'You haven't seen the *Courier*? What have you been doing all day?' He took a crumpled newspaper from his coat pocket and handed it to Beatrice. 'What I like about it is the irony.' He carefully withdrew the cork from the bottle of Bollinger making only a soft pop. 'You spend four days working round the clock, five of you, on a grand expensive wedding dress and what gets into the newspaper?' He poured the champagne. 'Old clothes you put on as an afterthought and hats made in half an hour.' He lifted his glass and toasted them, 'Congratulations!'

The two hats that had taken half an hour to make were a turban twisted out of multi-coloured silk remnants which Beatrice had worn back to front and a short pale grey silk snood worn with purple bands across her forehead by Evangeline. The photograph showed Beatrice standing behind Evangeline and the caption read, 'Chic Sheikh'.

'So, you see, we can't keep all the money, it's made from something so horrible.' Beatrice finished her champagne.

392

'I feel as if somebody had punched me in the stomach.' Evangeline put down her glass which she had hardly touched. 'No, no more.' She moved her hand over it as Jack picked up the bottle. 'That's rather a lot to hear at one go, you know, Bea. You've been learning it gradually.' She gave a short laugh. 'And you say I keep secrets from you. I think we're equal now.'

'That's not fair, Evie.' Jack put a calming hand on Beatrice's shoulder. 'She was trying to protect you.'

'Mm, that was my excuse too,' she said with bitterness. 'You say we can't keep all the money. How much is tainted? And how much isn't?'

'Don't, Evie. It's all over now.' Beatrice rose and put her arms around Evangeline. 'Papa is dead, Arthur is no longer your guardian, we're free to get on with our lives. I'm sorry it was such a shock, I always suspected you knew a little about it.'

Evangeline patted Beatrice and withdrew from her embrace. 'It's all right, I'll be all right. I'm glad now that I didn't know Mama, I can't imagine her pain.' She buried her face in her hands for a moment then flung her head back. 'No. I want to be practical. What about the money?'

'I think we can keep the money from the

sale of Cadogan Mews because it must have been Mama's money that he used to buy it.'

'And the rest?' Jack said. 'The ill-gotten gains?'

'We'll give it to a charity,' Beatrice said simply.

Evangeline frowned. 'A charity, which one?'

'We only know one.'

'You mean . . . ?' Evangeline didn't want to say the name in case she was wrong.

'Yes, I mean the East End Mission. After all, we know quite a few people who will benefit from it.'

'Hooray, that makes me feel much better. And you'll still get married?'

'Oh, I think so, don't you, Jack?'

'Don't forget, her bottom's bigger than mine.' Molly regarded her own neatly shaped one sideways in the mirror. 'Mine is like an apple, hers is like a pear,' she announced.

'I'll keep that in mind, Molly, thank you,' said Tilly with a mouthful of pins. Picking up some marking chalk, Letty ran a white line down both sides of the skirt. 'We'll release it there,' she said, winking at Tilly.

'That was the employment agency.' Evangeline came in carrying a bale of fine black silk jersey. 'They can let us have one person

394

each morning for a week and one in the afternoon but after that they are both available.'

'That suits us, don't it, Miss Evie? You can take it off now, Molly, that's the last fitting.' Tilly helped Molly step out of the skirt. 'That way you can choose who you like best.'

'And who you like, Letty. They must fit in.'

'Very considerate, Miss. Did Miss Haycock settle on how many dresses she wants?'

'Bea cut it down to three each.'

'Nice and easy order — we can cut them together.'

'Glad this is the last fitting, I am,' Molly grumbled, as she put on her thick calico skirt. 'I was getting fond of it — wouldn't mind wearing it tomorrow.'

'Where are you going, Molly? Where's he taking you?'

'Don't know yet, he'll tell me tonight when we go for our walk.' She didn't want to tell the girls that he hadn't suggested taking her anywhere. These days when they went for a walk they always met that Patrick; she didn't know why he wanted her there at all.

Daphne Haycock also looked at her bottom in the long mirror in the office, but with less approval than Molly. 'I don't think health suits me, I used to be flat all over, now I have bumps.'

'They're known as curves, Daphne.'

'Eek, don't say that, it's a dirty word.'

Beatrice helped her on with her coat. 'I hope you'll be happy there, Daphne, or happier.'

'I must be, I will be.' She picked up Beatrice's hand and kissed it. 'Imagine, an apartment on the Île St Louis. You and Jack can come and see us.'

'Will you be singing in French?'

'Pour moi et ma fille?' She laughed and rubbed her nose angrily. 'I'm too sophisticated to cry.'

'Idiot. You're not sophisticated at all.'

'That's what Renée says. 'Bye, send the dresses as soon as possible, or we'll have to sing naked.'

'If I wasn't doing myself out of a job, I'd say that was a good idea.'

Daphne laughed. 'Oh dear, St Beatrice, your halo is slipping.'

The front door closed with a loud bang. 'For a girl as skinny as that she makes a lot of noise,' said Tilly as she bent over the sketch Evangeline was drawing. Pointing, Evangeline said, 'I'd like to wear it next week, I'm going to a dinner party at Olivia Stett-Gittins'.'

'She'd be bound to order one, she likes all your funny ideas.' Tilly picked up some small diamanté beads and placed them in a semi-circle round the high neck of the black silk jersey fabric that Letty had cut to resemble a jumper. 'Like this, so they look like a necklace?'

'Right — and the other idea, well, that might be too difficult.' Evangeline drew another sketch.

'I can only try,' Tilly said.

'It sounds mad, but could you in the same sort of semi-circle as if it was a necklace sew in diamanté this word?' She drew on the sketch, DIAMONDS.

'It's a winner, Miss Evie, it's the most brilliant idea anyone's ever had.' Letty patted Tilly on the back. 'You can do that, easy.'

'Tell you what, Miss Evie,' Tilly took the pencil and sketch, 'it'd be easier still if I used . . .' she drew PEARLS, 'not so many letters.'

Evangeline crept down the back-stairs into the kitchen and left Molly's birthday presents on the table. A birthday card containing a postal order from them both, another card with a credit note from Jackson's, hope she laughed at that, a parcel from her mother in Ireland, a big one, probably a cake and a hand-knitted jumper, and a large signed photograph of Rudolph Valentino as the Sheikh that Jack had found. Nothing had arrived from Michael but Molly was seeing him tonight. She left the kitchen on tiptoe and went back upstairs. Stopping outside her bedroom she looked up the stairs to the studio, which would soon be her new bedroom. Which had already been her bedroom last night between eight and ten o'clock. Hugo had arrived to take her out to dinner, but she felt on edge and wasn't hungry. She had been showing him the studio, asking his advice about the alterations, when he'd leant against the wall and said, 'Take your clothes off.' She had undressed slowly and carefully, then sitting on the dilapidated sofa she pulled her knees up to roll down her stockings and unbutton her shoes. She then undressed him, delicately, hardly touching him and led him to the sofa where she lay on top of him and moved him inside her.

It was ten o'clock when she said he must go, they were lying on a heap of velvet curtains and cushions. His body was wet with perspiration. The two hours they had spent making love had removed for now the thoughts of her unknown sad mother. When she returned from the dressing room, washed and partly dressed, he was putting on his clothes and looking out of the dark window lit only by a distant gas-lamp.

'I don't think my feelings for you will change.' His voice was thoughtful. 'I can't imagine a time when I won't want you as passionately as I did tonight.' She sat on the sofa buttoning her shoes and didn't reply. 'So, Evangeline, I'm going to ask you a shocking question.'

She looked up with a shy smile. 'I doubt if you can shock me.'

'Will you marry me?'

She was shocked. She stood up and looked at herself in the mirror, adjusting her belt. It was something she'd thought about, wondered about; but it was an easy decision after all.

'No.' In the half light, without his glasses, he couldn't see her, and taking a step towards him, she said again, 'No. Ever since we met you've been training me to be your mistress, Hugo, and that is what I am. I expect I will get married one day and have children, but not yet.'

'And not me?'

'No. I'm your mistress, Hugo, you got what you wanted.'

'But not, I think, what I needed.' His voice hadn't changed, it was still thoughtful. He had been perfectly good-humoured afterwards: they had made sandwiches and taken them to the small sitting room. She had told him some of the story about her father, to which he had listened attentively, advising her that it was

399

the past, not to forget it but to leave it in the past and not stay behind with it. He was leaving as Jack delivered Beatrice back. 'Goodbye,' he had said, 'I'll see you when I get back from Vienna.' She shivered. The Indian summer was over.

'Miss Evie, I come early to have a word.' Letty hung her coat on the long rack that held various garments in different stages of readiness. 'I don't like hanging my coat, dirty from the tube, next to Mrs Whatsit's taffeta.'

'The alterations won't take long, Letty.' Thanks to Arthur's windfall. They had discussed, Jack, Beatrice and she, investing the money wisely, or converting the house, and nobody had voted for a wise investment. A real couture house was what they wanted.

'Sorry, Letty, I was miles away.'

'Would you give this note to Miss Maddox tonight, you said you were seeing her. It's to say thanks.'

'Thanks?'

'Yes. I saw Charlie's mum last night. She'd been to the Scrubs to see him and that lawyer had told him not to worry about his fee, Miss Maddox had put in a word for him at some trust run by her East End Mission, pays poor people's law fees. Not that he would charge much, shouldn't think. After all, he's a socialist.'

'Yes, I'll give it to her. Very thoughtful of you.'

'Next thing, Miss Evie, I've 'ad an idea about what I'd call a trademark for you, if you'd be interested.'

'Very, Letty.' Evangeline was amused but sceptical. 'Go on.'

'Well, take your sister's initial B, your initial E, the initial of your surname E, put them together you get . . . ?'

'A bee!'

'Exactly, so you have a design of a little bumble-bee on all your clothes.' Letty was triumphant.

'It's a very good idea, Letty.' Evangeline was serious. 'And if we use it, we'll pay you for it.'

'Of course. Now what about Molly?' Letty's voice dropped to a theatrical whisper. 'Give her the suit after the last fitting, all right? Be about half past five.'

'Yes, we'll ask her to try it on and then tell her it's hers.' Evangeline went to the rack and removed an eau-de-Nil crêpe-de-Chine dress.

'I want to get this tea gown ready. Phew! Five fittings, Letty, we're too successful!'

'Ssh, don't tempt Providence,' Letty said darkly.

Beatrice put her head round the workroom

door. 'Where's Molly?'

'Madame Roncard gone?'

'Yes, and she's ordered something else. I'm not surprised, that ballgown is one of the best things we've ever done. Absolute simplicity with exquisite detail.' The three faces smiled at the compliment.

'She won't be as pleased as Molly will be. I'll get her.' When Evangeline returned with Molly they were all busy sewing. 'It's just a tiny adjustment, won't take long.'

'I don't mind at all, I was only doing me ironing.' She'd felt a bit down all day. It was nice of the Misses to give her the money and all but Tilly and Letty had forgotten, and her twenty-first as well. Evangeline finished buttoning the jacket, straightened the high white collar and tied the astrakhan collar on.

'What do you think, Molly?'

'I think it's perfect, Miss, it don't need no adjusting.'

Letty lifted her hand to conduct: 'Happy Birthday to You, Happy Birthday to You, Happy Birthday dear Molly, Happy Birthday to You.'

She stood there, her mouth wide open. 'I don't understand.'

'It's yours, we made it for you. We made it for someone with a bottom like an apple.' Tilly prodded the undoubtedly apple-like bottom.

'But it's cashmere,' Molly said with awe, stroking the jacket tenderly. 'Oh, Miss Bea, Miss Evie, all of ye, I'm just over the moon. Thank you a thousand million times.'

'You can wear it tonight — Molly, what is it? You're not going to cry?' Evangeline touched her face gently.

'No, Miss, but it's that there isn't going to be any tonight.' Last night she'd gone to meet Michael for his two hours' off, but he hadn't been at their usual place, the corner of Wardley Mews. That Patrick had been there instead. He had hurried her off, not saying much till they had crossed Park Lane and were at Hyde Park Corner behind the Duke of Wellington's house.

In answer to her repeated questions, 'Where is he? What's the matter?' he had said, 'Michael's fine. He's sailing for America.' He pulled her on again towards Kensington — she was breathless and not a little frightened. Patrick kept looking behind him and he was walking with her on the outside. Not like a gentleman at all.

Finally he let her sit on a bench on the edge of Rotten Row, shaded by a large elm tree. 'It's better for you not to know any more, Molly. He'll be writing to you when he gets there.'

'It's the Republican Army, isn't it? He's

been up to something.'

He repeated, 'Better not to know.'

'Maybe it is, and maybe it would have been better not to have met him.' He shrugged and looked around anxiously.

He wanted to be off, she could tell. She told him to go, she would find her own way home. 'Tell him not to write, there's no point. Oh, it isn't the IRA stuff, Patrick, we were never really suited, we never did have much in common, except being Irish.' Walking slowly home, she decided Jackson's might be good for cheese and chocolates but it wasn't any good for picking up fellows.

'So, I'm not crying, but I am good and fed up. All dressed up and nowhere to go.' She stroked the cashmere again, so soft you could hardly feel it. She'd omitted some of the details in her story, altering Patrick's name and not mentioning America. She also left out the information that Patrick or someone else would be near the Albert Memorial the first Tuesday of the month between six and seven o'clock, in case she needed anything or wanted to help the cause.

'You will have somewhere to go, Molly.' Beatrice had a brainwave. 'You can either eat here with us and Jack, but we'll be talking about all the wedding preparations, or —'

'But then I won't be wearing me beautiful

suit,' she said sadly.

'You can wear it at Miss Bea's wedding,' Letty reminded her.

'That's next week and it's me birthday today.'

'Or,' Beatrice continued, 'we'll treat you all to high tea at Lyons' Corner House.'

'Good gracious, that would be somewhere for me to show me clothes. Oh, thank you again. Can you two come?' She was holding back from being too excited in case they said no.

'Try and stop us. We can walk there so you get full use of the suit and we can get a bus home from the top of Shaftesbury Avenue,' Letty said, ever practical.

'I feel as if it's my birthday too. What a treat. I'd just like to finish this jacket, I'm half-way through the revers, then I'll wash and tidy up.' Tilly picked up the white broadcloth jacket she was working on.

'White's very hard on your eyes. Talking of white, Miss Bea, what are you doing about your wedding dress?'

'It isn't a wedding dress as such, Tilly. We're leaving immediately after for the train, no time to change, just dash back here to pick up my suitcase and off to Victoria station.'

'The Golden Arrow, very romantic.' Molly sighed, picturing herself in a cabin lying in the arms of Douglas Fairbanks who had recently superseded the Sheikh.

'I'm too old for a lot of fuss. I've been working on it in the office. It's only a coat, really.'

'Only a coat,' Letty whispered to Tilly as Beatrice walked up the aisle of the tiny church, the thin autumn sunshine scattering brilliant blue and amber light through the stained-glass windows. Her coat was made of white bouclé wool; it was high-necked and high-waisted and stopped just above her ankles, its only decoration the horn buttons which fastened it. On her glossy reddish hair, which was massed on top of her head, was perched a Cossack-style hat in the same material with a gold feather cockade pinned at the front.

Evangeline was surprised to find herself in tears when the couple exchanged vows very clearly, 'I do.' 'I do.' But it was a happy ending for Bea, after thirty years of sadness and anger. No, not a happy ending, a happy beginning.

The small congregation left the church and piled into two motor cars, Piggy driving one with Evangeline seated next to him and Mr and Mrs Maddox in the back, Penelope driving hers with Molly next to her and Tilly and Letty in the dickey seat.

'What are you three doing when they leave?

Can't work, can you, with all the workmen in the house?'

'No, Miss Maddox.' Molly looked over her shoulder to the dickey seat. 'We've got other plans. Letty is helping Miss Evie deal with the workmen in Green Street and Tilly and I are taking the workmen at Mr Jack's house fish and chips for their dinners.' Molly had hopes of a young cockney painter she'd taken a shine to when she'd let Mr Allen and his helpers into the Holland Park house this morning. He'd been cheeky about her tight skirt and that was all to the better, she thought.

'So many secrets.' Penelope parked the motor next to Piggy's.

Letty nudged Tilly. 'And that's not all,' she whispered, pointing to the rather large bag she was carrying.

'Confetti?' Penelope had noticed the little exchange.

'Not exactly, Miss Maddox, more in the way of a present.' They took some things out of the bag and went up to the door purposefully.

'That's it, Evie, I'm ready, we must go. Are you all right, darling?' Beatrice gave Jack her small suitcase. 'Hugo didn't get back from Vienna. Were you disappointed?'

'Oh, he'll be back, Bea, I know that.' They walked out of the front door.

'And when you return,' Letty said, as she

waved her hand triumphantly at the house, 'this will be,' Tilly slammed the front door and pointed to a gleaming brass plate, 'The House of Eliott.'